A NOTE FROM THE AUTHOR

Ever since the third or fourth of the Darkover novels, my surprisingly faithful readers have been writing in to me, asking, in essence, "Why don't you write a novel about the Ages of Chaos?"

For a long time I demurred, hesitating to do this; to me the essence of the Darkover novels seemed to be just this—the clash of cultures between Darkovan and Terran. If I had acceded to their request to write about a time "before the coming of the Terrans," it seemed to me, the very essence of the Darkover novels would have been removed, and what remained would be very much like any of a thousand other science-fantasy novels dealing with alien worlds where people have alien powers and alien concerns.

It was my readers who finally persuaded me to attempt this. If every reader who actually writes to an author represents only a hundred who do not (and I am told the figure is higher than this) there must be, by now, several *thousand* readers out there who are interested and curious about the time known as the Ages of Chaos; the time before the Comyn had firmly established an alliance of their seven Great Houses to rule over the Domains; and also the height of the Towers, and of that curious technology known then as "starstone" and later becoming the science of matrix mechanics.

Readers of *The Forbidden Tower* will want to know that *Stormqueen* deals with a time *before* Varzil, Keeper of Neskaya, known as "the Good," perfected the techniques allowing women to serve as Keepers in the Towers of the Comyn.

In *The Shattered Chain,* Lady Rohana says;

> "There was a time in the history of the Comyn when we did selective breeding to fix these gifts in our racial heritage; it was a time of great tyranny, and not a time we are very proud to remember."

This is a story of the men and women who lived under that tyranny, and how it affected their lives, and the lives of those who came after them on Darkover.

—MARION ZIMMER BRADLEY

Stormqueen!

A DARKOVER NOVEL

by
Marion Zimmer Bradley

DAW Books, Inc.
Donald A. Wollheim, Publisher

1633 Broadway, New York, N.Y. 10019

DEDICATION

To Catherine L. Moore

First Lady of Science Fiction

I have ceased, I hope, the imitation which is said to be the sincerest form of flattery. I shall never outgrow, I hope, the desire to emulate; nor the admiration, the affection, and the inspiration which she has created in every woman who writes science fiction and fantasy—and in most of the men, too!

—MZB

First Printing, June 1978

7 8 9 10 11 12

 DAW TRADEMARK REGISTERED
U.S. PAT. OFF. MARCA
REGISTRADA, HECHO EN U.S.A.

PRINTED IN U.S.A.

CHAPTER
ONE

The storm was wrong somehow.

That was the only way Donal could think of it . . . *wrong somehow*. It was high summer in the mountains called the Hellers, and there should have been no storms except for the never-ending snow flurries on the far heights above the timberline, and the rare savage thunderstorms that swooped down across the valleys, bouncing from peak to peak and leaving flattened trees and sometimes fire in the path of their lightnings.

Yet, though the sky was blue and cloudless, thunder crackled low in the distance, and the very air seemed filled with the tension of a storm. Donal crouched on the heights of the battlement, stroking with one finger the hawk cradled in the curve of his arm, crooning half-absently to the restless bird. It was the storm in the air, the electric tension, he knew, which was frightening the hawk. He should never have taken it from the mews today—it would serve him right if the old hawkmaster beat him, and a year ago he would probably have done so without much thought. But now things were different. Donal was only ten, but there had been many changes in his short life. And this was one of the most drastic, that within the change of a few moons hawkmaster and tutors and grooms now called him—not that-brat-Donal, with cuffs and pinches and even blows, merited and unmerited, but, with new and fawning respect—young-master-Donal.

Certainly life was easier for Donal now, but the very change made him uneasy; for it had not come about from anything he had done. It had something to do with the fact that his mother, Aliciane of Rockraven, now shared the bed

of Dom Mikhail, Lord of Aldaran, and was soon to bear him
a child.

Only once, a long time ago (two midsummer festivals had
come and gone), had Aliciane spoken of these things to her
son.

"Listen carefully to me, Donal, for I shall say this once
only and never again. Life is not easy for a woman unprotected." Donal's father had died in one of the small wars, which
raged among the vassals of the mountain lords, before Donal
could remember him; their lives had been spent as unregarded poor relations in the home of one kinsman after another, Donal wearing castoffs of this cousin and that, riding
always the worst horse in the stables, hanging around unseen
when cousins and kinsmen learned the skills of arms, trying
to pick up what he could by listening.

"I could put you to fosterage; your father had kinsmen in
these hills, and you could grow up to take service with one of
them. Only for me there would be nothing but to be drudge
or sewing-woman, or at best minstrel in a stranger's household, and I am too young to find that endurable. So I have
taken service as singing-woman to Lady Deonara; she is frail,
and aging, and has borne no living children. Lord Aldaran is
said to have an eye for beauty in women. And I am beautiful, Donal."

Donal had hugged Aliciane fiercely; indeed she was beautiful, a slight girlish woman, with flame-bright hair and gray
eyes, who looked too young to be the mother of a boy eight
years old.

"What I am about to do, I do it at least partly for you,
Donal. My kin have cast me off for it; do not condemn me if
I am ill-spoken by those who do not understand."

Indeed it seemed, at first, that Aliciane had done this more
for her son's good than her own: Lady Deonara was kind
but had the irritability of all chronic invalids, and Aliciane
had been quenched and quiet, enduring Deonara's sharpness
and the shrewish envy of the other women with goodwill and
cheerfulness. But Donal for the first time in his life had whole
clothing made to his measure, horse and hawk of his
own, shared the tutor and the arms-master of Lord Aldaran's
fosterlings and pages. That summer Lady Deonara had borne
the last of a series of stillborn sons; and Mikhail, Lord of Aldaran, had taken Aliciane of Rockraven as *barragana* and

sworn to her that her child, male or female, should be legitimated, and be heir to his line, unless he might someday father a legitimate son. She was Lord Aldaran's acknowledged favorite—even Deonara loved her and had chosen her for her lord's bed—and Donal shared her eminence. Once, even, Lord Mikhail, gray and terrifying, had called Donal to him, saying he had good reports from tutor and arms-master, and had drawn him into a kindly embrace. "I would indeed you were mine by blood, foster-son. If your mother bears me such a son I will be well content, my boy."

Donal had stammered, "I thank you, kinsman," without the courage, yet, to call the old man "foster-father." Young as he was, he knew that if his mother should bear Lord Aldaran his only living child, son or daughter, then he would be half-brother to Aldaran's heir. Already the change in his status had been extreme and marked.

But the impending storm . . . it seemed to Donal an evil omen for the coming birth. He shivered; this had been a summer of strange storms, lightning bolts from nowhere, ever-present rumblings and crashes. Without knowing why, Donal associated these storms with *anger*—the anger of his grandsire, Aliciane's father, when Lord Rockraven had heard of his daughter's choice. Donal, cowering forgotten in a corner, had heard Lord Rockraven calling her *bitch*, and *whore*, and names Donal had understood even less. The old man's voice had been nearly drowned, that day, by thunder outside, and there had been a crackle of angry lightnings in his mother's voice, too, as she had shouted back, "What am I to do, then, Father? Bide here at home, mending my own shifts, feeding myself and my son upon your shabby honor? Shall I see Donal grow up to be a mercenary soldier, a hired sword, or dig in your garden for his porridge? You scorn Lady Aldaran's offer—"

"It is not *Lady* Aldaran I scorn," her father snorted, "but it is not she whom you will serve and you know it as well as I!"

"And have you found a better offer for me? Am I to marry a blacksmith or charcoal-burner? Better *barragana* to Aldaran than wife to a tinker or ragpicker!"

Donal had known he could expect nothing from his grandsire. Rockraven had never been a rich or powerful estate; and it was impoverished because Rockraven had four sons to provide for, and three daughters, of whom Aliciane was the youngest. Aliciane had once said, bitterly, that if a man has no sons, that is tragedy; but if he has too many, then worse for him, for he must see them struggle for his estate.

Last of his children, Aliciane had been married to a younger son without a title, and he had died within a year of their marriage, leaving Aliciane and the newborn Donal to be reared in strangers' houses.

Now, crouching on the battlements of Castle Aldaran and watching the clear sky so inexplicably filled with lightning, Donal extended his consciousness outward, outward—he could almost *see* the lines of electricity and the curious shimmer of the magnetic fields of the storm in the air. At times he had been able to call the lightning; once he had amused himself when a storm raged by diverting the great bolt where he would. He could not always do it, and he could not do it too often or he would grow sick and weak; once when he had felt through his skin (he did not know how) that the next bolt was about to strike the tree where he had sheltered, he had somehow *reached out* with something inside him, as if some invisible limb had grasped the chain of exploding force and flung it *elsewhere*. The lightning bolt had exploded, with a sizzle, into a nearby bush, crisping it into blackened leaves and charring a circle of grass, and Donal had sunk to the ground, his head swimming, his eyes blurred. His head had been splitting in three parts with the pain, and he could not see properly for days, but Aliciane had hugged and praised him.

"My brother Caryl could do that, but he died young," she told him. "There was a time when the *leroni* at Hali tried to breed storm-control into our *laran*, but it was too dangerous. I can *see* the thunder-forces, a little; I cannot manipulate them. Take care, Donal; use that gift only to save a life. I would not have my son blasted by the lightnings he seeks to control." Aliciane had hugged him again, with unusual warmth.

Laran. Talk of it had filled his childhood, the gifts of extrasensory powers which were so much a preoccupation with the mountain lords—yes, and far away in the lowlands, too. If he had had any truly extraordinary gift, telepathy, the ability to force his will upon hawk or hound or sentry-bird, he would have been recorded in the breeding charts of the *leroni*, the sorceresses who kept records of parentage among those who carried the blood of Hastur and Cassilda, legendary forebears of the Gifted Families. But he had none. Merely storm-watch, a little; he sensed when thunderstorms or even forest fire struck, and someday, when he was a bit older, he would take his place on the fire-watch, and it would help him, to know, as he already knew a little, where the fire would move next. But this was a minor gift, not worth breeding for. Even at Hali they had abandoned it, four generations before, and Donal knew, not knowing precisely how he knew, that this was one reason why the family of Rockraven had not prospered.

But this storm was far beyond his power to guess. Somehow, without clouds or rain, it seemed to center here, over the castle. *Mother*, he thought, *it has to do with my mother*, and wished that he dared run to seek her, to assure himself that all was well with her, through the terrifying, growing awareness of the storm. But a boy of ten could not run like a babe to sit in his mother's lap. And Aliciane was heavy now and ungainly, in the last days of waiting for Lord Aldaran's child to be born; Donal could not run to her with his own fears and troubles.

He soberly picked up the hawk again, and carried it down the stairs; in air so heavy with lightning, this strange and unprecedented storm, he could not loose it to fly. The sky was blue (it looked like a good day for flying hawks) but Donal could *feel* the heavy and oppressive magnetic currents in the air, the heavy crackle of electricity.

Is it my mother's fear that fills the air with lightning, as sometimes my grandsire's anger did? Suddenly Donal was overwhelmed with his own fear. He knew, as everyone knew, that women sometimes died in childbirth; he had tried hard not to think about that, but now, overwhelmed with terror for his mother, he could feel the crackle of his own fear in the lightning. Never had he felt so young, so helpless. Fiercely he wished he were back in the shabby poverty of Rockraven, or ragged and unregarded as a poor cousin in some kinsman's stronghold. Shivering, he took the hawk back to the mews, accepting the hawkmaster's reproof with such meekness that the old man thought the boy must be sick!

Far away in the women's apartments, Aliciane heard the continuing roll of thunder; more dimly than Donal, she sensed the strangeness of the storm. And she was afraid.

The Rockravens had been dropped from the intensive

breeding program for *laran* gifts; like most of her generation, Aliciane thought that breeding program outrageous, a tyranny no free mountain people would endure in these days, to breed mankind like cattle for desired characteristics.

Yet all her life she had been reared in loose talk of lethal genes and recessives, of bloodlines carrying desired *laran*. How could any woman bear a child without fear? Yet here she was, awaiting the birth of a child who might well be heir to Aldaran, knowing that his reason for choosing her had been neither her beauty—although she knew, without vanity, that it had been her beauty which first caught his eye—nor the superb voice which had made her Lady Deonara's favorite ballad-singer, but the knowledge that she had born a strong and living son, gifted with *laran*; that she was of proven fertility and could survive childbirth.

Rather, I survived it once. What does that prove, but that I was lucky?

As if responding to her fear, the unborn child kicked sharply, and Aliciane drew her hand over the strings of her *rryl*, the small harp she held in her lap, pressing the side-bars with her other hand and sensing the soothing effect of the vibrations. As she began to play, she sensed the stir among the women who had been sent to attend her, for Lady Deonara genuinely loved her singing-woman, and had sent her own most skillful nurses and midwives and maids to attend her in these last days. Then Miknail, Lord Aldaran, came into her room, a big man, in the prime of life, his hair prematurely grayed; and indeed he was far older than Aliciane, who had turned twenty-four but last spring. His tread was heavy in the quiet room, sounding more like a mailed stride on a battle-field than a soft-shod indoor step.

"Do you play for your own pleasure, Aliciane? I had thought a musician drew most of her pleasure from applause, yet I find you playing for yourself and your women," he said, smiling, and hitched a light chair around to sit in it at her side. "How is it with you, my treasure?"

"I am well but weary," she said, also smiling. "This is a restless child, and I play partly because the music seems to have a calming effect. Perhaps because the music calms *me*, and so the child is calm, too."

"It may well be so," he said, and when she put the harp from her, said, "No, sing, Aliciane, if you are not too tired."

"As you will, my lord." She pressed the strings of the harp into chords, and sang, softly, a love song of the far hills:

"Where are you now?
  Where does my love wander?
  Not on the hills, not upon the shore,
    not far on the sea,
  Love, where are you now?

"Dark the night, and I am weary,
  Love, when can I cease this seeking?
  Darkness all around, above, beyond me,
  Where lingers he, my love?"

Mikhail leaned toward the woman, drew his heavy hand gently across her brilliant hair. "Such a weary song," he said softly, "and so sad; is love truly such a thing of sadness to you, my Aliciane?"

"No, indeed not," Aliciane said, assuming a gaiety she did not feel. Fears and self-questioning were for pampered wives, not for a *barragana* whose position depended on keeping her lord amused and cheery with her charm and beauty, her skills as an entertainer. "But the loveliest love songs are of sorrow in love, my lord. Would it please you more if I choose songs of laughter or valor?"

"Whatever you sing pleases me, my treasure," Mikhail said kindly. "If you are weary or sorrowful you need not pretend to gaiety with me, *carya*." He saw the flicker of distrust in her eyes, and thought, *I am too sensitive for my own good; it must be pleasant never to be too aware of the minds of others. Does Aliciane truly love me, or does she only value her position as my acknowledged favorite? Even if she loves me, is it for myself, or only that I am rich and powerful and can make her secure?* He gestured to the women, and they withdrew to the far end of the long room, leaving him alone with his mistress; present, to satisfy the decencies of the day that dictated a childbearing woman should never be unattended, but out of earshot.

"I do not trust all these women," he said.

"Lord, Deonara is truly fond of me, I think. She would not put anyone among my women with ill will to me or my child," Aliciane said.

"Deonara? No, perhaps not," Mikhail said, remembering

that Deonara had been Lady of Aldaran for twice ten years and shared his hunger for a child to be heir to his estate. She could no longer promise him even the hope of one; she had welcomed the knowledge that he had taken Aliciane, who was one of her own favorites, to his bed and his heart. "But I have enemies who are not of this household, and it is all too easy to plant a spy with *laran*, who can relay all the doings of my household to someone who wishes me ill. I have kinsmen who would do much to prevent the birth of a living heir to my line. I marvel not that you look pale, my treasure; it is hard to credit wickedness that would harm a little child, yet I have never been sure that Deonara was not victim to someone who killed the children unborn in her womb. It is not hard to do; even a little skill with matrix or *laran* can break a child's fragile link to life."

"Anyone who wished you ill, Mikhail, would know you have promised me that my child will be legitimated, and would turn her evil will to me," Aliciane soothed. "Yet I have borne this child without illness. You fear needlessly, my dear love."

"Gods grant you are right! Yet I have enemies who would stop at nothing. Before your child is born, I will call a *leronis* to probe them; I will have no woman present at your confinement who cannot swear under truthspell that she wishes you well. An evil wish can snap a newborn child's fight for life."

"Surely that strength of *laran* is rare, my dearest lord."

"Not as rare as I could wish it," Mikhail, Lord Aldaran, said. "Yet of late I have strange thoughts. I find these gifts a weapon to cut my own hand; I who have used sorcery to hurl fire and chaos upon my enemy, I feel it now that they have strength to hurl them upon me, too. When I was young I felt *laran* as a gift of the gods; they had appointed me to rule this land, and dowered me with *laran* to make my rule stronger. But as I grow old I find it a curse, not a gift."

"You are not so old, my lord, and surely no one now would challenge your rule!"

"No one who dares do so openly, Aliciane. But I am alone among those who hover waiting for me to die childless. I have meaty bones to pick . . . all gods grant your child is a son, *carya*."

Aliciane was trembling. "And if it is not . . . oh, my dear lord. . . ."

"Why, then, treasure, you must bear me another," he said

gently, "but even if you do not, I shall have a daughter whose dower will be my estate, and who will bring me the strong alliances I need; even a woman-child will make my position that much stronger. And *your* son shall be foster-brother and paxman, shield in trouble and strong arm. I truly love your son, Aliciane."

"I know." How could she have been trapped this way . . . finding that she loved the man whom, at first, she had simply thought to ensnare with the wiles of her voice and her beauty? Mikhail was kind and honorable, he had courted her when he might have taken her as lawful prey, he had assured her, unasked, that even if she failed to give him a living son, Donal's future was secure. She felt safe with him, she had come to love him, and now she feared *for* him, too.

Caught in my own trap!

She said, almost laughing, "I need no such reassurance, my lord. I have never doubted you."

He smiled, accepting that, the courtesy of a telepath. "But women are fearful at such times, and it is sure now that Deonara will bear me no child, even if I would ask it of her after so many tragedies. Do you know what it is like, Aliciane, to see children you have longed for, desired, love even before they were born, to see them die without drawing breath? I did not love Deonara when we were wed; I had never seen her face, for we were given to one another for family alliances; but we have endured much together, and although it may seem strange to you, child, love can come from shared sorrow as well as shared joy." His face was somber. "I love you well, *carya mea*, but it was neither for your beauty nor even for the splendor of your voice that I sought you out. Did you know Deonara was not my first wife?"

"No, my lord."

"I was wed first when I was a young man; Clariza Leynier bore me two sons and a daughter, all healthy and strong. . . . Hard as it is to lose children at birth, it is harder yet to lose sons and daughter grown almost to manhood and womanhood. And yet I lost them—one after another, as they grew to adolescence. I lost them all three, with the descent of *laran*; they died in crisis and convulsions, all of them, of that scourge of our people. I myself was ready to die of despair."

"My brother Caryl died so," Aliciane whispered.

"I know; yet he was the only one of your line, and your father had many sons and daughters. You yourself told me that your *laran* did not descend at adolescence, playing havoc with mind and body, but that you grew slowly into it from babyhood, as with many of the Rockraven folk. And I can see that this is dominant in your line, for Donal is barely ten years old, and though I do not think his *laran* is full developed yet, still he has much of it, and he at least is not like to die on the threshold. I knew that for your children, at least, I need not fear. Deonara, too, came from a bloodline with early onset of *laran*, but none of the children she bore me lived long enough for us to know whether they had *laran* or no."

Aliciane's face twisted in dismay and he laid his arm tenderly about her shoulders. "What is it, my dear one?"

"All my life I have felt revulsion for this—to breed men like cattle!"

"Man is the only animal that thinks not to improve his race," Mikhail said fiercely. "We control weather, build castles and highways with the strength of our *laran*, explore greater and greater gifts of the mind—should we not seek to better ourselves as well as our world and our surroundings?" Then his face softened. "But I understand that a woman as young as you thinks not in terms of generations, centuries; while one is yet young, you think only of self and children, but at my age it is natural to think in terms of all those who will come after us when we and our children are many centuries gone. But such things are not for you unless you wish to think of them; think of your child, love, and how soon we will hold her in our arms."

Aliciane shrank, whispering, "You know, then, that it is a daughter I am to bear you—you are not angry?"

"I told you I would not be angry; if I am distressed it is only that you did not trust me enough to tell me this when first you knew," Mikhail said, but the words were so gentle they were hardly a reproof. "Come, Aliciane, forget your fears; if you give me no son, at least you have given me a sturdy foster-son, and your daughter will be a powerful strength in bringing me a son-in-law. And our daughter will have *laran*."

Aliciane smiled and returned his kiss; but she was still taut with apprehension as she heard the distant crackle of the unprecedented summer thunder, which seemed to come and go in tune with the waves of her fear. *Can it be that Donal is afraid of what this child will mean to him?* she wondered, and wished passionately that she had the precognitive gift, the *laran* of the Aldaran clan, so that she might *know* that all would be well.

CHAPTER
TWO

"Here is the traitor!"

Aliciane trembled at the anger in Lord Aldaran's voice as he strode wrathfully into her chamber, thrusting a woman ahead of him with his two hands. Behind him the *leronis*, his household sorceress, bearing the matrix or blue starstone which somehow amplified the powers of her *laran*, tiptoed; a fragile pale-haired woman, her pallid features drawn with terror of the storm she had unleashed.

"Mayra," Aliciane said in dismay, "I thought you my friend, and friend to Lady Deonara. What has befallen that you are my enemy and my child's?"

Mayra—she was one of Deonara's robing-women, a sturdy middle-aged dame—stood frightened but defiant between Lord Aldaran's hard hands. "No, I know nothing of what that sorceress-bitch has said of me; is she jealous of my place here, having no useful work but to meddle with the minds of her betters?"

"It will not serve you to put ill names on me," said the *leronis* Margali. "I asked all these women but one question, and that under the truthspell, so that I would hear in my mind if they lied. Is your loyalty to Mikhail, Lord Aldaran, or to the *vai domna*, his lady Deonara? And if they said me *no*, or said *yes* with a doubt or a denial in their thoughts, I asked only, again under truthspell, if their loyalty were to husband or father or home-lord. From this one alone I got no honest answer, but only the knowledge that she was concealing all. And so I told Lord Aldaran that if there was a traitor among his women it could be only she."

Mikhail let the woman go and turned her around to face

16

him, not ungently. He said, "It is true that you have been long in my service, Mayra; Deonara treats you with the kindness of a foster-sister. Is it me you wish evil, or my lady?"

"My lady has been kind to me; I am angered to see her set aside for another," said Mayra, her voice shaking. The *leronis* behind her said, in passionless tone, "No, Lord Aldaran, there she speaks no truth, either; she holds no love for you nor for your lady."

"She lies!" Mayra's voice rose to a half-shriek. "She lies—I wish you no ill save what you have brought on yourself, lord, by taking the bitch of Rockraven to your bed. It is she who has put a spell on your manhood, that bitch-viper!"

"*Silence!*" Lord Aldaran quivered as if he would strike the woman, but the word was enough; everyone within range was smitten dumb, and Aliciane trembled. Only once before had she heard Mikhail use what was called, in the language of *laran*, the command-voice. There were not many who could summon enough control over their *laran* to use it; it was not an inborn gift, but one that required both talent and skilled training. And when, in that voice, Mikhail, Lord Aldaran, commanded *silence*, none within earshot could form an audible word.

The silence in the room was so extreme that Aliciane could hear the smallest of sounds: some small insect clicking in the woodwork of the paneling, the frightened breathing of the women, the far-off crackle of thunder. *It seems,* she thought, *that all through this summer we have had thunder, more than I can remember in any year before. . . . What nonsense to have in my thoughts now, when I stand before a woman who might have meant my death, had she attended my childbed. . . .*

Mikhail glanced at her, where she stood trembling and propping herself upright by the arm of a chair. Then he said to the *leronis*, "Attend the lady Aliciane, help her to sit, or to lie down on her bed if she feels better so . . ." and Aliciane felt Margali's strong hands supporting her, easing her into the chair. She shook with anger, hating the physical weakness she could not control.

This child saps my strength as never Donal did. . . . Why am I so weakened? Is it that woman's evil will, wicked spells . . . ? Margali laid her hands on Aliciane's forehead and she felt soothing calm radiating out from them. She tried to relax under them, to breathe evenly, to calm the frantic restlessness she could sense in the movements of her child within her body. *Poor little one . . . she is afraid, too, and no wonder. . . .*

"You—" Lord Aldaran's voice commanded, "Mayra, tell me why you bear me ill will, or would seek to harm the lady Aliciane or her child!"

"Tell *you*?"

"You will, you know," Mikhail of Aldaran said. "You will tell us more than you ever believed you would say, whether you do so of your free will and painlessly, or whether it is dragged from you shrieking! I have no love for torturing womenfolk, Mayra, but I will not harbor a scorpion-ant within my chamber, either! Save us this struggle." But Mayra faced him, silent and defiant, and Mikhail shrugged faintly, a tautness Aliciane knew—and would not have dared defy— settling down over his face. He said, "On your own head, Mayra. Margali, bring your starstone—no. Better still, send for *kirizani*."

Aliciane trembled, though Mikhail was showing mercy in his own way. *Kirizani* was one of half a dozen drugs distilled from the plant resins of kireseth flowers, whose pollen brought madness when the Ghost-wind blew in the hills; *kirizani* was that part of the resin which lowered the barriers against telepathic contact, laying the mind bare to anyone who would probe within it. It was better than torture, and yet . . . She quailed, looking at the raging purpose on Mikhail's face, at the smiling defiance of the woman Mayra. They all stood silent while the *kirizani* was brought, a pale liquid in a vial of transparent crystal.

Mikhail uncapped it and said quietly, "Will you take it without protest, Mayra, or shall the women hold you and pour it down your throat like a horse being dosed?"

Mayra's face flushed; she spit at him. "You think you can make me speak with your sorcery and drugs, Lord Mikhail? Ha—I defy you! You need no evil will of mine—enough lurks already in your house and in the womb of your bitch-mistress there! A day will come when you pray you had died childless—and there will be no other! You will take no other to your bed, no more than you have done while the bitch of Rockraven grew heavy with her witch-daughter! My work is done, *vai dom!*" She flung the respectful term at him like a taunt. "I need no more time! From this day you will father

neither daughter nor son—your loins will be empty as a winter-killed tree! And you will cry out and pray—"

"Silence that evil banshee!" Mikhail said, and Margali,
starting upright from the fainting Aliciane, raised her jeweled
matrix, but the woman spit again, laughed hysterically,
gasped, and crumpled to the floor. In the stunned silence
Margali went to her, laid a perfunctory hand to her breast.

"Lord Aldaran, she is dead! She must have been spelled to
die on questioning."

The man stared in dismay at the lifeless body of the
woman, unanswered questions unspoken on his lips. He said,
"Now we shall never know what she has done, or how, or
who was the enemy who sent her here to us. I would take my
oath Deonara knows nothing of it." But the words held a
question, and Margali laid her hand on the blue jewel and
said quietly, "On my life, Lord Aldaran, the Lady Deonara
has no ill will to Lady Aliciane's child; this she has told me
often, that she is glad for you and for Aliciane, and I know
when I am hearing truth."

Mikhail nodded, but Aliciane saw the lines around his
mouth deepen. If Deonara, jealous of Lord Aldaran's favor,
had wished Aliciane some harm, that at least would have
been understandable. But who, she wondered, knowing little
of the feuds and power struggles of Aldaran, could wish evil
to a man so good as Mikhail? Who could hate him so much
as to plant a spy among his wife's waiting-women, to do evil
to the child of a *barragana*, to cast, perhaps, *laran*-powered
curses on his manhood?

"Take her away," Aldaran said at last, his voice not entirely steady. "Hang her body from the castle heights for
kyorebni to pick; she has earned no faithful servant's burial
rites." He waited, impassive, while tall guardsmen came and
bore away Mayra's dead body, to be stripped and hanged for
the great birds of prey to peck asunder. Aliciane heard thunder crackling in the distance, then nearer and nearer, and Aldaran came toward her, his voice now softened to tenderness.

"Have no more fear, my treasure; she is gone and her evil
will with her. We will live to laugh at her curses, my darling." He sank into a chair nearby, taking her hand in gentle
fingers, but she sensed, through the touch, that he, too, was
distressed and even frightened. And she was not strong
enough to reassure him; she felt as if she were fainting again.
Mayra's curses rang in her ears, like the reverberating echoes

in the canyons around Rockraven when as a child she had shouted into them for the amusement of hearing her own voice come back to her multiplied a thousandfold from all quarters of the wind.

You will father neither daughter nor son. . . . Your loins will be empty as a winter-killed tree. . . . A day will come when you pray you had died childless. . . . The reverberating remembered sound swelled, overwhelmed her; she lay back in the chair, near to losing consciousness.

"Aliciane, Aliciane—" She felt his strong arms around her, raising her, carrying her to her bed. He laid her down on the pillows, sat beside her, gently stroking her face.

"You must not be frightened of shadows, Aliciane."

She said, trembling, the first thing that came into her head. "She cursed your manhood, my lord."

"I feel not much endangered," he said with a smile.

"Yet—I myself have seen and wondered . . . you have taken no other to your bed in these days when I am so heavy, as would have been your custom."

A faint shadow passed over his face, and at this moment their minds were so close that Aliciane regretted her words; she should not have touched on his own fear. But he said, firmly putting away fear in cheerfulness, "Why, as for that, Aliciane, I am not so young a man that I cannot live womanless for a few moons. Deonara is not sorry to be free of me, I think; my embraces have never meant more to her than duty, and dying children. And in these days, it seems, except for you, women are not so beautiful as they were when I was young. It has been no hardship to me, to forbear asking what is no pleasure to you to give; but when our child is born and you are well again, you shall see if that fool woman's words have any evil effect on my manhood. You may yet give me a son, Aliciane, or, if not, at least we shall spend many joyous hours together."

She said, shaking, "May the Lord of Light grant it, indeed." He bent and kissed her tenderly, but the touch of his lips again brought them close, with shared fear and, abruptly, shared pain, tearing at her.

He straightened as if shocked, calling to her women. "Attend my lady!"

She clung to his hands. "Mikhail, I am frightened," she whispered, and picked up his thought, *Indeed this is no good omen, that she should go into labor with the sound of that witch's curses still in her ears. . . .* She felt, too, the strong discipline with which he curbed and controlled even the thought, that fear might not spiral, heightened by each mind through which it passed. He said, with gentle command, "You must try to think of our child only, Aliciane, and lend her strength; think of our child only—and of my love."

It was nearing sunset. Clouds massed on the heights beyond Castle Aldaran, tall stormclouds piling higher and higher, but where Donal soared the sky was blue and cloudless. His slight body lay stretched along a wooden framework of light woods, between wide wings of thinnest leather built out on a narrow frame. Borne up by the currents of air, he soared, dipping a hand to either side to balance on the strong gusts to left or to right. The air bore him aloft, and the small matrix-jewel fastened along the crosspiece. He had made the levitation glider himself, with only a little help from the stable-men. Several of the boys in the household had such toys, as soon as their training in the use of the starstones was such as to maintain their levitation skills without undue danger. But most of the lads in the household were at their lessons; Donal had slipped away to the castle heights and soared away alone, even though he knew that the penalty would be to forbid him the use of the glider, perhaps for days. He could feel the stresses, the fear, everywhere in the castle.

A traitor executed, dying before touched, a death-spell on her. She had cursed Lord Aldaran's manhood. . . .

Gossip had run around Castle Aldaran like wildfire, fueled by the few women who had actually been in Aliciane's chamber and seen anything; they had seen too much to keep silent, too little to give a true account.

She had flung curses at the little *barragaña* and Aliciane of Rockraven had fallen down in labor. She had cursed Lord Aldaran's manhood—and it was true that he had taken no other to his bed, he who had always before taken a new woman with every change of the moons in the sky. A new, ominous question in the gossiping made Donal shiver: Was it the Lady of Rockraven who had spelled his manhood so he would desire no other, that she might keep her place in his arms and in his heart?

One of the men, a coarse man-at-arms, had laughed, a deep, suggestive laugh, and said, "That one needs no spells; if

Lady Aliciane cast her pretty eyes on me, I would gladly pawn my manhood," but the arms-master said firmly, "Be still, Radan. Such talk is unseemly among young lads, and look, you—see who stands among them? Go to your work; do not stand here and gossip and tell dirty tales." When the man had gone, the arms-master said kindly, "Such talk is unseemly, but it is only jesting, Donal; he is distressed because he has no woman of his own, and would speak so of any fair woman. He means no disrespect to your mother, Donal. Indeed, there will be great rejoicing at Aldaran if Aliciane of Rockraven gives him an heir. You must not be angry at unthinking speech; if you listen to every dog that barks, you will have no leisure to learn wisdom. Go to your lessons, Donal, and do not waste time resenting what ignorant men say of their betters."

Donal had gone, but not to his lessons; he had taken his glider to the castle heights and soared out on the air currents, and now rode them, distressing thoughts left behind, memory in abeyance, wholly caught up in the intoxication of soaring, bird-fashion, now swooping to the north, now turning back west to where the great crimson sun hung low on the peaks.

A hawk must feel like this, hovering. . . . Under his sensitive fingertips, the wood-and-leather wing tilted downward faintly, and he focused on the current, letting it bear him down the draft. His mind sunk into the hyperawareness of the jewel, seeing the sky not as blue emptiness but as a great net of fields and currents which were his to ride, now floating down, down until it seemed he would strike on a great crag and be dashed asunder, then at the last minute letting a sharp updraft snatch him away, hovering down the wind. . . . He floated, mindless, soaring, wrapped in ecstasy.

The green moon, Idriel, hung low, a gibbous semi-shape in the reddening sky; the silver crescent of Mormallor was the palest of shadows; and violent Liriel, the largest of the moons, near to full, was just beginning to float up slowly from the eastern horizon. A low crackle of thunder from the massy clouds hanging behind the castle roused memory and apprehension in Donal. He might not be chastised for slipping away from lessons at a time like this, but if he remained out after sunset he would certainly be punished. Strong winds sprang up at sunset, and about a year ago, one of the page-boys at the castle had smashed his glider and broken an elbow on one of the rocks below. He had been lucky, they knew, not to kill himself. Donal cast a wary eye back at the walls of the castle, seeking for an updraft that would carry him to the heights—otherwise he must drift down to the slopes below the castle and carry his glider, which was light but hugely awkward, all the way up again. Feeling the faintest of air pressures, magnified through the awareness of the matrix, he caught an updraft which, if he rode it carefully, would carry him above and behind the castle, and he could float down to the roofs.

Riding up it, he could see, with a shiver, the swollen naked figure of the woman who hung there, her face already torn by the *kyorebni* who hovered and swooped there. Already she was unrecognizable, and Donal shuddered. Mayra had been kind to him in her own way. Had she truly cursed his mother? He shuddered with his first real awareness of death.

People die. They really die and are pecked to bits by birds of prey. My mother could die in childbirth, too. . . . His body twitched in sudden terror and he felt the fragile wings of the glider, released from control of his mind and body, flutter and slip downward, falling. . . . Swiftly he mastered it, brought it up, levitating his body until he caught a current again. But now he could feel the faint tension and shock in the air, the building static.

Thunder crackled above him; a bolt of lightning flashed to the heights of Castle Aldaran, leaving a smell of ozone and a faint burned smell in Donal's nostrils. Behind the deafening roar, Donal saw without hearing the flare and play of lightning in the massed clouds above the castle. In sudden fright, he thought, *I must get down, out of here; it is not safe to fly in an oncoming storm. . . .* He had been told again and again to scan the sky for lightning in the clouds before letting his glider take off.

A sudden violent downdraft caught him, sent the fragile wood-and-leather apparatus plummeting down; Donal, really frightened, clung hard to the handholds, with sense enough not to try to fight it too soon. It felt as if it would smash him down on the rocks, but he forced himself to lie limp along the struts, his mind searching ahead for the crosscurrent. At just the right moment he tensed his body, focusing into the matrix awareness, felt levitation and the crosscurrent carry him up again.

Now. Quickly, and carefully. I must get up to the level of the castle, catch the first current that glides down. There is no time to waste. . . . But now the air felt heavy and thick and Donal could not read it for currents. In growing dread, he sent his awareness out in all directions, but he sensed only the strong magnetic charges of the growing storm.

This storm is wrong, too! It's like the one the other day. It's not a real storm at all, it's something else. Mother! Oh, my mother! It seemed to the frightened child, clinging to the struts of the glider, that he could hear Aliciane crying out in terror, "Oh, Donal, what will become of my boy," and he felt his body convulse in terror, the glider slipping from his control, falling . . . falling. . . . If it had been less light, less broad-winged, it would have smashed onto the rocks, but the air currents, even though Donal could not read them, bore him along. After a few moments his fall stopped, and he began to drift sideways again. Now, using *laran*—the levitational strength given body and mind by the matrix jewel— and his trained awareness searching for the traces of currents through the magnetic storm, Donal began to fight for his life. He forced away the voice he could almost hear, his mother's voice crying out in terror and pain. He forced away the fear which let him see his own body lying broken into bits on the crags below. He forced himself to submerge wholly into his own heightened *laran*, making the wood-and-leather wings extensions of his own outstretched arms, feeling the currents that blew and battered at them as if they buffeted his own hands, his own legs.

Now . . . ride it upward . . . just so far . . . try to gain a few lengths toward the west. . . . He forced himself to go limp as another smashing bolt of lightning leaped from a cloud, feeling it burst beyond him. *No control . . . it isn't going anywhere . . . it has no awareness . . .* and the maxims of the kindly *leronis* who had taught him what little he knew: *The trained mind can always master any force of nature.* . . . Ritually, Donal reminded himself of that.

I need not fear wind or storm or lightning, the trained mind can master. . . . But Donal was only ten years old, and resentfully he wondered if Margali had ever flown a glider in a thunderstorm.

A deafening crash socked him momentarily mindless; he felt the sudden drench of rain along his chilled body, and fought to stop the trembling which sought to wrest control of the fluttering wings from his mind.

Now. Firmly. Down, and down, along this current . . .

*right to the ground, along the slope . . . no time to play with
another updraft. Down here I will be safe from the lightning. . . .*

His feet had almost touched the ground when another
harsh upcurrent seized the wide wings and flung him upward
again, away from the safety of the slopes. Sobbing, fighting
the mechanism, he fought to force it down again, throwing
himself over the edge and hanging vertically, grasping the
struts over his head, letting the wide wings slow his fluttering
fall. He sensed, through his skin, the lightning bolt and all his
strength went out to divert it, to thrust it *elsewhere.* His
hands clung frantically to the struts above his head as he
heard the lightning and the deafening blast, saw with dazed
eyes one of the great standing rocks on the slope split asunder with a great crashing roar. His feet touched ground; he
fell hard, rolling over and over, feeling the glider's struts
smash and break to splinters. Pain cannoned through his
shoulder as he fell, but he had enough strength and awareness
left to go limp, as he had been taught to do in arms-practice,
to fall without the muscular resistance which could
break bones. Alive, bruised, sobbing, he lay stunned on the
rocky slope, feeling the currents of lightning darting, aim-
lessly, around him, thunder rolling from peak to peak.

When he had recovered his breath, he picked himself up.
Both wing-struts of the glider were smashed, but it could be
repaired; he was lucky that his arms were not smashed like the
struts. The sight of the splintered rock turned him sick and
dizzy, and his head throbbed; but he realized that with all
this, he was lucky to be alive. He picked up the broken toy,
letting the splintered wings hang folded, and began slowly to
trudge up the slope toward the castle gates.

"She hates me," Aliciane cried in terror. "She does not
want to be born!"

Through the darkness that seemed to hover around her
mind she felt Mikhail catch and hold her flailing hands.

"My dearest love, that is folly," he murmured, holding the
woman against him, firmly controlling his own fears. He, too,
sensed the strangeness of the lightning which flashed and
crackled around the high windows, and Aliciane's terror reinforced his own dread. It seemed there was another in the
room, besides the frightened woman, besides the calm
presence of Margali, who sat with her head bent, not looking

at either of them, her face blue-lighted with the glimmer of the matrix stone. Mikhail could feel the soothing waves of calm Margali sent out, trying to surround them all with it; he tried to let his own mind and body surrender to the calm, relax to it. He began the deep rhythmic breathing he had been taught for control, and after a little he felt Aliciane, too, relax and float with it.

Where, then, whence the terror, the struggle . . .

It is she, the unborn . . . it is her fear, her reluctance . . .

Birth is an ordeal of terror; there must be someone to reassure her, someone who awaits her with love. . . . Aldaran had done this service at the birth of all his children; sensing the formless fright and rage of the unformed mind, thrust by forces it could not comprehend. Now, searching his memories (had any of Clariza's children been so strong? Deonara's babes, none of them had been able even to fight for their lives, poor little weaklings . . .), he reached out, searching for the unfocused thoughts of the struggling child, torn by awareness of the mother's pain and fright. He sought to send out soothing thoughts of love, of tenderness; not in words, for the unborn had no knowledge of language, but he formed them into words for his own sake and Aliciane's, to focus their emotions, to give a feeling of warmth and welcome.

You must not be afraid, little one; it will soon be over . . . you will breathe free and we will hold you in our arms and love you . . . you are long awaited and dearly loved. . . . He sought to send out love and tenderness, to banish from his mind the frightening thought of the sons and daughter he had lost, when all his love could not follow them into the darkness their developing *laran* had cast on their minds. He tried to blot out memory of the weak and pitiful struggles of Deonara's children, who had never lived to draw breath. . . . *Did I love them enough? If I had loved Deonara more, would her children have fought harder to live?*

"Draw the curtains," he said after a moment, and one of the women in the chamber tiptoed to the window and closed out the darkening sky. But the thunder roared in the room, and the flare of the lightning could be seen even through the drawn curtains.

"See how she does, the little one," the midwife said, and Margali rose quietly, came to lay gentle hands around Aliciane's body, sinking her awareness into the woman, to monitor her breathing, the progress of the birth. A woman with *laran,* bearing a child, could not be physically examined or touched, for fear of hurting or frightening the unborn with a careless pressure or touch. The *leronis* must do this, using the perception of her own telepathic and psychokinetic powers. Aliciane felt the soothing touch, and her troubled face relaxed, but as Margali withdrew she cried out in sudden terror.

"Oh, Donal, Donal—what will become of my boy?"

Lady Deonara Ardais-Aldaran, a slight aging woman, tiptoed to Aliciane's side, and took the slender fingers in hers. She said soothingly, "Do not fear for Donal, Aliciane. Avarra forbid it should be needful, but I swear to you that I will, from this day forth, be foster-mother to him, as tenderly as if he were one of my own sons."

"You have been kind to me, Deonara," Aliciane said, "and I sought to take Mikhail from you."

"Child, child—this is no time to think of this; if you can give Mikhail what I could not, then you are my sister and I will love you as Cassilda loved Camilla, I swear it." Deonara bent and kissed Aliciane's pale cheek. "Set your mind at rest, *breda*; think only of this little one who comes to our arms. I will love her too."

Held tenderly in the arms of her child's father, of the woman who had sworn to welcome her child as her own, Aliciane knew that she should be comforted. Yet, as lightning flared on the heights and rumbled around the walls of the castle, she felt terror all through and pervading her. *Is it the child's terror or mine?* Her mind swam into darkness under the soothing of the *leronis,* under the flooding reassurances of Mikhail, pouring out love and tenderness. *Is it for me or only for the child?* It no longer seemed to matter; she could see no further. Always before, she had had some faint sense of what would come after, but now it seemed there was nothing in the world but her own fear, the child's fear, the formless, wordless rage. It seemed to her that the rage focused with the thunder, that the birth pains tearing her were brightening and darkening as the lightning came and went . . . thunder crashing not on the heights outside but in and around her own violated body . . . terror, rage, fury expending itself within her . . . the lightning bringing fury and pain. She struggled for breath and cried out and her mind sank, almost with relief, into dark, and silence, and nothingness. . . .

"Ai! She is a little fury," the midwife said, gingerly holding the struggling child. "You must calm her, *domna*, before I cut her life from her mother's, or she will struggle and bleed overmuch—but she is strong, a hearty little woman!"

Margali bent over the shrieking infant. The face was dark red, contorted into a furious scream of rage; the eyes, squinted almost shut, were a blazing blue. The round little head was covered with thick red fuzz. Margali laid her slender hands along the naked body of the child, crooning softly to her. Under the touch the baby calmed a little and stopped fighting; and the midwife was able to sever the umbilical cord and tie it. But when the woman took the infant and wrapped her in a warmed blanket, she began to shriek again and struggle and the woman laid her down, drawing back a shocked hand.

"Ai! Evanda have mercy, she is one of *those*! Well, when she is grown, the little maiden need not fear rape, if she can strike already with *laran*. I have never heard of this in a babe so young!"

"You frightened her," Margali said, smiling; but as she took the child, her smile slid off. Like all of Deonara's women, she had loved the gentle Aliciane. "Poor child, to lose so loving a mother, so soon!"

Mikhail of Aldaran knelt, his face drawn with anguish, beside the body of the woman he had loved. "Aliciane! Aliciane, my beloved," he mourned. Then he raised his face, in bitterness. Deonara had taken the wrapped infant from Margali and was holding it, with the fierce hunger of thwarted motherhood, to her meager breast.

"You are not ill content, are you, Deonara—that none will vie with you to mother this child?"

"That is not worthy of you, Mikhail," Deonara said, holding Aliciane's child close. "I loved Aliciane well, my lord; would you have me cast aside her child, or can I best show my love by rearing her as tenderly as if she were my own? Take her, then, my husband, until you find another love." Try as she would, Lady Aldaran could not keep the bitterness from her voice. "She is your only living child. And if already she has *laran*, she will need much care to rear her. My poor babes never lived even this long." She put the child into Dom Mikhail's arms, and he stood looking down, with infinite tenderness and grief, at his only child.

Mayra's curse rang in his mind: *You will take no other to*

your bed . . . your loins will be empty as a winter-killed tree.
As if his own dismay communicated itself to the infant in his
arms she began to struggle again and shriek in the blanket.
Beyond the window the storm raged.

Dom Mikhail looked into the face of his daughter. Infinitely precious she seemed to the childless man; the more so if
the curse should be true. She was rigid in his arms, squalling,
her small face contorted as if she were trying to outshout the
rage of the storm outside, her tiny pink fists clenched with
rage. Yet already he could see in her face a miniature blurred
copy of Aliciane's—the arched brows and high cheekbones,
the eyes blazing blue, the fuzz of red hair.

"Aliciane died to give me this great gift. Shall we give her
her mother's name, in memory?"

Deonara shuddered and flinched. "Would you bestow on
your only daughter the name of the dead, my lord? Seek a
name of better omen!"

"As you will. Give her what name pleases you, *domna*."

Deonara said, faltering, "I would have named our first
daughter Dorilys, had she lived long enough to be named. Let
her bear that name, in token that I will be a mother to her."
She touched the rose-petal cheek with a finger. "How do you
like that name, little woman? Look—she sleeps. She is weary
with so much crying. . . ."

Beyond the windows of the birth-chamber the storm muttered into silence and died away, and there was no sound but
the slow dripping of the last raindrops outside.

CHAPTER
THREE

* * * *Eleven Years Later* * * *

It was the dark hour before dawn. Snow fell silently over the monastery of Nevarsin, already buried under deep snow.

There was no bell, or if there was, it rang silently, unheard, in Father Master's quarters. Yet in every cell and dormitory, brothers and novices and students moved silently, as if on that single noiseless signal, out of sleep.

Allart Hastur of Elhalyn came awake sharply, something in his mind tuned and receptive to the call. In his first years he had often slept through it, but no one in the monastery might waken another; part of the training here was that the novices should hear the inaudible and see what was not there to be seen.

Nor did he feel cold, though he was covered, by rule, only with the outer cowl of his long robe; he had by now disciplined his body so that it would generate heat to warm him as he slept. With no need of light, he rose, drew the cowl over the simple inner garment he wore night and day, and thrust his feet into rude sandals woven of straw. Into his pockets he thrust the small bound prayer book, the pen case and sealed ink-horn, his own bowl and spoon; now in the pockets of the robe were all the items which a monk might own or use. Dom Allart Hastur was not yet a fully sworn brother of Saint-Valentine-of-the-Snows at Nevarsin. It would be a year before he could achieve that final detachment from the world which lay below him—a troubling world, and one which he remembered every time he fastened the leather strap of his sandals; for in the world of the Domains below him, *sandal-*

wearer was the ultimate insult for a male, implying effeminate behavior, or worse. Even now, as he fastened the sandal-strap, he was forced to calm his mind from that memory by the three slow breaths, pause, three more breaths paced to a murmured prayer for the cause of the offense; but Allart was painfully aware of the irony in this.

To pray for peace for my brother, who put this insult on me, when it was he who drove me here, for my very sanity's sake? Aware that he still felt anger and resentment, he did the breathing ritual again, firmly dismissing his brother from his mind, remembering the words of the Father Master.

"You have no power over the world or the things of the world, my son; you have renounced all desire for that power. The power you have come here to attain is the power over the things within. Peace will come only when you become fully aware that your thoughts are not from outside yourself; they come from within, and thus are wholly yours, the only things in this universe over which it is legitimate to have total power. You, not your thoughts and memories, rule your mind, and it is you, no other, who bid them to come and go. The man who allows his own thoughts to torment him is like the man who clasps a scorpion-ant to his breast, bidding it bite him further."

Allart repeated the exercise, and at the end of it, the memory of his brother had vanished from his mind. *He has no place here, not even in my mind and memory.* Calm now, his breathing coming and going in a small white cloud about his mouth, he left the cell and moved silently down the long corridor.

The chapel, reached by a brief passage through the falling snow, was the oldest part of the monastery. Four hundred years ago, the first band of brothers had come here to be above the world they wished to renounce, digging their monastery from the living rock of the mountain, hollowing out the small cave in which, it was said, Saint-Valentine-of-the-Snows had lived out his life. Around the hermit's remains, a city had grown: Nevarsin, the City of Snows. Now several buildings clustered here, each one built with the labor of monkish hands, in defiance of the ease of these days; it was the brothers' boast that not a single stone had been moved with the aid of any matrix, or with anything other than the toil of hands and mind.

The chapel was dark, a single small light glowing in the

shrine where the statue of the Holy Bearer of Burdens stood, above the last resting-place of the saint. Allart, moving quietly, eyes closed as the rule demanded, turned into his assigned place on the benches; as one, the brotherhood knelt. Allart, eyes still closed by rule, heard the shuffle of feet, an occasional stumble of some novice who must still rely on the outer instead of the inner sight to move his clumsy body about the darkness of the monastery. The students, unsworn, with minimal teaching, stumbled in the darkness, ignorant of why the monks neither allowed nor required light. Whispering, pushing one another, they stumbled and sometimes fell, but eventually they were all in their assigned places. Again there was no discernible sound, but the monks rose with a single disciplined movement, following again some invisible signal from Father Master, and their voices rose in the morning hymn:

> "One Power created
> Heaven and Earth
> Mountains and valleys
> Darkness and light;
> Male and female
> Human and nonhuman.
> This Power cannot be seen
> Cannot be heard
> Cannot be measured
> By anything except the mind
> Which partakes of this Power;
> I name it Divine. . . ."

This was the moment of every day when Allart's inward questions, searchings, and dismay wholly vanished. Hearing the voices of his brothers singing, old and young, treble with childhood or rusty with age, loosing his own voice in the great affirmation, he lost all sense of himself as a separate, searching, questing entity. He rested, floating, in the knowledge that he was a part of something greater than himself, a part of the great Power which maintained the motion of moons, stars, sun, and the unknown Universe beyond; that here he had a true place in the harmony; that if he vanished, he would leave an Allart-sized hole in the Universal Mind, something never to be replaced or altered. Hearing the singing, he was wholly at peace. The sound of his own voice, a finely trained tenor, gave him pleasure, but no more than the sounds of each voice in the choir, even the rusty and untuneful quavering of old Brother Fenelon next to him. Whenever he sang with his brothers, he recalled the first words he had ever read of Saint-Valentine-of-the-Snows, words which had come to him during the years of his greatest torment, and which had given him the first peace he had known since he left his childhood behind.

"Each one of us is like a single voice within a great choir, a voice like no other; each of us sings for a few years within that great choir and then that voice is forever silenced, and other voices take its place; but every voice is unique and none is more beautiful than another, or can sing another's song. I call nothing evil but the attempt to sing to another's tune or in another's voice."

And Allart, reading those words, had known that from childhood he had been attempting, at the command of his father and brothers, tutors, arms-masters and grooms, servants and superiors, to sing to a tune, and in a voice, which could never be his own. He had become a *cristoforo*, which was believed unseemly for a Hastur; a descendant of Hastur and Cassilda, a descendant of gods, one who bore *laran*; a Hastur of Elhalyn, near to the holy places at Hali where the gods once had walked. All the Hasturs, from time immemorial, had worshiped the Lord of Light. Yet Allart had become a *cristoforo*, and a time had come when he had left his brethren and renounced his inheritance and come here to be Brother Allart, his lineage half forgotten even by the brethren of Nevarsin.

Forgetful of self, and yet all-mindful of his own individual and unique place in the choir, in the monastery, in the Universe, Allart sang the long hymns; later he went, his fast still unbroken, to his assigned work of the morning, bringing breakfast to the novices and students in the outer refectory. He carried the steaming jugs of tea and hot bean-porridge to the boys, pouring the food into stoneware bowls and mugs, noticing how the cold young hands curved around the heat to try to warm themselves. Most of the boys were too young to have mastered the techniques of internal heat, and he knew that some of them wore their blankets wrapped under their cowls. He felt a detached sympathy for them, remembering his own early sufferings with the cold before his untrained mind could learn how to warm his body; but they had hot food and slept under extra blankets and the more they felt the cold, the sooner they would apply themselves to conquering it.

He kept silence (though he knew he should have reproved them) when they grumbled about the coarseness of the food; here in the quarters of the children, food rich and luxurious, by contrast, was served. He himself had tasted hot food only twice since entering the full monastic regimen; both times when he had done extraordinary work in the deep passes, rescuing snowbound travelers. Father Master had judged the chilling of his body had gone to a point where it endangered his health, and had ordered him to eat hot food and sleep under extra blankets for a few days. Under ordinary conditions, Allart had so mastered his body that summer and winter were indifferent to him, and his body made full use of whatever food came his way, hot or cold.

One disconsolate little fellow, a pampered son of the Lowland Domains with carefully cut hair curled around his face, was shivering so hard, wrapped in cowl and blanket, that Allart while spooning him out a second portion of porridge—for the children were allowed to eat as much as they wished, being growing boys—said gently, "You will not feel the cold so much in a little while. The food will warm you. And you are warmly clad."

"Warmly?" the child said, disbelieving. "I haven't my fur cloak, and I think I am going to die of the cold!" He was near to tears, and Allart laid a hand compassionately on his shoulder.

"You won't die, little brother. You will learn that you can be warm without clothes. Do you know that the novices here sleep with neither blanket nor cowl, naked on the stone? And no one here has died of the cold yet. No animal wears clothing, their bodies being adapted to the weather where they live."

"Animals have fur," protested the child, sulkily. "I've only got my skin!"

Allart laughed and said, "And that is proof you do not need fur; for if you needed fur to keep warm, you would have been born furred, little brother. You are cold because since childhood you have been told to be cold in the snow and your mind has believed this lie; but a time will come, even before summer, when you too will run about barefoot in the snow and feel no discomfort. You do not believe me now, but remember my words, child. Now eat up your porridge, and feel it going to work in the furnace of your body, to bring heat to all your limbs." He patted the tearstained cheek, and went on with his work.

He, too, had rebelled against the harsh discipline of the monks; but he had trusted them, and their promises had been truthful. He was at peace, his mind disciplined to control, living only one day at a time with none of the tormenting pressure of foresight, his body now a willing servant, doing what it was told without demanding more than it needed for well-being and health.

In his years here he had seen four batches of these children arrive, crying with cold, complaining about harsh food and cold beds, spoiled, demanding—and they would go away in a year, or two, or three, disciplined to survival, knowing much of their past history and competent to judge their own future. These, too, including the pampered little boy who was afraid he would die of cold without his fur cloak, would go away hardened and disciplined. Without deliberation, his mind moved into the future, trying to see what would become of the child, to reassure himself. He knew it—his sternness with the child was justified. . . .

Allart tensed, his muscles stiffening as they had not done since his first year here. Automatically, he breathed to relax them, but the sudden dread remained.

I am not here. I cannot see myself at Nevarsin in another year. . . . Is it my death I see: Or am I to go forth? Holy Bearer of Burdens, strengthen me. . . .

It had been this that brought him here. He was not, as some Hasturs were, *emmasca*, neither male nor female, long-lived but mostly sterile; though there were monks in this monastery who had indeed been born so, and only here had they found ways to live with this, which in these days was an affliction. No; he had known from childhood that he was a man, and had been so trained, as was fitting to the son of a royal line, fifth from the throne of the Domains. But even as a child, he had had another trouble.

He had begun to see the future almost before he was able to talk; once, when his foster-father had come to bring him a horse, he had frightened the man by telling him that he was glad he had brought the black instead of the gray he had started out with.

"How did you know I started to bring you the gray?" the man had asked.

"I saw you giving me the gray," Allart had said, "and then I saw you giving me the black, and I saw that your pack fell and you turned back and did not come at all."

"Mercy of Aldones," the man had whispered. "It is true that I came near to losing my pack in the pass, and if I had lost it I would have had to turn back, having little food for the journey."

Only slowly had Allart begun to realize the nature of his *laran*; he saw, not the one future, the true future alone, but all possible futures, fanning out ahead of him, every move he made spawning a dozen new choices. At fifteen, when he was declared a man and went before the Council of Seven to be tattooed with the mark of his Royal House, he found his days and nights torture, for he could see a dozen roads before him at every step, and a hundred choices each spurting new choices, till he was paralyzed, never daring to move for terror of the known and the new unknown. He did not know how to shut it out, and he could not live with it. In arms-training he was paralyzed, seeing at every stroke a dozen ways a movement of his own could disable or kill another, three ways every stroke aimed at him could land or fail to land. The arms-training sessions became such a nightmare that eventually he would stand still before the arms-master, cowering like a frightened girl, unable even to lift his sword. The *leronis* of his household tried to reach his mind and show him the way out of this labyrinth, but Allart was paralyzed with the different roads he could see for her training, and with his own growing sensitivity to women, could see himself seizing her mindlessly, and in the end he hid himself in his room, letting them call him coward and idiot, refusing to move or take a single step for fear of what would happen, knowing himself a freak, a madman. . . .

When Allart had finally stirred himself to make his long, terrifying journey—at every step seeing the false step which could plunge him into the abyss, to be killed or lie broken for days on the crags below the path, seeing himself fleeing, turning back—Father Master had welcomed him and heard his story, saying, "Not a freak or a madman, Allart, but much afflicted. I cannot promise you will find your true road here, or be cured, but perhaps we can teach you to live with it."

"The *leronis* thought I could learn to control it with a matrix, but I was afraid," Allart had confessed, and it was the first time he had felt free to speak of fear; fear was the forbidden thing, cowardice a vice too unspeakable to mention for a Hastur.

Father Master nodded and said, "You did well to fear the matrix; it might have controlled you through your fear. Perhaps we can show you a way to live without fear; failing that, perhaps you can learn a way to live with your fears. First you will learn that they are *yours*."

"I have always known this. I have felt guilty enough about them—" Allart protested, but the old monk had smiled.

"No. If you truly believed they were *yours*, you would not feel guilt, or resentment, or anger. What you see is from outside yourself, and may come, or not, but is beyond your control. But your fear is yours, and yours alone, like your voice, or your fingers, or your memory, and therefore yours to control. If you feel powerless over your fear, you have not yet admitted that it is yours, to do with as you will. Can you play the *rryl*?"

Startled at this mental jump, Allart admitted that he had been taught to play the small, handheld harp after a fashion.

"When your strings would not at first make the sounds you wished, did you curse the instrument, or your unskilled hands? Yet a time came, I suppose, when your fingers were responsive to your will. Do not curse your *laran* because your mind has not yet been trained to control it." He let Allart think that over for a moment, then said, "The futures you see are from outside, generated by neither memory nor fear; but the fear arises within you, paralyzing your choice to move among those futures. It is you, Allart, who create the fear; when you learn to control your fear, then you can look unafraid at the many paths you may tread and choose which you will take. Your fear is like your unskilled hand on the harp, blurring the sound."

"But how can I help being afraid? I do not *want* to fear."

"Tell me," Father Master said mildly, "which of the gods put the fear into you, like a curse?" Allart was silent, shamed, and the monk said quietly, "You speak of *being* afraid. Yet fear is something you generate in yourself, from your mind's lack of control; and you will learn to look at it and discover for yourself when you choose to be afraid. The first thing you must do is to acknowledge that the fear is *yours*, and you can bid it come and go at will. Begin with this; whenever you feel fear that prevents choice, say to yourself: 'What has made me feel fear? Why have I chosen to feel this fear preventing my choice, instead of feeling the freedom to choose?' Fear is a way of not allowing yourself to choose freely what you will do next; a way of letting your body's reflexes, not the needs of your mind, choose for you. And as you have told me, mostly, of late, you have chosen to do nothing, so that none of the things you fear will come upon you; so your choices are not made by you but by your fear. Begin here, Allart. I cannot promise to free you of your fear, only that a time will come when you are the master, and fear will not paralyze you." Then he had smiled and said, "You came here, did you not?"

"I was more afraid to stay than to come," Allart said, shaking.

Father Master had said, encouragingly, "At least you could still select between a greater and a lesser fear. Now you must learn to control the fear and look beyond it; and then a day will come when you will know that it is yours, your servant, to command as you will."

"All the Gods grant it," Allart had said, shivering.

So his life here had begun . . . and had endured for six years now. Slowly, one by one, he had mastered his fears, his body's demands, learning to seek out among the bewildering fan-shaped futures the one least harmful. Then his future had narrowed, until he saw himself only here, living one day at a time, doing what he must . . . no more and no less.

Now, after six years, suddenly what he saw ahead was a bewildering flow of images: travel, rocks and snow, a strange castle, his home, the face of a woman. . . . Allart covered his face with his hands, again in the grip of the old paralyzing fear.

No! No! I will not! I want to stay here, to live my own destiny, to sing to no other man's tune and in no other man's voice. . . .

For six years he had been left to his own destiny, subject only to the futures determined by his own choices. Now the outside was breaking in on him again; was someone outside the monastery making choices in which he must be involved, one way or another? All the fear he had subdued in the last six years crowded in on him again; then, slowly, breathing as he had been taught, he mastered it.

My fear is my own; I am in command of it, and I alone can choose. . . . Again he sought to see, among the thronging images, one path in which he might remain Brother Allart, at peace in his cell, working for the future of his world in his own way. . . .

But there was no such future path, and this told him something; whatever outside choice was breaking in on him, it would be something which he could not choose to deny. A long time he struggled, kneeling on the cold stone of his cell, trying to force his reluctant body and mind to accept this knowledge. But in the end, as he now knew he had power to do, he mastered his fear. When the summons came he would meet it unafraid.

By midday, Allart had faced enough of the bewildering futures which spread out, diverging endlessly, before him, to know at least a part of what he faced. He had seen his father's face—angry, cajoling, complaisant—often enough in these visions to know, at least in part, what was the first trial facing him.

When Father Master summoned him, he could face the ancient monk with calm and an impassive control.

"Your father has come to speak with you, my son. You may see him in the north guest chamber."

Allart lowered his eyes; when at last he raised them, he said, "Father, must I speak with him?" His voice was calm, but the Father Master knew him too well to take this calm at face value.

"I have no reason to refuse him, Allart."

Allart felt like flinging back an angry reply, "I have!" but he had been trained too well to cling to unreason. He said quietly, at last, "I have spent much of this day schooling myself to face this; I do not want to leave Nevarsin. I have found peace here, and useful work. Help me to find a way, Father Master."

The old man sighed. His eyes were closed—as they were most of the time, since he saw more clearly with the inner sight—but Allart knew they beheld him more clearly than ever.

"I would indeed, for your sake, son, that I could see such a way. You have found content here, and such happiness as a man bearing your curse can find. But I fear your time of content is ended. You must bear in mind, lad, that many men never have such a time of rest to learn self-knowledge and discipline; be grateful for what you have been given."

Oh, I am sick of this pious talk of acceptance of those burdens laid upon us—Allart caught back the rebellious thought, but Father Master raised his head and his eyes, colorless as some strange metal, met Allart's rebellious ones.

"You see, my boy, you have not really the makings of a monk. We have given you some control over your natural inclinations, but you are by nature rebellious and eager to change what you can, and changes can be made only *down there*." His gesture took in a whole wide world outside the monastery. "You will never be content to accept your world complacently, son, and now you have the strength to fight rationally, not to lash out in blind rebellion born of your own pain. You must go, Allart, and make such changes in your world as you may."

Allart covered his face with his hands. Until this moment he had still believed—*like a child, like a credulous child!*—that the old monk held some power to help him avoid what must be. He knew that six years in the monastery had not helped him grow past this; now he felt the last of his childhood drop away, and he wanted to weep.

Father Master said with a tender smile, "Are you grieving that you cannot remain a child, in your twenty-third year, Allart? Rather, be grateful that after all these years of learning, you have been made ready to be a man."

"You sound like my father!" Allart flung at him angrily. "I had that served up to me morning and night with my porridge—that I was not yet manly enough to fill my place in the world. Do not *you* begin to speak so, Father, or I shall feel my years here were all a lie!"

"But I do not mean what your father means, when I say you are ready to meet what comes as a man," Father Master said. "I think you know already what I mean by manhood, and it is not what my lord Hastur means; or was I mistaken when I heard you comfort and encourage a crying child this morning? Don't pretend you do not know the difference, Allart." The stern voice softened. "Are you too angry to kneel for my blessing, child?"

Allart fell to his knees; he felt the touch of the old man on his mind.

"The Holy Bearer of Burdens will strengthen you for what must come. I love you well, but it would be selfish to keep you here; I think you are too much needed in that world you tried to renounce." As he rose, Father Master drew Allart into a brief embrace, kissed him, and let him go.

"You have my leave to go and clothe yourself in secular garments, if you will, before you present yourself to your father." Again, for the last time, he touched Allart's face. "My blessing on you always. We may not meet again, Allart, but you will be often in my prayers in the days to come. Send your sons to me, one day, if you will. Now go." He seated himself, letting his cowl drop over his face, and Allart knew he had been dismissed from the old man's thoughts as firmly as from his presence.

Allart did not avail himself of Father Master's permission to change his garments. He thought angrily that he was a monk, and if his father liked it not, that was his father's trouble and none of his own. Yet part of this rebellion came from the knowledge that when he turned his thoughts ahead he could not see himself again in the robes of a monk, nor here in Nevarsin. Would he never come again to the City of Snows?

As he walked toward the guest chamber, he tried to discipline his breathing to calm. Whatever his father had come to say to him, it would not be bettered by quarreling with the old man as soon as they met. He swung open the door and went into the stone-floored chamber.

Beside the fire burning there, in a carven chair, an old man sat, erect and grim, his fingers clenched on the chair-arms. His face had the arrogant stamp of the lowland Hasturs. As he heard the measured sweep of Allart's robe brushing on the stone, he said irritably, "Another of you robed spooks? Send me my son!"

"Your son is here to serve you, *vai dom*."

The old man stared at him. "Gods above, is it you, Allart? How dare you present yourself before me in this guise!"

"I present myself as I am, sir. Have you been received with comfort? Let me bring you food or wine, if you wish."

"I have already been served so," the old man said, jerking his head at the tray and decanter on the table. "I need nothing more, except to speak with you, for which purpose I undertook this wretched journey!"

"And I repeat, I am here and at your service, sir. Had you a hard journey? What prompted you to make such a journey in winter, sir?"

"You!" growled the old man. "When are you going to be ready to come back where you belong, and do your duty to clan and family?"

Allart lowered his eyes, clenching his fists till his nails cut deep in his palm and drew blood; what he saw in this room, a few minutes from now, terrified him. In at least one of the futures diverging now from his every word, Stephen Hastur, Lord Elhalyn, younger brother of Regis II, who sat on the throne of Thendara, lay here on the stone floor, his neck broken. Allart knew that the anger surging in him, the rage he had felt for his father since he could remember, could all too easily erupt in such a murderous attack. His father was speaking again, but Allart did not hear, fighting to force mind and body to composure.

I do not want to fall upon my father and kill him with my two hands! I do not, I—do—not! And I will not! Only when he could speak calmly, without resentment, he said, "I am sorry, sir, to displease you. I thought you knew that I wished to spend my life within these walls, as a monk and a healer. I would be allowed to pronounce my final vows this year at midsummer, to renounce my name and inheritance and dwell here for the rest of my life."

"I knew you had once said so, in the sickness of your adolescence," Dom Stephen Hastur said, "but I thought it would pass when you were restored to health of body and mind. How is it with you, Allart? You look well and strong. It seems that these *cristoforo* madmen have not starved you nor driven you quite mad with deprivations—not yet."

Allart said amiably, "Indeed they have not, sir. My body, as you can see, is strong and well, and my mind at peace."

"Is it so, son? Then I shall not begrudge the years you have spent here; and by whatever methods they achieved this miracle, I shall forever be grateful to them."

"Then compound your gratitude, *vai dom*, by giving me leave to remain here where I am happy and at peace, for the rest of my life."

"Impossible! Madness!"

"May I ask why, sir?"

"I had forgotten that you did not know," Lord Elhalyn said. "Your brother Lauren died, three years ago; he had your *laran*, only in worse form still, for he could not manage to distinguish between past and future; and when it came upon him in all strength, he withdrew inside himself and never spoke again, or responded to anything outside, and so died."

Allart felt grieved. Lauren had been the merest child, a stranger, when he left home; but the thought of the boy's sufferings dismayed him. How narrowly he himself had escaped that fate! "Father, I am sorry. What pity you could not have sent him here; they might have been able to reach him."

"One was enough," Dom Stephen said. "We need no weakling sons; better die young than pass on such a weakness in the blood. His Grace, my brother Regis, has but a single heir; his elder son died in battle against those invaders at Serrais, and his only remaining son, Felix, who will inherit his throne, is frail in health. I am next, and then your brother Damon-Rafael. You stand within four places of the throne, and the king is in his eightieth year. You have no son, Allart."

Allart said, with a violent surge of revulsion, "With such a curse as I bear, would you have me pass it to another? You have told me how it cost Lauren his life!"

"Yet we need that foresight," Stephen Hastur said, "and you have mastered it. The *leroni* of Hali have a plan for fixing it in our line without the instability which endangered your sanity and killed Lauren. I tried to speak of this to you before you left us, but you were in no shape to think of the needs of the clan. We have made compact with the Aillard clan for a daughter of their line, whose genes have been so modified that they will be dominant, so that your children will have the sight, and the control to use it without danger. You will marry this girl. Also she has two *nedestro* sisters, and the *leroni* of the Tower have discovered a technique which will assure that you will father only sons on all of these. If the experiment succeeds, your sons will have the foresight and the control, too." He saw the disgust in Allart's face and said, enraged, "Are you no more than a squeamish boy?"

"I am a *cristoforo*. The first precept of the Creed of Chastity is *to take no woman unwilling*."

"Good enough for a monk, not a man! Yet none of these will be unwilling when you take her, I assure you. If you wish, the two who are not your wives need not even know your name; we have drugs now which will mean that they carry away only the memory of a pleasant interlude. And every woman wishes to bear a child of the lineage of Hastur and Cassilda."

Allart grimaced in revulsion. "I want no woman who must

be delivered to me drugged and unconscious. *Unwilling* does not only mean fighting in terror of rape; it would also mean a woman whose ability to give, or refuse, free consent had been destroyed by drugs!"

"I would not suggest it," said the old man angrily, "but you have made it clear that you are not ready to do your duty by caste and clan of your own free will! At your age, Damon-Rafael had a dozen *nedestro* sons by as many willing women! But you, you sandal-wearer—"

Allart bent his head, fighting the reflex of anger which prompted him to take that frail old neck between his hands and squeeze the life out of it. "Damon-Rafael spoke his mind often enough on the subject of my manhood, Father. Must I hear it from you as well?"

"What have you done to give me a better opinion of you? Where are *your* sons?"

"I do not agree with you that manhood must be measured by sons alone, sir; but I will not argue the point with you now. I do not wish to pass on this curse in my blood. I know something of *laran*. I feel you are wrong in trying to breed for greater strength in these gifts. You can see in me—and in Lauren, even more—that the human mind was never intended to bear such weight. Do you know what I mean if I speak of *recessives* and *lethal genes*?"

"Are you going to teach me my business, youngster?"

"No, but in all respect, Father, I will have no part in it. If I were ever to have sons—"

"There is no *if* about it. You must have sons."

The old man's voice was positive, and Allart sighed. His father simply did not hear him. Oh, he heard the words with his ears. But he did not listen; the words went through and past him, because what Allart was saying did not agree with the fixed belief of Lord Elhalyn—that a son's prime duty was to breed the sons who would carry on the fabled gifts of Hastur and Cassilda, the *laran* of the Domains.

Laran, sorcery, psi power, which enabled these families to excel in the manipulation of the matrix stones, the starstones amplifying the hidden powers of the mind; to know the future, to force the minds of lesser men to their own will, to manipulate inanimate objects, to compel the minds of animal and bird—*laran* was the key to power beyond imagining, and for generations the Domains had been breeding for it.

"Father, hear me, I beg you." Allart was not angry or argumentative now, but desperately in earnest. "I tell you, nothing but evil can come of this breeding program, which makes of women only instruments to breed monsters of the mind, without humanity! I have a conscience; I cannot do it."

His father sneered, "Are you a lover of men, that you will not give sons to our caste?"

"I am not," Allart said, "but I have known no woman. If I have been cursed with this evil gift of *laran*—"

"Silence! You blaspheme our forefathers and the Lord of Light who gave us *laran*!"

Now Allart was angry again. "It is you who blaspheme, sir, if you think the gods can be bent to human purposes this way!"

"You insolent—" His father sprang up, then, with an enormous effort, controlled his rage. "My son, you are young, and warped by these monkish notions. Come back to the heritage to which you were born, and you will learn better. What I ask of you is both right and needful if the Hasturs are to prosper. No"—he gestured for silence when Allart would have spoken— "on these matters you are still ignorant, and your education must be completed. A male virgin"—try as he might, Lord Elhalyn could not keep the contempt from his voice— "is not competent to judge."

"Believe me," Allart said, "I am not indifferent to the charms of women. But I do not wish to pass on the curse of my blood. And I will not."

"That is not open to discussion," Dom Stephen said, menace in his voice. "You will not disobey me, Allart. I would think it disgrace if a son of mine must father his sons drugged like some reluctant bride, but there are drugs which will do that to you, too, if you leave us no choice."

Holy Bearer of Burdens, help me! How shall I keep from killing him as he stands here before me?

Dom Stephen said more quietly, "This is no time for argument, my son. You must give us a chance to convince you that your scruples are unfounded. I beg of you, go now and clothe yourself as befits a man and a Hastur, and make ready to ride with me. You are so needed, my dear son, and—do you not know how much I have missed you?"

The genuine love in his voice thrust pain through Allart's heart. A thousand childhood memories crowded in on him, blurring past and future with their tenderness. He was a pawn to his father's pride and heritage, yes, but with all this,

Lord Elhalyn sincerely loved all his sons, had been genuinely afraid for Allart's health and sanity—or he would never have sent him to a *cristoforo* monastery, of all places on the face of this world! Allart thought, *I cannot even hate him; it would be so much easier if I could!*

"I will come, Father. Believe me, I have no wish to anger you."

"Nor I to threaten you, lad." Dom Stephen held out his arms. "Do you know, we have not yet greeted one another as kinsmen? Do these *cristoforos* bid you renounce kin-ties, son?"

Allart embraced his father, feeling with dismay the bony fragility of the old man's body, knowing that the appearance of domineering anger masked advancing weakness and age. "All the gods forbid I should do so while you live, my father. Let me go and make ready to ride."

"Go, then, my son. For it displeases me more than I can say, to see you in this garb so unfitting for a man."

Allart did not answer, but bowed and went to change his clothes. He would go with his father, yes, and present the appearance of a dutiful son. With certain limits, he would be so. But now he knew what Father Master had meant. Changes were needful in his world, and he could not make them behind monastery walls.

He could see himself riding forth, could see a great hawk hovering, the face of a woman . . . a woman. He knew so little of women. And now they meant to deliver up to him not one but three, drugged and complaisant . . . *that* he would fight to the end of his will and conscience; he would be no part of this monstrous breeding program of the Domains. *Never.* The monkish garb discarded, he knelt briefly, for the last time, on the cold stones of his cell.

"Holy Bearer of Burdens, strengthen me to bear my share of the world's weight . . ." he murmured, then rose and began to clothe himself in the ordinary dress of a nobleman of the Domains, strapping a sword at his side for the first time in over six years.

"Blessed Saint-Valentine-of-the-Snows, grant I may bear it justly in the world . . ." he whispered, then sighed, and looked for the last time on his cell. He knew, with a sorrowful inner knowledge, that he would never set eyes on it again.

CHAPTER
FOUR

The *chervine*, the little Darkovan stag-pony, picked its way fastidiously along the trail, tossing its antlers in protest at the new fall of snow. They were free of the mountains now, Hali no more than three days' ride away. It had been a long journey for Allart, longer than the seven days it had taken to ride the actual distance; he felt as if he had traveled years, endless leagues, great chasms of change; and he was exhausted.

It took all the discipline of his years at Nevarsin to move securely through the bewilderment of what he now saw, legions of possible futures branching off ahead of him at every step, like different roads he might have taken, new possibilities generated by every word and action. As they traveled the dangerous mountain passes, Allart could see every possible false step which might lead him over a precipice, to be smashed, as well as the safe step he actually took. He had learned at Nevarsin to thread his way through his fear, but the effort left him weak and weary.

And another possibility was always with him. Again and again, as they traveled, he had seen his father lying dead at his feet, in an unfamiliar room.

I do not want to begin my life outside the monastery as a patricide! Holy Bearer of Burdens, strengthen me . . . ! He knew he could not deny his anger; that way lay the same paralysis as in fear, to take no step for fear it would lead to disaster.

The anger is mine, he reminded himself with firm discipline. *I can choose what I will do with my anger, and I can choose not to kill.* But it troubled him to see again and again, in that unfamiliar scene which grew familiar as he traveled

47

with the vision, the corpse of his father, lying in a room of green hangings bordered with gold, at the foot of a great chair whose very carvings he could have drawn, so often had he seen it with the sight of his *laran*.

It was hard, as he looked upon the face of his living father, not to look upon him with the pity and horror he would feel for the newly and shockingly dead; and it was a strain on him to show nothing of this to Lord Elhalyn.

For his father, as they traveled, had put aside his words of contempt for Allart's monkish resolution, and ceased entirely to quarrel with him about it. He spoke only kindly to his son, mostly of his childhood at Hali before the curse had descended on Allart, of their kinfolk, the chances of the journey. He spoke of Hali, and the mining done in the Tower there, by the powers of the matrix circle, to bring copper and iron and silver ore to the surface of the ground; of hawks and *chervines*, and the experiments which his brother had made breeding, with cell-deep changes, rainbow-colored hawks, or *chervines* with fantastic jewel-colored antlers like the fabled beasts of legend.

Day by day Allart recaptured some of his childhood love for his father, from the days before his *laran* and the *cristoforo* faith had separated them, and again he felt the agony of mourning, seeing that accursed room with the green hangings and gold, the great carven chair, and his father's face, white and stark and looking very surprised to be dead.

Again and again on this road other faces had begun to come out of the dimness of the unknown into the possible future. Most of them Allart ignored as he had learned in the monastery, but two or three returned repeatedly, so that he knew they were not the faces of people he *might* meet, but people who *would* come into his life; one, which he dimly recognized, was the face of his brother Damon-Rafael, who had called him sandal-wearer and coward, who had been glad to be rid of his rivalry, that he alone might be Elhalyn's heir.

I wish that my brother and I might be friends and love one another as brothers should. Yet I see it nowhere among all the possible futures. . . .

And there was the face of a woman, returning continually to the eyes of his mind, though he had never seen her before. A small woman, delicately made, with eyes dark-lashed in her colorless face and hair like masses of spun black glass; he saw her in his visions, a grave face of sorrow, the dark eyes

turned to him in anguished pleading. *Who are you?* he wondered. *Dark girl of my visions, why do you haunt me this
way?*

Strange for Allart after the years in the monastery, he had
begun to see erotic visions, too, of this woman, see her laughing, amorous, her face lifted to his own for a caress, closed
under the rapture of his kiss. *No!* he thought. No matter how
his father should tempt him with the beauty of this woman,
he would hold firm to his purpose; he would father no child
to bear this curse of his blood! Yet the woman's face and
presence persisted, in dreams and waking, and he knew she
was one of those his father would seek as a bride for him.
Allart thought it would indeed be possible that he would be
unable to resist her beauty.

Already I am half in love with her, he thought, *and I do
not even know her name!*

One evening, as they rode down toward a broad green valley, his father began to speak again of the future.

"Below us lies Syrtis. The folk of Syrtis have been Hastur
vassals for centuries; we will break our journey there. You
will be glad to sleep in a bed again, I suppose?"

Allart laughed. "It is all one, Father. During this journey I
have slept softer than ever I did at Nevarsin."

"Perhaps I should have had such monkish discipline, if old
bones are to make such journeys! I will be glad of a mattress,
if you will not! And now we are but two days' ride from
home, and we can plan for your wedding. You were handfasted at ten years old to your kinswoman Cassandra Aillard, do
you not remember?"

Try as he might, Allart could remember nothing but a festival where he had had a suit of new clothes and had been
made to stand for hours and listen to long speeches by the
grown-ups. He told his father so, and Dom Stephen said,
genial once more, "I am not surprised. Perhaps the girl was
not even there; I think she was only three or four years old
then. I confess I, too, had doubts about this marriage. Those
Aillards have *chieri* blood, and they have an evil habit of
bearing, now and then, daughters who are *emmasca*—they
look like beautiful women, but they never become ripe for
mating, nor do they bear children. Their *laran* is strong,
though, so I risked the handfasting, and when the girl had become a woman, I had our own household *leronis* examine her
in the presence of a midwife, who gave it as her opinion that

the girl was a functioning female and could bear children. I
have not seen her since she was a tiny girl, but I am told she
has grown up to be a fine-looking maiden; and she is Aillard,
and that family is a strong alliance to our clan, one we need
greatly. You have nothing to say, Allart?"

Allart forced himself to speak calmly.

"You know my will on that matter, Father. I will not quarrel with you about it, but I have not changed my mind. I
have no wish to marry, and I will father no sons to carry on
this curse in our blood. I will say no more."

Again, shockingly, the room with the green and gold hangings, and his father's dead face, swam before his mind, so
strongly that he had to blink hard to see his father riding at
his side.

"Allart," his father said, and his voice was kind, "during
these days when we have journeyed together, I have come to
know you too well to believe that. You are my own son, after
all, and when you are back in the world where you belong,
you will not long keep these monkish notions. Let us not
speak of it, *kihu caryu*, until the time is upon us. The gods
know I have no will to quarrel with the last son they have
left me."

Allart felt his throat tighten with grief.

*I cannot help it. I have come to love my father. Is this how
he will break my will at last, not with force but with
kindness?* And again he looked on his father's dead face in
the room hung with gold and green, and the face of the dark
maiden of his visions swam before his blurring eyes.

Syrtis Great House was an ancient stone keep, fortified
with moat and drawbridge, and there were great outbuildings
of wood and stone, and an elaborate courtyard, under shelter
of a glasslike canopy of many colors; underfoot were colored
stones, laid together with a precision no workman could have
accomplished, so that Allart knew the Syrtis folk were of the
new-rich, who could make full use of the ornamental and difficult matrix technology to have such beautiful things constructed. *How can he find so many of the* laran-*gifted to do
his will?*

The old lord Syrtis was a plump soft man, who came into
the courtyard himself to welcome his overlord, falling to his
knees in fawning politeness, rising with a smile that was almost a smirk when Dom Stephen drew him into a kinsman's

embrace. He embraced Allart, too, and Allart flinched from the man's kiss on his cheek.

Ugh, he is like a fawning house cat!

Dom Marius led them into his Great Hall, filled with sybaritic luxury, seated them on cushioned divans, called for wine. "This is a new form of cordial, made from our apples and pears; you must try it. . . . I have a new amusement; I will talk of it when we have dined," Dom Marius of Syrtis said, leaning back into the billowy cushions. "And this is your younger son, Stephen? I had heard some rumor that he had forsaken Hali and become a monk among the *cristoforos,* or some such nonsense. I am glad it is only a vicious lie; some people will say *anything*."

"I give you my word, kinsman, Allart is no monk," Dom Stephen said. "I gave him leave to dwell at Nevarsin to recover his health; he suffered greatly in adolescence from threshold sickness. But he is well and strong, and came home to be married."

"Oh, is it so?" Dom Marius said, regarding Allart with his wide, blinking eyes, encased in wide pillows of fat. "And is the fortunate maiden known to me, dear boy?"

"No more than to me," Allart said in grudging politeness. "I am told she is my kinswoman Cassandra Aillard; I saw her but once, when she was a baby girl."

"Ah, the *domna* Cassandra! I have seen her in Thendara; she was present at the Festival Ball in Comyn Castle," Dom Marius said with a leer.

Allart, thought, disgusted, *He only wants us to know he is important enough to be invited there!*

Dom Marius called servants to bring their supper. He followed the recent fad for nonhuman servants, *cralmacs,* artificially bred from the harmless trailmen of the Hellers, with matrix-modified genes by human insemination. To Allart the creatures seemed ugly, neither human nor trailman. The trailmen, strange and monkeylike though they were, had their own alien beauty. But the *cralmacs,* handsome though some of them undeniably were, had for Allart the loathsomeness of something unnatural.

"Yes, I have seen your promised bride; she is fair enough to make even a true monk break his vows," Dom Marius sniggered. "You will have no regrets for the monastery when you lie down with her, kinsman. Though all those Aillard

girls are unlucky wives, some being sterile as *riyachiyas* and
others so fragile they cannot carry a child to birth."

He is one of those who like to foretell catastrophe, too, Allart thought. "I am in no great hurry for an heir; my elder
brother is alive and well and has fathered *nedestro* sons. I
will take what the gods send." Eager to change the subject,
he asked, "Did you breed the *cralmacs* on your own estate?
Father told me as we rode of my brother's experiments in
breeding ornamental *chervines* through matrix-modification;
and your *cralmacs* are smaller and more graceful than those
bred at Hali. They are good, I remember, only for mucking
out stables and such heavy work, things it would be unsuitable to ask one's human vassals to do."

He said this with a sudden pang—*How quickly I forget!*—remembering that in Nevarsin he had been taught that
no honest work was beneath the dignity of a man's own
hands. But the words had diverted Dom Marius again into
boasting.

"I have a *leronis* from the Ridenow, captured in battle,
who is skillful with such things. She thought I was kind to
her, when I assured her she would never be used against her
own people—but how could I trust her in such a
battle?—and she made no trouble about doing other work for
me. She bred me these *cralmacs,* more graceful and shapely
indeed than any I had before. I will give you breeding stock,
male and female, if you will, for a wedding gift, Dom Allart;
no doubt your lady would welcome handsome servants. Also
the *leronis* bred for me a new strain of *riyachiyas*; will you
see them, cousin?"

Lord Elhalyn nodded, and when they finished the meal the
promised *riyachiyas* were brought in. Allart looked on them
with an inner spasm of revulsion: exotic toys for jaded
tastes. In form they were women, fair of face, slender, with
shapely breasts lifting the translucent folds of their draperies,
but too narrow of hip and slender of waist and long of leg to
be genuine women. There were four of them, two fair-
haired, two dark; otherwise identical. They knelt at Dom
Marius's feet, moving sinuously, the curve of their slender
necks, as they bowed, swanlike and exquisite, and Allart,
through his revulsion, felt an unaccustomed stirring of desire.

*Zandru's hells, but they are beautiful, as beautiful and un-
natural as demon hags!*

"Would you believe, cousin, that they were borne in *cral-*

mac wombs? They are of my seed, and that of the *leronis*," he said, "so that a fastidious man, if they were human, might say they were my daughters, and indeed, the thought adds a little—a little something," he said, sniggering. "Two at a birth—" He pointed to the fair-haired pair and said, "Lella and Rella; the dark ones are Ria and Tia. They will not disturb you with much speech, though they can talk and sing, and I had them taught to dance and to play the *rryl* and to serve food and drink. But, of course, their major talents are for pleasure. They are matrix-spelled, of course, to draw and bind—I see you cannot take your eyes from them, nor"—Dom Marius chuckled— "can your son."

Allart started and angrily turned away from the horribly enticing faces and bodies of the inhumanly beautiful, lust-inspiring creatures.

"Oh, I am not greedy; you shall have them tonight, cousin," Dom Marius said, with a lewd chuckle. "One or two, as you will. And if you, young Allart, have spent six years of frustration in Nevarsin, you must be in need of their services. I will send you Lella; she is my own favorite. Oh, the things that *riyachiya* can do, even a sworn monk would yield to her touch." He grew grossly specific, and Allart turned away.

"I beg you, kinsman," he said, trying to conceal his loathing, "do not deprive yourself of your favorite."

"No?" Dom Marius's cushiony eyes rolled back, in feigned sympathy. "Is it so? After so many years in a monastery, do you prefer the pleasures to be found among the brethren? I myself seldom desire a *ri'chiyu*, but I keep a few for hospitality, and some guests desire a change now and then. Shall I send you Loyu? He is a beautiful boy indeed, and I have had all of them modified to be almost without response to pain, so that you can use him any way you choose, if you desire."

Dom Stephen said quickly, seeing that Allart was about to explode, "Indeed, the girls will do well enough for us. I compliment you on the skill of your *leronis* at breeding them."

When they had been taken to the suite of rooms allotted to them, Dom Stephen said, enraged, "You will *not* disgrace us by refusing this courtesy! I will not have it gossiped here that my son is less than a man!"

"He is like a great fat toad! Father, is it a reflection on my manhood that the thought of such filth overwhelms me with loathing? I would like to fling his foul gifts in his sniggering face!"

"You weary me with your monkish scruples, Allart. The *leroni* never did better than when they bred us the *riyachiyas*; nor will your wife-to-be thank you if you refuse to have one in your household. Can you be so ignorant as not to know that if you lie with a breeding woman, she may miscarry? It is part of the price we pay for our *laran*, which we have bred with such difficulty into our line, that our women are fragile and given to miscarry, so that we must spare them when they are with child. If you turn your desires on a *riyachiya* only she need not be jealous, as if you had given your affections to a real girl who would have some claim on your thoughts."

Allart turned his face away; in the Lowlands this kind of speech between the generations was the height of indecency, had been from the days when group marriage was commonplace and any man of your father's age could be your father, any woman of an age to be your mother could have been your mother indeed; so that the sexual taboo was absolute between generations.

Dom Stephen said defensively, "I would never so far forget myself, Allart, except that you have not been willing to do your duty by our caste. But I am sure you are enough my son that you will come to life with a woman in your arms!" He added, crudely, "You need not be scrupulous; the creatures are sterile."

Allart thought, sick with disgust, *I may not wait for the room with the green and gold hangings, I may kill him here and now,* but his father had turned away and gone into his own chamber.

He thought, enraged, as he made ready for bed, of how corrupt they had become. *We, the sacred descendants of the Lord of Light, bearing the blood of Hastur and Cassilda—or was that only a pretty fairy tale?* Were the *laran* gifts of the families descended from Hastur no more than the work of some presumptuous mortal, meddling with gene-matter and brain-cells, some sorceress with a matrix jewel modifying germ plasm as Dom Marius's *leronis* did with those *riyachiyas,* making exotic toys for corrupt men?

The gods themselves—if indeed there are any gods—must turn sick at the sight of us!

The warm, luxurious room sickened him; he wished himself back at Nevarsin, in the solemn night silence. He had turned out the light when he heard an almost noiseless foot-

step and the girl Lella, in her flimsy draperies, stole softly
across the floor to his side.

"I am here for your contentment, *vai dom*."

Her voice was a husky murmur; her eyes alone betrayed
that she was not human, for they were dark brown animal
eyes, great soft, strange unreadable eyes.

Allart shook his head.

"You can go away again, Lella. I will sleep alone tonight."

Sexual images tormented him, all the things he *might* do,
all the possible futures, an infinitely diverging set of probabilities hinging on this moment. Lella sat on the edge of the
bed; her soft slender fingers, so delicate that they seemed almost boneless, stole into his. She murmured, pleading, "If I
do not please you, *vai dom*, I will be punished. What would
you have me do? I know many, many ways to give delight."

He knew his father had maneuvered this situation. The
riyachiyas were bred and taught and spelled to be irresistible;
had Dom Stephen hoped she would break down Allart's inhi-
bitions?

"Indeed, my master will be very angry if I fail to give you
pleasure. Shall I send for my sister, who is as dark as I am
fair? And she is even more skilled. Or would it give you
pleasure to beat me, Lord? I like to be beaten, truly I do."

"Hush, hush!" Allart felt sick. "No one would want anyone
more beautiful than you." And indeed, the shapely young
body, the enchanting little face, the loose scented hair falling
across him, were enticing. She had a sweet, faintly musky
scent; somehow before he touched her he had believed that
the *riyachiyas* would smell animal, not human.

Her spell is on me, he thought. How then could he resist?
With a sense of deathly weariness, as he felt her slender fingertips trace a line of awareness down his bare neck from
earlobe to shoulder, he thought, *What does it matter? I had
indeed resolved to live womanless, never to pass on this curse
I bear. But this poor creature is sterile, I cannot father a
child on her if I would. Perhaps when he knows I have done
his will in this, he will be less ready to put insults on me and
call me less than a man. Bearer of Burdens, strengthen me! I
but make excuses for what I want to do. Why should I not?
Why must I alone resist what is given by right to every man
of my caste?* His mind was spinning. A thousand alternate futures spun out before him: in one he seized the girl in his
hands and wrung her neck like the animal he knew her to be;

in another he saw himself and the girl entwined in tenderness, and the image swelled, driving the awareness of lust into his body; in another he saw the dark maiden lying dead before him. . . . *So many futures, so much death and despair.* . . . Spasmodically, desperately, trying to blot out the multiple futures, he took the girl in his arms and drew her down on the bed. Even as his lips came down on hers, he thought of despair, futility. *What does it matter, when there is all this ruin before me . . . ?*

He heard, as if from nowhere, her small cries of pleasure, and in his wretchedness, thought, *At least she is not unwilling,* and then he did not think again at all, which was an enormous relief.

CHAPTER
FIVE

When he woke, the girl was gone, and Allart lay without moving for a moment, overcome with sickness and self-contempt. *How shall I keep from killing that man, that he brought this upon me . . . ?* But as his father's dead face swam before his eyes in the familiar room with green and gold hangings, he reminded himself sternly, *The choice was mine; he provided only the opportunity.*

Nevertheless, he felt overwhelming self-contempt as he moved around the room, making ready to ride. In the night past he had learned something about himself that he would rather not have known.

In his six years in Nevarsin it had been no trouble to him to keep to the womanless precincts of the monastery, to live without thought of women; he had never been tempted, even at midsummer festival when even the monks were free to join in the revelry, to seek love or its counterfeit in the lower town. So it had never occurred to him that he would find it difficult to keep his resolve—not to marry, not to father children bearing the monstrous curse of *laran*. Yet, even through his loathing and revulsion for the thing Lella was, not even human, six years of self-imposed celibacy had been cast aside in minutes, at the touch of a *riyachiya*'s obscenely soft fingertips.

Now what is to become of me? If I cannot keep my resolve for a single night. . . . In the crowding, diverging futures he saw before his every step, there was a new one, and it displeased him: that he might become some such creature as old Dom Marius, refusing marriage indeed, sating his lust with these unnaturally bred pleasure girls, or worse.

He was grateful that their host did not appear at breakfast; he found it hard enough to face his father, and the vision of his father's dead face came near to blotting out the real, live presence of the old man, good-natured over his buttered bread and porridge. Sensing his son's unspoken anger (Allart wondered if his father had had reports from servants, or even if he had stooped low enough to question the girl Lella, to verify that Allart had proved his masculinity), Dom Stephen kept silence until they were donning their riding-cloaks, then said, "We will leave the riding-animals here, son; Dom Marius has offered us an air-car which will take us directly to Hali, and the servants can bring the riding-animals on in a few days. You have not ridden in an air-car since you were very small, have you?"

"I do not remember that I rode in one even then," said Allart, interested against his will. "Surely they were not common in such times."

"No, very uncommon, and of course they are toys for the wealthy, demanding a skilled *laran* operator as they do," Lord Elhalyn said. "They are useless in the mountains; the crossdrafts and winds would dash any heavier-than-air vehicle against the crags. But here in the Lowlands it is safe enough, and I thought such a flight would divert you."

"I confess I am curious," Allart said, thinking that Dom Marius of Syrtis certainly spared no pains to ingratiate himself with his overlord. First he put his favorite pleasure girls at their disposal, and now this! "But I heard at Nevarsin that these contrivances were not safe in the Lowlands either. While war rages between Elhalyn and Ridenow, they are all too easily attacked."

Dom Stephen shrugged, saying, "We all have *laran*; we can make short work of any attackers. After six years in a monastery, no doubt your fighting skills are rusty when it comes to sword and shield, but I have no doubt you could strike anyone who attacked us out of the sky. I have fire-talismans." He looked shrewdly at his son, then said, "Or are you going to tell me that the monks have made you such a man of peace that you will not defend your life or the life of your kinsmen, Allart? I seem to remember that as a boy you had no stomach for fighting."

No, for at every stroke I saw death or disaster for myself or another, and it is cruel of you to taunt me with childish weakness which was no fault of mine, but of your own ac-

cursed hereditary Blood-Gift. . . . But aloud Allart said, forcing himself to ignore the shocking dead face of his father which persisted in appearing before his eyes, blurring his father's living face, "While I live, I will defend my father and my Lord to the death, and the gods do so to me and more also if I fail or falter."

Startled, warmed by something in Allart's voice, Lord Elhalyn put out his arms and embraced his son. For the first time Allart could remember, to him or anyone, the old man said, "Forgive me, dear son, that was not worthy of me. I should not so accuse you unmerited," and Allart felt tears stinging his eyes.

Gods forgive me. He is not cruel, or if he is, it is only out of fear for me, too. . . . He truly wills to be kind. . . .

The air-car was long and sleek, made of some gleaming glassy material, with ornamental stripes of silver down the length of it, a long cockpit with four seats, open to the sky. *Cralmacs* rolled it out from its shed, onto the ornamented paving of the inner courtyard, and the operator, a slender young man with the red hair which proclaimed the minor nobility of the Kilghard Hills, approached them with a curt bow, a mere perfunctory reverence; a highly trained expert, a *laranzu* of this kind, needed to be deferential to no man, not even to the brother of the king at Thendara.

"I am Karinn, *vai dom.* I have orders to take you to Hali. Please take your seats."

He left it to the *cralmacs* to lift Dom Stephen into his seat, and to fasten the straps around him, but as Allart took a place, Karinn lingered a moment before going to his own seat. He said, "Have you ever ridden in one of these, Dom Allart?"

"Not since I can remember. Is it powered by such a matrix as you alone can handle? That would seem beyond belief!"

"Not entirely; in there"—Karinn pointed— "is a battery charged with energy to run the turbines; it would indeed demand more power than one man has at his command, to levitate and move such an apparatus, but the batteries are charged by the matrix circles, and my *laran*, at this moment, is needed only to guide and steer—and to be aware of attackers and evade them." His face was somber. "I would not defy my overlord, and it is no part of my duty to refuse to do as I am bid. but—have you *laran*?"

As Karinn spoke, the unease in Allart clarified, with a sudden sharp vision of this air-car bursting asunder, exploding, falling out of the sky like a stone. Was this only a distant probability or did it truly lie before them? He had no way of knowing.

"I have *laran* enough to be uneasy at trusting myself to this contraption. Father, we will be attacked. You know that?"

"Dom Allart," Karinn said, "this contraption, as you call it, is the safest means of transport ever devised by starstone technology. You are vulnerable to attack between here and Hali, should you go a-horse, for three days; in an air-car you will be there before midday and they must place their attackers very precisely. Furthermore, it is easier to defend yourself with *laran* than against such weapons as they may send against you with armed men. I can see a day coming on Darkover when all the Great Houses will have such weapons and devices to protect themselves against envious rivals or rebellious vassals; and then there will be no more wars, either, for no sane men will risk *this* kind of death and destruction. Such *contraptions* as this, *vai dom*, may be only expensive toys for rich men now, but they will bring us such an age of peace as Darkover has never known!"

He spoke with such conviction and enthusiasm that Allart doubted his own rising vision of dreadful warfare with weapons ever more dreadful. Karinn must be right. Such weapons would surely restrain sane men from making war at all, and so he who invented the most terrible weapons worked the harder for peace.

Taking his seat, Allart said, "Aldones, Lord of Light, grant you speak with true vision, Karinn. And now let us see this miracle."

I have seen many possible futures which never came to pass. I have found this morning that I love my father well, and I will cling to the belief that I will never lay hands upon him, no more than I would wring the neck of that poor harmless little riyachiya *in the night past. I will not fear attack, either, but I will guard against it, while I take pleasure in this new means of travel.* He let Karinn show him how to fasten the straps that would hold him in his seat if the air became turbulent, and the device that swiveled his seat behind a magnified pane of glass, giving him instant view of any attackers or menace.

He listened closely as the *laranzu*, taking his own seat and fastening himself into place, bent his head in alert concentration and the battery-powered turbine began to roar. He had practiced enough in boyhood, in the tiny gliders levitated by small matrixes and soaring on the air currents around the Lake of Hali, to be aware of the elementary principles of heavier-than-air flight, but it was incredible to him that a matrix circle, a group of close-linked telepath minds, could charge a battery strongly enough to power such enormous turbines. Yet *laran* could be powerful, and a matrix could amplify the electric currents of the brain and body enormously, a hundredfold, a thousandfold. He wondered how many minds with *laran* it took, operating for how long, to charge such batteries with the tremendous humming power of those roaring turbines. He would have liked to ask Karinn—but would not disturb the *laranzu's* concentration—why such a vehicle could not be adapted to ground transit, but quickly realized that for any ground vehicle roads and highways were needed. Someday, perhaps, roads would be practical, but on the rough terrain from the Kilghard Hills north, ground transit would probably always be limited to the feet of men and animals.

Quickly, with the humming power, they skimmed along a level runway surfaced with glassy material which must have been poured there by matrix-power, too; then they were airborne, rising swiftly over treetops and forests, moving into the very clouds with an exhilarating speed that took Allart's breath away. It was as far beyond the soaring he had done on gliders, as the gliders were above the slow plodding of a *chervine!* Karinn motioned, and the air-car turned its vast wings southward and flew over the forests to the south.

They had flown for a considerable time. Allart was beginning to feel the straps constricting his body, and wished he might loosen them for a little, when he felt within himself, with a spurt of sudden excitement, alertness and fear.

We are seen, pursued—we will be attacked!

Look to the west, Allart—

Allart squinted his eyes into the light. Small shapes appeared there, one, two, three—were they gliders? If they were, such an air-car could outrun them swiftly. And, indeed, Karinn, with swift motions of his hands, was turning the air-car to evade the pursuers. For a moment it seemed they would not be followed; one of the gliding forms—*These are not gliders! Are they hawks?*—soared up, up, above them,

higher and higher. It was indeed a hawk, but Allart could
feel human intelligence, human awareness, watching them
with malevolent will. No natural hawk had ever had eyes
which glittered so, like great jewels! *No, this is no normal
bird!* Restless with unease, he watched the soaring flight of
the bird as it went higher and higher, winging with long, swift
flapping strokes into the sky above them. . . .

Suddenly a narrow, gleaming shape detached itself from
the bird and fell down, plummeting, arrowlike, toward the
car. Allart's vision, even before thought, provided him with
the knowledge of what would happen if that long, deadly
shape, gleaming like glass, should strike the air-car: they
would explode into fragments, each fragment coated with the
terrible *clingfire*, which clung to what it touched and went on
burning and burning, through metal and glass and flesh and
bone.

Allart grasped the matrix he wore about his neck, jerked it
with shaking fingers from the protecting silks. *There is so
little time*. . . . Focusing into the depths of the jewel, he altered his awareness of time so that now the glassy shape fell
ever more slowly, and he could focus on it, as if taking it between invisible fingers of force. . . . Slowly, slowly, carefully. . . . he must not risk having it break while it could fall
into the air-car and fragments of *clingfire* destroy flesh and
car. His slowed awareness spun accelerated futures through
his mind—he saw the air-car exploding in fragments, his father slumping over and blazing up with *clingfire* in his hair,
Karinn going up like a torch, and the air-car falling out of
control, heavier than a stone . . . but none of those things
would be allowed to happen!

With infinite delicacy, his mind focused into the pulsing
lights of his matrix, and his eyes closed, Allart manipulated
the glassy shape away from the air-car. He sensed resistance,
knew the one guiding the device was fighting him for control
of it. He struggled silently, feeling as if his physical hands
were trying to keep hold of a greased and wriggling live thing
while *other* hands fought to wrest it away, to fling it at him.

*Karinn, quickly, get us higher if you can so that it will
break below us*. . . .

He felt his body slump against the straps as the air-car
angled sharply upward; saw, with a fragment of his mind, his
father collapse in his seat, thinking with swift contrition, *He
is old, frail, his heart cannot take much of this* . . . but the

main part of his mind was still in those fingers of force that struggled with the now-writhing device, which seemed to squirm under the control of his mind. They were nearly free of it now—

It exploded with a wild crash that seemed to rock all space and time, and Allart felt sharp burning pain in his hands; swiftly he withdrew his consciousness from the vicinity of the exploded device, but the burning still resonated in his physical hands. Now he opened his eyes and saw that the device had indeed exploded well below them, and fragments of *clingfire* were falling in a molten shower to set ablaze the forests below. But one fragment of the glassy shell had been flung upward, over the rim of the air-car, and the thin fire was spreading along the edge of the cockpit, reaching fingers of flame toward where his father lay slumped and unconscious.

Allart fought against his first impulse—to lean over and beat out the fire with his hands. *Clingfire* could not be extinguished that way; any fragment that touched his hands would burn through his clothing and his flesh and through to the bone, as long as there was anything left to be consumed. He focused again into the matrix—there was no time to take out the fire-talisman Karinn had given him, he should have had it ready!—calling his own fire and flaring it out toward the *clingfire*. Briefly it flamed high, then with a last gutter of light, the *clingfire* died and was gone.

"Father—" he cried, "are you hurt?"

His father held out shaking hands. The outer edge and the littlest finger were seared, blackened, but there was, as far as Allart could see, no greater hurt. Dom Stephen said in a weak voice, "The gods forgive me that I called your courage into question, Allart. You saved us all. I fear I am too old for such a struggle. But you mastered the fire at once."

"Is the *vai dom* wounded?" Karinn called from the controls. "Look! They have fled." Indeed, low on the horizon, Allart could see the small retreating shapes. Did they put real birds under spell by matrix to carry their vicious weapons? Or were they some monstrous, mutant-bred things, no more birds than the *cralmacs* were human; or some dreadful matrix-powered mechanical device that had been brought to deliver their deadly weapon? Allart could not guess, and his father's plight was such that he did not feel free to pursue their attackers even in thought.

"He is shocked and a little burned," he called anxiously to Karinn. "How long will it be before we are there?"

"But a moment or two, Dom Allart. I can see the gleam of the lake. There, below—"

The air-car circled, and Allart could see the shoreline and the glimmering sands, like jewels, along the shores of Hali. . . . *Legend says that the sands where Hastur, son of Light, walked, were jeweled from that day.* . . . And there the curious lighter-than-water waves that broke incessantly along the shore. To the north were shining towers, the Great House of Elhalyn, and at the far end of the lake, the Tower of Hali, gleaming faintly blue. As Karinn glided downward, Allart unfastened his restraining straps and clambered to his father's side, taking the burned hands in his own, focusing into the matrix to look with the eyes of his mind and assess the damage. The wound was minor indeed; his father was only shocked, his heart racing, more frightened than hurt.

Below them, Allart could see servants in the Hastur colors running out on the landing field as the air-car descended, but he held his father's hands in his own, trying to blot out all that he could foresee. *Visions, none of them true . . . the air-car did not explode in flame . . . what I see need not come—it is only what may come, borne of my fears. . . .*

The air-car touched the ground. Allart called, "Bring my lord's body-servants! He is hurt; you must carry him within!" He lifted his father in his arms, and lowered him into the waiting arms of the servants, then followed as they carried the frail figure within.

From somewhere a familiar voice, hateful from years ago, said, "What has come to him, Allart? Were you attacked in the air?" and he recognized the voice of his elder brother, Damon-Rafael.

Briefly he described the encounter, and Damon-Rafael said, nodding, "That is the only way to handle such weapons. They used the hawk-things, then? They have sent them upon us only once or twice before, but once they burned an orchard of trees, and nuts were scarce that year."

"In the name of all the gods, brother, who are these Ridenow? Are they of the blood of Hastur and Cassilda, that they can send such *laran* weapons upon us?"

"They are upstarts," Damon-Rafael said. "They were Drytowns bandits in the beginning, and they moved into Serrais and forced or bullied the old families of Serrais to give them their women as wives. The Serrais had strong *laran*, some of them, and now you can see the result—they grow stronger. They talk truce, and I think we must make truce with them, for this fighting cannot go on much longer. But their terms will not compromise. They want unquestioned ownership of the Domain of Serrais, and they claim that with their *laran* they have a right to it. . . . But this is no time to speak of war and politics, brother. How does our father? He seemed not much hurt, but we must get a healer-woman to him at once, come—"

In the Great Hall, Dom Stephen had been laid on a padded bench and a healer-woman was kneeling at his side, smearing ointments on the seared fingers, bandaging them in soft cloths. Another woman held a wine cup to the old lord's lips. He stretched a hand to his sons as they hurried toward him, and Damon-Rafael knelt at his side. Looking at his brother, Allart thought it was a little like looking into a blurred mirror; seven years his senior, Damon-Rafael was a little taller, a little heavier, like himself fair-haired and gray-eyed as were all the Hasturs of Elhalyn, his face beginning to show signs of the passing years.

"The gods be praised that you are spared to us now, Father!"

"For that you must thank your brother, Damon; it was he who saved us."

"If only for that, I give him welcome home," Damon-Rafael said, turning and drawing his brother into a kinsman's embrace. "Welcome, Allart. I hope you have come back to us in health, and without the sick fancies you had as a boy."

"Are you hurt, my son?" Dom Stephen asked, looking up at Allart with concern. "I saw you were in pain."

Allart spread out his hands before him. He had not been touched physically by the fire at all, but with the touch of his mind he had handled the fire-device, and the resonances had vibrated to his physical hands. There were red seared marks all along his palms, spreading up to his wrists, but the pain, though fierce, was dreamlike, nightmarish, of the mind and not of damaged flesh. He focused his awareness on it and the pain receded as the reddish marks began slowly to fade.

Damon-Rafael said, "Let me help you, brother," and took Allart's fingers in his own hands, focusing closely on them. Under his touch the red marks paled to white. Lord Elhalyn smiled.

"I am well pleased," he said. "My younger son has come back to me strong and a warrior, and my sons stand together as brothers. This day's work has been well done, if it has shown you—"

"Father!" Allart leaped toward him as the voice broke off with shocking suddenness. The healer-woman moved swiftly to his side as the old man fought for breath, his face darkening and congesting; then he slumped again, slid to the floor, and lay without moving.

Damon-Rafael's face was drawn with horror and grief. "Oh, my father—" he whispered, and Allart, standing in shock and dread at his side, looked up for the first time around the Great Hall, seeing for the first time what he had not seen in the confusion: the green and gold hangings, the great carved chair at the far end of the room.

So it was my father's Great Hall where he lay dead, and I did not even see till it was too late. . . . My foresight was true, but I mistook its cause. . . . Even knowing the many futures does nothing to avoid them. . . .

Damon-Rafael bent his head, weeping. He said to Allart, holding out his arms, "He is dead; our father has gone into the Light," and the brothers embraced, Allart trembling with shock at the sudden and unexpected descent of the future he had foreseen.

All around them, one by one, the servants knelt, turning to the brothers; and Damon-Rafael, his face drawn with grief, his breath coming ragged, forced himself to composure as the servants spoke the formula.

"Our Lord is dead. Live long, our Lord," and kneeling, held out their hands in homage to Damon-Rafael.

Allart knelt and, as was fitting and right under the law, was the first to pledge to the new overlord of Elhalyn, Damon-Rafael.

CHAPTER
SIX

Stephen, Lord Elhalyn, was laid to rest in the ancient burying ground by the shores of Hali; and all the Hastur kin of
the Lowland Domains, from the Aillards on the plains of Valeron, to the Hasturs of Carcosa, had come to do him honor.
King Regis, stooped and old, looking almost too frail to ride,
had stood beside the grave of his half-brother, leaning heavily
on the arm of his only son.

Prince Felix, heir to the throne of Thendara and the crown
of the Domains, had come to embrace Allart and Damon-
Rafael, calling them "dear cousins." Felix was a slight, effeminate young man with gilt hair and colorless eyes, and he
had the long, narrow pale face and hands of *chieri* blood.
When the funeral rites were ended there was a great ceremony. Then the old king, pleading age and ill health, was
taken home by his courtiers, but Felix remained to do honor
to the new Lord of Elhalyn, Damon-Rafael.

Even the Ridenow lord had sent an envoy from far Serrais,
proffering an unasked truce for twice forty days.

Allart, welcoming guests in the hall, came suddenly upon a
face he knew—though he had never set eyes upon her before.
Dark hair, like a cloud of darkness under a blue veil; gray
eyes, but so darkly lashed that for a moment the eyes themselves seemed as dark as the eyes of some animal. Allart felt
a strange tightening in his chest as he looked upon the face
of the dark woman whose face had haunted him for so many
days.

"Kinsman," she said courteously, but he could not lower
his eyes as custom demanded before an unmarried woman
who was a stranger to him.

*I know you well. You have haunted me, dreams and wak-
ing, and already I am more than half in love with
you.* . . . Erotic images attacked him, unfitting for this company, and he struggled with them.

"Kinsman," she said again, "why do you stare at me in such
unseemly fashion?"

Allart felt the blood rising in his face; indeed it was discourtesy, almost indecency, to stare so at a woman who was
a stranger to him, and he colored at the thought that she
might possess *laran,* might be aware of the images that tormented him. He finally found a scrap of his voice.

"But I am no stranger to you, *damisela.* Nor is it discourtesy that a man shall look his handfasted bride directly in the
face; I am Allart Hastur, and soon to be your husband."

She raised her eyes and returned his gaze fairly. But there
was tension in her voice. "Why, is it so? Still, I can hardly
believe that you have borne my image in your mind since
you last looked on my face, when I was an infant girl of four
years. And I had heard, Dom Allart, that you had withdrawn
yourself to Nevarsin, that you were ill or mad, that you
wished to be a monk and renounce your heritage. Was it only
idle gossip, then?"

"It is true that I had such thoughts for a time. I dwelt for
six years among the brethren of Saint-Valentine-of-the-Snows,
and would gladly have remained there."

*If I love this woman, I will destroy her . . . I will father
children who will be monsters . . . she will die in bearing
them. . . . Blessed Cassilda, foremother of the Domains, let
me not see so much, now, of my destiny, since I can do so
little to avert it. . . .*

"I am neither ill nor mad, *damisela*; you need not fear
me."

"Indeed," said the young woman, meeting his eyes
again. "You do not seem demented, only very troubled. Is it
the thought of our marriage which troubles you, then,
cousin?"

Allart said, with a nervous smile, "Should I not be well-
content, to see what beauty and grace the gods have given me
in a handfasted bride?"

"Oh!" She moved her head, impatient. "This is no time for
pretty speeches and flatteries, kinsman! Or are you one of

those who think a woman is a silly child, to be turned away with a courtly compliment of two?"

"Believe me, I meant you no discourtesy, Lady Cassandra," he said, "but I have been taught that it is unseemly to share my own troubles and fears when they are still formless."

Again the quick, direct look from the dark-lashed eyes.

"Fears, cousin? But I am harmless and a girl? Surely a lord of the Hasturs is afraid of nothing, and surely not of his pledged bride!"

Before the sarcasm he flinched. "Would you have the truth, Lady? I have a strange form of *laran*; it is not foresight alone. I do not see only the future which *will* be, but the futures which *might* come to pass, those things which may happen with ill luck or failure; and there are times when I cannot tell which of them are generated by causes now in motion, and which are born of my own fear. It was to master this that I went to Nevarsin."

He heard her sharp indrawn breath.

"Avarra's mercy, what a curse to carry! And have you mastered it, then, kinsman?"

"Somewhat, Cassandra. But when I am troubled or uncertain, it rushes in upon me again, so that I do not see only the joy which marriage to one such as you might bring me." Like a physical pain in his heart, Allart felt the bitter awareness of all the joys they *might* know, if he could bring her to return his love, the years ahead which might turn to brightness. . . . Fiercely he slammed the inner door, closing his mind against it. Here was no *riyachiya*, to be taken without thought, for a moment's pleasure!

He said harshly, and did not know how his own pain brought a rasp to his voice and coldness to his speech, "But I see, as well, all the griefs and catastrophe which may come; and till I can see my way through the false futures born of my own fears, I can take no joy in the thought of marriage. It is intended as no discourtesy to you, my lady and my bride."

She said, "I am glad you told me this. You know, do you not, that my kinsmen are angry because our marriage did not take place two years ago, when I was legally of age. They felt you had insulted me by remaining in Nevarsin. Now they wish to be sure you will claim me without further delay." Her dark glance glinted with humor. "Not that they care a *sekal* for my wedded bliss, but they are never done reminding me how near you stand to the throne, and how fortunate I am, and how I must captivate you with my charm so you will not escape me. They have dressed me like a fashion puppet, and dressed my hair with nets of copper and silver, and loaded me with jewels, as if you were going to buy me in the market. I half expected you to open my mouth and look at my teeth to be sure my loins and withers were strong!"

Allart could not help laughing. "On that score your kinfolk need have no fear, Lady; surely no man living could find any flaw in you."

"Oh, but there is," she said ingenuously. "They were hoping you would not notice, but I will not try to hide it from you." She spread her narrow, ringed hands before him. The slender fingers were laden with jewels, but there were six of them, and as his eyes fell on the sixth, Cassandra colored deeply and tried to draw them under her veil. "Indeed, Dom Allart, I beg you not to stare at my deformity."

"It seems to me no deformity," he said. "Do you play the *rryl*? It seems to me that you could strike chords with more ease."

"Why, so it does—"

"Then let us never again think of it as defect or deformity, Cassandra," he said, taking the slight six-fingered hands in his own and pressing his lips to them. "In Nevarsin, I saw children with six or seven fingers where the extra fingers were boneless or without tendons, so that they could not be moved or flexed; but you have full control of them, I see. I, too, am something of a musician."

"Truly? Is it because you were a monk? Most men have no patience for such things, or little time to learn them with the arts of war."

"I would rather be musician than warrior," Allart said, pressing the narrow fingers again to his lips. "The gods grant us enough peace in our days that we may make songs instead of war." But as she smiled into his eyes, her hand still against his lips, he noted that Ysabet, Lady Aillard, was watching them, and so was his brother Damon-Rafael, and they looked so self-satisfied that he turned sick. They were manipulating him into doing their will, despite his resolve! He let her hand go as if it had burned him.

"May I conduct you to your kinswoman, *damisela*?"

As the evening progressed, the festivities decorous but not

somber—the old lord had been decently laid to rest, and he had a proper heir, so there was no doubt the Domain would prosper—Damon-Rafael sought out his brother. Despite the feasting, Allart noticed he was still quite sober.

"Tomorrow we ride for Thendara, where I shall be invested Lord of the Domain. You must ride with us, brother; you must be warden and heir-designate for Elhalyn. I have no legitimate sons, only *nedestro*; they will not legitimate a *nedestro* heir until it is certain that Cassilde will give me none." He looked across the room at his wife, a cold, almost bitter look. Cassilde Aillard-Hastur was a pale, slight woman, sallow and worn.

"The Domain will be in your hands, Allart, and in a sense I am at your mercy. How runs the proverb? 'Bare is back without brother.' "

Allart wondered how, in the name of all the gods, brothers could be friends, or anything but the cruelest of rivals, with such inheritance laws as these? Allart had no ambition to displace his brother as head of the Domain, but would Damon-Rafael ever believe that? He said, "I would indeed that you had left me within the monastery, Damon."

Damon-Rafael's smile was skeptical, as if he feared that his brother's words concealed some devious plot. "Is it so? Yet I watched you speaking with the Aillard woman, and it was obvious you could hardly await the ceremony. You are like to have a legitimate son before I do; Cassilde is frail, and your bride looks strong and healthy."

Allart said with concealed violence, "I am in no hurry to wed!"

Damon-Rafael scowled. "Yet the Council will not accept a man of your years as heir unless you agree to marry at once; it is scandalous that a man in his twenties should be still unwedded and without even any natural sons." He looked sharply at Allart. "Can it be that I am luckier than I think? Are you, perhaps, an *emmasca*? Or even a lover of men?"

Allart grinned wryly. "I grieve to disappoint you. But as for being *emmasca*, you saw me stripped and shown to Council when I came to manhood. And if you wished for me to become a lover of men, you should have made certain that I never came among the *cristoforos*. But I will return to the monastery, if you like."

He thought, for a moment, almost in elation, that this would be the answer to his torment and perplexities. Damon-

Rafael did not want him to breed sons who might be rivals to
his own; and so perhaps he could escape the curse of fathering sons who would carry his own tragic *laran*. If he were to
return to Nevarsin . . . he was surprised at the pain of the
thought.

Never to see Cassandra again. . . .

Damon-Rafael shook his head, not without regret. "I dare
not anger the Aillards. They are our strongest allies in this
war; and they are vexed that Cassilde has not cemented the
alliance by giving me an heir of Elhalyn and Aillard blood. If
you avoid the marriage I will have another enemy, and I cannot afford the Aillards for enemies. Already they fear I have
found a better match for you. But I know our father had
reserved two *nedestro* half-sisters of the Aillard clan for you,
with modified genes, and what will I do if you should have
sons by all three of them?"

Revulsion, as when Dom Stephen had first spoken of this,
surged in Allart again. "I told my father I had no wish for
that."

"I would rather that any sons of Aillard blood should be
mine," Damon-Rafael said, "yet I cannot take your pledged
wife; I have a wife of my own, and I cannot make a lady of
such an exalted clan into my *barragana*. It would be a matter
for blood-feud! Although if Cassilde were to die in childbirth,
as she has been likely to do any time these past ten years,
and may do at any time in the future, then—" His eyes
sought out Cassandra where she stood near her kinswomen,
appraisingly moving up and down her body; and Allart felt a
quite unexpected anger. How dare Damon-Rafael talk that
way? Cassandra was *his!*

Damon-Rafael said, "Almost I am tempted to delay your
marriage for a year. Should Cassilde die in bearing the child
she now carries, I would be free to make Cassandra my wife.
I suppose they would even be grateful, when she came to
share my throne."

"You speak treason," Allart said, genuinely shocked now.
"King Regis still sits on the throne, and Felix is his legitimate
son and will succeed him."

Damon-Rafael's shrug was contemptuous. "The old king?
He will not live a year. I stood by his side today by our father's grave; and I, too, have some of the foresight of the
Hasturs of Elhalyn. He will lie there before the seasons turn
again. As for Felix—well, I have heard the rumors, and no

doubt you have heard them, too. He is *emmasca*; one of the elders who saw him stripped was bribed, they say, and another had faulty eyesight. Whatever the truth, he has been married seven years, and his wife looks not like a woman who has been well treated in her marriage bed; nor has there ever been so much as a rumor that she was breeding. No, Allart. Treason or no, I tell you I will be on the throne within seven years. Look with your own foresight."

Allart said very quietly, "On the throne, or dead, my brother."

Damon-Rafael looked at him with enmity and said, "Those old she-males of the Council might prefer the legitimate son of a younger brother to the *nedestro* of the elder. Will you thrust your hand within the flame of Hali and pledge to support the claim of my son, legitimate or no?"

Allart fought to find the true sight through images of a kingdom raging in flames, a throne within his grasp, storms raging across the Hellers, a keep tumbling as if blasted by earthquake—*no!* He was a man of peace; he had no will to fight with his brother for a throne, see the Domains run red with the blood of a terrible fratricidal war. He bowed his head.

"The gods ordained it, Damon-Rafael, when you were born my father's eldest son. I will swear what oath you require of me, my brother and my lord."

In Damon-Rafael's look triumph mingled with contempt. Allart knew that if their positions had been reversed, he would have had to fight to the death for his inheritance. He tensed with dislike as Damon-Rafael embraced him and said, "So, I will have your oath and your strong hand to guard my sons; then perhaps the old saying is true, and I need not feel my back bare and brotherless."

He looked with regret across the room again at Cassandra, wrapped in her blue veil. "I suppose—No, I am afraid you must take your bride. All the Aillards would be offended if I made her *barragana*, and I cannot keep you both unwed for another year against the possibility that Cassilde might die and I should be free to wed again."

Cassandra—in his hands? Damon-Rafael, who thought of her only as a pawn for a political alliance, to cement the support of her kinfolk? The thought sickened him. Yet Allart recalled his own resolve: to take no wife, to father no sons to bear the curse of his *laran*. He said, "In return for my support, then, brother, spare me this marriage."

"I cannot," Damon-Rafael said regretfully, "though I would willingly take her myself. But I dare not offend the Aillards that way. Never mind, you may not long be burdened with her; she is young, and many of those Aillard women have died in bearing their first child. It is likely she will do so, too. Or she may be like Cassilde, fertile enough, but bearing only stillborn babes. If you keep her breeding and miscarrying for a few years, my sons will be safe and no one would claim you had not done your best for our clan; it will be *her* fault, not yours."

Allart said, "I would not want to treat any woman so!"

"Brother, I care not at all how you treat her, so that you wed her and bed her and the Aillards are bound to us by kin-ties. I did but suggest a way you might be rid of her without discredit to your own manhood." He shrugged, dismissing the matter. "But enough of this. We will ride for Thendara tomorrow, and when the heirship is settled, then we will ride here for your wedding again. Will you drink with me?"

"I have drunk enough," Allart lied, eager to avoid further contact with his brother. His foresight had seen truly. Not in all the worlds of probability was it written anywhere that he and Damon-Rafael would be friends, and if Damon-Rafael should come to the throne—and Allart's *laran* told him that might very well be—it might be that Allart must even guard his life, and the lives of his sons.

Holy Bearer of Burdens, strengthen me! Another reason I should father no sons to come after me—that I must fear for them, too, at my brother's hands!

CHAPTER
SEVEN

In amiable mood, eager to do honor to his young kinsman, His Grace Regis II had agreed to perform the ceremony of marriage; his lined old face glowed with kindliness as he spoke the ritual words and locked the copper-chased bracelets, the *catenas*, first on Allart's wrist and then on Cassandra's.

"Parted in fact," he said, unlocking the bracelets, "may you never be so in spirit or in heart." They kissed, and he said, "May you be forever one."

Allart felt Cassandra trembling as they stood, hands joined by the precious metal.

She is afraid, he thought, *and no wonder. She knows nothing of me; her kinsmen sold her to me as they might have sold a hawk or brood mare.*

In earlier days (Allart had read something of Domain history at Nevarsin), marriages like this would have been unthinkable. It had been considered a form of selfishness for women to bear children to one man alone, and the gene pool had been broadened by increasing the number of possible combinations. Briefly Allart wondered if that had been how they first bred the accursed *laran* into their race; or was it true that they were descended from the children of gods who came here to Hali and fathered sons to rule over their kindred? Or were the tales true of crosses with the nonhuman *chieri,* who gave their caste both the sexless *emmasca,* and the gift of *laran*?

Whatever had happened, these long-past and mostly forgotten days of group marriage had vanished as families began to climb to power; inheritance, and the breeding program, had

75

made exact knowledge of paternity important. *Now a man is judged only by his sons, and a woman by her abilities as a breeder of sons—and she knows it is only for this that she has been given to me!*

But the ceremony had come to a close, and Allart felt his wife's hands cold and shaking in his as he bent to touch her lips, briefly, in the ritual kiss which ended it, and led her out to dance in an explosion of congratulations, goodwill, and applause from his gathered kinsmen and peers. Allart, hypersensitive, felt the sharp-edged overtones in the congratulatory words, and thought that few of them meant their goodwill. His brother Damon-Rafael probably meant his goodwill sincerely. Allart had stood before the holy things at Hali that morning, thrusting his hand into the cold fire that did not burn unless the speaker knew himself forsworn, and pledged his honor as Hastur to support his brother's wardenship of the clan, and his sons' succession to the throne. The other kinsmen congratulated him because he had made a politically powerful alliance with the strong clan of the Aillards of Valeron, or because they hoped to ally themselves with him by marriage through the sons and daughters this marriage might engender, or simply because they took pleasure in the sight of a wedding, and the drinking and dancing and revelry, making a welcome break from the official mourning for Dom Stephen.

"You are silent, my husband," Cassandra said.

Allart started, hearing a pleading note in her voice. *It is worse for her, poor girl. I was consulted—somewhat—about this marriage; she was not even allowed to say yea or nay. Why do we do this to our women, since it is through them that we keep these precious inheritances which have come to mean so much to us!*

He said gently, "My silence was not meant for you, *damisela*. This day has given me much to think about; that is all. But I am churlish to think so deeply in your presence."

The level eyes, so deeply lashed that they appeared dark, met his, with a gleam of humor in their depths. "Again you are treating me like a maiden to be flattered into silence with a pretty compliment; and I presume to remind you, my lord, that it is hardly seemly to call me *damisela* when I am your wife."

"God help me, yes," he said, despairing, and she looked at him, a faint frown stitching itself across her smooth brow.

"Is it so unwilling that you have been wed? I was brought up since childhood to know I must marry as my kinsmen bade me; I thought a man more free to choose."

"I think no man is free; at least, not here in the Domains." He wondered if this was why there was so much revelry at a wedding, so much dancing and drinking—in order that the sons and daughters of Hastur and Cassilda might forget they were being bred like stud-animals and brood-mares for the sake of the accursed *laran* that brought power to their line!

But how could he forget? Allart was again in the grip of the out-of-focus time sense which was the curse of his *laran*, futures diverging from this very moment with the land flaming in war and struggle, hovering hawks like those which had flung *clingfire* at his air-car, great broad-winged gliders with men hanging from them, fires rising in the forests, strange snowcapped peaks from the ranges beyond Nevarsin which he had never seen, the face of a child surrounded with the pale blaze of lightnings. . . . *Are all these things coming into my life, truly, or are they only things which* may *come?*

Did he have any control over any of them at all, or would some relentless fate thrust them all upon him? As they had thrust Cassandra Aillard upon him as his wife, this woman standing before him. . . . A dozen Cassandras, not one, looking up at him—aglow with love and passion he knew he could arouse, torn with hatred and loathing (yes, he could rouse that, too), limp with exhaustion, dying with a curse, dying in his arms. . . . Allart closed his eyes in a vain effort to shut out the faces of his wife.

Cassandra said, in real alarm, "My husband! Allart! Tell me what is wrong with you, I beg!"

He knew he had frightened her, and sought to control the crowding futures, to put to practice the techniques he had learned at Nevarsin, to narrow down the dozen women she had become—might become, *would* become—into the one who stood before him now.

"It is not anything you have done, Cassandra. I have told you how I am cursed."

"Is there nothing that can help you?"

Yes, he thought savagely, *it would have helped most of all if neither of us had ever been born; if our ancestors, may they freeze forever in Zandru's darkest hell, could have refrained from breeding this curse into our line!* He did not speak it, but she picked up the thought, and her eyes widened in dismay.

But just then kinsmen and kinswomen burst in on their momentary solitude. Damon-Rafael claimed Cassandra for a dance with an arrogant, "She will be all yours soon enough, brother!" and someone else thrust a glass into his hand, demanding that he join in the revelry which, after all, was in his honor!

Trying to conceal rage and rebellion—after all, he could not blame his guests for the whole system!—he let himself be persuaded to drink, to dance with young kinswomen who evidently had so little to do with his future that their faces remained reassuringly one, not altered continually by the crisscrossing probabilities of his *laran*. He did not see Cassandra again until Damon-Rafael's wife Cassilde, and their kinswomen, were leading her from the hall for the formal bedding.

Custom demanded that the bride and husband be put to bed in the presence of their assembled peers, as proof that the marriage had been duly made. Allart had read at Nevarsin that there had been a time, soon after the establishment of marriage for inheritance and the *catenas*, when public consummation had been required, too. Fortunately Allart knew that would not be demanded of him. He wondered how anyone had ever managed it!

It was not long before they led him, in a tumult of the usual jokes, into the presence of his bride. Custom demanded, too, that a bride's bedding-gown should be more revealing than anything she had ever worn before—or would ever wear again. In order, Allart thought cynically, that all might see she had no hidden flaw that would impair her value as breeding-stock.

The gods grant they have not drugged her into complaisance. . . . He looked sharply to see if her eyes were drug-blurred, whether they had dosed her with aphrodisiacs. He supposed this was merciful for a girl given unwilling to a complete stranger; no one, he supposed, would have much heart for fighting a terrified girl into submission. Again conflicting futures, conflicting possibilities and obligations crowded into his mind with images of lust fighting for place with other futures in which he saw her lying dead in his arms. What had Damon-Rafael told him? That all of her sisters had died with the birth of their first child. . . .

With a chorus of congratulations, the kinsmen withdrew, leaving them alone. Allart rose and threw down the bar of the lock. Returning to her side, he saw the fear in her face and the gallant effort she made to hide it.

Does she fear I shall fall on her like a wild animal? But aloud he said only, "Have they drugged you with *aphrosone* or some such potion?"

She shook her head. "I refused it. My foster-mother would have made me drink it, but I told her I did not fear you."

Allart asked, "Then why are you trembling?"

She said, with that flash of spirit he had seen in her before, "I am *cold*, my lord, in this near-naked gown they insisted I must wear!"

Allart laughed. "It seems I have the better of it, then, being robed in fur. Cover yourself, then, Lady—it would have not needed that for me to desire you—I forgot, you do not like to be complimented, or flattered!" He came up and sat on the edge of the great bed beside her. "May I pour you some wine, *domna?*"

"Thank you." She took the glass, and as she sipped he saw the color come back into her face. Gratefully she tugged the fur robe up, to her shoulders. He poured some for himself, turning the stem of the goblet in his fingers, trying to think how he must say what must be said without offending her. Again the crowding futures and possibilities threatened to overwhelm him, so that he could see himself ignoring his scruples, taking her into his arms with all the pent-up passion of his life. How she would come alive with passion and love, the years of joy they would share . . . and again, confusingly, blurring the face of the woman and the moment before him, another woman's face, tawny and laughing, surrounded by masses of copper hair. . . .

"Cassandra," he said, "did you want this marriage?"

She did not look at him. "I am *honored* by this marriage. We were handfasted when I was too young to remember. It must be different for you, you are a man and have choice, but I had none. Whatever I did as a child, I heard nothing but this or that will or will not be suitable when you are wed to Allart Hastur of Elhalyn."

He said, the words wrung from him, "What joy it must be to have such security, to see only one future instead of a dozen, a hundred, a thousand . . . not to have to tread your way among them like an acrobat who dances upon a stretched rope at Festival Fair!"

"I never thought of that. I thought only that your life was more free than mine, to choose. . . ."

"Free?" He laughed without amusement. "My fate was as sealed as yours, Lady. Yet we may still choose among the futures I can see, if you are willing."

She said in a low voice, "What is left for us to choose now, my lord? We are wedded and bedded; it seems to me that no more choice is possible. Only this; you can use me cruelly or gently, and I can bear all with patience or disgrace my caste by fighting you away and forcing you, like the victim of some old bawdy song, to bear the marks of my nails and teeth. Which indeed," she said, her eyes glinting up at him in a laugh, "I would think it shameful to do."

"The gods forbid you should have cause," he said. For a moment, so poignant were the images roused by her words, it seemed that all other futures had really been wiped out. She was his wife, given to him consenting, even willing, and wholly at his mercy. He could even make her love him.

Then why do we not yield together to our destiny, my love . . . ?

But he forced himself to say, "A third choice remains still, my lady. You know the law; whatever the ceremony, this is no marriage until we make it so, and even the *catenas* can be unlocked, if we petition."

"If I should so anger my kinsmen, and bring the wrath of the Hasturs upon them, then the string of alliances on which the reign of the Hasturs is built will come crashing down. If you seek to return me to my kinsmen because I found no favor with you, there will be no peace for me, and no happiness." Her eyes were wide and desolate.

"I thought only— A day might come when you could be given to one more to your liking, my girl."

She said shyly, "What makes you think I could find one more to my liking?"

He realized with sudden dread that the worst had happened. Fearing she would be given to an insensitive brute who would think of her only as a brood-mare, finding that instead he spoke to her as to an equal, the girl was ready to adore him!

If he so much as touched her hand, he knew, his resolve would vanish; he would cover her with kisses, draw her into his arms—if only to wipe out the crowding futures he could see building up from this crucial moment, wipe them all out in a single moment by *some* positive action, whatever it might be.

His voice sounded strained, even to himself. "You know the curse I bear. I see not the true future alone, but a dozen futures, any one of which may come true, or mock me by never coming to pass. I had resolved never to marry, that I might never transmit this curse to any son of mine. This was why I had resolved to renounce my heritage and become a monk; I can see, all too clearly, what marriage with you might bring about. Gods above," he cried out, "do you think me indifferent to you?"

"Are your visions always true, Allart?" she pleaded. "Why must we deny our destiny? If these things are ordained, they will come about, whatever we do now, and if not, they cannot trouble us." She raised herself to her knees, flung her arms around him.

"I am not unwilling, Allart. I—I—I love you."

For the barest instant Allart could not help tightening his arms around her. Then, fighting the shamed memory of how he had surrendered to the temptation of the *riyachiya*, he seized her shoulders in his hands and thrust her away with all his strength. He heard his own voice harsh and ice-cold, as if it belonged to someone else.

"Do you still expect me to believe they have not drugged you with aphrodisiacs, my lady?"

She went rigid, tears of anger and humiliation welling in her eyes. He wanted, as he had never wanted anything in his life, to draw her back to rest against his heart.

"Forgive me," he begged. "Try to understand. I am fighting to—to find my way out of this trap they have led us into. Don't you know what I have seen? All roads lead there, it seems—that I will do what is expected of me, that I will breed monsters, children tormented worse by *laran* than ever I was, dying as my young brother died, or worse, living to curse us that they were ever born. And do you know what I have seen for you, at the end of every road, my poor girl? Your death, Cassandra, your death in bearing my child."

She whispered, her face white, "Two of my sisters so died."

"Yet you wonder why. I am not rejecting you, Cassandra. I am trying to avoid the frightful destiny I have seen for both of us. God knows, it would be easy enough. . . . Along most of the lines of my future, I see it, the course it would be easiest to take; that I should love you, that you should love me, that we will walk hand in hand into that terrible tragedy the future holds for us. Tragedy for you, Cassandra. And for me. I—" He swallowed, trying to steady his voice. "I would not bear the guilt of your death."

She began to sob. Allart dared not touch her; he stood looking down at her, heart-wrung, wretched. "Try not to cry," he said, his voice ragged. "I cannot bear it. The temptation is always there, to do the easiest thing, and trust to luck to lead us through; or if all else fails, to say, 'It is our destiny and no man can fight against fate.' For there are other choices. You might be barren, you might survive childbirth, our child might escape the curse of our joint *laran*. There are so many possibilities, so many temptations! And I have resolved that this marriage shall be no marriage at all, until I see my way clear before me. Cassandra, I beg you, agree to this."

"It seems that I have no choice," she said, and looked up at him, desolate. "Yet there is no happiness, either, in our world, for a woman who finds no favor with her husband. Until I am pregnant, my kinswomen will give me no peace. They have *laran*, too, and if this marriage is not consummated, sooner or later they will know that, too, and the same troubles we foresaw from refusing the marriage will be on us. Either way, my husband, it seems that we are the game who may stay in the trap or walk to the cookpot; either way lies ruin."

Calmed by the seriousness with which she sought to think about and evaluate their predicament, Allart said, "I have a plan, if you will follow me in it, Cassandra. Most of our kinsmen, before they come to my age, take their turn in a Tower, using their *laran* in a matrix circle which can give energy and power and a good life to our people. I was excused this duty because of my poor health, but the obligation should be filled. Also, the life of the court is not the best life for a young wife who—" He choked on the words. "Who might be breeding. I will petition for leave to take you to the Tower of Hali, where we will do our share of work in a matrix circle. So we will not face your kinswomen or my brother, and we can dwell apart without provoking talk. Perhaps, while we are there, we can find some way out of this dilemma."

Cassandra's voice was submissive. "Let it be as you will.

But our kin will think it strange that we choose this during the first days of our marriage."

"They may think what they will," Allart said. "I think it no crime to give false coin to thieves, or to lie to one who questions beyond courtesy. If I am questioned by anyone who has a right to an answer, I shall say that I shirked this obligation during my early manhood, and I wish to satisfy it now, so that you and I may go away together with no remaining unfulfilled obligations overshadowing our lives. You, my lady, may say what you will."

Her smile glinted at him; again Allart felt the wrench of heartbreak.

"Why, I will say nothing at all, my husband. I am your wife and I go where you choose to go, needing no more explanation than that! I do not say that I love this custom, nor that if you chose to demand it of me, I should obey without strife. I doubt you would find me such a submissive wife after all, Dom Allart. But I can use the custom where it suits my purposes!"

Holy Bearer of Burdens, why could not my fate have given me a woman I would be glad to put aside, not this one it would have been so easy for me to love! Exhausted with relief, he bowed his head, took up her slender fingers and kissed them.

She saw the broken weariness in his face and said, "You are very weary, my husband. Will you not lie down now and sleep?"

Again the erotic images were torturing him, but he pushed them aside. "You do not know much of men, do you, *chiya?*"

She shook her head. "How could I? Now it seems I am not to know," she said, and looked so sad that, even through his resolve, Allart felt a distant regret.

"Lie down and sleep if you will, Cassandra."

"But will you not sleep?" she asked naïvely, and he had to laugh.

"I will sleep on the floor; I have slept in worse places, and this is luxury after the stone cells of Nevarsin," he said. "Bless you, Cassandra, for accepting my decision!"

She gave him a faint smile. "Oh, I have been taught that it is a wife's duty to obey. Though it is a different obedience than I foresaw, still, I am your wife and will do as you command. Good night, my husband."

The words were gently ironic. Stretched on the soft rugs of

the chamber, Allart summoned all the discipline of his years
at Nevarsin and finally managed to blot out from his mind all
the images of Cassandra awakened to love; nothing remained
but the moment, and his resolve. But once, before dawn, he
thought he could hear the sound of a woman crying, very
softly, as if muffling the sound in silks and coverlets.

The next day they departed for Hali Tower; and there they
remained for half a year.

CHAPTER
EIGHT

Early spring again in the Hellers, Donal Delleray, called Rockraven, stood on the heights of Castle Aldaran, wondering idly if the Aldaran forefathers had chosen this high peak for their keep because it commanded much of the country around. It sloped down toward the distant plains, and behind it rose toward the far impassable peaks where no human thing dwelled, but only trailmen and the half-legendary *chieri* of the far Hellers, in their fastnesses surrounded by eternal snow.

"They say," he said aloud, "that in the farthest of these mountains, so far in the snows that even the most skilled mountaineer would fail before he found his way through the peaks and crevasses, there is a valley of unending summer, and there the *chieri* have withdrawn since the coming of the children of Hastur. That is why we never see them now, in these days. There the *chieri* dwell forever, immortal and beautiful, singing their strange songs and dreaming immortal dreams."

"Are the *chieri* really so beautiful?"

"I do not know, little sister; I have never seen a *chieri*," Donal said. He was twenty now, tall and whiplash thin, dark-tanned, dark-browed, a straight and somber young man who looked older than he was. "But when I was very small, my mother told me once that she had seen a *chieri* in the forests, behind a tree, and that she had the beauty of the Blessed Cassilda. They say, too, that if any mortal wins through to the valley where the *chieri* dwell, and eats of their food and drinks of their magical waters, he, too, will be gifted with immortality."

85

"No," Dorilys said. "Now you are telling me fairy tales. I am too old to believe such things."

"Oh, you are so old," Donal teased. "I look daily to see your back stoop over with age and your hair turn gray!"

"I am old enough to be handfasted," Dorilys said with dignity. "I am eleven years old, and Margali says I look as if I were already fifteen."

Donal gave his sister a long, considering look. It was true; at eleven Dorilys was already taller than many women, and her slender body had already some hint of a woman's shapely roundness.

"I do not know if I want to be handfasted," she said, suddenly sulky. "I do not know anything of my cousin Darren! Do you know him, Donal?"

"I know him," Donal said, and his face went bleak. "He was fostered here, with many other lads, when I was a boy."

"Is he handsome? Is he kind and well-spoken? Do you like him, Donal?"

Donal opened his mouth to speak and then shut it again. Darren was the son of Lord Aldaran's younger brother, Rakhal. Mikhail, Lord Aldaran, had no sons, and this marriage would mean that their children would inherit and consolidate the two estates; this was the way great Domains were built. It would be pointless to prejudice Dorilys against her promised husband because of boyish differences.

"You must not judge by that, Dorilys; we were children when we knew one another, and we fought as boys do; but he is older now, and so am I. Yes, he is good-looking enough, I suppose, as women judge such things."

"It seems hardly fair, to me," Dorilys said. "You have been more than a son to my father. Yes, he said so himself! Why can *you* not inherit his estate, since he has no son of his own?"

Donal forced himself to laugh. "You will understand these things better when you are older, Dorilys. I am no blood kin to Lord Aldaran, though he has been a kind foster-father to me, and I can expect no more than a fosterling's part in his estate; and that only because he pledged my mother—and yours—that I should be well provided for. I look for no more inheritance than this."

"That is a foolish law," Dorilys said vehemently, and Donal, seeing the signs of angry emotion in her eyes, said quickly, "Look down there, Dorilys! See, between the fold in the hills, you can see the riders and the banners. That will be Lord Rakhal and his entourage riding up toward the castle, come for your handfasting. So you must run down to your nurse and let her make you beautiful for the ceremony."

"Very well," Dorilys said, diverted, but she scowled as she started down the stairway. "If I do not like him, I will not marry him. Do you hear me, Donal?"

"I hear you," he said, "but that is a little girl speaking, *chiya*. When you are a woman you will be more sensible. Your father has chosen carefully to make a marriage which will be suitable; he would not give you in marriage unless he were sure this would be the best for you."

"Oh, I have heard that again and again, from Father, from Margali. They all say the same, that I must do as I am told and when I am older I will understand why! But if I do not like my cousin Darren I will not marry him, and you know there is no one who can make me do anything I do not want to do!" She stamped her foot, her rosy face flushed with pettish anger, and ran toward the stairway leading down into the castle. As if in echo to her words, there was a faint, faraway roll of thunder.

Donal remained looking over the railing, lost in somber thought. Dorilys had spoken with the unconscious arrogance of a princess, of the pampered only daughter of Lord Aldaran. But it was more than that, and even Donal felt a qualm of dread when Dorilys spoke so positively.

There is no one who can make me do anything I do not want to do. It was all too true. Willful since birth, no one had ever dared to cross her too seriously, because of the strange *laran* with which she had been born. No one quite knew the extent of this strange power; no one had ever dared to provoke it knowingly. Even while she was still unweaned, anyone who touched her against her will had felt the power she could fling—expressed, then, only as a painful shock— but the gossip of servants and nurses had exaggerated it and spread frightening tales. When, even as a baby, she screamed in rage, or hunger, or pain, lightnings and thunder had rolled and crashed about the heights of the castle; not only the servants, but the children fostered in the castle, had learned to fear her anger. Once, in her fifth year, when a fever had laid her low, delirious for days, raving and unconscious, not recognizing even Donal or her father, lightning bolts had crashed wildly all those nights and days, striking dangerously near the towers of the castle, random, terrifying. Donal, who could control the lightnings a little himself (though nothing like this), had wondered what phantoms and nightmares pursued her in delirium, that she struck so violently against them.

Fortunately as she grew older she longed for approval and affection, and Lady Deonara, who had loved Dorilys as her own, had been able to teach her some things. The child had Aliciane's beauty and her pretty ways, and in the last year or two, she had been less feared and better liked. But still the servants and children feared her, calling her witch and sorceress when she could not hear; not even the boldest of the children dared offend her to her face. She had never turned on Donal, nor on her father, nor on her foster-mother Margali, the *leronis* who had brought her into the world; nor, during Lady Deonara's lifetime, had she ever gone against Deonara's will.

But since Deonara's death, Donal thought (sadly, for he, too, had loved the gentle Lady Aldaran), *no one has ever gainsaid Dorilys.* Mikhail of Aldaran adored his pretty daughter, and denied her nothing, in or out of reason, so that the eleven-year-old Dorilys had the jewels and playthings of a princess. The servants would not, because they feared her anger and the power which gossip had exaggerated so enormously. The other children would not, partly because she was highest in rank among them, and partly because she was a willful little tyrant who never shrank from enforcing her domination with slaps, pinches, and blows.

It is not too bad for a little girl—a pretty, pampered little girl—to be willful beyond all reason, and for everyone to fear her, and give her everything she wants. But what will happen when she grows to womanhood, if she does not learn that she cannot have all things as she will? And who, fearing her power, will dare to teach her this?

Troubled, Donal turned down the stairs and went inside, for he, too, must be present at the handfasting, and at the ceremonies beforehand.

In his enormous presence-chamber, Mikhail, Lord Aldaran, awaited his guests. The Aldaran lord had aged since the birth of his daughter; a huge, heavy man, stooped now and graying, he had something still of the look of an ancient, molting hawk; and when he raised his head it was not unlike the stir-

ring of some such ancient bird on its block—a ruffle of
feathers, a hint of concealed power, in abeyance and still
there, dormant.

"Donal? Is it you? It is hard to see in this light," Lord Aldaran said, and Donal, knowing that his foster-father did not
like to admit that his eyes were not as sharp as they had
been, came toward him.

"It is I, my lord."

"Come here, dear lad. Is Dorilys ready for the ceremony
tonight? Do you think she is content with the idea of this
marriage?"

"I think she is too young to know what it means," Donal
said. He had dressed in an ornate dyed-leather suit, high indoor boots fringed at the top and carved, his hair confined in
a jeweled band; about his neck a firestone flashed crimson.
"Yet she is curious. She asked me if Darren were handsome
and well-spoken, if I liked him. I gave her small answer to
that, I fear, but I told her she must not judge a man on a
boy's quarrels."

"Nor must you, my boy," Aldaran said, but he said it
gently.

"Foster-father—I have a boon to ask of you," Donal said.

Aldaran smiled and said, "You have long known, Donal,
any gift within reason that I can give is yours for the asking."

"This will cost you nothing, my lord, except some thought.
When the Lord Rakhal and Lord Darren come before you
tonight to discuss the matter of Dorilys's marriage gifts, will
you introduce me to the company by my father's name, and
not as Donal of Rockraven as you are used to do?"

Lord Aldaran's nearsighted eyes blinked, giving him more
than ever the air of some gigantic bird of prey blinded by the
light. "How is this, foster-son? Would you disown your
mother, or her place here? Or yours?"

"All gods forbid," Donal said.

He came and knelt at Lord Aldaran's side. The old man
laid a hand on his shoulder, and at the touch the unspoken
words were clear to both of them: *But only a bastard wears
his mother's name. I am orphaned, but no bastard.*

"Forgive me, Donal," the old man said at last. "I am to
blame. I wished—I wished not to remember that Aliciane had
ever belonged to any other man. Even when she had—had
left me, I could not bear to remind myself that you were not,

in sober truth, my own son." It was like a cry of pain. "I
have so often wished that you were!"

"I, too," said Donal. He could remember no other father,
wished for no other. Yet Darren's bullying voice seemed as
fresh in his ears as it had been ten years ago:

"Donal of Rockraven; yes, I know, the *barragana's* brat.
Do you even know who fathered you, or are you a son of the
river? Did your mother lie in the forest during a Ghost-wind
and come home with no-man's son in her belly?" Donal had
flown at him, then, like a banshee, clawing and kicking, and
they had been dragged apart, still howling threats at each
other. Even now, it was not pleasant to think of young Darren's scornful gaze, the taunts he had made.

There was tardy apology in Lord Aldaran's voice. "If I
have wronged you out of my own hunger to call you my son,
believe I never meant to throw doubt on the honor of your
own lineage, nor to conceal it. I think in what I mean to do
tonight you will find how truly I value you, dear son."

"I need nothing but that," Donal said, and sat beside him
on a low footstool.

Aldaran reached for his hand and they sat like that until a
servant, bringing lights, proclaimed: "Lord Rakhal Aldaran
of Scathfell, and Lord Darren."

Rakhal of Scathfell was like his brother had been ten years
ago, a big hearty man in the prime of life, his face open and
jovial, with that good-fellowship devious men often assume as
a way of proclaiming that they are concealing nothing, when
the truth is often quite the reverse. Darren was like him, tall
and broad, no more than a year or two older than Donal,
sandy-red hair swept back from a high forehead, a straight-
forward look which made Donal think, at first glance, *Yes,
he is handsome, as girls reckon such things. Dorilys will like
him. . . .* He told himself that his faint sense of foreboding
was no more than a distaste for seeing his sister taken from
his own exclusive protection and charge and given to another.

*I cannot look that Dorilys should remain with me always.
She is heir to a great Domain; I am her half-brother, no
more, and her well-being must lie in other hands than mine.*

The lord Aldaran rose from his seat and advanced a few
steps toward his brother, taking his hands warmly.

"Greetings, Rakhal. It is too long since you have come to
me here at Aldaran. How goes all at Scathfell? And Darren?"
He embraced his kinsmen, one after the other, leading them

to sit near him. "And you know my foster-son, half-brother to your bride, Darren. Donal Delleray, Aliciane's son."

Darren lifted his eyebrows in recognition and said, "We were taught arms-practice together, and other things. Somehow I had thought his name was Rockraven."

"Children are given to such misconceptions," Lord Aldaran said firmly. "You must have been very young then, nephew, and lineage means little to young lads. Donal's grandparents were Rafael Delleray and his wife *di catenas* Mirella Lindir. Donal's father died young, and his widowed mother came here as singing-woman. She bore me my only living child. Your bride, Darren."

"Indeed?" Rakhal of Scathfell looked on Donal with a courteous interest, which Donal suspected of being as spurious as the rest of his good humor.

Donal wondered why it should matter to him what the Scathfell clan thought of him.

Darren and I are to be brothers-by-marriage. It is not a relationship I would have sought. He, Donal, was honorably born, honorably fostered in a Great House; that should have been enough. Looking at Darren, he knew it would never be enough, and wondered why. Why should Darren Aldaran, heir to Scathfell, bother to hate and resent the half-brother of his promised wife, the fosterling of her father?

Then, looking at Darren's falsely hearty smile, suddenly he knew the answer. He was not much of a telepath, but Darren might as well have shouted it at him.

Zandru's hells, he fears my influence over Lord Aldaran! The laws of inheritance by blood are not yet so firm, in these mountains, that he is certain of what may happen. It would not be the first time a nobleman had sought to disinherit his lawful heir for one he considered more suitable; and he knows my foster-father thinks of me as a son, not a fosterling.

To do Donal credit, the thought had never crossed his mind before. He had known his place—bound to Lord Aldaran by affection, but not by blood—and accepted it. Now, the thought awakened because the men of Scathfell had provoked it, he wondered why it could *not* be so; why could the man he called "Father," to whom he had been a dutiful son, not name his heir as he chose? The Aldarans of Scathfell had *that* inheritance; why should they swell their holdings almost to the size of a kingdom by adding Aldaran itself to their estate?

But Lord Rakhal had turned away from Donal, saying heartily, "And now we are brought together over the matter of this marriage, so that when we are gone, our young people may hold our joined lands for their doubled portion. Are we to see the girl, Mikhail?"

Lord Aldaran said, "She will come to greet the guests, but I felt it more suitable to settle the business part of our meeting without her presence. She is a child, not suited to listen while gray beards settle matters of dowries and marriage gifts and inheritance. She will come to pledge herself, Darren, and to dance with you at the festivities. But I beg of you to remember that she is still very young and there can be no thought of actual marriage for four years at least, perhaps more."

Rakhal chuckled. "Fathers seldom think their daughters ripe to marry, Mikhail!"

"But in this case," Aldaran said firmly, "Dorilys is no more than eleven; the marriage *di catenas* must take place no sooner than four years from now."

"Come, come. My son is already a man; how long must he wait for a bride?"

"He must wait those years," Aldaran said firmly, "or seek one elsewhere."

Darren shrugged. "If I must wait for a little girl to grow up, then I suppose I must wait. A barbarous custom this, to pledge a grown man to a girl who has not yet put aside her dolls!"

"No doubt," Rakhal of Scathfell said, in his hearty and jovial manner, "but I have felt this marriage was important ever since Dorilys was born, and have spoken often of it to my brother in the past ten years."

Darren said, "If my uncle was so opposed before this, why has he given way now?"

Lord Aldaran's shoulders went up and down in a heavy shrug. "I suppose because I am growing old and am at last resigned to the knowledge that I should have no son; and I would rather see the estate of Aldaran pass into the hands of kinfolk, than into the hands of a stranger."

Why, at this moment, after ten years, Aldaran wondered, should he think of a curse flung by a sorceress many years dead? *From this day your loins shall be empty.* It was true that he had never thought seriously, from Aliciane's death, of taking another woman to his bed.

"Of course it could be argued," Rakhal of Scathfell said, "that *my* son is lawful heir to Aldaran, anyway. The lawgivers might well argue that Dorilys deserves no more than a marriage portion, and that a lawfully born nephew is nearer in inheritance than a *barragana*'s daughter."

"I do not grant the right of those so-called lawgivers to offer any judgment in that matter!"

Scathfell shrugged. "In any case this marriage will settle it without appeal to the law, with the two claimants to marry. The estates shall be joined; I am willing to settle Scathfell on Dorilys's eldest son, and Darren shall hold Castle Aldaran as warden for Dorilys."

Aldaran shook his head.

"No. In the marriage contract it is provided; Donal shall be his sister's warden till she is five-and-twenty."

"Unreasonable," protested Scathfell. "Have you none other way to feather your fosterling's nest? If he has no property from father or mother, can you not settle some on him by gift?"

"I have done so," Aldaran said. "When he came of age, I gave him the small holding of High Crags. It is derelict, since those who held it last spent their time in making war on their neighbors, and not in farming; but Donal, I think, can bring it back to fruitfulness. It only remains to find him a suitable wife, and that shall be done. But he shall be warden for Dorilys."

"This looks not as if you trusted us, Uncle," protested Darren. "Think you, truly, we would deprive Dorilys of her rightful heritage?"

"Of course not," said Aldaran, "and since you have no such thoughts, how can it matter to you who is warden for her fortune? Of course, if you had indeed some such notion, you would have to protest Donal's choice. A paid hireling as warden could be bribed, but certainly not her brother."

Donal heard all this in amazement. He had not known, when his foster-father sent him to report on the estate of High Crags, that Aldaran designed it for *him*; he had reported fairly on the work it would take to put it in order, and on its fine possibilities, without believing his foster-father would give him such an estate. Nor did he have any idea that Aldaran would use this marriage-contract to make him Dorilys's guardian.

On second thought, this was reasonable. Dorilys was nothing to the Aldarans of Scathfell except an obstacle in their way to Darren's inheriting. If Lord Aldaran should die tomorrow, only he, as warden, could prevent Darren from taking Dorilys immediately in marriage despite her extreme youth, after which Darren could make use of her estate as he chose. It would not be the first time a woman had been quietly made away with, once her inheritance was safely in her husband's hands. They might wait till she had borne a child, to make it look legal; but everyone knew that young wives were prone to die in childbirth, and the younger they were, the more likely to die so. Tragic, of course, but not uncommon.

With Donal as her warden, and the wardenship extended until Dorilys was a full five-and-twenty, not just old enough to marry legally and bear children, then even if she should die, Donal would be there as her warden and guardian of any child she might bear; and her estate could not fall undisputed into Darren's hands.

He thought, *My foster-father spoke truly when he said I should know tonight how much he valued me. It may be that he trusts me because he has no one else to trust. But at least he knows that I will protect Dorilys's interests even before my own.*

Aldaran of Scathfell had not accepted this peacefully; he was still arguing the point and did not cede it until Lord Aldaran reminded his brother that three other mountain lords had all made suit for Dorilys, and that she might have been handfasted at any time to anyone her father chose, even to one of the Lowlands Hasturs or Altons.

"Indeed she was pledged once before, since Deonara's Ardais kinfolk were eager to handfast her to one of their sons. They felt they had the best claim, since Deonara never bore me a living son. But the boy died shortly afterward."

"Died? How did he die?"

Aldaran shrugged. "An accident of some sort, I heard. I do not know the details."

Nor did Donal. Dorilys had been visiting her Ardais kin at the time, and had come home shocked by the death of her promised husband, even though she had hardly known him and had not really liked him. She had told Donal, "He was a big, rough, rude boy and he broke my doll." Donal had not questioned her. Now he wondered. Young as Donal was, he knew that if some child stood in the way of an advantageous alliance, that child might not live long.

And the same could be said of Dorilys. . . .

"On this point, my mind is made up," Lord Aldaran said, with an air of good nature, but firmly. "Donal, and Donal alone, shall be warden for his sister."

"This is an insult to your kin, Uncle," Darren protested, but the Lord of Scathfell silenced his son.

"If it must be, then it must be," he said. "We should be grateful that the maiden who is to be one of our family has a trustworthy kinsman to protect her; her interests are ours, of course. It shall be as you wish, Mikhail." But his look at Donal, eyes veiled and thoughtful, put the young man on his guard.

I must look to myself, he thought. *There is probably no danger till Dorilys is grown and the marriage consummated, since if Aldaran still lived he could name another warden.*

But if Aldaran should die, or Dorilys once wedded and taken to Scathfell, my chances would not be great to live very long.

He wished suddenly that Lord Aldaran were not dealing with kinsmen. If he had been dealing with strangers he would have had a *leronis* present, with truthspell to make lying or double-dealing impossible. But, although Aldaran might not trust his kinsmen overmuch, he could not insult them by insisting on having a sorceress, and a truthspell, to bind the bargains.

They set their hands on it, and signed the contract provided—Donal, too, was required to sign—and the matter was done. Then they were all embracing as kinsmen and going down into the room where the other guests had assembled to celebrate this occasion with feasting, dancing, and revelry.

But Donal, seeing Darren of Scathfell's eyes on him, thought again, coldly, *I must guard myself.*

This man is my enemy.

CHAPTER
NINE

When they went down into the Great Hall, Dorilys was
there with her foster-mother, the *leronis* Margali, receiving
their guests. For the first time, she was dressed not as a little
girl but as a woman, in a long gown of blue, embroidered at
neck and sleeves with gold traceries. Her shining copper hair
was braided low on her neck and caught into a woman's butterfly-clasp. She looked far older than her years; she might
have been fifteen or sixteen, and Donal was struck by her
beauty, yet he was not wholly pleased to see this abrupt
change.

His foreboding was justified when Darren, presented to
Dorilys, blinked at her, obviously smitten. He bowed over her
hand, saying gallantly, "Kinswoman, this is a pleasure. Your
father had given me to believe I was being handfasted to a
little girl, and here I find a lovely woman awaiting me. It is
even as I thought—no father ever believes his daughter ripe
for marriage."

Donal was stricken with sudden foreboding. Why had Margali done this? Aldaran had written it so carefully into the
marriage contract that there could be no marriage until Dorilys had reached fifteen. He had emphasized strongly that she
was only a little girl, and now they had given the lie to that
argument by presenting Dorilys before all the assembled
guests as a grown woman. As Darren, still murmuring gallant
words, led Dorilys out for the first dance, Donal looked after
them, troubled.

He asked Margali about this, and she shook her head.

"It was not by my will, Donal; Dorilys would have it so. I
would not cross her when her mind was so strongly set to it.

You know as well as I do that it is not wise to provoke Dorilys when she *will* have something. The gown was her mother's, and although I am sorry to see my little girl so grown up, still, if she is grown to it—"

"But she is *not*," Donal said, "and my foster-father spent a considerable time convincing Lord Scathfell that Dorilys was still a child, and far too young to marry. Margali, she *is* only a little girl, you know that as well as I!"

"Yes, I know, and a very childish one, too," Margali said, "but I could not argue with her on the eve of a festival. She would have made her displeasure felt all too greatly! You know as well as I, Donal. I can sometimes get her to do my will in important things, but if I tried to enforce my will on her in little things, she would soon stop listening to me when I sought to command her in the most serious ones. Does it matter, really, what dress she wears for her handfasting, since Lord Aldaran has written it, you say, into the marriage contract, that she shall not be bound till she is fifteen?"

"I suppose not, while my foster-father is still hale and strong enough to enforce his will," Donal said, "but the memory of this may cause trouble later, if something should happen within the next few years." Margali would not betray him—she had been kind to him from earliest childhood, she had been his mother's friend—but still it was unwise to speak so of the lord of a Domain and he lowered his voice. "Lord Scathfell would have no scruples in forcing the child into marriage for his own ambitions, and to seize Aldaran for his own; nor would Darren. If she had been shown tonight for the child she is, public opinion might put some damper, however small, on any such plan. Now those who see her tonight dressed in a woman's garments, and evidently already full-grown, will not be inclined to inquire about her real age; they will simply remember that at her handfasting she looked like a grown woman, and assume that those folk of Scathfell had right on their side, after all."

Margali looked worried now, too, but she tried to shrug it aside. "I think you are letting yourself make nightmares without cause, Donal. There is no reason to think Lord Aldaran will not live another score of years; certainly long enough to protect his daughter from being taken in marriage before she is old enough. And you know Dorilys—she is a creature of whim; tonight it may please her to play the lady in her mother's gowns and jewels, but tomorrow it will be forgotten and she will be playing at leapfrog and jackstones with the other children, so that no one living could think her anything but the little child she is in truth."

"Merciful Avarra, grant it may be so," said Donal gravely.

"Why, I see no reason to doubt it, Donal. . . . Now you must do your duty by your foster-father's guests, too; there are many women waiting to dance with you, and Dorilys, too, will be wondering why her brother does not lead her out to dance."

Donal tried to laugh, seeing Dorilys, returning at Darren's side, entirely surrounded by a group of the young men, the minor nobility of the hills, Aldaran's Guardsmen. It might be true that Dorilys was amusing herself, playing the lady, but she was making a very successful pretense of it, laughing and flirting, all too obviously enjoying the flattery and admiration.

Father will not remonstrate with her. She looks all too much like our mother; and he is proud of his beautiful daughter. Why should I worry, or grudge Dorilys her amusements? No harm can come to her among our kinsmen, at a formal dance, and tomorrow, no doubt, it will be as Margali foresaw, Dorilys with her skirts tucked up to her knees and her hair in a long tail, tearing about like the little hoyden she is, and Darren can see the real Dorilys, the child who is young enough to enjoy dressing up in her mother's frock but still far from womanhood.

Trying to thrust aside his misgivings, Donal applied himself to his duties as host, chatting politely with a few elderly dowagers, dancing with young women who had somehow been forgotten or neglected, unobtrusively coming between Lord Aldaran and importunate hangers-on who might trouble him by making inconvenient requests too publicly to be refused. But whenever his eyes turned in Dorilys's direction, he saw her surrounded by recurrent waves of young men, and she was all too evidently enjoying her popularity.

The night was far advanced before Donal had a chance to dance, at last, with his sister; so far that she thrust out her lip, pouting like the child she was, when he came up to her.

"I thought you would not dance with me at all, brother, that you would leave me to all these strangers!"

Her breath was sweet, but he smelled the traces on it of wine, and asked with a slight frown, "Dorilys, how much have you been drinking?"

She dropped her eyes guiltily. "Margali said to me that I

should drink no more than one cup of wine, but it is a sad thing if at my own handfasting I am to be treated as a little girl who should be put to bed at nightfall!"

"Indeed I think you are no more," Donal said, almost laughing at the tipsy child. "I should tell Margali to come and take you to your nurse. You will be sick, Dorilys, and then no one will think you a lady, either."

"I do not feel sick, only happy," she said, leaning her head back and smiling up at him. "Come, Donal, don't scold me. All evening I have waited to dance with my darling brother; won't you dance with me?"

"As you will, *chiya*." He led her onto the dance floor. She was an expert dancer, but halfway through the dance she tripped over the unaccustomed long skirt of her gown and fell heavily against him. He caught her close to keep her from falling, and she threw her arms about him, laying her head on his shoulder, laughing.

"O-oh, maybe I have drunk too much, as you said—but each of my partners offered to drink with me at the end of a dance and I did not know how to refuse and be polite. I must ask Margali what is polite to say in such circum—circumstanshes." Her tongue tripped on the word and she giggled. "Is this what it feels like to be drunk, Donal, giddy and feeling as if all my joints were made of strung beads like the dolls the old women sell in the markets of Caer Donn? If it is, I think I like it."

"Where is Margali?" Donal asked, looking about the dance floor for the *leronis*; inwardly he resolved there should be some harsh words spoken to the lady. "I will take you to her at once, Dori."

"Oh, poor Margali," Dorilys said with an innocent stare. "She is not well; she said she was so blinded with headache that she could not see, and I made her go to lie down and rest." She added, with a defensive pout, "I was tired of having her standing over me with that reproving scowl, as if *she* were Lady Aldaran and I only a servant! I will not be ordered about by servants!"

"Dorilys!" Donal reproved angrily. "You must not speak so. Margali is a *leronis* and a noblewoman, and Father's kinswoman; you must not speak of her that way! She is no servant! And your father saw fit to put you in her care, and it is your duty to obey her, until you are old enough to be responsible for yourself! You are a very naughty little girl! You must not give your foster-mother headaches, and speak to her rudely. Now, look—you have disgraced yourself by getting tipsy in company as if you were some low-bred wench from the stables! And Margali is not even here to take charge of you!" Inwardly he was dismayed. Donal himself, her father, and Margali were the only persons on whom Dorilys had never turned her willfulness.

If she will no longer allow herself to be ruled by Margali, what are we to do with her? She is spoiled and uncontrollable, and yet I had hoped Margali could keep her in hand till she was grown.

"I am really ashamed of you, Dorilys, and Father will be very displeased when he knows how you have served Margali, who has always been so good and kind to you!"

The child said, lifting her stubborn little chin, "I am Lady Aldaran and I can do exactly what I want to do!"

Donal shook his head in dismay. The incongruity of this struck him, that she looked so much like a grown woman—and a very lovely one, at that—and spoke and acted like the spoiled and passionate child she was. *I would that Darren could see her now; he would realize what a baby she is, beyond the gown and jewels of a lady.*

Yet, Donal thought, she was not quite a baby; the *laran* she carried, already strong as his own, had allowed her to give Margali a violent headache. *Perhaps we should think ourselves fortunate that she does not seek to bring thunder and lightning upon us, as I am sure she could do if she were really angry!* Donal thanked the gods that for all Dorilys's strange *laran*, she was not a telepath and could not read his thoughts, as he could sometimes read the thoughts of those around him.

He said, coaxingly, "But you should not stay here in company when you are drunken, *chiya*; let me take you to your nurse, upstairs. The hour is late, and soon our guests will be going to their beds. Let me take you away, Dorilys."

"I don't want to go up to bed," Dorilys said sulkily. "I have had only this one dance with you, and Father has not yet danced with me, and Darren made me promise that he should have other dances later. Look—now he comes to claim them."

Donal urged, in a troubled whisper, "But you are in no state to dance, Dorilys; you will be falling over your own feet."

"No, I will not, truly. . . . Darren," she said, moving toward her handfasted partner, raising her eyes to his with a guile that looked adult. "Dance with me; Donal has been scolding me as an older brother thinks he has the right to do, and I am weary of listening to him."

Donal said, "I was trying to convince my sister that this party has gone on long enough for a girl so young. Perhaps she will be more ready to hear wisdom from you, Darren, who are to be her husband." *If he is drunk,* Donal thought angrily, *I will not give her into his charge, even if I must quarrel with him in this public place.*

But Darren seemed well in command of his faculties. He said, "Indeed it is late, Dorilys; what do you think—"

Abruptly there was an outcry of shouting at the far end of the hall.

"Good God!" Darren exclaimed, turning toward the clamor. "It is Lord Storn's younger son and that young whelp from Darriel Forst. They will be at blows; they will draw steel."

"I must go," Donal said in consternation, recalling his duties as his father's master of ceremonies, official host at this occasion, but he glanced, troubled, at Dorilys. Darren said, with unusual friendliness, "I will look after Dorilys, Donal. Go and see to them."

"I thank you," Donal said, hastily. Darren was sober, and he would have a vested interest in keeping his affianced wife from behaving too scandalously in public. He hurried toward the sound of the angry words, where the two youngest members of the rival families were engaged in a loud and angry dispute. Donal was skilled at such tactics. He came quickly up to them, and by joining in the dispute, convinced each of the quarreling men that he was on *his* side; then tactfully eased them apart. Old Lord Storn took charge of his quarrelsome son, and Donal took young Padreik Darriel into his own charge. It was some time before the young man sobered, apologized, and sought out his kinsmen to take his leave; then Donal looked around the ballroom for his sister and Darren. But he could see no sign of them, and wondered if Darren had managed to persuade his sister to leave the dance floor and go to her nurse.

If he has influence over Dorilys, perhaps we should even be grateful for that. Some of the Aldarans have the command-

*ing voice; Father had it when he was younger. Has Darren
managed to use it on Dorilys?*

His eyes sought for Darren, without success, and he began
to feel a vague sense of foreboding. As if to emphasize his
fears, he heard a faint, distant roll of thunder. Donal could
never hear thunder without thinking of Dorilys. He told himself not to be ridiculous; this was the season for storms in
these mountains. Nevertheless, he was afraid. Where was
Dorilys?

As soon as Donal had hurried away toward the quarreling
guests, Darren laid his hand under Dorilys's arm. He said,
"Your cheeks are flushed, *damisela*; is it the heat of the ballroom, with so many people, or have you danced to weariness?"

"No," Dorilys said, raising her hands to her hot face, "but
Donal thinks I have drunk too much wine and came to scold
me. As if I were a little girl still in his care, he wanted me to
be put to bed like a child!"

"It does not seem to me that you are a child," Darren said,
smiling, and she moved closer to him.

"I knew you would agree with me!"

Darren thought, *Why did they tell me she was a little girl?*
He looked up and down the slender body, emphasized by the
long close-fitting gown. *No child this! And still they think to
put me off! Does that old goat of an uncle of mine think to
play for time in the hopes of making a more advantageous
marriage, or give himself time to declare the bastard of
Rockraven his heir?*

"Truly, it is hot here," Dorilys said, moving still closer to
Darren, her fingers warm and sweaty on his arm, and he
smiled down at her.

"Come, then. Let us go out on the balcony where it is
cooler," Darren urged, drawing her toward one of the cur-
tained doors.

Dorilys hesitated, for she had been carefully brought up by
Margali and knew it was not considered proper for a young
woman to leave a dancing floor except with a kinsman. But
she thought, defensively, *Darren is my cousin, and also my
promised husband.*

Dorilys felt the cool air from the mountains towering over
Castle Aldaran, and drew a long sigh, leaning against the balcony rail.

"Oh, it was so hot in there. Thank you, Darren. I am glad to be out of that crowded place. You are kind to me," she said, so ingenuously that Darren, frowning, looked at the young woman in surprise.

How childish she was for a girl so obviously adult! He wondered, fleetingly, if the girl were feeble-minded or even an idiot. What did it matter, though? She was heir to the Domain of Aldaran, and it only remained for Darren to engage her affections, so that she would protest if her kinsmen sought for some reason to deprive him of his due by breaking off the marriage. The sooner it took place, the better; it was disgraceful, that his uncle wanted him to wait four years! The girl was obviously marriageable now, and the insistence on delay seemed to him completely unreasonable.

And if she were so childish, his task would be all the easier! He pressed the hand she laid trustingly in his and said, "No man living would hesitate an instant to do such a *kindness,* Dorilys—to maneuver for a moment alone with his promised bride! And when she is as lovely as you, even the kindness becomes more of a pleasure than a duty."

Dorilys felt herself coloring again at the compliment. She said, "Am I beautiful? Margali told me so, but she is only an old woman, and I do not think she is any judge of beauty."

"You are indeed most beautiful, Dorilys," Darren said, and in the dim light streaming in patches from the ballroom, she saw his smile.

She thought, *Why, he really means it; he is not only being kind to me!* She felt the first childish stirrings of awareness of her own power, the power of beauty over men. She said, "I have been told my mother was beautiful; she died when I was born. Father says I look like her; did you ever see her, Darren?"

"Only when I was a boy," Darren said, "but it is true. Aliciane of Rockraven was counted one of the loveliest women from the Kadarin to the Wall around the World. There were those who said she had put a spell on your father, but she needed no witchcraft but her own beauty. You are indeed very like her. Have you her singing voice as well?"

"I do not know," Dorilys said. "I can sing in tune, so my music-mistress says, but she says I am too young to know whether I will have a fine voice, or only a love of music and some little skill. Are you fond of music, Darren?"

"I know little about it," he said, smiling and moving closer to her, "and it needs not a beautiful voice to make a woman lovely in my eyes. Come—I am your cousin and kinsman and your promised husband; will you kiss me, Dorilys?"

"If you want me to," she said pliantly, and turned her cheek to him for his kiss. Darren, wondering again if the girl were teasing him or simply dim-witted, took her face between his hands, turning it toward him, and kissed her on the lips, his arms going around her to draw her against him.

Dorilys, submitting to the kiss, and through the tipsy blur of her sensations, felt a faint, wary stir of caution. Margali had warned her. *Oh, Margali is always trying to spoil my fun!* She leaned against Darren, letting him draw her tight against him, enjoying the touch, opening her mouth to his repeated kisses. Dorilys was no telepath, but she had *laran*, and she picked up a diffuse blur of his emotion, the arousal within him, the dim sense, *This may not be so bad after all*, and wondered why that should surprise him. Well, after all, she supposed it must be annoying for a young man to be told he was to be married off to a cousin he did not know, and she felt fuzzily glad that Darren thought her beautiful. He went on kissing her, slowly, repeatedly, sensing that she did not protest the kisses. Dorilys was too drunk, too unaware, to realize very clearly what was happening, but when his fingers moved to unlace her bodice, moving inside to cup over her bare breasts, she felt suddenly abashed and pushed him away.

"No, Darren, it is unseemly. Really, you must not," she protested, feeling her tongue thick in her mouth. For the first time she was aware that perhaps Donal was right; she should *not* have drunk so much. Darren's face was flushed, and he seemed unwilling to let her go. She took his hands firmly between her firm little fingers and pushed them away.

"No, Darren, don't!" Her hands went to cover her exposed breasts; she fumbled to relace the strings.

"No, Dorilys," he said thickly, so thickly that she wondered if he had drunk too much, too. "It's all right; it is not unseemly. We can be married as soon as you will. You will like being married to me; won't you?" He drew her close and kissed her again, hard and insistently. He murmured, "Dorilys, listen to me. If you will let me take you, now, then your father will allow the marriage rites to take place at once."

Now Dorilys was beginning to be wary; she drew her mouth away from his, moved away from him, beginning, through the blur, to wonder if she should have come out here at all, alone with him. She was still innocent enough not to be quite sure what it was he wanted of her, but she knew it was something she ought not to do, and even more, something he ought really not to ask. She said, her hands trembling as she sought to lace her bodice, "My father—Margali says I am not yet old enough to be married."

"Oh, the *leronis*. What does an old virgin know of love and marriage?" Darren said. "Come here and kiss me again, my little love. No, now, be still in my arms. Here, let me kiss you—like this—"

She could feel the intensity now in the kiss, frightening, his face the face of a stranger, swollen, dark with intent, his hands no longer caressing but strong, insistent.

"Darren, let me go," she begged him. "Really, really, you must not!" Her voice was trembling in panic. "My father will not like it. Take your hands from me! I beg you, kinsman—cousin!" She pushed at him, but she was a child, and still half drunk, and Darren was a grown man, cold sober. Her blurred *laran* picked up his intent, his determination, the touch of cruelty behind it.

"No, don't fight me," he muttered. "When it is over, your father will be all too glad to give you to me at once, and that will not displease you; will it, my little one, my beauty? Here, let me hold you."

Dorilys began to struggle, in sudden terror. "Let me go, Darren! Let me go! My father will be very angry; Donal will be angry with you. Let me go, Darren, or I will cry out for help!"

She saw the awareness of that threat in his eyes, and she opened her mouth to shriek for help, but he was aware of her intent and his hand, hard and determined, clasped over her mouth, smothering the cry, while he drew her closer to him. Terror suddenly gave way to anger in Dorilys. *How dare he!* Under the flooding rage, she *reached out*, in a way she had been able to do since babyhood if one touched her against her will, *striking. . . .*

Darren's hand fell from hers, and with a smothered cry, he grated with pain, "Ah, you little demon, how dare you!" and swung back his hand, striking her so hard on the cheek that she was knocked nearly senseless. "No woman alive does this to me! You are not unwilling; you want to be teased and flattered! No more; it is too late for that!"

As she fell to the floor, he knelt beside her, tearing at his clothes. Dorilys, in wild rage and fright, *struck out* again, hearing the crash of thunder through her own shriek, seeing the brilliant white flare that struck Darren. He reeled back, his face contorted, fell heavily atop her. In terror, she pushed him aside and scrambled up, gasping, sick, exhausted. He lay insensible, not moving. Never, never had she struck so hard, never. . . . *Oh, what have I done!*

"Darren," she pleaded, kneeling beside his motionless form. "Darren, get up! I didn't mean to hurt you, only you mustn't try to maul me like that. I don't like it. Darren! Darren! Did I really hurt you? Cousin, kinsman, speak to me!" But he was silent, and in sudden terror, heedless of her disheveled hair and torn gown, she ran toward the door of the ballroom.

Donal! It was the only thought in her mind. *Donal will know what to do! I must find Donal!*

Donal, alert to his sister's cry of panic, resounding in his mind even though it was not audible within the ballroom, had made a hasty excuse to the elderly friend of his grandfather who had come to speak with him, and hurried in search of her, led by the soundless cry.

That bastard Darren! He opened the balcony door and his sister fell into his arms, her hair half unbound, her dress open at the throat.

"Dorilys! *Chiya*, what has happened?" he said, his heart pounding, his throat sticking with dread. Gods above, would even Darren presume to lay rough hands on a girl of eleven?

"Come, *bredilla*. No one must see you like this. Come, smooth your hair, *chiya*; lace your bodice, quickly," he urged, thinking grimly that this must be kept from their father. He would quarrel with his kinsmen of Scathfell. It never crossed Donal's mind that such a quarrel might redound to his personal benefit. "Don't cry, little sister. No doubt he was drunk and did not know what he was doing. Now you see why a young woman must not drink so much she has not her wits about her, to keep young men from getting such ideas. Come, Dorilys, don't cry," he begged.

She said, her voice shaking, "It's Darren . . . I hurt him. I don't know what's wrong; he just lies there and will not speak to me. He kissed me too roughly. At first I wanted him to kiss me, but then he grew rough and I made him stop, and he hit me—and I was angry and I—I made the lightning come, but I didn't want to hurt him, really I didn't. Please, Donal, come and see what is wrong with him."

Avarra, merciful goddess! Donal, his breath coming in gasps, followed his sister onto the dark balcony, kneeling beside Darren, but already he knew what he should find. Darren, his face raised to the dark sky, lay motionless, his body already growing cold.

"He's dead, Dorilys; you've killed him," he said, drawing her into his arms in fierce protectiveness, feeling her whole body shaking like a tree in the wind. Around the heights of Castle Aldaran the thunders crashed and rolled, slowly fading into silence.

CHAPTER
TEN

"And now," said Lord Scathfell somberly, "if the gods will, we shall hear the truth of this dreadful business."

The guests had been cleared away, escorted to their rooms or to their horses. Over the heights of Castle Aldaran the great red sun was beginning to show a wet crimson face through the heavy banks of cloud. Darren's body had been carried to the chapel deep in tht heart of the castle. Donal had never liked Darren, but he could not keep back pity as he saw the young man lying stark and astonished, his clothing disarrayed, his head flung back in the spasm of agony and terror which had ended his life. *He came to an undignified end*, Donal thought, and would have arranged the young man's clothing in more seemly fashion; then it occurred to him that this would remove all traces of Dorilys's only defense.

Blood-guilt on so young a child, he thought with a shudder, and stepped back from the corpse and went out to Lord Aldaran's presence-chamber.

Margali had been roused from the heavy sleep which had fallen over her at the cessation of pain; she was there, a thick shawl thrown over her night-robe, Dorilys sobbing in her arms. The girl looked like an exhausted child now, her face blotched with long crying, her hair coming down in stray locks and tendrils, her swollen eyelids drooping sleepily over her eyes. She had almost stopped crying, but every now and then a renewed spasm of sobs would shake her thin shoulders. She was sitting in Margali's lap like the child she was, though her long legs dragged on the floor. Her elaborate gown was bedraggled and crushed.

Over the child's head Margali looked at Lord Mikhail of Aldaran and said, "Will you have truthspell, then, my lord? Very well, but let me at least call her nurse and put the child to bed. She has been awake all night, and you can see—" She moved her head, indicating the weeping, disheveled Dorilys, clinging to her.

"I am sorry, *mestra*. Dorilys must remain," Aldaran said. "We must hear what she has to say, too, I fear, and under truthspell. . . . Dorilys"— his voice was gentle—"let go of your foster-mother, my child, and go and sit there beside Donal. No one will hurt you; we only want to know what happened."

Reluctantly, Dorilys loosed her grip from Margali's neck. She was rigid, gripped with terror. Donal could not help but think of a rabbithorn before a pack of mountain beasts. She came and sat on the low bench beside him. Donal put out his hand to her and the childish fingers gripped it, painfully tight. With her free hand she wiped her smeared face on the sleeve of her gown.

Margali took her matrix from the silken bag around her throat, gazed for a moment into the blue jewel, and her low, clear voice was distinctly audible, though she was almost whispering, in the silence of the presence-chamber.

"In the light of the fire of the jewel, let the truth lighten this room where we stand."

Donal had seen the setting of truthspell many times, and it had never ceased to awe him. From the small blue jewel, a glow began, slowly suffused the face of the *leronis*, crept out into the room, creeping slowly from face to face. Donal felt the shimmer of the light on his own face, saw it glowing on the blotched face of the child at his side, saw it lightening the face of Rakhal of Scathfell and the paxman who stood motionless at his back. In the blue light Mikhail of Aldaran looked more than ever like some aged and molting bird of prey, motionless on his block, but when he raised his head the power and the menace were there, silent potential.

Margali said, "It is done, my lord. The truth alone may be spoken here while this light endures."

Donal knew that if falsehoods were knowingly spoken under the truthspell, the light would vanish from the face of the speaker, showing instantly that he lied.

"Now," said Mikhail of Aldaran, "you must tell us what you know of this, Dorilys. How came Darren to die?"

Dorilys raised her face. She looked pitiable, her face smeared and blotched with weeping, her eyes swollen, and again she wiped her nose on the elaborate sleeves of her gown. She clung hard to Donal's hand, and he could feel her trembling. Aldaran had never before used the commanding voice on his daughter. After a moment she said, "I—I didn't know he was dead," and blinked rapidly as if she were about to cry again.

Rakhal of Scathfell said, "He is dead. My eldest son is dead. Have no doubt about that, you—"

"*Silence!*" With the sound of the commanding voice, even Lord Scathfell let his voice die into quiet. "Now, Dorilys, tell us what befell between Darren and you. How came the lightnings to strike him?"

Dorilys slowly gained command of her voice. "We were warm from dancing, and he said we should go out on the balcony. He began to kiss me, and he—" Her voice shook again, uncontrollably. "He unlaced my gown and touched me, and he would not stop when I bade him." She blinked hard, but the truthlight on her face did not falter. "He said I should let him take me now so that Father could not delay the marriage. And he kissed me roughly; he hurt me." Her hands went up to cover her face, and she shook with a fresh outburst of sobs.

Aldaran's face was set like stone. He said, "Don't be afraid, my daughter; but you must let our kinsmen see your face."

Donal took Dorilys's hands in his. He could feel the agony of her fear and shame as if it were pulsing out through her small hands.

She said, stammering, into the unflickering truthlight, "He—he hit me hard when I pushed him away, and he knocked me down on the floor, and then he got down on the floor beside me, and I was—I was scared, and I hit him with the lightnings. I didn't want to hurt him; I only wanted him to take his hands off me!"

"You! You killed him, then! You struck him with your witch-lightnings, you fiend from hell!" Scathfell rose, advanced from his seat, his hand raised as if to strike.

"Father! Don't let him hurt me!" Dorilys cried out in shrill terror. A blue blaze of lightning struck outward, and Rakhal of Scathfell reeled back, stopped dead in his tracks, clutching at his heart. The paxman came and supported his faltering lord to his seat.

Donal said, "My lords, if she had not struck him down, I would myself have called challenge on him! To seek to ravish a girl of eleven!" His hand clutched at his sword as if the dead man stood before him.

Aldaran's voice was filled with sorrow and bewilderment as he turned to Lord Scathfell. "Well, my brother, you have seen. I regret this, more than I can say; but you have seen the truthlight on the child's face, and it seems to me there is little fault in her, either. How came your son to attempt a thing so unseemly at his own handfasting—to try to rape his intended bride?"

"It never occurred to me that he would need to rape," Scathfell said, anger beating through his words. "It was I who told him, simply, to make sure of her. Did you truly think we would agree to wait for years while you sought out a more advantageous marriage? A blind man could have seen that the girl was marriageable, and the law is clear: if a handfasted couple lie together, the marriage is legal from that moment. It was I who told my son to make sure of his bride."

"I should have known," Aldaran said bitterly. "You did not trust me, brother? But here stands the *leronis* who brought my daughter to the light. Under truthspell, Margali, how old is Dorilys?"

"It is true," the *leronis* said into the blue truthlight. "I took her from Aliciane's dead body eleven summers ago. But even if she had been of marriageable age, my lord of Scathfell, why should you connive at the seduction of your own niece?"

"Yes, we should hear that, too," Mikhail of Aldaran said. "Why, my brother? Could you not trust the dues of kin?"

"It is you who have forgotten kinship's dues," Scathfell flung at him. "Need you ask, brother? When you would have had Darren wait years while you schemed to find some way to give all to the bastard of Rockraven, whom you call fosterling. That bastard son you will not even acknowledge!"

Without stopping to think, Donal rose from his seat and stepped to the paxman's place, three steps behind Mikhail of Aldaran. His hand hovered a few inches above his sword-hilt. Lord Aldaran did not look around at Donal, but the words were wrenched from him.

"Would to all the gods that your words were true! Would that Donal had been born of my blood, lawfully or unlawful!

No man could ask more in kinsman or son! But alas—alas, with grief I say it—and in the light of truthspell, Donal is not my son."

"Not your son? Truly?" Scathfell's voice was contorted with fury. "Why, then, why else would an old man so forget kinship's dues if he were not unseemly besotted with the boy? If not your son, then it must be he is your minion!"

Donal's hand flashed to sword-hilt. Aldaran, sensing his intent, reached out and gripped Donal's wrist in steel fingers, squeezing until Donal's hand relaxed and he let the sword slide back into the scabbard, undrawn.

"Not beneath this roof, foster-son; he is still our guest." Then he let Donal's wrist go, advancing on the lord of Scathfell, and Donal thought again of a hawk swooping on his prey. "Had any man but my brother spoken such words I would tear the lie from his throat. Get out! Take up the body of that foul ravisher you called son, and all your lackeys, and get you gone from my roof before indeed I forget the dues of kin!"

"Your roof indeed, but not for long, my brother," Scathfell said between his teeth. "I will tear it down stone from stone around your head, ere it goes to the bastard of Rockraven!"

"And I will burn it over my own head, before it goes to any son of Scathfell," Lord Aldaran retorted. "Be gone from my house before high noon, else my servants shall drive you forth with whips! Get you back to Scathfell, and think lucky I do not harry you forth from that stronghold as well, which you hold by my favor. I make allowance for your grief, or I would have revenge in your heart's blood for what you have said and done here today! Get you gone to Scathfell, or where you will, but come into my presence no more, nor call me again brother!"

"Brother no more, nor overlord," Scathfell said in a rage. "The gods be thanked, I have other sons, and a day will come when we hold Scathfell of our own right, and not by your leave and favor. A day will come when we hold Aldaran as well, and yonder murdering sorceress who hides behind the mask of a weeping girl-baby shall be held to account with her own blood! From hence, Mikhail of Aldaran, look to yourself, and your witch-daughter, and to the bastard of Rockraven whom you will not own your son! The gods alone know what hold he has on you! Some filthy spell of witchcraft! I will breathe no longer this air polluted with the foul sorceries of this place!" Turning, his paxman at his heels, Lord Scathfell went forth, with a slow and measured step, from Aldaran's presence-chamber. His last look was for Dorilys, a look so full of loathing that Donal turned cold.

When brethren are at odds, enemies step in to widen the gap, Donal thought. Now his foster-father had quarreled with all his kin. *And I, who alone stand by him now—I am not even his son!*

When the folk of Scathfell had departed, Margali said firmly, "Now, my lord, by your leave, I shall take Dorilys away to her bed."

Aldaran, starting out of a brooding apathy, said, "Yes, yes, take the child away, but return to me here when she sleeps."

Margali took the sobbing child away, and Aldaran sat motionless, head down, lost in thought.

Donal forbore to disturb him, but when Margali returned, he asked, "Shall I go?"

"No, no, lad, this concerns you, too," Aldaran said, sighing as he looked up at the *leronis.* "No blame to you, Margali, but what are we to do now?"

Margali said, shaking her head, "I cannot control her anymore, my lord. She is strong and willful, and soon the stresses of puberty will be upon her. I beg you, Dom Mikhail, to place her in charge of someone stronger than I, and better fitted to teach her control of her *laran,* or worse things than this may follow."

Donal wondered, *What could be worse than this?*

As if picking up the unspoken question, Aldaran said, "Every other child I have fathered has died in adolescence of the threshold sickness which is the curse of our line. Must I fear that for her, too?"

Margali said, "Have you thought, my lord, of sending her to the *vai leroni* of Tramontana Tower? They would care for her, and teach her the uses of her *laran.* If anyone alive could bring her through adolescence unharmed, it is they."

Donal thought, *That is certainly the right solution.* "Yes, Father," he said eagerly. "You will remember how kind they were to me whenever I went there. They would have been glad to have me among them, if you could have spared me from your side. Even so, they always welcomed me among them as guest and friend, and they taught me much about the use of my *laran,* and would have gladly taught me more. Send Dorilys to them, Father."

Aldaran's face had brightened imperceptibly; then he frowned again. "To Tramontana? Would you shame me before my neighbors, then, Donal? Am I to show my weakness, that they can spread the word abroad to all the folk in the Hellers? Am I to be made the subject of gossip and scorn?"

"Father, I think you wrong the folk of Tramontana," Donal said, but he knew it would do no good. He had reckoned without Dom Mikhail's pride.

Margali said, "If you will not entrust her to your neighbors at Tramontana, Dom Mikhail, then I beg of you to send her to Hali or Neskaya, or to one of the Towers in the Lowlands. I am no longer young enough, or strong enough, to teach her or control her. All the gods know, I have no wish to part with her. I love her as if she were my own child, but I cannot handle her anymore. In a Tower they are schooled to do so."

Aldaran thought about that for some time. Finally he said, "I think she is too young to be sent to a Tower. But there are old ties of friendship between Aldaran and Elhalyn. For the sake of that old friendship, perhaps the lord of Elhalyn will send a *leronis* from Hali Tower to care for her. This would excite no comment. Any household with *laran* has need of some such person, to teach the young people of that household. Will you go, Donal, and ask that someone shall come to Aldaran to dwell in our household and teach her?"

Donal rose and bowed. The thought of Dorilys, safe in Tramontana Tower among his friends, had attracted him; but perhaps it had been too much to ask that his foster-father should make his weakness known to his neighbors. "I shall ride today, if you will, my lord, as soon as I can assemble an escort befitting your rank and dignity."

"No," Aldaran said, heavily. "You will ride alone, Donal, as befits a suppliant. I have heard that there is a truce between the Elhalyn and the Ridenow; you will be safe enough. But if you go alone, it will be clear that I am beseeching their help."

"As you will," Donal said. "I can ride tomorrow, then. Or even this night."

"Tomorrow will be time enough," Aldaran said. "Let the folk of Scathfell get well away to their homes. I want no word of this to get around the mountains."

CHAPTER
ELEVEN

At the far end of the Lake of Hali, the Tower rose, a narrow, tall structure, made of pale translucent stone. Most of the more demanding work of the matrix circle was done at night. At first Allart had not understood this, thinking it superstition or meaningless custom. As time passed, however, he had begun to realize that the night hours, while most people slept, were the most free of intruding thoughts, the random vibrations of other minds. In the deserted night hours, the matrix circle workers were free to send their conjoined minds into the matrix crystals which enormously amplified the electronic and energon vibrations of the brain, transforming power into energy.

With the tremendous power of the linked minds and the giant artificial matrix lattices which the technicians could build, these mental energies could mine deep-buried metals to the surface in a pure molten flow; could charge batteries for the operation of air-cars or the great generators which lighted the castles of Elhalyn and Thendara. Such a circle had raised the glistening white towers of the castle at Thendara from the living rock of the mountain peak where it stood. From the many Towers like this one flowed all the energy and technology of Darkover, and it was the men and women of the Tower circles who created it.

Now, in the shielded matrix chamber—shielded, not only by taboo and tradition, and the isolation of Hali, but by force-fields which could strike an intruder dead or mindless—Allart Hastur sat before a low, round table, hands and mind linked with the six others of his circle. All the energies of his brain and body were concentrated into a single flow toward the Keeper of the circle. The Keeper was a slight, steel-strong young man; his name was Coryn, and he was a cousin of Allart's, about his own age. Seated before the giant artificial crystal, he seized the massed energon flows of the six who sat around the table, pouring them through the intricate inner crystal lattices, directing the stream of that energy into the rows of batteries ranged before them on the low table. Coryn did not move or speak, but as he pointed a narrow, commanding hand toward one battery after another, the linked, blank-faced members of the circle poured every atom of their focused energies into the matrix and through the body of the Keeper, sending enormous charges of energy into the batteries, one by one.

Allart was ice-cold, cramped, but he did not know it; he was unaware of his body, unaware of anything except the pouring streams, the flow of energy which rushed through him. Dimly, without thought, it reminded him of the ecstatic union of minds and voices of the morning hymns of Nevarsin, this sense of unique blending and separateness, of having found his own place in the music of the universe. . . .

Outside the circle of linked hands and minds, a white-robed woman sat, her face in her hands, nothing visible but the falling streams of her long copper-colored hair. Her mind moved ceaselessly around and around the circle, monitoring one after another of the motionless figures. She eased the tension of a muscle before it could impair concentration, soothed a sudden cramp or itch before it could intrude into the concentration of the man or woman in the circle; made certain breathing did not falter, nor any of the small automatic movements which kept the neglected bodies in good order—the rhythmic blinks of the eyes to avoid strain, the faint shift of position. If breathing faltered, she went into rapport with the breather and starting the smooth rhythm again, lending smooth pace to a faltering heart. The linked members of the circle were not conscious of their own bodies, had not been conscious of them for hours. They were aware only of their linked minds, floating in the blazing energies they poured into the batteries. Time had stopped for them in an endless instant of massive union; only the monitor was conscious of the passing hours. Now, not seeing but sensing that the hour of sunrise was still some time away, she was aware of some tension in the circle that should not be there, and sent her questing mind from one to another of the linked figures.

Coryn. The Keeper himself, trained for years in mind and body to endure just this strain . . . no, he was in no distress. He was cramped, and she checked his circulation; he was cold but was not yet aware of it. His condition had not altered since the early hours of the night. Once his body was linked and locked into one of the comfortably balanced postures he could maintain unmoving for hours, it was well with him.

Mira? No, the old woman who had been monitor before Renata herself was calm and unaware, floating peacefully in the energy nets, focused on the outflows of force, random dreaming, blissful.

Barak? The sturdy, swarthy man, the technician who had built the artificial matrix lattice to the requirements of this circle, was cramped. Automatically Renata descended into his body-awareness, eased a muscle before pain could intrude into his concentration. Nothing else was amiss with him.

Allart? How had a newcomer to the circle come to have such control? Had it been his Nevarsin training? His breathing was deep and slow, unfaltering, the flow of oxygen to his limbs and heart unceasing. He had even learned the most difficult trick of a matrix circle, the long hours unmoving, without undue pain or cramping.

Arielle? She was the youngest of the circle in years, yet at sixteen she had spent a full two years here in Hali, and had achieved the rank of mechanic. Renata checked her carefully: breathing, heart, the sinuses which sometimes gave Arielle trouble because of the dampness here in the lake country. Arielle was from the southern plains. Finding nothing amiss, Renata checked further. No, nothing wrong, not even a full bladder to cause tension. Renata thought, *I wondered if Coryn had made her pregnant, but it is not that. I checked her carefully before she entered the circle, and Arielle knows better than that. . . .*

It must be the other newcomer, then, Cassandra. . . . Carefully monitoring, she checked heart, breathing, circulation. Cassandra was cramped, but not in much pain from it, not enough to notice. Renata felt Cassandra's awareness, a random troubled flutter, and sent a quick, reassuring thought to calm her before it could disturb the others. Cassandra was new to this work, and had not yet come to take the routine intrusion of a monitor's touch on body and mind with complete acceptance. It took Renata some seconds to soothe Cassandra before she could go into the deeper internal monitoring.

Yes, it is Cassandra. It is her strain we are all sharing. . . . She should not have come into the circle at this time, with her woman's cycles about to come upon her. I thought she knew better than that. . . . But Renata never thought of blaming Cassandra, only herself. *I should have made certain of that.* Renata knew how hard it was, in the early days of learning, to confess weakness or admit to limitations.

She moved into rapport with Cassandra, trying to calm her tension, but she realized Cassandra was not yet able to work with her in that kind of total closeness. She sent a careful, warning thought to Coryn, a gentle touch akin to the softest of murmurs.

We must break soon . . . be ready when I signal to you.

The flow of energies did not pause or falter, but the barest outside flutter of Coryn's attention replied, *Not yet; there is still an entire row of batteries which must be charged,* then he sank back into the linkage of the circle without a ripple.

Now Renata was troubled. The word of the Keeper was law in the circle; yet it was the responsibility of the monitor to keep custody of the well-being of the bodies of the linked members. So far she had carefully shielded her thoughts and her concern from all of them, but from somewhere she felt, now, a faint awareness, a withdrawal of total energy from the circle, which should not have been there. *Allart is aware of Cassandra. He is too aware of her for this stage. He should not, linked into the circle like this, know she is alive, any more than another.* As yet it was only a flicker and she compensated by gently nudging Allart's awareness back to his own focus of energy. She tried to hold Cassandra steady, as if, on a steep stairway, she had lent the other woman the support of her arm. But once the intensity of concentration was broken, something in the stream of energies faltered, wavered, as a wind ruffles the face of the waters. One by one she felt the disturbance run around the circle, only a flicker, but at this high level of concentration, disrupting. Barak shifted his weight uneasily. Coryn coughed. Arielle snuffled. and Renata felt Cassandra's breathing falter, grow heavy. Now imperative, she sent out a second warning:

We must break, Coryn. It is near time. . . .

This time the backlash was definitely irritable, and it reverberated through all the linked minds like an alarm bell. Allart heard the sound in his mind as he had heard the soundless bells of Nevarsin, and began slowly to recover his independent focus. Coryn's irritation was like a stinging slap; he felt it like the twitching of some internal strand as he felt Cassandra's consciousness drop away. It was like plucking forth an ingrown strand, as if some deep root planted in his being was jerked forth all bloody. One by one he felt the circle break and disintegrate, not the gentle withdrawal it had been in the earlier times, but this time falling apart painfully. He heard Mira gasping with effort, Arielle sniffle as if she were going to cry. Barak groaned, stretching a painfully cramped limb. Allart knew enough not to move too quickly at first; he moved with the slowest, most careful of motions, as if coming awake from a very deep sleep. But he was troubled and distressed. What had happened to the circle? Certainly their work had not been completed. . . .

One by one, around the table, the others were coming up from the depths of the matrix trance. Coryn looked white and shattered. He did not speak, but the intensity of his anger, directed at Renata, was painful to them all.

I told you, not yet. Now we will have this all to do again, for less than a dozen batteries. . . . Why did you break just now? Was there anyone in this circle too weak to endure for just a little more? Are we children playing jackstones, or a responsible mechanics' circle?

But Renata paid no attention, and Allart, his conscious mind flicking back into focus, saw that Cassandra had fallen sideways, her long dark hair scattered along the tabletop. He shoved back his low chair and sprang to her side, but Renata was there before him.

"No," she said, and with a flicker of dismay, Allart heard the commanding voice focused against him. *"Don't touch her!* This is my responsibility!" In his extreme sensitization Allart picked up the thought Renata had not spoken aloud: *You have done too much already; you are responsible for this. . . .*

I? Holy Bearer of Burdens, strengthen me! I, Renata?

Renata was kneeling beside Cassandra, her fingertips spread at the back of Cassandra's neck, just touching her at the nerve center there. Cassandra stirred, and Renata said soothingly, "It's all right, love; you're all right now."

Cassandra murmured, "I'm so cold, so cold."

"I know. it will pass in a few minutes."

"I'm so sorry. I didn't mean—I was sure—" Cassandra looked around, dazed, at the edge of tears. She flinched before Coryn's angry glare.

"Let her alone, Coryn. It's not her fault," Renata said, not looking up.

Coryn said, with a gesture of deep irony, *"Z'par servu, vai leronis. . . .* Have we your leave to test the batteries? While you minister to our bride?"

Cassandra was struggling against sobs. Renata said, "Don't mind Coryn; he is as tired as we all are. He didn't mean that as it sounded."

Arielle went to a side table, took up a metal tool—the matrix circles had first call on all the scarce metals of Darkover—and, wrapping her hand in insulating material, went to the batteries, touching them one after another to elicit the spark indicating they were fully charged. The other members of the circle rose cautiously, stretching cramped bodies. Renata still knelt at Cassandra's side; finally she withdrew her hands from the pulse circuits at the other woman's throat.

"Try to stand up now. Move around if you can."

Cassandra chafed her thin hands together. "I am as cold as if I had spent the night in Zandru's coldest hell. Thank you, Renata. How did you know?"

"I am a monitor. It is my duty to know such things." Renata Leynier was a slight, tawny young woman, with masses of copper-gold hair, but her mouth was too wide for beauty, her teeth somewhat crooked, her nose splotched with freckles. Her eyes, though, were wide and gray and beautiful.

"When you have had a little more training, Cassandra, you will be able to sense them for yourself, and tell us when you are not well enough to join a circle. At such a time, as I thought you knew, your psychic energy leaves your body with your blood, and you need all your strength for yourself. Now you must go to bed and rest for a day or two. Certainly you must not work in the circle again, or do any work demanding so much effort and concentration."

Allart came toward them, troubled. "Are you ill, Cassandra?"

Renata answered for her. "Overwearied, no more, and in need of food and rest." Mira had gone to a cupboard at the far end of the room and was setting out some of the food and wine kept there so that the circle members could refresh themselves at once from the tremendous energy-drains of their work. Renata went and searched among the provisions for a long bar of compressed nuts, sticky with honey. She put it into Cassandra's hand, but the dark-haired woman shook her head.

"I do not like sweets. I will wait for a proper breakfast."

"Eat it," Renata said, in command voice. "You need the strength."

Cassandra broke off a piece of the sticky confection and put it into her mouth. She grimaced at the cloying taste, but chewed it obediently. Arielle joined them, and throwing down the tool and taking a handful of dried fruits, she put them greedily into her mouth. When she could speak plain she said, "The last full dozen of the batteries are not charged, and the last three we finished will have to be done again; they are not to full capacity."

"What a nuisance!" Coryn glared at Cassandra.

"Let her alone!" Renata insisted. "We have all been beginners!"

Coryn poured himself some wine and sipped it. "I am sorry, kinswoman," he said at last, smiling at Cassandra, his normal good nature taking over again. "Are you wearied, cousin? You must not exhaust yourself for a few batteries."

Arielle wiped her fingers, sticky with the honeyed fruit. "If there is any work more tedious from Dalereuth to the Hellers than charging batteries, I cannot imagine it."

"Better that than mining," Coryn said. "Whenever I work with metals, I come out exhausted for half a moon. I am glad there is no more work to be done this year. Every time we go into the earth for mining, I come back to consciousness feeling as if I had lifted every spoonful of it with my own two hands!"

Allart, disciplined by the years of arduous physical and mental training at Nevarsin, was less weary than the others, but his muscles were aching with tension and inactivity. He saw Cassandra break another piece of the sticky honey-nut confection, felt her grimace as she put it into her mouth. They were still in rapport and he felt her revulsion for the oversweet stuff as if he were eating it himself.

"Don't eat that if you don't like it. Surely on the shelves

there is something more to your liking," he said, and turned
to rummage in them.

Cassandra shrugged. "Renata said this would restore me
more quickly than anything else. I don't mind."

Allart took a piece of it himself. Barak, who had been sip-
ping a cup of wine, finished it and came toward them.

"Are you recovered, kinswoman? The work is indeed fa-
tiguing when you are new to it, and there are no suitable
restoratives here." He laughed aloud. "Perhaps you should
have a spoonful or so of kireseth honey; it is the best of all
restoratives after long weariness, and you especially should—"
Abruptly he coughed and turned away, pretending he had
choked on the last swallow in his glass, but they all heard the
words in his mind as if he had spoken them aloud. *You especially should take such restoratives, since you are so new-
made a bride and have more need of them*. . . . but before
the words had escaped his tongue, Barak had recalled what
indeed they all knew, having been in close telepathic rapport
with Allart and Cassandra: the real state of affairs between
them.

The only amend he could make for the tactless jest was to
turn away, pretend the words unthought as they had been unspoken. There was a brief silence in the matrix chamber and
then they all began talking very loudly and all at once about
something else. Coryn took up the metal tool and checked a
couple of the batteries himself. Mira rubbed her cold hands
and said she was ready for a hot bath and a massage.

Renata put an arm around Cassandra's waist.

"You, too, sweetheart. You are cold and cramped. Go
down now; send for some proper breakfast and have a hot
bath. I will send my own bath-woman; she is extra skilled at
massage, and can loosen those tight muscles and nerves of
yours so you can sleep. Don't feel guilty. All of us over-
worked in our first season here. No one likes to admit
weakness, and we have all done it. When you have had some
hot food and a bath and massage, then lie down and sleep.
Have her put hot bricks at your feet and cover you well."

Cassandra demurred. "I do not like to deprive you of her
services."

"*Chiya*, I do not let myself get into such a state anymore.
Go now. Tell Lucetta I said to tend you as she does me when
I am out of the circle. Do as you are told, cousin. This is my
business, to know what you need even when you do not know

it yourself," she said. Allart thought she sounded motherly, as if she were a generation Cassandra's senior, instead of a girl Cassandra's own age or less.

"I will go down, too," Mira said. Coryn drew Arielle's hand through his arm and they left together. Allart was about to follow when Renata laid a feather-light hand on his arm.

"Allart, if you are not too weary, I would like a word with you."

Allart had been thinking of his luxurious room on a lower floor, and a cool bath, but he was not really weary; he said so, and Renata nodded.

"If this is the training of the Nevarsin brethren, perhaps we should acquire it for our circles. You are as steady and unwearied as Barak, and he has been part of our circles almost as long as I have been alive. You should teach us something of your secrets! Or do the brethren pledge you to secrecy?"

Allart shook his head. "It is only a discipline of breathing."

"Come. Shall we walk outdoors in the sunshine?"

Together they went down to the ground level, stepped through the force-field which protected the Tower circle against intrusion when they were working, and went into the growing brilliance of the morning. Allart walked silently beside Renata. He was not unduly tired, but he was tense and sleepless, his nerves jangling. As always when he relaxed his barriers even a little, his *laran* wove conflicting futures around him, diverging but just as perceptible as the green lawns sloping away toward the lake and the cloudy shores of Hali.

Silent, they walked side by side along the shore. Liriel, the violet moon, just past full, was setting dimly over the lake. Green Idriel, the palest of crescents, hung high and pale over the faraway rim of mountains.

Allart knew—he had known when first he set eyes on Renata—that this was the other of the two women he had seen again and again, and again, in the diverging futures of his life. From that first day in the Tower he had been on guard against her, speaking no more than the barest courtesies, avoiding her as much as it was possible to avoid anyone in the close quarters of the Tower. He had come to respect her competence as a monitor, to value her quick laughter and good humor, and this morning, watching her ministering to Cassandra's collapse, he had been touched by her kindness.

But until this moment they had never exchanged a single word outside the line of their duties in the circle.

Now hampered by fatigue he saw Renata's face, not as it was—gentle, impersonal, withdrawn, the look of a Tower-trained monitor at work, speaking of professional things—but as it might be in any of the diverging, fanning futures which *might* come to pass. Although he had barricaded himself against it, never allowing such thoughts freedom, he had seen her warmed by love, known the tenderness she could summon, had possessed her as if in a dream. This, overlaid upon the real state of affairs between them, confused and embarrassed him, as if he must face a woman about whom he had dreamed erotically, and conceal it from her. No. No woman had any part in his life except Cassandra, and he had firmly resolved how limited *that* part should be. He steeled himself against any lowering of these barriers and looked on Renata with the cold, impersonal gaze, almost hostile, of the Nevarsin monk.

They walked together, hearing the whispering sound of the soft cloud-waves. Allart had grown up on the shores of Hali, and had heard it all his life, but now he seemed to hear it freshly through Renata's ears.

"I never tire of this sound. It is so like, and so unlike, water. I suppose no one could swim in this lake?"

"No, you would sink. Slowly, it is true, but you would sink; it will not hold you up. But you can breathe it, you know, so it does not matter if you sink. Many times in my boyhood I have walked along the lake-bottom to watch the strange things within it."

"You can breathe it? And you will not drown?"

"No, no, it is not water at all—I do not know what it is. If you breathe it too long, you will become faint, and feel too weary even to take breaths, and there is some danger that you will become unconscious and die without remembering to breathe. But for a little while it is exhilarating. And there are strange creatures. I do not know whether to call them fish or bird, nor could I say whether they swim in the cloud or fly through it, but they are very beautiful. They used to say that to breathe the cloud of the lake conferred long life and that was why we Hasturs are long-lived. They say, too, that when Hastur, the son of the Lord of Light, fell to the shores at Hali, he gave immortality to those who dwelt there, and that we Hasturs lost that gift because of our sinful lives. But these things are all fairy tales."

"You think so being a *cristoforo*?"

"I think so being a man of reason," Allart said, smiling. "I cannot conceive of a god who would meddle with the laws of the world he created."

"Yet the Hasturs are long-lived, in truth."

"I was told at Nevarsin that all those of the blood of Hastur bear *chieri* blood; and the *chieri* are all but immortal."

Renata sighed. "I have heard, too, that they are *emmasca*, neither man nor woman, and thus free of the perils of being either. I think I envy them that."

It struck Allart that Renata gave tirelessly of her own strength; yet there was none to care if she herself was over-wearied.

"Go and rest, kinswoman. Whatever you have to say to me, it cannot be so urgent that it cannot wait till you have had the food and rest to which you were so quick to send my dear lady."

"But I would rather say it while Cassandra is sleeping. I must say it to one of you, and though I know you will think it an intrusion, you are older than Cassandra and better able to endure what I must say. Well, enough of apology and preamble. . . . You should not have come here with Cassandra new-made a bride and your marriage still unconsummated."

Allart opened his mouth to speak, but she gestured him to silence. "I warned you, remember, that you would think it an intrusion of your privacy and hers. I have been in the Tower since I was fourteen; I know the courtesies of such things. But also I am monitor here, and responsible for the well-being of everyone in the Tower. Anything which interferes— no, hear me out, Allart—anything which impairs your functioning, disrupts us all. I knew before you had been here three days that your bride was virgin still, but I did not intrude, not then. I thought perhaps you had been married for political reasons and did not like one another. But now, after half a year, it is obvious that you are madly in love. The tension between you is disrupting us all, and making Cassandra ill. She is so tense all the time that she cannot even properly monitor the state of her own nerves and body, which she should be able to do by now. I can do it for her, a little, when you are in the circle, but I cannot do it all the time and

I ought not to do for her what she should learn to do for herself. Now, I am sure you had some good reason for coming here in this state, but whatever your reasons, you knew too little of how a Tower circle must function. You can endure this; you have had the Nevarsin training and you can function even when you are unhappy. Cassandra cannot. It is as simple as that."

Allart said defensively, "I did not think Cassandra was so unhappy."

Renata looked at him and shook her head. "If you do not know, it is only that you have not allowed yourself to know. The wisest thing would be to take her away until things are settled between you; then, if you wish, you can return. We are always in need of trained workers, and your training at Nevarsin is very valuable. As for Cassandra, I think she has the talent to become a monitor, even a technician if the work interests her. But not now. This is a time for the two of you to be alone, not disrupting us all with your unsolaced needs."

Allart listened, cold with dismay. His own life had been lived so long under iron discipline that it had never occurred to him that his own needs, or Cassandra's unhappiness, could interfere to a hair's weight with the circle. But of course he should have known.

"Take her away, Allart. Tonight would not be too soon."

Allart said through mounting misery, "I would give all I possess, I think, if I were free to do that. But Cassandra and I have pledged one another—"

He turned away, but the thoughts were clear in his mind, and Renata looked at him in dismay.

"Cousin, what could prompt you to a vow so rash? I do not speak only of your duty to kinsmen and clan."

"No," said Allart. "Don't speak of that, Renata, not even in friendship. I have heard all too much of that and I need no one to remind me. But you know what kind of *laran* I have and what a curse it has been to me. I would not perpetuate it in sons and grandsons. This breeding program among those families with *laran*, which prompts you to speak of duty to caste and kin, it is wrong, it is evil. I will not pass it on!" He spoke vehemently, trying to blot out the sight of Renata's face, not as it was, grave with kindly concern, but as it might be, all pity wakened, tenderness and passion.

"A curse indeed, Allart! I, too, have many fears and doubts about the breeding program. I do not think any woman in the Domains is ever free of them. Yet, Cassandra's unhappiness, and yours, is needless."

"There is more, and worse," Allart said desperately. "At the end of every road I can foresee, it seems, Cassandra lies dead in bearing my child. Even if I could compromise my conscience to father a child who might bear this curse, I could not bring that fate on her. So we have pledged to live apart."

"Cassandra is very young and a virgin," Renata said, "and may be excused for knowing no better than that, though it seems wicked to me to keep a woman in ignorance of anything which may so closely affect her life. But surely the choice you have made is too extreme, since it is apparent even to outsiders that you love each other. You can hardly be unaware that there are ways—" She turned her face away, embarrassed, as she spoke. Such things were not spoken of much even between husband and wife. Allart was embarrassed, too.

She cannot be older than Cassandra! In the name of all the gods, how does a young woman, gently reared, of good family and still unmarried, come to know of such things?

The thought was very clear in his mind, and Renata could not help picking it up. She said dryly, "You have been a monk, cousin, and for that reason alone I am willing to admit that perhaps you really do not know the answer to that question. Perhaps you still believe that it is men alone who have such needs, and that women are immune to them. I do not want to scandalize you, Allart, but women in the Tower need not, and cannot, live by the foolish laws and customs of this time, which pretend that women are no more than toys to serve men's desires, with none of their own, save to breed sons for their clans. I am no virgin, Allart. Any one of us— man or woman—must learn, before we have been long in the circle, to face our own needs and desires, or we cannot put all our strength into the work we do. Or, if we try, such things happen as befell this morning—or worse, much worse."

Allart looked away from her, embarrassed. His first, almost automatic thought was pure reaction to his childhood teachings. *The men of the Domains know this, and still let their women come here?*

Renata shrugged, answering the unspoken question.

"It is the price they pay for the work we do—that we women shall to some extent be freed, for our term here, of the laws which emphasize inheritance and breeding. I think most of them choose not to inquire too closely. Also, it is not safe for a woman working in the circles to interrupt her term with pregnancy." She added after a moment, "If you wish, Mira can instruct Cassandra—or I myself. Perhaps she would take it more easily from a girl her own age."

If anyone had told me, while I dwelt at Nevarsin, that there was any woman alive with whom I could speak openly of such things, and that woman neither wife nor kinswoman, I would never have believed it. I had never thought there could be simple honesty between man and woman, this way.

"That would solve our worst fears, indeed, while we dwelt in the Tower. Perhaps we can have—this much. Indeed, we spoke of this, a little." Cassandra's words echoed in his mind as if they had been spoken only moments ago, not half a season gone by:

"I can bear it, as things are now, Allart, but I do not know if I could hold to such a resolve. I love you, Allart. I cannot trust myself. Sooner or later I would want your child, and it is easier this way, without the possibility and the temptation. . . ."

Hearing the echo in his mind, Renata said indignantly, "Easier for *her*, perhaps—" and stopped herself. "Forgive me, I have no right. Cassandra, too, is entitled to her own needs and desires, not to what you or I think she *ought* to feel. When a girl has been taught, since she was old enough to understand the words, that a woman's reason for living is to bear children to her husband's caste and clan, it is not easy to change that, or to find some other purpose for living." She fell silent, and Allart thought her voice sounded too bitter for her youth. He wondered how old she was, and they were so close in rapport that Renata answered the unspoken question.

"I am only a month or two older than Cassandra. I am not yet free of the desire to bear a child someday, but I had fears very like yours about this breeding program. Of course it is only men who are allowed to voice such fears and qualms; women are not supposed to think of such things. I sometimes feel that women in the Domains are not supposed to think at all! But my father was indulgent with me, and I won the promise that I should not marry till I was twenty, and that I might have training in a Tower, and I have learned much. For instance, Allart, if you and Cassandra chose to have a child, and she became pregnant, then with the aid of a monitor she could probe the unborn deeply, into the very germ plasm. If it should bear the kind of *laran* you fear, or any lethal recessive which could kill Cassandra in bearing it, she need not bring it to birth."

Allart said violently, "It is evil enough that we Hasturs meddle with the stuff of life of breeding *riyachiyas* and such abominations by genetic manipulation of our seed! But to do that with my own sons and daughters? Or to destroy, willingly, a life I myself have given? The thought sickens me!"

"I am not the keeper of your conscience, or of Cassandra's," Renata said. "This is only one choice; there must be others more to your liking. Yet I think it a lesser evil. I know that someday I shall be forced to marry, and if I am pledged to bear children to my caste, I will find myself caught between two choices which seem to me almost equally cruel: to bear, perhaps, monsters of *laran* to my caste, or to destroy them unborn in my womb." Allart saw her shudder.

"It was for this I became a monitor, that I might not contribute, unknowing, to this breeding program which has brought these monstrosities into our race. Now, *knowing* what I must do has made it the less endurable; I am not a god, to determine who will live and who will die. Perhaps you and Cassandra have done right after all, to give no life you must take away again."

"And while we await these choices," Allart said bitterly, "we charge batteries that idle folk may play with air-cars, and light their homes without dirtying their hands on resin and pitch, and mine metals to spare others the labor of bringing them from the ground, and we create weapons ever more fearful, to destroy lives over which we have no shadow of right."

Renata went very white. "No! Now, *that* I had not heard. Allart, is this your foresight, is war to break out again?"

"I saw, and spoke unthinking," Allart said, staring at her in dread. The sounds and sights of war were already around him, blurring her presence, and he thought, *Perhaps I will be killed in battle, be spared further wrestling with destiny or conscience!*

"It is your war and none of mine," she said. "My father has no quarrel with Serrais and no allegiance to Hastur; if the war breaks out anew, he will send for me, demanding again that I return home to marry. Ah, merciful Avarra, I am filled with good advice as to how you and your lady shall conduct your marriage and I have neither courage nor wisdom to face my own! Would that I had your foresight, Allart, to know which of many evil choices would bring the least of wrong."

"Would that I could tell you," he said, taking her hands for a moment. With the gesture Allart's *laran* clearly showed Renata and himself riding away northward together . . . where? For what purpose? The image faded and was gone, to be replaced by a whirl of images: The swooping flight of a great bird—or was it truly a bird? A child's face terrified, frozen in the glare of lightnings. A rain of *clingfire* falling, a great tower breaking, crumbling, smashing into rubble. Renata's face all ablaze with tenderness, her body under his own. . . . Dazed with the swirling pictures, he struggled to shut away the crowding futures.

"Perhaps *this* is the answer!" Renata said with sudden violence. "To breed monsters and let them loose on our people, make weapons ever more fearful, wipe out our accursed race and let the gods make another, a people without this dreadful, monstrous curse of *laran!*"

In the aftermath of her outburst it was so still that Allart could hear somewhere the morning sounds of wakening birds chirping, the soft wet sounds of the cloud-waves along the shores of Hali. Renata drew a long, shuddering breath. But when she spoke again she was calm, the disciplined monitor.

"But this is afar from what it was laid on me to say to you. For the sake of our work, you and Cassandra must not again work in the same matrix circle until all is well with you; till you have given and received your love and come to terms with it, or until you have decided for all time that it shall never be so, and you can be friends without indecision or desire. For the time, perhaps, you can be placed in different circles for working; after all, there are eighteen of us here, and you can work separately. But if you do not go away together, one of you must go. Even in separate circles, there is too much tension between you for you to dwell together under this roof. I think you should be the one to go. You have had, at Nevarsin, some teaching to master your *laran*, and Cassandra has not. But it is for you to say, Allart. In law, your marriage has made you Cassandra's master, and if you wish to exercise the right, the keeper of her will and conscience, too."

He ignored the irony. "If you think it would profit my lady to remain," he said, "then she shall stay and I will go." Bleakness came over him. He had found happiness at Nevarsin and been driven forth, never to return. Now he had found useful work here, the full possession of his *laran* gift, and was he to go forth from here, too?

Is there no place for me on the face of this world? Must I forever be driven, homeless, by the winds of circumstance? Then he was wryly amused at himself. He complained because his *laran* showed him too many futures, now he was dismayed because he saw none. Renata, too, was driven by choices not under her own control.

"You have worked all the night, cousin," he said, "and then you have stayed here and wrestled with my troubles and my wife's, and taken no thought for your own weariness."

Her smile glinted deep in her eyes, though it did not reach her mouth. "Oh, it has eased me to think of troubles other than my own; didn't you know that? The burdens of others are light to the shoulders. But I will go and sleep. And you?"

Allart shook his head. "I am not sleepy. I think perhaps I will go and walk in the lake for a little while, look at the strange fish or birds or whatever they may be and try to decide again what they are. Did our forefathers breed them, I wonder, with their passion for breeding strange things? Perhaps I, too, will find peace in regarding something afar from my own troubles. Bless you, kinswoman, for your kindness."

"Why? I solved nothing. I have given you more worries, that is all," she said. "But I will go and sleep, and perhaps dream an answer to all our troubles. Is there such a *laran* as that, I wonder?"

"Probably," Allart said, "but no doubt it has been given to someone who knows not how to use it for his own good; that is how these things happen in this world. Otherwise we might somehow find our way out of these worries and be like the game-pawn which manages to wriggle off the board without being captured. Go and sleep, Renata. All gods forbid you should bear the burden of our fears and worries, even in dreams."

CHAPTER
TWELVE

That evening, when Allart joined the members of his circle in the lower hall at Hali, he found them all talking excitedly, the six who had worked with him that morning, and all the others. Across the room he caught Renata's eyes; she was pale with dread. He asked Barak, who stood at the edge of the circle, "What is it, what's happened?"

"The war is upon us again. The Ridenow have launched an attack with bowmen and *clingfire* arrows, and Castle Hastur, in the Kilghard Hills, is under siege by air-cars and incendiaries. Every able-bodied man of Hastur and Aillard allegiance is out to combat the fire raging in the forests, or to defend the castle. We had word from the relays at Neskaya. Arielle was in the relay nets and heard—"

"Gods above," Allart said, and Cassandra came and stood looking up at him, troubled.

"Will the lord Damon-Rafael send for you, my husband? Must you go to the war?"

"I do not know," he said. "I was long enough in the monastery that my brother may think me too little skilled in campaign and strategy, and wish another of his paxmen to command the men." He fell silent, thinking, *If one of us must go, perhaps it is better if I go to war. If I do not come back, then she will be freed, and we will be out of this hopeless impasse.* The woman was looking up at him, her eyes filled with tears, but he kept his face cold, impassive, the disciplined and impersonal glance of the monk. He said, "Why are you not resting, my lady? Renata said you would be ill. Should you not keep your bed?"

"I heard the talk of war and I was frightened," she said,

132

seeking for his hand, but he gently drew it away, turning to Coryn.

The Keeper said, "I would think you better employed here, Allart. You have the strength that makes our work easier, and since the war has broken out again, we are sure to be asked to make *clingfire* for weapons. And since we are to lose Renata—"

"Are we to lose Renata?"

Coryn nodded. "She is a neutral in this war; her father has already sent word on the relays that she must be sent home under a safe-conduct. He wishes her out of the combat area at once. I am always sorry to lose a good monitor," Coryn added, "but I believe, with training, Cassandra will be equally skillful. Monitoring is not difficult, but Arielle is better as a technician. Do you think, Renata, that you will have time to instruct Cassandra in the techniques of monitoring before you go?"

"I will try," Renata said, coming toward them, "and I will stay as long as I can. I do not want to leave the Tower—" and she looked up at Allart helplessly. He remembered what she had told him only that morning.

"I shall be sorry to see you go, kinswoman," he said, taking her hands gently in his own.

"I would rather stay here with you," she said. "Would that I were a man like you and free to choose."

"Ah, Renata," he said, "men are not free either, not free to refuse war and dangers. I who am a Hastur lord can be sent unwilling into battle as if I were the least of my brother's vassals."

They stood for a moment, hands clasped, unaware of Cassandra's eyes on them, nor did either of them see her leave the hall. Then Coryn came up to them.

"How we shall need you, Renata! Lord Damon-Rafael has sent to us already for a new supply of *clingfire* and I have devised a new weapon that I am eager to experiment with." He took a careless seat in the window, as merrily as if he were devising a new sport or game. "A homing device set to a trap-matrix to kill only a particular enemy, so that if we aim it—for instance—at Lord Ridenow, it will do no good for his paxmen to throw himself in front of his lord's body. Of course we would have to get his thought-pattern, resonances from some captured article of his clothing, perhaps, or better yet, jewelry he has worn next to his body. Or by probing some captured man of his. Such a weapon will harm no one else, for nothing but the particular pattern of *his* mind will detonate it; it will fly to *him*, and him *only*, and kill him."

Renata shuddered, and Allart absentmindedly stroked her hand.

"*Clingfire* is too hard to make." Arielle said. "I wish they could find some better weapon. First we must mine the red stuff from the ground, then separate it atom by atom by distilling at high heat, and that is dangerous. Last time I worked with it, one of the glass vessels exploded; fortunately I was wearing protective clothing, but even so—" She thrust out her hand, showing a wicked scar, round, cicatrized, a deep depression in the flesh. "Only a fragment, only a grain, but it burned to the bone and had to be cut away."

Coryn lifted the girl's hand to his lips and kissed it. "You bear an honorable scar of war, *preciosa*. Not many women do. I have devised vessels which will not break at whatever heat; we have all put a binding spell on them so that they cannot shatter no matter what happens. Even if they should crack or break, the binding spell will hold them so that they stay in their shape and will not fly and shatter and injure the bystanders."

"How did you do that?" Mira asked.

"It was easy," Coryn said. "You set their pattern with a matrix so they can take no other shape. They can crack, and their contents can leak out, but they cannot fly asunder. If they are smashed the pieces will sooner or later settle gently down—we cannot put gravity wholly in abeyance—but they will not fly with enough strength to cut anyone. But to work with a ninth-level matrix, as we must do when refining *clingfire*, we need a circle of nine, and a technician, or better yet, another Keeper, to hold the binding spell on the vessels. I wonder," Coryn added, gazing at Allart, "would you make a Keeper, given training?"

"I have no such ambitions, kinsman."

"Yet it would keep you away from the war," Coryn said frankly, "and if you feel guilt at that, remember you will be better employed here, and not without risk. None of us is free of scars. Look," he added, holding up his hands, showing a deep, long-healed burn. "I took a backflow once, when a technician faltered. The matrix was like a live coal. I thought it would burn to the bones of my hands like *clingfire*. As for suffering—well, if we are to be working circles of nine, night and day, for the making of weapons—well, we will suffer, and our women with us, if we must spend so much time in the circles."

Arielle colored as the men standing around began to chuckle softly; they all knew what Coryn meant: the major side effect of matrix work, for men, was a long period of impotence. Seeing Allart's stiff smile, Coryn chuckled again.

"Perhaps we should all be monks, and trained to endure *that*, with cold and hunger," he said, laughing. "Allart, tell me. I have heard that on your way from Nevarsin you were attacked by a *clingfire* device which exploded—but you managed to wrest it loose so that it exploded at a distance. Tell me about that."

Allart told what he could remember of the episode, and Coryn nodded gravely. "I had thought of such a missile, making it superfragile, to be filled either with *clingfire* or with ordinary incendiaries. I have one which will set an entire forest ablaze, so that they must withdraw fighting men to fight the fire. And I have a weapon which is like those fancy drops our artisans make, which can be struck with hammers or trodden on by beasts, and will not break, but the merest touch against the long glass tail and they shatter into a thousand fragments. This one cannot be prematurely exploded as you did with the one sent against your father, because nothing, *nothing*, will explode it except the detonating thoughts of the one who sent it. I am not sorry for the end of the truce. We must have a chance to try these weapons somewhere!"

"Would they might stay forever untried!" Allart said with a shudder.

"Ah, there speaks the monk," Barak said. "A few years will cure you of such treasonous nonsense, my lad. Those Ridenow usurpers who would crowd their way into our Domain are many and fertile, some of the fathers with six or seven sons, all land-hungry and quarrelsome. Of *my* father's seven sons, two died at birth and another when *laran* came on him at adolescence. Yet it seems to me almost worse to have many sons who survive to manhood, so that an estate must be cut into slivers to support them all; or they must range outward, as those Ridenow have done, seeking lands enough for them to rule, and conquer."

Coryn smiled without even a trace of mirth. "True," he said. "One son is needful, so needful they will do anything to insure that one survives; but if two should live, it is too many.

I was the younger son, and my elder brother is well pleased that I should dwell here as Keeper, powerless in the great events of our time. *Your* brother is more loving, Allart—at least he has given you in marriage!"

"Yes," Allart said, "but I have sworn to uphold his claim to the throne, should anything befall King Regis—may his reign be long!"

"Already his reign has been overlong," said a Keeper from one of the other circles. "But I am not looking forward with any pleasure to what will come when your brother and Prince Felix begin to struggle for the throne. War with Ridenow is evil enough, but a war of brethren within the Hastur Domain would be far worse."

"Prince Felix is *emmasca*, I have heard," Barak said. "I do not think he will fight to keep his crown—eggs can't fight stones!"

"Well, he js safe enough while the old king lives," Coryn said. "But after that it is only a matter of time till he is challenged and exposed. Who, I wonder, did they bribe, to let him be named as heir in the first place? But perhaps you were fortunate, Allart, for your brother needed your support badly enough to find you a wife, and a lovely and winning lady she is indeed."

"I thought I had seen her here but a moment ago," said the other Keeper, "but now she is gone."

Allart looked around, suddenly filled with a nameless foreboding. A group of the younger women of the Tower were dancing at one end of the long room; he had thought her among them. Again he saw her lying dead in his arms . . . but he dismissed the picture as an illusion born of fear and his mental disquiet.

"Perhaps she has gone upstairs to her room again. Renata bade her keep her bed, for she was not well, and I was surprised she had come down at all tonight."

"But she is not in her room," Renata said, coming to them, picking up his thought, her face white. "Where can she have gone, Allart? I went to ask if she wished me to instruct her as a monitor, and she is not within the Tower at all."

"Merciful Avarra!" Suddenly the diverging futures crashed in upon him again and Allart knew where Cassandra had gone. Without a word of leavetaking he turned away from the men and hurried out, going through halls and corridors, stepping through the force-field and out of the Tower.

The sun, a great crimson ball, hung like fire on the distant hills, coating the lake with flame.

She saw me with Renata. I would not touch her hand, though she was weeping; yet I kissed Renata before her eyes. Only in friendship, as I might have comforted a sister, only because I could touch Renata without that agony of love and guilt. But Cassandra saw and did not understand. . . .

He shouted Cassandra's name, but there was no reply, only the soft splashing sound of the cloud-waters. He flung off his outer garment and began to run. At the very edge of the sand he saw two small high-heeled sandals, dyed blue, not kicked this way and that but lined up with meticulous care, as if she had knelt here, delaying. Allart kicked off his boots and ran into the lake.

The strange cloud-waters enfolded him, dim, strange, and the thick, foggy sensation surrounded him. He breathed it in, feeling the curious exhilaration it gave at first. He could see quite clearly, as if through a thin morning mist. Brilliant creatures—fish or bird?—glided past him, their shimmering orange and green colors like nothing he had ever seen, except the lights behind his eyes when he had been given a dose of *kirian*, the telepathic drug which opened the brain . . . . Allart felt his feet falling lightly on the weedy bottom of the lake as he began to run along the lake bed.

Something had passed this way, yes. The fish-birds were gathering, drifting in the cloud-currents. Allart felt his running feet slowing. The heavy gas of the cloud was beginning to oppress him now. He sent out a despairing cry: *"Cassandra!"* The cloud of the lake would not carry sound; it was like being at the bottom of a very silent well, silence engulfing and surrounding him. Even at Nevarsin he had never known such silence. The fish-birds drifted past him, noiseless, curious, their luminescent colors stirring reflections in his brain. He was dizzy, light-headed. He forced himself to breathe, remembering that in the strange gaseous cloud of the lake, there was none of that element which triggered the breath reflex in the brain. He must breathe by effort and will; his brain would not keep his body breathing automatically.

"Cassandra!"

A faint, distant flicker, almost pettish. . . . *"Go away. . . ."* and it was gone again.

Breathe! Allart was beginning to tire; here the weeds were deeper, thicker, and he had to force his way through him.

Breathe! In and out, remember to breathe. . . . He felt a long slimy trail of weed lock around his ankle, had to stoop and disengage it. *Breathe!* He forced himself to struggle on, even as the brilliantly colored fish-birds began to cluster around him, their colors blurring before his eyes. His *laran* rushed upon him, as always when he was troubled or fatigued, and he saw himself sinking down and down into the gas and ooze, lying there quiet and content, suffocating in happy peace because he had forgotten how to breathe. . . . *Breathe!* Allart struggled to draw in another damp breath of the gas, reminding himself that it would support life indefinitely; the only danger was forgetting to breathe it in. Had Cassandra already reached this point? Was she lying, comfortably dying—a painless ecstatic death—here at the bottom of the lake?

She wanted to die, and I am guilty. . . . *Breathe! Don't think of anything now, just remember to breathe.* . . .

He saw himself carrying Cassandra from the lake, still, lifeless, her long hair lying black and dripping across his arm . . . saw himself bending over her, lying in the swaying grasses in the lake bed, taking her in his arms, sinking down beside her . . . no more *laran.* no trouble, no more fear, the family curse ended forever for them both.

The fish-birds moved, agitated, around him. Before his feet, he saw a flicker of pale blue, no color ever to be seen at the bottom of the lake. Was it the long sleeve of Cassandra's gown? *Breathe.* . . . Allart bent over her. She was lying there, on her side, her eyes open and still, a faint joyous smile on her lips, but she was too far gone to see Allart. His heart clutching, he bent over her, lifted her lightly into his arms. She was unconscious, faint, her body lolling against him in the drifting weeds. *Breathe! Breathe into her mouth; it is the gas in our expelled breath which triggers breathing.* . . . Allart tightened his arms about her and laid his lips against hers, forcing his breath into her lungs. As if in reflex, she breathed, a long deep breath, and was still again.

Allart lifted her and began to carry her back along the lake bed, in the dim cloudy light reddened now by the setting sun, and terror suddenly struck him. *If it grows dark, if the sun sets, I will never find my way to the shore in the darkness. We will die here together.* Again he bent over her, forcing his expelled breath into her mouth; again he felt her breathe. But the automatic breathing-mechanism was gone in

Cassandra, and he did not know how long she could survive without it, even with the oxygen of the reflex breaths he forced her to take, every two or three steps, by breathing into her mouth. And he had to hurry, before the light was gone. He struggled along in the growing darkness, holding her in his arms, but he had to stop every two or three breaths, to breathe life into her again. Her heart was beating. If she would only breathe. . . if he could only rouse her enough to remember to breathe. . . .

The last few steps were nightmare. Cassandra was a slight woman, but Allart was not a big man, either. As the cloud-fog grew shallower, he finally abandoned any attempt to carry her and dragged her along, stooping and holding her under the shoulders, every two or three steps stopping to force his breath into her lungs. At last his head broke out into air and he gasped air convulsively, hearing it sob in and out of his lungs. Then, with a final effort, he grabbed Cassandra up and held her with her head out of the cloudy gas, stumbling drunkenly toward the shore, collapsing beside her on the grass. He lay beside her, breathing into her mouth, pressing her ribs, until after several breaths she shuddered and gasped and let out a strange wailing cry, not unlike the cry of a newborn child as his lungs filled with the first breath. Then he heard her begin to breathe normally again. She was still unconscious, but after a little, in the gathering darkness, he felt her thoughts touch his. Then she whispered, still faintly, only a breath, "Allart? Is it you?"

"I am here, my beloved."

"I am so cold."

Allart caught up the garment he had flung away, wrapped it tightly around her. He held her, close-folded, murmuring hopeless endearments.

"Preciosa . . . bredhiva . . . my treasure, my cherished, why . . . how . . . I thought I had lost you forever. Why did you want to leave me?"

"Leave you? No," she whispered. "But it was so peaceful in the lake, and all I wanted was to stay there forever in the silence, and not to fear anymore, or cry anymore. I thought I could hear you calling me, but I was so weary. . . . I only lay down to rest a little, and I was so tired, I could not rise. I could not seem to breathe, and I was afraid . . . and then you came . . . but I knew you did not love me."

"Not love you? Not want you? Cassandra—" Allart found

that he could not speak. He pulled her close to him, kissed her on the cold lips.

Moments later he took her up again in his arms and carried her into the Tower, through the lower hall. The other members of the matrix circles, assembled there, stared at him with shock and amazement, but there was something in Allart's eyes that kept them from speaking or approaching the couple. He felt Renata watching them, felt the curiosity and horror from them all. Briefly, without thinking about it, he saw himself as he must appear in their eyes, soaked and bedraggled, bootless, Cassandra's drenched garments soaking the cloak he had wrapped around her, her long dark hair streaming dampness and entangled weeds. Before the grim concentration in his face they drew aside as he went through the hall and up the long stairs; not to the room where she had slept, alone, since they had come here, but along a wide hallway on the lower floors of the Tower, to his own room.

He shut and locked the door behind him and knelt beside her, with shaking hands removing the soaked clothing, wrapping her warmly in his own blankets. She was still as death, pale and unmoving against the pillow, her damp hair hanging lifelessly down.

"No," she whispered. "You are to leave the Tower and you did not even tell me. I felt it would be better to die than to stay here alone, with all the others mocking me, knowing I am wed and no wife, that you did not love me or want me."

"Not love you?" Allart whispered again. "I love you as my blessed forefather loved Robardin's daughter on the shores of Hali centuries ago. Not want you, Cassandra?" He held her to him, covering her with kisses, and he felt that his kisses were breathing life into her as the breath of his lungs had given her life at the depths of the lake. He was almost beyond thought, beyond remembering the pledge they had made to one another, but a final, despairing thought crossed his mind before he drew the blankets aside.

I can never let her go, not now. Merciful Avarra, have pity on us!

CHAPTER
THIRTEEN

Allart sat at Cassandra's side, looking into her sleeping face. Physically she was not much the worse for her experience in the lake. Even now he was not certain whether it had been a genuine attempt at suicide, or only an impulse born of deep unhappiness, compounded by illness and exhaustion. But in the days since then he had hardly left her side. He had come so close to losing her!

The others in the Tower had left them much to themselves. As they had known the state of affairs between himself and Cassandra, he sensed they knew the change that had come, but it did not seem to matter.

Now, he knew, as soon as Cassandra was able to leave her bed, some decision must be made. Should he leave the Tower and take her with him, send her to a place of safety (for if they were making weapons here, the Tower would be under attack), or should he go away himself and leave her here for the *laran* training he knew she must have?

Yet again and again, his own *laran* gave him visions of riding away to the north, Renata at his side. Cassandra's absence from these visions frightened him. What was to become of her?

He saw strange banners overhead, war, the clashing of swords, the explosion of strange weapons, fire, death. *Maybe that would be best for us both. . . .*

He found it impossible to keep to the disciplined calm he had learned at Nevarsin. Cassandra was ever-present in his mind, his thoughts and emotions as hypersensitive to her as his body.

He had broken the pledge they had made to one another.

After seven years in Nevarsin, I am still weak, still driven by the senses and not by the mind. I took her without thought, as if she had been one of old Dom Marius's pleasure girls.

He heard the soft knock at the door, but even before it registered on his ears, he knew—*it has come.* He stooped and kissed the sleeping woman, with an aching sense of farewell, then went to the door, opening it in a split second after the knock, so that Arielle blinked in surprise.

"Allart," she whispered. "Your brother, the lord Elhalyn, is below in the Stranger's Hall and asks to speak with you. I will remain with your wife."

Allart went down to the Stranger's Hall, the only room in the Tower into which outsiders were permitted to come. Damon-Rafael was there, his paxman noiseless and unmoving at his back.

"You lend us grace, brother. How may I serve you?"

"I suppose you have heard of the truce's end?"

"Then you have come to summon me to arms?"

Damon-Rafael said with a contemptuous laugh, "Do you suppose I should come myself for that? Anyhow, you would serve me better here; I have little faith, after all those years of monkish seclusion, in your skill at arms or any of the manly arts. No, brother, I have another mission for you, if you will accept it."

It took all of Allart's hard-won discipline to remain silent at the taunt, remarking quietly that he was at the service of his brother and his overlord.

"You have dwelled beyond the Kadarin; have you ever traveled to the Aldaran lands, near Caer Donn?"

"Never; only to Ardais and Nevarsin."

"Still, you must know that clan grows over-powerful. They hold Castle Aldaran at Caer Donn, as well as Sain Scarp and Scathfell; and they make alliances with all the others, with Ardais and Darriel and Storn. They are of Hastur kin, but Lord Aldaran came not to my accession as lord of Elhalyn, nor has he come to midsummer festival in Thendara for many years. Now, with this war breaking forth again, he is like a great hawk in his mountain aerie, ready to swoop down on the Lowlands whenever we are torn by strife and cannot resist him. If all those who owe allegiance to Aldaran were to strike us at once, Thendara itself could not hold. I can foresee a day when all the Domains from Dalereuth to the Kilghard Hills might lie under the lordship of Aldaran."

Allart said, "I knew not you had the foresight, brother."

Damon-Rafael moved his head with a quick, impatient gesture. "'Foresight? That takes not much reading! *When kinsmen quarrel, enemies step in to widen the gap.* I am trying to negotiate another truce—it profits us nothing to set the land aflame—but with our cousins of Castle Hastur under seige, it is not easy. Our carrier-birds are flying night and day with secret dispatches. Also, I have *leroni* working in relays to send messages, but of course we can entrust nothing secret to them; what is known to one is known to all with *laran.* Now we come to the service I ask of you, brother."

"I listen," Allart said.

"It is long since a Hastur sent a kinsman on diplomatic mission to Aldaran. Yet we need such a tie. The Storns hold lands to the west of Caer Donn, close to Serrais across the hills, and they might find it useful to join with the Ridenow. Then all of the alliances within the Hellers could be drawn into this war. Do you think you might persuade Lord Aldaran to hold himself and his liegemen neutral in this war? I do not think he would join it on our side, but he might be willing to stay out of it entirely. You are Nevarsin-trained; you know the language of the Hellers well. Will you go for me, Allart, and try to keep Mikhail, Lord Aldaran, from joining in this war?"

Allart studied his brother's face. This seemed all too simple a mission. Did Damon-Rafael plot some treachery, or did he simply want Allart out of the way, so that the Hasturs of Elhalyn would not have loyalties divided between the brothers?

"I am at your command, Damon-Rafael, but I know little diplomacy of that sort."

"You will carry letters from me," Damon-Rafael said, "and you will write secret dispatches and send them to me by carrier-birds. You will write open dispatches, which spies on both sides will certainly see; but you will also write secret dispatches, and send them under a matrix-lock which none but I can open or read. Surely you can arrange a lock spelled shut so that if other eyes fall upon them they will be destroyed?"

"That is simple enough," Allart said, and now he understood. There could not be many people to whom Damon-Rafael would willingly give the unique pattern of his own body and brain to set a matrix-lock; such a lock was a common tool for assassins, like the homing device Coryn had mentioned.

So I am one of the two or three persons living to whom Damon-Rafael will entrust that power over him; because I am sworn to defend him and his sons.

"I have arranged it so you will have a cover for your mission," Damon-Rafael said. "We have captured an envoy from Aldaran, fearing he had been sent to declare for the Ridenow. But the messenger, when my household *leronis* probed his sleep, told us he was on a personal mission for Lord Aldaran. I don't know all the details, but it has nothing to do with the war. His memory has been matrix-cleansed, and when he speaks with your Keeper, which he will do soon, I suppose, he will not know that he was ever captured or that he has been probed at all. I have arranged with our cousin Coryn that you will be, ostensibly, in charge of the truce flag which will escort Aldaran's messenger northward to the Kadarin. No one will notice if you simply continue and ride with them to Aldaran. Is that satisfactory to you?"

What choice have I? But I have known for days now that I must ride northward; only I did not know it was to Aldaran. And what has Renata to do with this? But aloud he said to Damon-Rafael only, "It seems you have thought of everything."

"At sunset, my paxman will ride here to give you documents qualifying you as my ambassador, and instructions for sending messages, and access to carrier-birds." He rose, saying, "If you wish, I will pay a courtesy visit to your lady. It should be thought this is a family visit without any secret purpose."

"I thank you," Allart said, "but Cassandra is not well, and has kept her bed. I shall convey her your respectful compliments."

"Do so, by all means," Damon-Rafael said, "although, I suppose, since you have chosen to dwell with her in the Tower, there is no reason to send congratulations. I do not imagine she is already carrying your child."

Not now, perhaps never. . . . Allart felt again the surge of desolation. He said aloud only, "No, we have not as yet any such good fortune." Damon-Rafael had no way of knowing the real state of affairs between himself and Cassandra, neither the pledge they had made one another nor the circum-

stances in which it had been broken. He was only twisting a
knife at random. There was no need to waste anger on his
brother's malice, but Allart was angry.

Still, he was bound to obey Damon-Rafael as overlord of
Elhalyn, and Damon-Rafael was so far right. If the North-
men from the Hellers joined this war, there would be ravage
and disaster.

I should be grateful, he thought, *that the gods have sent
me such an honorable way to serve in this war. If I can persuade the Aldarans to neutrality I will indeed do well for all
the vassals of Hastur.*

As Damon-Rafael rose to depart, Allart said, "Truly, I
thank you, brother, for entrusting me with this mission," and
his words were so heartfelt that Damon-Rafael stared at him
with surprise. When he embraced Allart at parting there was
a touch of warmth in the gesture. The two would never be
friends, but they were nearer to it at this moment than they
had been for years or Allart knew it sadly—were ever likely
to be again.

Later that night he was summoned again to the Stranger's
Hall, this time, he supposed, to meet with Damon-Rafael's
envoy, bearing safe-conducts and dispatches.

Coryn met him outside the door.

"Allart, do you speak the languages of the Hellers?"

Allart nodded, wondering if Damon-Rafael had taken
Coryn into his confidence and why.

"Mikhail of Aldaran has sent us a messenger," Coryn said,
"but his command of our language is uncertain. Will you
come and speak to him in his own tongue?"

"Gladly," Allart said, and thought, *Not Damon-Rafael's
envoy, then, but Aldaran's messenger. Damon-Rafael said he
had been mind-probed. I think that unjust, but, after all, this
is war.*

When he came with Coryn into the Stranger's Hall, he
recognized the messenger's face. His *laran* had shown it to
him again and again, though he had never known why: a
dark-haired, dark-browed, youthful face, looking at him with
tentative friendliness. Allart greeted him in the formal speech
of the Hellers.

"You lend us grace, *siarbainn,*" he said, giving it the special
inflection which made the archaic word for stranger mean,
friend-still-unknown. "How may I serve you?"

The strange youth rose and bowed.

"I am Donal Delleray, foster-son and paxman to Mikhail, Lord Aldaran. I bring his words, not my own, to the *vai leroni* of Hali Tower."

"I am Allart Hastur of Elhalyn; this, my kinsman and cousin, Coryn, *tenerézu* of Hali. Speak freely."

He thought, *Surely this is more than coincidence, that Aldaran should send a messenger just as my brother devises his plan. Or did he devise his plan to fit the messenger's coming? The gods strengthen me—I see plots and counterplots everywhere!*

Donal said, "First, *vai domyn*, I am to bear you Lord Aldaran's apologies for sending me in his place. He would not hesitate to come as suppliant and petitioner, but he is old, and hardly fitted to bear the long road from Aldaran. Also, I can ride more quickly than he. Indeed, I had thought to be here within eight days' ride, but I seem to have lost a day on the road."

Damon-Rafael and his damned mind-probing, Allart thought, but he said nothing, waiting for Donal to make his request.

Coryn said, "It is our pleasure to do courtesy to Lord Aldaran; what does he ask?"

"Lord Aldaran bids me say that his daughter, his only living child and heir, is cursed with *laran* such as he has never known before. The aged *leronis* who has cared for her since her birth no longer knows what to do with her. The child is of an age when my father fears lest threshold sickness destroy her. He comes, then, as suppliant, to ask of the *vai leroni* if they know of one who will come to care for her during these crucial seasons."

This was not unknown, that a Tower-trained *leronis* might go to guide and care for some young heir during the troubled years of adolescence, when threshold sickness took such toll of the sons and daughters of their caste. A *laranzu* from Arilinn Tower had first counseled Allart to seek sanctuary at Nevarsin. And, Allart thought, if Aldaran was beholden to Hali for such a service, Aldaran would be all the more ready to refrain from angering Elhalyn by coming into this war.

Allart said, "The Hasturs of Elhalyn, and those who serve them in Hali Tower, will be pleased to serve Lord Aldaran in this matter." He asked Coryn in their own language, "Who shall we send?"

"I thought you would go," Coryn said. "You are none too eager to remain and become entangled in this war."

"I shall go, indeed, at my brother's bidding and on his mission," Allart said, "but it is not seemly that a *laranzu* shall have the training of a maiden. Surely she needs a woman to guide her."

"Yet there is none to spare," said Coryn. "Now that I am to lose Renata, I shall need Mira for monitoring. And, of course, Cassandra is not even well enough trained for monitoring, far less for work of this sort, teaching a young girl to control her gift."

Allart said, "Could not Renata fulfill this mission? It seems to me that this would remove her from the combat zone, as much as returning to Neskaya."

"Yes, Renata is the obvious choice," Coryn said, "but she is not to go to Neskaya. Did you not hear? No," he answered his own question. "While Cassandra has been ill, you have stayed with her and you did not hear the word from the relays. Dom Erlend Leynier has sent word that she is not to go to Neskaya Towers but to go home to her wedding. It has twice been delayed already. I do not think she would wish to delay it again to go to some godforgotten corner of the Hellers, to teach some barefoot mountain girl how to handle her *laran!*"

Allart looked apprehensively at young Donal. Had he heard the offensive remark? But Donal, like a proper messenger, was staring straight before him, appearing neither to hear or see anything but what concerned him directly. If he *did* know enough of the Lowland tongue to understand Coryn's words, or had enough *laran* to read their thoughts, neither Coryn nor Allart would ever know.

"I do not think Renata is in such a great hurry to be married," Allart demurred.

Coryn chuckled. "I think you mean *you* are in no hurry for Renata to be married, cousin." Then, at the glare of rage in Allart's eyes, he said hastily, "I was but jesting, cousin. Tell young Delleray that we will ask the *damisela* Renata Leynier if she will undertake the journey northward."

Allart repeated the formal phrases to Donal, who bowed and replied, "Say to the *vai domna* that Mikhail, Lord Aldaran, would not have her make this tremendous service unremunerated. In gratitude, she will be dowered as if she were his younger daughter, when the time comes for her to marry."

"That is generous," Allart said, as indeed it was. The use of *laran* could not be bought or sold like ordinary service; tradition stated it should be used only in service to caste or clan and was not for hire. This was the usual compromise. The Leyniers were wealthy, but they had no such wealth as the Aldarans, and this would give Renata the dower of a princess.

After a few more courtesies, they had young Donal conducted to a chamber to await the final arrangements. Coryn said regretfully, as he and Allart went through the force-field into the main part of the Tower, "Perhaps I should have arranged this journey for Arielle. She is a Di Asturien, but she is *nedestro* and has no dower to speak of. Even if my brother would give me leave to marry, which is not likely, he would not allow me to wed with a poor girl." He laughed bitterly. "But it matters not . . . even if she were dowered with all the jewels of Carthon, a Hastur of Carcosa could not wed with a *nedestro* of Di Asturien; and if Arielle had such a dowry, her father would surely offer her to another, and I should lose her."

"You are long unmarried," Allart said, and Coryn shrugged.

"My brother is not eager for me to have an heir. I have *laran* enough, and I have fathered half a dozen sons for their accursed breeding program, on this girl and that, but I have not bothered to see the babes, though they say they all have *laran*. It is better not to get too fond of them, since I understand that every attempt to breed the Hastur gift to Aillard or Ardais has meant they die in threshold sickness, poor little brats. It is hard on their mothers, but I have no intention of letting myself be heart-wrung, too."

"How can you take it so casually?"

For a moment the mask of indifference broke and Coryn looked out at him in real distress.

"What else can I do, Allart? No son of Hastur has a life he can call his own, while the *leroni* of this damned stud-service they call our caste make all our marriages and even arrange the fathering of our bastards. But we are not all like you, able to tolerate living the life of a monk!" Then he was stony-faced, impassive again. "Well, it is not an unpleasant duty to my clan, after all. While I dwell here as Keeper, there are plenty of times when I am no use to any woman, which is almost as good as being a monk. . . . Arielle and I are willing to take what we can have when occasion permits. I am not like you, a romantic seeking a great love," he added defensively, and turned away. "Will you ask Renata if she will go, or shall I?"

"You ask her," Allart said. He knew already what she would say, knew they would ride northward together. He had seen it again and again; it could not be avoided.

Was it unavoidable, then, that he would love Renata, forgetting his love and his honor and his pledge to Cassandra?

I should never have left Nevarsin, he thought. *Would that I had flung myself from the highest crag before I let them force me away!*

CHAPTER
FOURTEEN

Renata hesitated at the door of the room, then, knowing that Cassandra was aware of her presence, went in without knocking. Cassandra was out of bed, although she still looked pale and exhausted. She had some needlework in her hands, and was setting small precise stitches in the petal of an embroidered flower, but as Renata's eyes fell on it Cassandra colored and put it aside.

"I am ashamed to waste time on so foolish and womanly a pastime."

Renata said, "Why? I, too, was taught never to let my hands sit idle, lest my mind find nothing to occupy itself but too much brooding on my own problems and miseries. Although my stitches were never so fine as yours. Are you feeling better now?"

Cassandra sighed. "Yes, I am well again. I suppose I can take my place among you. I suppose—" Renata, the empath, knew that Cassandra's throat closed, unable to speak the words. *I suppose they all know what I tried to do; they all despise me. . . .*

"There is not one of us feels anything for you save sympathy, sorrow that you could have been so unhappy among us, and none of us spoke or tried to ease your suffering," Renata said gently.

"Yet I hear whispers around me; I cannot read what is happening. What are you concealing from me, Renata? What are you all hiding?"

"You know that the war has broken out afresh," Renata began.

150

"Allart is to go to war!" It was a cry of anguish. "And he did not tell me."

"If he has hesitated to say this, *chiya*, surely it is only that he fears you might be overcome again by despair, and act rashly."

Cassandra lowered her eyes; gently as the words were spoken, they were a reproof, and well-deserved. "No, that will not happen again. Not now."

"Allart is not to go to war," Renata said. "Instead, he is being sent outside the combat area. A messenger has come from Caer Donn, and Allart is being sent to escort him, under a truce-flag. Lord Elhalyn has sent him on some mission to the mountain people there."

"Am I to go with him?" Cassandra caught her breath, a flush of such pure joy spreading over her face that Renata was reluctant to speak and banish it.

At last she said gently, "No, cousin. That is not your destiny now. You must stay here. You have great need of the training we can give, to master your *laran*, so that you will never again be overcome like that. And since I am to leave the Tower, you will be needed as a monitor here. Mira will begin at once to teach you."

"I? A monitor? Truly?"

"Yes. You have worked long enough in the circle so that your *laran* and your talents are known to us. Coryn has said that you will make a monitor of great skill. And you will be needed soon. With Allart's and my departure, there will hardly be enough trained workers here to form two circles, and not enough trained to monitor."

"So." Cassandra was silent a moment. "In any case, I have an easier lot than other women of my clan, who have nothing to do but watch their husbands ride forth to battle and perhaps death. I have useful work to do here, and Allart need have no fear that he leaves me with child." To answer Renata's questioning look, she said, "I am ashamed, Renata. Probably you do not know . . . Allart and I made one another a pledge, that our marriage would remain unconsummated. I—I tempted him to break that vow."

"Cassandra, Allart is not a child or an untried boy. He is a grown man, and fully capable of making such a decision for himself." Renata smothered an impulse to laugh. "I doubt he would be complimented by the thought that you ravished him against his will."

Cassandra colored. "Still, if I had been stronger, if I had been able to master my unhappiness——"

"Cassandra, it's done and past mending; all the smiths in Zandru's forges can't mend a broken egg. You are not the keeper of Allart's conscience. Now you can only look ahead. Perhaps it is just as well that Allart must leave you for a time. It will give you both the opportunity to decide what you wish to do in the future."

Cassandra shook her head. "How can I alone make a decision that concerns us both? It is for Allart to say what shall come afterward. He is my husband and my lord!"

Suddenly Renata was exasperated. "It is that attitude which has led women to where they are now in the Domains! In the name of the Blessed Cassilda, child, are you still thinking of yourself only in terms of a breeder of sons and a toy of lust? Wake up, girl! Do you think it is only for that Allart desires you?"

Cassandra blinked, startled. "What else am I? What else can any woman be?"

"You are not a woman!" Renata said angrily. "You are only a child! Every word you say makes it evident! Listen to me, Cassandra. First, you are a human being, a child of the gods, a daughter of your clan, bearing *laran*. Do you think you have it only that you may pass it on to your sons? You are a matrix worker; soon you will be a monitor. Do you honestly think you are no good to Allart for anything but to share his bed and to give him children? Gods above, girl, *that* he could have from a concubine, or a *riyachiya*. . . ."

Cassandra's cheeks flushed an angry red. "It is not seemly to talk about such things!"

"But only to *do* them?" Renata retorted, at white heat. "The gods created us thinking creatures; do you suppose they meant woman to be brood animals alone? If so, why do we have brains and *laran*, and tongues to speak our thoughts, instead of being given only fair faces and sex organs and bellies to bear our children and breasts to nourish them? Do you believe the gods did not know what they were doing?"

"I do not believe there are any gods at all," Cassandra retorted, and the bitterness in her voice was so great that Renata's anger vanished. She, too, had known that kind of bitterness; she was not yet free of it.

She put her arms around the other girl, and said tenderly, "Cousin, you and I have no reason to quarrel. You are young and untaught; as you learn, here, to use your laran, perhaps you will come to think differently about what you are, within yourself—not only as Allart's wife. Someday you may be the keeper of your own will and conscience, and not rely on Allart to make the decisions for both of you, nor lay on him the burden of your sorrows as well as his own."

"I never thought of that," said Cassandra, hiding her face against Renata's shoulder. "If I had been stronger, I would not have laid this burden upon him. I have put upon him the guilt for my own unhappiness which drove me into the lake. Yet he was only doing what he felt he must do. Will they teach me here to be strong, Renata? As strong as you?"

"Stronger, I hope, *chiya*," Renata said, kissing the other girl on the forehead, yet her own thoughts were grim. *I am full of good advice for her, yet I cannot handle my own life. For the third time, now, I run away from marriage, into this unknown mission at Aldaran, for a girl I do not know and for whom I care nothing. I should stay here and defy my father, not run away to Aldaran to teach some unknown girl how to use the* laran *that her foolish forefathers bred into her mind and body! What is this girl to me, that I should neglect my own life to help her gain command of hers?*

Yet she knew it had all been determined by what she was—a *leronis*, born with the talent, and fortunate enough to have been given Tower training to master it. Thus in honor bound to do whatever she could to help others less fortunate master their own unasked for, undesired *laran*.

Cassandra was calm now. She said, "Allart will not go without bidding me farewell . . . ?"

"No, no, of course not, my child. Coryn has already given him leave to withdraw from the circle, so this last night you spend under one roof, you may spend together to say your farewells." She did not tell Cassandra that she herself was to accompany Allart on his ride northward; that would be for Allart to tell her, in his own time and in his own way. She only said, "In any case, as things are between you now, one of you should go. You know that when serious work begins in the circle, you must remain apart and chaste."

"I do not understand that," Cassandra said. "Coryn and Arielle—"

"—have worked together for more than a year in the circle; they know the limits of what is allowed and what is dangerous," Renata said. "A day will come when you will

know it, too, but as you are now, it would be difficult to recall or keep to those limits. This is your time to learn, with
no distractions, and Allart would be"—she smiled at the
other girl, mischievously——"a distraction. Oh, these men, that
we can neither live at peace with them—nor without them!"

Cassandra's laughter was momentary. Then her face convulsed again with weeping. "I know that all you say is true,
and yet I cannot bear to have Allart leave me. Have you
never been in love, Renata?"

"No, not as you mean it, *chiya*." Renata held Cassandra
close to her, torn, with the empath *laran*, anguished with the
other woman's pain, as Cassandra sobbed helplessly against
her breast.

"What can I do, Renata? What can I do?"

Renata shook her head, staring bleakly into space. *Will I
ever know what it is to love that way? Do I want to know, or
is such love as this only a trap into which women walk of
their own free will, so that they have no more strength to rule
their own lives? Is this how the women of the Comyn have
become no more than breeders of sons and toys of lust?* But
Cassandra's pain was very real to her. At last she said, hesitating, shy before the depths of the other woman's emotion,
"You could make it impossible for him to leave you, if you
grieve like this, cousin. He would be too fearful for you, too
guilty at the thought of leaving you to such despair."

Cassandra struggled to control her sobs. Finally she said,
"You are right. I must not add to Allart's guilt and grief with
my own. I am not the first, nor the last wife of a Hastur who
must see him ride away from her, with no knowledge of
when, or ever, he will return; but his honor and the success of
his mission are in my hands, then. I must not hold that
lightly. Somehow"—she set her small chin stubbornly—"I
will find the strength to send him away from me; if not
gladly, at least I will try to make sure that he goes without
fear for me to add to his own."

It was a small party that rode north from Hali the next
day. Donal, as a suppliant, had ridden alone; Allart himself
had only the banner-bearer to which, as heir to Elhalyn, he
was entitled, and the messenger with a truce-flag; not so
much as a single body-servant. Renata, too, had dispensed
with lady companions, saying that in time of war such nice-
ties need not be observed; she had brought only her nurse

Lucetta, who had served her since childhood, and would have dispensed even with this attendance, save that an unmarried woman of the Domains could not travel without any female attendance.

Allart rode silently, apart from the rest, tormented by the memory of Cassandra at the moment of their parting, her lovely eyes filled with the tears she had struggled so valiantly not to shed before him. At least he had not left her pregnant; so far the gods had been merciful.

If there were any gods, and if they cared what befell mankind. . . .

Ahead he could hear Renata chatting lightheartedly with Donal. They seemed so young, both of them. Allart knew he was only three or four years older than Donal, but it seemed he had never been as young as that. *Seeing what will be, what may be, what may never be, it seems I live a lifetime in every day that passes.* He envied the boy.

They were riding through a land bearing the scars of war, blackened fields with traces of fire, roofless houses, abandoned farms. So few travelers passed them on the road that after the first day Renata did not even bother to keep her cloak modestly folded about her face.

Once an air-car flew low overhead; it circled, dipped low to scrutinize them, then turned about and flew back southward. The guardsman with the truce-flag dropped back to ride at Allart's side.

"Truce-flag or not, *vai dom,* I wish you had agreed to an escort. Those bastards of Ridenow may choose not to honor a truce-flag; and seeing your banners, it might occur to them that it would be worth much to capture the heir to Elhalyn and hold him to ransom from his Hastur kinfolk. It would not be the first time such a thing had happened."

"If they will not honor a flag of truce," Allart said reasonably, "it will avail us nothing to defeat them in this war, either, for they would not honor our victory or the terms of surrender. I think we must trust our enemies to abide by the rules of war."

"I have had small faith in the rules of war, Dom Allart, since first I saw a village burned to ashes by *clingfire*—not soldiers alone, but old men and women and little children. I would prefer to trust in the rules of war with a considerable escort at my back!"

Allart said, "I have not foreseen it with my *laran*, that we will be under attack."

The Guardsman only said dryly, "Then you are fortunate, *vai dom*. I have not the consolation of foresight or other sorcery," and fell into stubborn silence.

On the third day of the journey, they crossed a pass which led downward to the Kadarin River, which separated the Lowland Domains from the territories held by the mountain folk—Aldaran, Ardais, and the lesser lords of the Hellers. Before they rode downward, Renata turned back to look over the lands from which they had come, where most of the Domains lay spread out before them. Renata looked on the distant hills and Towers, then cried out in dismay—forest fire was raging across the Kilghard Hills away south.

"Look where it rages!" she cried. "Surely it will trespass on Alton lands." Allart and Donal, both telepaths, picked up her thought! *Will my home, too, lie in flames down there in a war which is none of ours?* Aloud she only said, her voice shaking, "Now I wish I had your foresight, Allart."

The panorama of the Domains below them blurred before Allart's eyes and he closed them in a vain attempt to shut out the diverging futures of his *laran*. If the powerful clan of the Altons was drawn into this war by an attack on their home country, no homestead or estate anywhere in the Domains would be safe. It would not matter to the Altons whether their homes were burned by fires deliberately set, or by those raging out of control after being set to attack elsewhere.

"How dare they use forest fire as a weapon," Renata demanded furiously, "knowing it cannot be controlled, but is at the mercy of winds over which they have no power."

"No," said Allart, trying to comfort her. "Some of the *leroni*—you know that—can use their powers to raise clouds and rain to dampen the fires, or even snow to smother them."

Donal drew his mount close to Renata's. "Where lies your home, Lady?"

She pointed a slender hand. "There, between the lakes of Miridon and Mariposa. My home is beyond the hills, but you can see the lakes."

Donal's dark face was intent, as he said, "Have no fear, *damisela*. See—it will move upward along that ridge"—he pointed—"and there the winds will drive it back upon itself. It will burn out before tomorrow's sunset."

"I pray you are right," she said, "but surely you are only guessing?"

"No, my lady. Surely you can see it, if you will only calm yourself. Certainly you, who are Tower-trained, can have no difficulty in reading how the air currents *there* will move this way, and the wind will rise *there*. You are a *leronis*; you must see that."

Allart and Renata regarded Donal in wonder and amazement. Finally Renata said, "Once when I was studying the breeding program, I read something of such a *laran* as that, but it was abandoned because it could not be controlled. But that was not in the Hastur kin, nor in the Delleray. Are you perhaps akin to the folk of Storn or Rockraven?"

"Aliciane of Rockraven—she who was fourth daughter to old Lord Vardo—was my mother."

"Is it so?" Renata looked at him with open curisoity. "I believed that *laran* extinct, since it was one of those which came on a child before birth and usually killed the mother who bore such a child. Did your mother survive your birth?"

"She did," Donal said, "but she died in bearing my sister Dorilys, who is to be in your care."

Renata shook her head. "So the accursed breeding program among the Hastur kin has left its mark in the Hellers, too. Had your father any *laran*?"

"I do not know. I cannot recall that I ever looked on his face," Donal said, "but my mother was no telepath, and Dorilys—my sister—cannot read thoughts at all. Such telepathy as I have must be the gift of my father."

"Did your *laran* come on you in infancy, or suddenly, in adolescence?"

"The ability to sense air currents, storms, has been with me as long as I can remember," Donal said. "I did not think it *laran* then, merely a sense everyone had to greater degree or less, like an ear for music. When I grew older I could control the lightning a little." He told how in childhood he had diverted a bolt of lightning which might, otherwise, have struck the tree under which he and his mother had sheltered. "But I can do it only rarely and in great need, and it makes me ill; so I try only to read these forces, not to control them."

"That is wisest," Renata confirmed. "Everything we know of the more unusual *laran* has taught us how dangerous it is to play with these forces; rain at one place is drought at another. It was a wise man who said, '*It is ill done to chain a dragon for roasting your meat.'* Yet I see you bear a star-stone."

"A little, and only for toys. I can levitate and control a glider, such things as that. Such small things as our household *leronis* could teach me."

"Were you a telepath from infancy, too?"

"No; that came on me when I was past fifteen, when I had ceased to expect it."

"Did you suffer much from threshold sickness?" Allart asked.

"Not much; dizziness, disorientation for half a season or so. Mostly I was distressed because my foster-father forbade me my glider for that time!" He laughed, but they could both read his thoughts: *I never knew how deeply my foster-father loved me, till I felt how deeply he feared then to lose me when I fell ill with threshold sickness.*

"No convulsions?"

"None."

Renata nodded. "Some strains have it more severely than others. You seem to have the relatively minor one, and Lord Aldaran's kin the lethal form. Is there Hastur blood in your family?"

"*Damisela*, I have not the faintest notion," Donal said stiffly, and the others heard his resentment as if he had spoken the words aloud: *Am I a racing chervine or a stud animal to be judged on my pedigree?*

Renata laughed aloud. "Forgive me, Donal. Perhaps I have dwelt too long in a Tower and had not considered how offensive another might consider such a question. I have spent so many years studying these things! Although indeed, my friend, if I am to care for your sister I must indeed study her lineage and pedigree as seriously as if she were a racing animal or a fine hawk, to find out how this *laran* came into her line, and what lethals and recessives she may be carrying. Even if they are quiet now, they could cause trouble when she comes to womanhood. But forgive me, I meant no offense."

"It is I should beg your pardon, *damisela*, for being churlish when you are studying ways to help my sister."

"Let us forgive one another then, Donal, and be friends."

Allart, watching them, felt sudden bitter envy of these young people who could laugh and flirt and enjoy life even when burdened with impending disasters. Then he was suddenly ashamed of himself. Renata had no light burden; she could have placed all the responsibility on father or husband, yet she had worked since her childhood to know what she should do, how best to take responsibility, even if it meant destroying the life of an unborn child and bearing the reproach toward a barren woman in the Domains. Donal had had no careless youth either, living with the knowledge of his own strange *laran* which could destroy him and his sister.

He wondered if every human being, indeed, walked through life on a precipice as narrow as his own. Allart realized that he had been acting as if he alone bore an intolerable curse, and all others were lighthearted, carefree. He watched Renata and Donal laughing and jesting, and then he thought, and it was a new and strange thought to him, *Perhaps Nevarsin gave me too exaggerated a seriousness about life. If they can live with the burdens they bear, and still be light of heart and enjoy this journey, perhaps they are wiser than I.*

When he rode forward to join them he was smiling.

They came to Aldaran late in the afternoon of a gray and rainy day, little spits of sleet hiding in the wind and rain. Renata had wrapped her cloak over her face and protected her cheeks with a scarf, and the banner-bearer had put away his flag to protect it and rode muffled in his thick cape, looking dour. Allart found that the increasing altitude made his heart pound, so that he felt light-headed. But with every day's ride Donal had seemed to cast off care and to look merry and youthful, as if the altitude and the worsening weather were only a sign of homecoming; even in the rain he rode bareheaded, the hood of his riding-cloak cast back, disregarding the sleet on his face, which was reddened with the wind and cold.

At the foot of the long slope that led upward to the castle, he paused and waved in a signal, laughing. Renata's nurse grumbled, "Are we to ride ordinary animals up that goattrack, or do they think we are hawks that can fly?" Even Renata looked a little daunted by the last steep path.

"*This* is the Aldaran keep? It seems as inaccessible as Nevarsin itself!"

Donal laughed. "No, but in the old days, when my fosterfather's forebears had to keep it by force of arms, this made it impregnable—my lady," he added, with sudden self-consciousness. During the days of the journey they had become

"Allart" and "Renata" and "Donal" to one another; Donal's sudden return to formal courtesy made them realize that whatever happened, this period of forgetfulness was ended and the burden of their separate destinies lay upon them again.

"I trust the soldiers on those walls know we are not come to attack," grumbled the guardsman who had borne the truce-flag.

Donal laughed and said, "No, we should be small indeed for a war party, I think. Look—there is my foster-father on the battlement, with my sister. Evidently he knew of our arrival."

Allart saw the blank look slide down over Donal's face, the look of the telepath in contact with those out of earshot.

A moment later Donal smiled gaily and said, "The horse path is not so steep, after all. On the far side of the castle there are steps carved from the rock, two hundred and eighty-nine of them. Would you prefer to climb up that way, perhaps? Or you, *mestra*?" he added to the nurse, and she made a sound of dismay. "Come, my foster-father awaits us."

During the long ride, Allart had made use of the techniques he had learned at Nevarsin, to keep the crowding futures at a distance. Since he could do nothing whatever about them, he knew that allowing himself to dwell upon them, with morbid fears, was a form of self-indulgence he could no longer give mental lease. He must deal with whatever came, and look ahead only when he had some reasonable chance of deciding which of the possible futures could be rationally affected by some choice actually within his own power to control. But as they reached the top of the steep slope, coming in out of the sleet and winds of the height into a sheltered courtyard, with servants crowding about to take the horses, Allart knew he had lived this scene before in memory or foresight. Through the momentary disorientation he heard a shrill childish voice crying out, and it seemed to him that he saw a flare of lightnings, so that he physically shrank from the voice, in the moment before he actually *heard* it clearly. It was simple after all, no danger, no flare of strange lightning, nothing but a joyous child's voice calling out Donal's name—and a little girl, her long plaits flying, ran from the shelter of an archway and wrapped him in her arms.

"I knew it must be you, and the strangers. Is this the woman who is to be my guardian and teacher? What is her

name? Do you like her? What is it like in the Lowlands? Do
flowers truly bloom there all year as I have heard? Did you
see any nonhumans as you traveled? Did you bring me back
any gifts? Who are these people? What kind of animals are
they riding?"

"Gently, gently, Dorilys," reproved a deep voice. "Our
guests will think us mountain barbarians indeed, if you chat-
ter like an ill-taught *gallimak*! Let your brother go, and greet
our guests like a lady!"

Donal let his sister cling tightly to his hand as he turned to
his foster-father, but he let her go as Mikhail of Aldaran took
him into a close embrace.

"Dearest lad, I have missed you greatly. Now will you not
present our honored guests?"

"Renata Leynier, *leronis* of Hali Tower," Donal said.
Renata made a deep curtsy before Lord Aldaran.

"Lady, you lend us grace; we are deeply honored. Allow
me to present my daughter and heir, Dorilys of Rockraven."

Dorilys lowered her eyes shyly as she curtsied.

"S'dia shaya, domna," she said bashfully.

Then Lord Aldaran presented Margali to Renata. "This is
the *leronis* who has cared for her since she was born."

Renata looked sharply at the old woman. Despite her pale,
fragile features, her graying hair and the lines of age in her
face, she still bore the indefinable stamp of power. Renata
thought, *If she has been in the care of a* leronis *since she was
born, and Aldaran felt still that she needed stronger care and
control—what, in the name of all the gods, does he fear for
this charming little girl?*

Donal was presenting Allart to his foster-father. Allart,
bowing to the old man, raised his eyes to look into the
hawklike face of Dom Mikhail, and knew abruptly that he
had seen this face before, in dreams and foresight, knew it
with mingled affection and fear. Somehow this mountain lord
held the key to his destiny, but he could see only a vaulted
room, white stone like a chapel, and flickering flames, and
despair. Allart fought to dismiss the unwelcome, confusing
images until some rational choice could be made among
them.

My laran *is useless,* he thought, *save to frighten me!*

As they were being led through the castle to their rooms,
Allart found himself nervously watching for the vaulted room

of his vision, the place of flames and tragedy. But he did not see it, and he wondered if it was anywhere at Castle Aldaran at all. Indeed, it might be anywhere—or, he thought bitterly, nowhere.

CHAPTER
FIFTEEN

Renata woke to sense the presence of an outsider; then she saw Dorilys's pretty, childish face peeping around a curtain.

"I am sorry," Dorilys said. "Did I wake you, *domna*?"

"I think so." Renata blinked, grasping vaguely at fragments of a disappearing dream, fire, the wings of a glider, Donal's face. "No, it does not matter, child; Lucetta would have waked me soon to go down to dinner."

Dorilys came around the curtain and sat on the edge of the bed. "Was the journey very tiring, *domna*? I hope you will have recovered soon from your fatigue."

Renata had to smile at the mixture of childishness and adult courtesy. "You speak *casta* very well, child; is it spoken so much here?"

"No," Dorilys said, "but Margali was schooled in the Domains, at Thendara, and she said I should learn to speak it well so that if I went to Thendara there would be none who could call me mountain barbarian."

"Then Margali did well, for your accent is very good."

"Were you trained in a Tower, too, *vai leronis*?"

"Yes, but there is no need to be so formal as all that," Renata said, spontaneously warming to the girl. "Call me cousin or kinswoman, what you will."

"You look very young to be a *leronis,* cousin," Dorilys said, choosing the more intimate of the two words.

Renata said, "I started when I was about your age." Then she hesitated, for Dorilys seemed childish for the fourteen or fifteen she looked. If she was to educate Dorilys, as a nobleman's daughter, she must quickly put a stop to so big a girl running about the courtyards with her hair flying, racing and shouting like a little girl. She wondered if, indeed, the girl was somewhat lacking in wit. "How old are you . . . fifteen?"

Dorilys giggled and shook her head. "Everyone says I look so, and Margali wearies me night and day with telling me I am too old to do this and too big to do that, but I am only eleven years old. I shall be twelve at summer harvest."

Abruptly Renata revised her perceptions of the girl. She was not, then, a childish and ill-educated young woman, as she looked, but a highly precocious and intelligent preadolescent girl. It was perhaps her misfortune that she looked older than her years, for everyone would expect Dorilys to have a degree of experience and judgment she could hardly possess at that age.

Dorilys asked, "Did you like being a *leronis*? What is a monitor?"

"You will find that out when I monitor you, as I must do before I begin to teach you about *laran*," Renata said.

"What did you do in the Tower?"

"Many things," Renata said. "Bringing metals to the surface of the ground for the smiths to work them, charging batteries for lights and air-cars, working in the relays to speak without voice to those in the other Towers, so that what was happening in one Domain could be known to all, much faster than a messenger could ride. . . ."

Dorilys listened, finally letting out a long, fascinated sigh. "And will you teach me to do those things?"

"Not all of them, perhaps, but you shall know such things as you have need to know, as the lady of a great Domain. And beyond that, such things as all women should know if they are to have control of their own lives and bodies."

"Will you teach me to read thoughts? Donal and Father and Margali can read thoughts and I cannot, and they can talk apart and I cannot hear, and it makes me angry because I know they talk about me."

"I cannot teach you that, but if you have the talent I can teach you to use it. You are too young to know whether you have it or not."

"Will I have a matrix?"

"When you can learn to use it," Renata said. She thought it strange that Margali had not already tested the child, taught her to key a matrix. Well, Margali was well on in years; perhaps she feared what her charge, headstrong and lacking in mature judgment, would do with the enormous power of a matrix. "Do you know what your *laran* is, Dorilys?"

The child lowered her eyes. "A little. You know what happened at my handfasting. . . ."

"Only that your promised husband died very suddenly."

Suddenly Dorilys began to cry. "He died—and everyone said I had killed him, but I didn't, cousin. I didn't want to kill him—I only wanted to make him take his hands off me."

Looking at the sobbing child, Renata's first, spontaneous impulse was to put her arms around Dorilys and comfort her. *Of course she hadn't meant to kill him! How cruel, to let a child so young carry blood-guilt!* But in the instant before she moved, an intuitive flash of second thought kept her motionless.

However young she was, Dorilys had *laran* which could kill. This *laran*, in the hands of a child too young to exercise rational judgment about it . . . the very thought made Renata shudder. If Dorilys was old enough to possess this terrifying *laran*, she was old enough—she would *have* to be old enough—to learn control, and its proper use.

Controlling *laran* was not easy. No one knew better than Renata, a Tower-trained monitor, how difficult it could be, the hard work and self-discipline which went even into the earliest stages of that control. How could a spoiled, pampered little girl, whose every word had been law to her companions and adoring family, find the discipline and the inner motivation to tread that difficult path? Perhaps the death she had wrought, and her guilt and fear about it, might be fortunate in the long run. Renata did not like to use fear in her teaching, but at the moment she did not know enough about Dorilys to throw away any slight advantage she might have in teaching the girl.

So she did not touch Dorilys, but let her cry, looking at her with a detached tenderness of which her calm face and manner gave not the slightest hint. At last she said, voicing the first thing she herself had been taught in the early discipline of Hali Tower, "*Laran* is a terrible gift and a terrible responsibility, and it is not easy to learn to control it. It is your own choice whether you will learn to control it, or whether it will control *you*. If you are willing to work hard, a time will come when you will be in command, when you will use your *laran* and not let it use you. That is why I have come here to teach you, so that such a thing cannot happen again."

"You are more than welcome here at Aldaran," Mikhail, Lord Aldaran said, leaning forward from his high seat and catching Allart's eyes. "It is long since I had the pleasure of entertaining one of my Lowland kin. I trust we will make you welcome. But I do not flatter myself that the heir to El- halyn did the service which any paxman or banner-bearer could do, just for the sake of showing me honor. Not when the Elhalyn Domain is at war. You want something of me— or the Elhalyn Domain wants something, which may not be the same thing at all. Will you not tell me your true mission, kinsman?"

Allart pondered a dozen answers, watching the play of fire- light on the old man's face, knowing it was the curious fore- sight of his *laran* which caused that face to wear a hundred aspects—benevolence, wrath, offended pride, anguish. Had his mission alone the power to raise all those reactions in Lord Aldaran, or was it something yet to pass between them?

At last, weighing each word, he said, "My lord, what you say is true, although it was a privilege to travel north with your foster-son, and I was not sorry to be at some distance from this war."

Aldaran raised an eyebrow and said, "I would have thought in time of war you would have been unwilling to leave the Domain. Are you not your brother's heir?"

"His regent and warden, sir, but I am sworn to support the claim of his *nedestro* sons."

"It seems to me you could have done better for yourself than that," Dom Mikhail said. "Should your brother die in battle, you seem better fitted to command a Domain than any flock of little boys, legitimate or bastard, and no doubt the folk of your Domain would rather have it so. There's a true saying: when the cat's a kitten, rats make play in the kitchen! So it goes with a Domain; in times like this, a strong hand is needful. In wartime a younger son, or one whose parentage is uncertain, can carve out for himself a position of power as he could never do at any other time."

Allart thought, *But I have no ambition to rule my Domain.* However, he knew that Lord Aldaran would never believe this. To men of his sort, ambition was the only legitimate emotion for a man born into a ruling house. *And it is this which keeps us torn with fratricidal wars.* . . . But he said nothing, if he did, Aldaran would immediately jump to the conclusion that he was an effeminate, or, worse, a coward. "My brother and overlord felt I could better serve my Domain on this mission, sir."

"Indeed? It must be more important than I had believed possible," Aldaran said, and he looked grim. "Well, tell me about it, kinsman, if it is a mission of such great moment to Aldaran that your brother must entrust it to his nearest rival!" He looked angry and guarded, and Allart knew he had not made a good impression. However, as Allart broached his mission, Aldaran slowly relaxed, leaning back in his chair, and when the young man had done he nodded slowly, letting out his breath with a long sigh.

"It is not so bad as I feared," he said. "I have foresight enough, and I could read your thoughts a little—not much; where did you learn to guard them so?—and I knew you came to speak of this war to me. I feared you had come, for the sake of the old friendship between your father and me, to urge me to join with your folk in this war. Though I loved your father well, *that* I would have been reluctant to do. I might have been willing to aid in the defense of Elhalyn, if you were hard pressed, but I would not have wished to attack the Ridenow."

"I have brought no such request, sir," Allart said, "but will you tell me why?"

"Why? Why, you ask? Well, tell me, lad," Aldaran said. "What grudge have you against the Ridenow?"

"I, myself? None, sir, save that they attacked an air-car in which I was riding with my father, and brought about his death. But all the Domains of the Lowlands have a grudge against the Ridenow because they have moved into the old Domain of Serrais and have taken their women in marriage."

"Is that such a bad thing?" Aldaran asked. "Did the women of Serrais ask your aid against these marriages, or prove to you that they had been married against their will?"

"No, but—" Allart hesitated. He knew it was not lawful for women of the Hastur kin to marry outside that kinfolk. As the thought crossed his mind, Aldaran picked it up and said, "As I thought. It is only that you want these women for your own Domain, and those close akin to you. I had heard that the male line of Serrais is extinct; it is this inbreeding which has brought that line to extinction. If the women of

Serrais wed back into the Hastur kin, I know enough of their bloodlines to predict that their *laran* will not survive another hundred years. They *need* new blood in that House. The Ridenow are healthy, and fertile. Nothing better could happen to the Serrais women than for the Ridenow to marry into their kindred."

Allart knew that his face betrayed his revulsion, though he tried to hide it. "If you will forgive plain speaking, sir, I find it revolting to speak of the relationships between men and women only in terms of this accursed breeding program in the Domains."

Aldaran snorted. "Yet you think it fitting to let the Serrais women be married off to Hasturs and Elhalyns and Aillards all over again? Isn't that breeding them for their *laran,* too? They wouldn't survive three more generations, I tell you! How many fertile sons have been born to Serrais in the last forty years? Come, come, do you think the lords who rule at Thendara are so charitable that they are trying to preserve the purity of Serrais? You are young, but you can hardly be so naïve as that. The Hastur kin would let Serrais die out before they let outlanders breed into it, but these Ridenow have other ideas. And that is the only hope for Serrais—some new genes! If you are wise, you people in the Domains will welcome the Ridenow and bind them to your own daughters with marriage ties!"

Allart was shocked. "The Ridenow—marry into the Hastur kin? They have no part in the blood of Hastur and Cassilda."

"Their sons will have it," Aldaran said bluntly, "and with new blood, the old Serrais line may survive, instead of breeding itself into sterility, as the Aillards are doing at Valeron, and as some of the Hasturs have done already. How many *emmasca* sons have been born into the Hasturs of Carcosa, or of Elhalyn, or Aillard, in the last hundred years?"

"Too many, I fear." Against his will Allart thought of the lads he had known in the monastery; *emmasca,* neither male nor wholly female, sterile, some with other defects. "But I have not studied the matter."

"Yet you presume to form an opinion on it?" Aldaran raised his eyebrows again. "I heard you had married an Aillard daughter; how many healthy sons and daughters have you? Though I need hardly ask. If you had, you would hardly be willing to swear allegiance to another man's bastards."

Stung, Allart retorted, "My wife and I have been wedded less than half a year."

"How many healthy legitimate sons has your brother? Come, come, Allart; you know as well as I that if your genes survive, they will do so in the veins of your *nedestro* children, even as mine. My wife was an Ardais, and bore me no more living children than your Aillard lady is likely to bear you."

Allart lowered his eyes, thinking with a spasm of grief and guilt, *It is no wonder the men of our line turn to riyachiyas and such perversions. We can take so little joy in our wives, between guilt at what we do to them, or fear for what will befall them!*

Aldaran saw the play of emotion on the young man's face and relented. "Well, well, there is no need to quarrel, kinsman; I meant no offense. But we have followed a breeding program, among the kin of Hastur and Cassilda, that has endangered our blood more than any upstart bandits could do—and salvation may take strange forms. It seems to me that the Ridenow will be the salvation of Serrais, if you folk at Elhalyn do not hinder them. But that is neither here nor there. Tell your brother that even if I wished to join in the war, which I do not, I could do nothing of the sort. I am myself hard-pressed; I have quarreled with my brother of Scathfell, and it troubles me that he has, as yet, sought no revenge. What is he plotting? I have meaty bones to pick, here at Aldaran, and it seems to me sometimes that the other mountain lords are like *kyorebni*, circling, waiting. . . . I am old. I have no legitimate heir, no living son at all, no single child of my own blood save my young daughter."

Allart said, "But she is a fair child—and a healthy one, it seems—and she possesses *laran*. If you have no son, surely you can find somewhere a son-in-law to inherit your estate!"

"I had hoped so," Aldaran said. "I think now it might even be well to marry her to one of those Ridenow, but *that* would bring down all the Elhalyn and Hastur kindred as well. It must depend, also, on whether your kinswoman can help her to survive the threshold at adolescence. I lost three grown sons and a daughter so. When I sought to wed into a line—such as my late wife, Deonara of Ardais—whose *laran* came early upon them, the children died before birth or in infancy. Dorilys survived birth and infancy, but with her *laran*, I fear she will not survive adolescence."

"The gods forbid she should die so! My kinswoman and I

will do all that we can. There are many ways now of preventing death in adolescence. I myself came near it, yet I live."

"If that is so," Aldaran said, "then am I your humble suppliant, kinsman. What I have is yours for the asking. But I beg you, remain and save my child from this fate!"

"I am at your service, Lord Aldaran. My brother has bidden me remain while I can be of use to you, or as long as needful to persuade you to remain neutral in this war."

"That I promise you," Aldaran said.

"Then you may command me, Lord Aldaran." Then Allart's bitterness broke through. "If you do not hold me too greatly in contempt, that I am not eager to return to the battlefield, since that seems to you the most fitting place for the young men of my clan!"

Aldaran bent his head. "I spoke in anger. Forgive me, kinsman. But I have no will to join this stupid war in the Lowlands, even though I feel the Hasturs should test the Ridenow before they admit them into their kindred. If the Ridenow cannot survive, perhaps they do not truly deserve to come into the line of Serrais. Perhaps the gods know what they are doing when they send wars among men, so that old lines of blood, softened by luxury and decadence, may die out, and new ones prevail, or come into them; new genetic material with traits tested by their ability to survive."

Allart shook his head. "This may have been true in the older days," he said, "when war was truly a test of strength and courage, so that the weaker did not survive to breed. I cannot believe it is so *now*, my lord, when such things as *clingfire* kill the strong and the weak alike, even women and little children who have no part in the quarrels of the lords . . ."

"*Clingfire!*" Lord Aldaran whispered. "Is it so, then—that they have begun to use *clingfire* in the Domains? But surely they can use it but little; the raw material is hard to mine from the earth and deteriorates so rapidly once it is exposed to the air."

"It is made by matrix circles in the Towers, my lord. This is one reason I was eager to leave the area of this war. I would not be sent cleanly into battle, but would be put to make the hellish stuff." Aldaran closed his eyes as if to shut out the unbearable.

"Are they all madmen, then, below the Kadarin? I had thought sheer sanity would deter them from weapons which must ravage conquerer and conquered alike! I find it hard to believe in any man of honor loosing such terrible weapons against his kin," Aldaran said. "Remain here, Allart. All the gods forbid I should send any man back into such dishonorable warfare!" His face twisted. "Perhaps, if the gods are kind, they will exterminate one another, like the dragons of legend who consumed one another in their fire, leaving their prey to build on the scorched ground beneath them."

CHAPTER
SIXTEEN

Renata, head lowered, hurried across the courtyard at Aldaran. In her preoccupation, she ran hard into someone, murmured an apology, and would have hurried on, but felt herself caught and held.

"Wait a moment, kinswoman! I have hardly seen you since I came here," Allart said.

Renata, raising her eyes, said, "Are you making ready to return to the Lowlands, cousin?"

"No, my lord of Aldaran has invited me to remain, to teach Donal something of what I learned at Nevarsin," Allart said. Then, looking full into her face, he drew a breath of consternation. "Cousin, what troubles you? What is so dreadful?"

Confused, Renata looked at him, saying, "Why, I do not know." Then, dropping into full rapport with his thoughts, she saw herself as she looked in his eyes—drawn, pale, her face twisted with grief and tragedy.

Is this what I am, or what I shall be? In sudden fear, she clung for a moment to him, and he steadied her, gently.

"Forgive me, cousin, that I frightened you. Indeed, I am beginning to feel that much of what I see exists only in my own fear. Surely there is nothing so frightful here, is there? Or is the *damisela* Dorilys such a little monster as the servants say?"

Renata laughed, but she still looked troubled. "No, indeed; she is the dearest, sweetest child, and as yet she has shown me only her most biddable and loving face. But— Oh, Allart, it is true! I am frightened for her; she bears a truly dreadful

laran, and I am afraid for what I must say to the lord Aldaran, her father! It cannot but make him angry!"

"I have seen her only for a few minutes," Allart said.
"Donal was showing me how he controls the glider-toys, and
she came down and begged to fly with us; but Donal said she
must ask Margali, that he would not take the responsibility of
letting her come. She was very cross, and went off in a great
sulk."

"But she did not strike at him?"

"No," said Allart. "She pouted and said he did not love
her, but she obeyed him. I would not want to let her fly until
she could control a matrix, but Donal said he was given one
when he was nine, and learned to use it without trouble. Evidently *laran* comes early on the Delleray kindred."

"Or on those of Rockraven," Renata said, "but she still
looked troubled. "I would not want to trust Dorilys with a
matrix yet; perhaps never. But we will speak of that later.
Lord Aldaran has agreed to receive me, and I must not keep
him waiting."

"Indeed you must not," Allart said, and Renata went
across the courtyard, frowning.

Outside the presence-chamber of the lord Aldaran, she
found Dorilys. The little girl looked more controlled and civilized today, her hair neatly plaited, her dress an embroidered
smock.

"I want to hear what you say to my father about me,
cousin," she said, sliding her hand confidingly into Renata's.

Renata shook her head. "It is not good for little girls to listen to the councils of their elders," she said. "I must say
many things which you would not understand. I give you my
word that everything concerning you will be told to you when
the proper time comes, but that proper time is not now,
Dorilys."

"I am not a little girl," Dorilys said, thrusting her lip out.

"Then you should not behave like one, pouting and stamping your foot as if you were five years old! Certainly such behavior will not convince me that you are old enough to listen
with maturity to talk about your future."

Dorilys looked more rebellious than ever. "Who do you
think you are, to talk that way to me? I am Lady of Aldaran!"

"You are a child who will one day be Lady of Aldaran,"
Renata said coldly, "and I am the *leronis* whom your father

saw fit to entrust with the task of teaching you proper behavior befitting that high place."

Dorilys pulled her hand free of Renata's, staring sulkily at the floor. "I will not be spoken to in that way! I will complain of you to my father, and he will send you away if you are not kind to me!"

"You do not know the meaning of the word unkindness," Renata said mildly. "When I entered the Tower of Hali as a novice to learn the art of monitor, no one was allowed to speak to me for forty days, nor to look into my eyes. This was to strengthen my reliance upon my *laran*."

"I wouldn't have put up with it," Dorilys said, and Renata smiled.

"Then they would have sent me home, knowing I did not have the strength and self-discipline to learn what I must learn. I will never be unkind to you, Dorilys, but you must master yourself before you are fit to command others."

"But it is different with me," Dorilys argued. "I am Lady of Aldaran, and already I command all the women in the castle, and most of the men, too. You are not the Lady of your Domain, are you?"

Renata shook her head. "No, but I am a Tower monitor. And even a Keeper is taught so. You have met your brother's friend, Allart. He is Regent of Elhalyn, yet at Nevarsin, for his training, he slept naked on stone for three winters, and never spoke in the presence of any monk superior to him."

"That's *horrible*," Dorilys said, making a face.

"No. We undertake these disciplines voluntarily, because we know we need to discipline our bodies and minds to obey us, so that our *laran* will not destroy us."

"If I obey you," Dorilys asked craftily, "will you give me a matrix and teach me to use it, so that I can fly with Donal?"

"I will when I think you can be trusted with it, *chiya*," Renata said.

"But I want it *now*," Dorilys argued.

Renata shook her head. "No," she said. "Now go back to your rooms, Dorilys, and I will see you when I have finished with your father." She spoke firmly, and Dorilys started to obey; then, after a few steps, she whirled around, stamping her foot angrily.

"You will not use command-voice on me again!"

"I will do what I think fit," said Renata, unmoved. "Your father has put me in charge of you. Must I tell him I find you disobedient, and ask him to command you to obey me in all things?"

Dorilys shrank. "No, please—don't tell Father on me, Renata!"

"Then obey me at once," Renata repeated, using the forbidden command-voice. "Go back and tell Margali you have been disobedient, and ask her to punish you."

Dorilys's eyes filled with tears, but she moved away, lagging, out of the courtyard, and Renata let her breath go.

How would I have forced her to obey if she had refused? And a time will come when she will refuse, and I must be prepared for that!

One of the servants was staring, wide-eyed, having observed the little interchange. Renata picked up the woman's thoughts without trying: *I have never seen my little lady obey like that . . . without a word of protest!*

So it was the first time Dorilys had to obey against her will, Renata thought. Margali, she knew, would punish Dorilys gently, only by setting her to sew long and uninteresting seams on skirts and shifts, and forbidding her to touch her embroidery-frames. *It will not hurt our little lady to learn to do tasks for which she has no liking or talent.*

But the confrontation had hardened her will for what she knew would be a difficult meeting with Lord Aldaran. She was grateful that he had agreed to receive her in the small study where he wrote his letters and saw the *coridom* about the business of his estates, rather than in the formal presence-chamber.

She found him dictating to his private secretary, but he broke off when she came in, and sent the man away. "Well, *damisela*, how are you getting along with my daughter? Do you find her obedient and biddable? She is headstrong, but very sweet and loving."

Renata smiled faintly. "She is not very loving at this moment, I fear," she said. "I have had to punish her, to send her to Margali to sit over her sewing for a while, and learn to think before she speaks."

Lord Aldaran sighed. "I suppose no child can be brought up without some punishment," he said. "I gave Donal's tutors leave to beat him, if they must, but I was gentler with him than my father with me, for I forbade his tutors to strike him hard enough to leave bruises; while as a boy I often was beaten so that I could not sit in comfort for days. But you will not need to beat my daughter, I hope?"

"I would prefer not to," Renata said. "I have always thought that solitary meditation over some tedious or boring task is punishment enough for most misbehavior. Still, I wish you would tell her, sometime, what you have told me, my lord. She seems to feel that her rank should excuse her from punishment or discipline."

"You would like me to tell her that my tutors had leave to beat me when I was a lad?" Lord Aldaran chuckled. "Very well, I shall do so, by way of reminding her that even I have had to learn to rule myself. But did you come only for leave to punish my daughter, Lady? I had thought that when I put her in your charge, you would take that for granted."

"And so I do," Renata said. "But I had something far more serious to discuss with you. You brought me here because you feared the strength of your daughter's *laran*, did you not? I have monitored her carefully, body and brain; she is still several moons short of puberty, I judge. Before that comes upon her, I would like to ask leave to monitor you, my lord, and Donal as well."

Lord Aldaran raised his eyebrows curiously. "May I ask why, *damisela?*"

"Margali has already told me all she can remember of Aliciane's pregnancy and confinement," Renata said, "so that I know some of what Dorilys inherited from her mother. But Donal, too, bears the heritage of Rockraven, and I would like to know what recessives Dorilys may be carrying. It is simpler to check Donal than to go into germ plasm. The same with you, my lord, since Dorilys bears not only your heritage but that of all your line. I would also like access to your genealogies, so that I can see if there are any traces in *your* line of certain kinds of *laran*."

Lord Aldaran nodded. "I can see that you should be armed with such knowledge," he said. "You may tell the keeper of the Aldaran archives that I give you freedom of all our records. Do you think, then, that she will survive threshold sickness in adolescence?"

"I will tell you that when I know more of what lies within her genes and heritage," Renata said. "I will do what I can for her, I swear it, and so will Allart. But I must know what I am facing."

"Well, I have no particular objection to being monitored,"

Lord Aldaran said, "although it is a technique with which I am not familiar."

"Deep monitoring of this sort was developed for the matrix circles working on the higher levels," Renata said. "When we had done using it for that, we found it had other uses."

"What must I do, then?"

"Nothing," Renata said. "Simply make your mind and body as quiet and relaxed as you can, and try to think of nothing at all. Trust me; I shall not intrude into your thoughts, but only into your body and its deeper secrets."

Aldaran shrugged. "Whenever you like," he said.

Renata reached out, beginning the slow monitoring process; first monitoring his breathing, his circulation, then going deeper and deeper into the cells of body and brain. After a long time she gently withdrew, and thanked him, but she looked troubled and abstracted.

"What is the verdict, *damisela?*"

"I would rather wait until I have seen the archives, and worked with Donal," she said, and bowed to him, leaving the room.

A few days later, Renata sent word asking if Lord Aldaran could receive her again.

When she came into his presence this time, she wasted no words.

"My lord, is Dorilys your only living child?"

"*Yes*, I told you that."

"I know she is the only child you acknowledge. But is that only a manner of speaking, or the literal truth? Have you any unacknowledged bastards, by-blows, any child at all born of your blood?"

Aldaran shook his head, troubled.

"No," he said. "Not one. I had several children by my first marriage, but they died in their adolescence, of threshold sickness; and Deonara's babes all died before they were weaned. In my youth I fathered a few sons here and there, though none survived adolescence. As far as I know, Dorilys alone, on the face of this world, bears my blood."

"I do not want to anger you, Lord Aldaran," Renata said, "but you should get you another heir at once."

He looked at her, and she saw the dismay and panic in his eyes.

"Are you warning me that she, too, will not survive adolescence?"

"No," said Renata. "There is every reason to hope she will survive it; she may even become something of a telepath. But your heritage should not rest on her alone. She might, as Aliciane did, survive the bearing of a single child. Her *laran*, as near as I can tell, is sex-linked; one of the few gifts that are. It is recessive in boys; Donal has the ability to read air currents and air pressure, to feel the winds and sense the movement of storms, and even to control the lightning a little, though not to draw it or to generate it. But this gift is dominant in females. Dorilys might survive the birth of a son. She could not survive the birth of a daughter gifted unborn with such *laran*. Donal, too, should be warned to father only sons, unless he wishes to see their mothers struck down by this *laran* in their unborn daughters."

Aldaran took this in slowly. At last he said, his face gray with torment, "Are you saying that Dorilys killed Aliciane?"

"I thought you knew that. This is one reason the Rockraven gift was abandoned by the breeding program. Some daughters, without the full strength of *laran* themselves, nevertheless had it to pass on to *their* daughters. I think Aliciane must have been one of these. And Dorilys had the full *laran*. . . . During her birth—tell me—was there a storm?"

Aldaran felt his breath catch in his throat, recalling how Aliciane had cried out, in terror, "She hates me! She doesn't want to be born!"

Dorilys killed her mother! She killed my beloved, my Aliciane. . . . Desperately, struggling for fairness, he said, "She was a newborn child! How can you blame her?"

"Blame? Who speaks of blame? A child's emotions are uncontrolled; they have had no training in controlling them. And birth is terrifying for a child. Did you not know that, my lord?"

"Of course! I was present when all of Deonara's babes were born," he said, "but I could calm them to some extent."

"But Dorilys was stronger than most babes," Renata said, "and in her fear and pain, she struck—and Aliciane died. She does not know this; I hope she will never know. But, knowing this, you can see why it is not safe to rely on her, alone, to pass your blood to future generations. Indeed, it would be safer for her never to marry, though I shall teach her, when she comes to womanhood, how to conceive sons only."

"Would Aliciane had had such teaching," said Lord Aldaran, with great bitterness. "I did not know this technique was known in the Domains."

"It is not very commonly taught," Renata said, "although those who breed *riyachiyas* know it, to breed nothing but females. It has not been taught lest the lords of great estates, hungry for sons, should upset the balance nature has given us, so that there would be too few women born. Yet, in such a case as this, I think, where such a frightful *laran* can strike the unborn, I think it justified. I will teach Dorilys, and Donal, too, if he wishes."

The old man bowed his head. "What am I to do? She is my only child!"

"Lord Aldaran," Renata said quietly, "I would like your permission, if I think it needful, to burn out her *laran* in adolescence to destroy her psi centers within the brain. It might save her life—or her reason."

He stared at her in horror. "Would you destroy her mind?"

"No. But she would be free of *laran*," Renata said.

"Monstrous! I refuse absolutely!"

"My lord," Renata said, and her face was drawn, "I swear to you. If Dorilys were the child of my own womb, I would ask you the same. Do you know she has killed three times?"

"Three? *Three*? Aliciane; Darren, my brother's son—but that was justified, he attempted to ravish her!"

Renata nodded. She said, "She was handfasted once before, and the child died, did he not?"

"I thought that was an accident."

"Why, so it was," said Renata. "Dorilys was not six years old. She knew only that he had broken her doll. She had blocked it from her mind. When I forced her to remember it, she cried so pitifully, I think it would have melted the heart of Zandru's self! So far she strikes only in panic. She would not, I think, even have killed the kinsman who tried to rape her, but she had no control. She could not stun, only kill. And she may kill again. I do not know if anyone living can teach her enough control over this kind of *laran*. I would not burden her with guilt, if she strikes again in a moment of fear or panic."

Renata hesitated. Finally she said, "It is well known: power corrupts. Even now, I think, she knows no one dares to defy her. She is headstrong and arrogant. She may like the knowledge that everyone fears her. A girl on the threshold of adolescence has many troubles; at such times girls dislike their faces, their bodies, the color of their hair. They think others dislike them, because they have so many anxieties they cannot yet focus. If Dorilys comforts herself for these anxieties with the knowledge of her power—well, I know *I* would be frightened of her under these conditions!"

Aldaran stared at the floor of the room, black and white and inlaid with a mosaic of birds. "I cannot consent to having her *laran* destroyed, Renata. She is my only child."

"Then, my lord," Renata said bluntly, "you should marry again and get you another heir before it is too late; and at your age you should lose no time."

"Do you think I have not tried that?" Aldaran said bitterly. Then, hesitating, he told Renata of the curse.

"My lord, surely a man of your intelligence knows that the power of such a curse is upon your mind, not your manhood."

"So I told myself for many years. Yet I felt no desire for any woman, for many years after Aliciane died. After Deonara died, and I knew I had only a single *nedestro* girl-child surviving, I took others to my bed; yet none of them quickened. Of late I have begun to believe the curse had struck me before the sorceress voiced it, for while Aliciane was heavy with my child I took no other. For me that was unknown, that I should live half a year with no woman for my bed." He shook his head, apologetically. "Forgive me, *damisela*. Such talk is unseemly to a woman of your years."

"Speaking of such things I am not a woman but a *leronis*, my lord. Don't trouble yourself about that. Have you never been monitored to test this, my lord?"

"I did not know such a thing was possible."

"I will test it, if you will," Renata said matter-of-factly. "Or if you would rather—Margali is your kinswoman, and nearer to your years—if it would trouble you less. . . ."

The man stared at the floor. "I would feel less shamed before a stranger, I think," he said in a low voice.

"As you will." Renata quieted herself and sank deep into the monitoring of body and brain; cell deep.

After a time she said regretfully, "You are cursed, indeed, my lord. Your seed bears no spark of life."

"Is such a thing possible? Did the woman merely know my shame, or did she cause this—this—" His voice died, between rage and dismay.

Renata said quietly, "I have no way of knowing, my lord. I suppose it is possible that some enemy could have done this to you. Although no one trusted with a matrix in the Towers would be capable of such a thing. We are sworn with many oaths against such abuse of our powers."

"Can it be reversed? What the powers of sorcery have done, can they not undo?"

"I fear not, sir. Perhaps if it had been known at once, something—but after so many years, I fear it is an impossible task."

Aldaran bowed his head. "Then I must pray to all the gods that you can somehow bring Dorilys undamaged through adolescence. She alone bears the heritage of Aldaran."

Renata pitied the old man; he had had to face some painful and humiliating truths today. She said gently, "My lord, you have a brother, and your brother has sons. Even if Dorilys should not survive this—although, indeed, I pray Avarra may guard her from all harm—the Aldaran heritage will not be wholly lost. I beg you, sir, be reconciled to your brother."

Aldaran's eyes blazed with sudden, terrible exploding rage.

"Have a care, my girl! I am grateful for all you have done, and all you will do, for my child, but there are some things even you cannot say to me! I have sworn that I will tear down this castle stone by stone ere it falls to any son of Scathfell! Dorilys will reign here after me, or none!"

Cruel, arrogant old man! Renata found herself thinking. *It would serve you right if that came, indeed, to pass! His pride is stronger than his love for Dorilys, or he would spare her this terrible destiny!*

She bowed. "Then there is no more to be said, my lord. I will do what I can for Dorilys. Yet I beg you to remember, sir, that the world will go as it will, and not as you or I would have it go."

"Kinswoman, I beg you, be not angry. I beg you not to let your anger at this sharp-tongued old man make you any less a friend to my little girl."

"Nothing could do that," Renata said, softening against her will to the old man's charm. "I love Dorilys, and I will guard her as much as I may, even against herself."

When she had left Aldaran, she walked for a long time on the battlements, troubled. She faced a very serious ethical problem. Dorilys probably could not survive childbirth. Could she reconcile it to her own strict code, to let the girl come unknowing to womanhood with that shocking curse? Should she warn Dorilys of what lay ahead for her?

She thought, angry again, that Lord Aldaran would expose Dorilys to such a death rather than accept the knowledge that his brother of Scathfell might inherit his domain.

Cassilda, blessed mother of the Hastur kin, she thought. *All gods be praised that I am not lord of a Domain!*

CHAPTER
SEVENTEEN

Summer in the Hellers was beautiful; the snows receded to the highest peaks, and even at dawn there was little rain or snow.

"A beautiful season, but dangerous, cousin Allart," Donal said, standing at the height of the castle. "We have fewer fires than the Lowland Domains. for our snows remain longer, but our fires rage longer because of the resin-trees, and in the heat of these days they give off the volatile oils which ignite so quickly when the summer lightning storms rage. And when the resin-trees ignite—" He shrugged, spreading his hands, and Allart understood; he, too, had seen the volatile trees catch fire and go up like torches, throwing off showers of sparks which fell in liquid rain, spreading flame through the whole forest.

"It is a miracle that there are any resin-trees left, if this happens year after year!"

"True; I think if they grew less swiftly, these hills would be bare and the Hellers a wasteland from the Kadarin to the Wall around the World. But they grow swiftly, and in a year the slopes are re-covered."

Allart said, fastening the straps of the flying-harness around his waist, "I have not flown in one of these since I was a boy. I hope I have not lost the knack!"

"You never lose it," Donal said. "When I was fifteen and ill with threshold sickness, I could not fly for almost a year. I was dizzy and disoriented and when I was well again I thought I had forgotten how to fly. But my body remembered, as soon as I was airborne."

Allart drew the last buckle tight. "Have we far to fly?"

"Riding, it would be more than most animals could do in two days; it lies by paths mostly straight up and down. But as the *kyorebni* fly, it is little more than an hour's flight."

"Would it not be simpler to take an air-car?" Then Allart remembered he had seen none in the Hellers.

Donal said, "The folk of Darriel experimented with such things. But there are too many crosscurrents and cross-drafts among the peaks here; even with a glider you must pick your day carefully for flying, and be wary of storms and changes in the wind. Once I had to sit on a crag for hours, waiting for a summer storm to subside." He chuckled with the memory. "I came home as bedraggled and sad as a rabbithorn who has had to yield his hole to a tree-badger! But today, I think, we will have no such trouble. Allart, you are Tower-trained, do you know the folk at Tramontana?"

"Ian-Mikhail of Storn is Keeper there," Allart said, "and I spoke with all of them in the relays, from time to time, during my half-year at Hali. But I have never been to Tramontana in the flesh."

"They have always welcomed me there; indeed, I think they are always glad of visitors. They sit like hawks in their aerie, seeing no one from midsummer festival to midwinter night. It will be a pleasure for them to welcome you, cousin."

"And for me," Allart said. Tramontana was the most distant and farthest northward of the Towers, in almost total isolation from the others, though its workers passed messages through the relay-nets and exchanged information about the work they had done in developing new uses for matrix science. It had been the workers at Tramontana, he remembered, who devised the chemicals for fire-fighting, where they could be found in the deep caves under the Hellers, refining them, devising new ways to use them, all with the matrix arts.

"Is it not true that they have worked with matrixes to the twenty-fifth level?"

"I think so, cousin. There are thirty of them there, after all. It may be the farthest of the Towers, but it is not the smallest."

"Their work with chemicals is brilliant," Allart said, "although I think I would be afraid to do some of the things they have done. Yet their technicians say that once the lattices are mastered, a twenty-sixth-level matrix is no more dangerous than a fourth-level. I do not know if I would wish to trust myself to the concentration of twenty-five other people."

Donal smiled ruefully. "I wish I knew more of these things. I know only what Margali has taught me, and what little they have had leisure to tell me, when I visit there, and I have seldom been given leave to stay more than a single day."

"Indeed, I think you would have made a mechanic, or perhaps even a technician," Allart said, thinking of how swiftly the lad had responded to his teaching, "but you have another destiny."

"True; I would not abandon my father, nor my sister, and they need me here," Donal said. "So there are many things I shall never do with a matrix, for they need the safety of a Tower. But I am glad to have learned what I could, and for nothing am I more glad than this," he added, touching the leather-and-wood struts of the glider. "Are we ready to go, cousin?"

He stepped to the edge of the parapet, fluttered the long extended leather flaps of the glider wings to catch the air current, then stepped off into the air, soaring upward. Allart, his senses extended, could just feel the edge of the current; he stepped to the parapet edge, feeling an inner cramping at the height, the glimpse of the fearful gulf below him. Yet if a boy like Donal could fly without fear over that height. . . . He focused on the matrix, stepped free, and felt the sudden dizziness of the long drop and swoop outward, the tug of the current that bore him upward. His body swiftly balanced itself, lying along the inner struts, leaning this way and that as he mastered the balance of the toy. He saw Donal's glider, soaring hawklike above him, and caught an updraft carrying him along until they flew side by side.

For the first minutes Allart was so preoccupied with the mastery of the glider that he did not look down at all, his entire consciousness caught up into the delicate balances, the pressure of the air and the energy currents he could dimly sense, all around him. Somehow it made him think of his days at Nevarsin, when he had first mastered his *laran* and had learned to see human beings as swirls, energy-nets of force like streaming currents, without the awareness of flesh and blood, of his *solid* body. Now he sensed that the insubstantial air was filled with the same streaming currents of force. *If I have taught Donal much, he has given me no less in return, teaching me this mastery of air currents and the streams of force which permeate the air as they do the land and the waters.* . . . Allart had never before been aware of these currents in the air; now he could almost *see* them, could pick and choose among them, riding them up, up to a height where the winds dashed against the frail glider, racing along on the tremendous airstream, then picking a convenient current to dip down again to a safer height. He began, as he lay along the struts now, leaving a fragment of his consciousness to control the glider, to look down at the mountain panorama laid out below him.

Below them a quiet mountainous countryside stretched out, slope after slope of hills covered with dark forest, now and then the thickness giving way to slanted rows of trees, marching mechanically up and down a hillside—nut-farms, or plantations of edible fungus in the forest. Hillsides had been cleared for grasses where herds grazed, dotted with small huts where the herd-keepers lived, and now and again, beside the course of a racing mountain stream, a waterwheel set up for the making of cheeses, or the fibers which, matrix-enhanced, could be extracted from the bulk of the milk after whey and curds had been pressed out. He smelled the odd reek of a felting-mill, and another of a mill where the scraps left after timbering were pressed into paper. On a rocky slope, he saw the entrance to a network of caves where the forge-folk lived and saw the glow of their fires, where flying sparks could not endanger forests or populated areas.

As they flew on, the hills became higher and more deserted. He felt Donal's touch on his thoughts—the boy was developing into a skilled telepath who could attract his attention without troubling it— and Allart followed him down a long draft between two hills, to where the white glareless stone of Tramontana Tower gleamed in the noonlight. He saw a sentry on the heights raise his hand in greeting, and followed as Donal swooped down, folding the wings of his glider as he landed on his feet, sinking gracefully to his knees and rising in a single controlled movement, whipping off the glider wings in a long trail behind him; but Allart, less skilled at this game, found himself knocked off his feet, in a disorderly tangle of struts and ropes. Donal, laughing, came to help him disentangle himself.

"Never mind, cousin, I have landed that way many times myself," he said, though Allart wondered how many years it had been since he had done so. "Come, Arzi will take your glider and keep it safe against our return," he added, gesturing to the bent old man who stood beside him.

"Master Donal," said the old man, in a dialect so thick that even Allart, who knew most of the Hellers dialects, found it hard to follow. "A joy, as ever, to welcome ye back among us. Y' lend us grace, *dom'yn*," he added, including Allart in his rude bow.

Donal said, "This is my old friend Arzi, who has served the Tower since before I was born, and welcomed me here three or four times a year since I was ten years old. Arzi— my cousin, Dom Allart Hastur of Elhalyn."

"Vai dom." Arzi's bow was almost comical in its depth and deference. "Lord Hastur lends us grace. Ah, it's a happy day—the *vai leronyn* will be glad indeed to welcome ye, Lord Hastur."

"Not Lord Hastur," Allart said gently, "only Lord Allart, my good man, but I thank you for your welcome."

"Ah, it's been many, many years since a Hastur came among us," Arzi said. "Be pleased t' follow me, *vai domyn*."

"Look what the winds have brought us," called a merry voice, and a young girl, tall, slender, with hair as pale as snow on the distant peak, came running toward Donal, holding out her hands to him in welcome. "Donal, how glad we all are to see you again! But you have brought a guest to us!"

"I am glad to return, Rosaura," Donal said, embracing the girl as if they were long-lost kin. The girl stretched out her hands to welcome Allart, with the swift touch of telepaths to whom this was more natural than the touch of fingertips. Allart, of course, had known who she was even before Donal spoke the name, but as they brushed against one another her face lighted again with a quick smile.

"Oh, but you are Allart, who was at Hali for half a year. I had heard you were in the Hellers, of course, but I had no notion fortune would bring you here to us, kinsman. Have you come to work with Tramontana Tower?"

Donal was watching with amazement at this meeting. "But you have not been here before, cousin," he said to Allart.

"That is true," Rosaura said. "Until this hour, none of us have looked upon our kinsman's face, but we have touched him in the relays. This is a glad day for Tramontana, kinsman! Come and meet the rest of us." Rosaura took them inside, and quickly they were surrounded by more than a dozen young men and women—some of the others were at work in the relays, others asleep after a night of work—all of whom welcomed Donal almost as one of themselves.

Allart's emotions were mixed. He had managed not to think too much about what he had left behind at Hali Tower, and now he was meeting, face to face, minds he had touched in the relays there, putting faces and voices and personalities to people he had known only in the elusive, bodiless touch of mind to mind.

"Are you coming to Tramontana to stay, cousin? We can use a good technician."

Regretfully, Allart shook his head. "I am committed elsewhere, though nothing would please me more, I think. But I have been long at Aldaran, without much news from the outside world. How goes the war?"

"Much as before," said Ian-Mikhail of Storn, a slight, dark young man with curling hair. "There was a rumor that Alaric Ridenow, him they call the Red Fox, had been slain, but it was false. King Regis lies gravely ill, and Prince Felix has summoned the Council. If he should die, may his reign be long, there will be need for another truce while Felix is crowned, should he ever be crowned. And among your own kinsmen, Allart, word came through the relays that a son was born to your brother's lady in the first tenday of the rose month. The boy does well, though the lady Cassilde has not recovered her strength and could not suckle him herself. There is some fear that she will not recover. But the boy has been proclaimed your brother's heir."

"The gods be thanked, and Evanda the merciful smile on the child." Allart spoke the formula with real relief.

Now Damon-Rafael had a legitimate son; there was no question whether the Council would choose a legitimate brother over a *nedestro* son.

Yet, among the crowding futures, Allart saw himself crowned at Thendara. Angrily he tried to slam the door on his *laran* and the unwelcome possibilities. *Have I some taint of my brother's kind of ambition, after all?*

"And," said Rosaura, "I spoke with your lady but three days ago, in the relays."

Allart's heart seemed to clutch painfully and knock against his ribs. Cassandra! How long had it been since he had called her image to mind? "How does my lady?"

"She seems well and content," Rosaura said. "You knew,

did you not, that she has now been appointed full monitor for Coryn's circle at Hali?"

"No, I had not heard."

"She is a powerful telepath in the relay-nets. I wonder you could bring yourself to leave her behind. You have not been long married, have you?"

"Not yet a year," Allart said. *No, not long, a painfully short time to leave a beloved wife. . . .* He had forgotten that he was among trained telepaths, a Tower circle; for a moment he had dropped his barriers, saw the pain in his thoughts reflected all around him.

He said, "The fortunes of war, I suppose. The world will go as it will and not as you or I would have it." He felt sententious, prim, as he mouthed the cliché, but they displayed the bland unrevealing non-contact, the mental turning-away which is the courtesy among telepaths when truths too revealing have been shown. He recovered his composure while Donal spoke of their errand.

"My father sent me for the first of the fire-chemicals to be taken to the station at the heart of the resin-tree forest; the others can be sent more slowly, with pack-animals. We are building a new fire station on the peak. The talk became general, of fire-fighting, of the season and the early storms.

One of the *leronyn* took Donal to make up a packet of the chemicals which could be carried back on the gliders, and Rosaura drew Allart aside.

"I regret the necessities which parted you so soon from your bride, kinsman; but if you like, and if Cassandra is in the relays, you can speak with her."

Faced with the possibility, Allart felt his heart clench. He had resigned himself, told himself that if he never saw Cassandra again, at least they avoided the grimmest of the futures he had seen. Yet he knew he could not forbear this chance to speak with her.

The matrix chamber was like any other, the vaulted roof and blue window-lights below it admitting soft radiance, the monitor screen, the great relay lattice. A young woman in the soft loose robe of a matrix worker knelt before it, her face blank and calm with the distant look of a matrix technician with the mind attuned elsewhere, thoughts caught up in the relay-nets that linked all the telepaths in all the Towers of Darkover.

Allart took his place beside the girl in the relays, the inner part of his thoughts still troubled.

What shall I say to her? How can I meet her again, even this way?

But the old discipline held, the ritual breaths to calm his mind, his body locking itself in one of the effortless postures which could be maintained indefinitely without too much fatigue.

He cast himself into the vast spinning darkness, like the swoop of the glider over the great gulf. Thoughts whirled and spun past him like distant conversation in a crowded room, meaningless because he was unaware of their origin or context. Slowly, as he became more aware of the structure of the relay-net tonight, he felt a more definite touch, Rosaura's voice.

Hali. . . .

We are here, what would you have?

If the lady Cassandra Aillard-Hastur is among you, her husband is with us at Tramontana and begs a word with her. . . .

Allart, is it you? As recognizable as her bright hair, her gay girlish smile, he touched Arielle. *I think Cassandra is sleeping, but for this she will be glad to be wakened. Bear my greetings to my cousin Renata; I think of her often with love and blessings. I will waken Cassandra for you.*

Arielle was gone. Allart was back in the floating silence, messages slipping past him without impinging on any part of his mind which could remember or register them. Then, without warning, she was *there,* beside him, around him, a presence almost physical. . . . *Cassandra!*

Allart, my beloved. . . .

The texture of tears, of amazement, disbelief, reunion; an instant, timeless (three seconds? three hours?), of absolute, ecstatic joining, like an embrace. It was like nothing except the moment when he had first possessed her and in that moment felt the barriers drop, felt her mind yield and blend into his, a joining more complete, a mutual surrender more total than the union of their bodies. Wordless, but complete; he was lost in it, felt her lose herself in it.

It could not be sustained for long at such a level; he felt it drop away, recede into ordinary thought, ordinary contact.

Allart, how came you to Tramontana?

With the foster-son of Aldaran, to collect the first of the fire-fighting chemicals for the high fire season; it is upon us in the Hellers. He flashed to her a picture of the long, ecstatic flight here, the swoop of the glider, the wind racing past head and body.

We have had fires here, too. The Hali Tower was attacked with air-cars and incendiaries. He saw ravening flames on the shore, explosions, an air-car struck down and burning like a meteor as it fell, exploded by the linked minds of eleven at Hali, the dying shrieks of the flyer who had brought it in, drugged and suicidal. . . .

But you are safe, my beloved?

I am safe, although we are all weary, working day and night. . . . Many things have happened to me, my husband. I shall have much to tell you. When will you return to me?

That must be as the gods will, Cassandra, but I shall not delay any longer than I must. . . . As he formed the word-thoughts he knew they were true. The part of wisdom might be never to see her again. But even now he could foresee a day when he would hold her in his arms again, and he knew abruptly that even if death were the penalty, he would not turn away . . . nor would she.

Allart, are we to fear the entrance of the Aldarans into this war? Since you left us for the Hellers, we have all feared that more than anything else.

No, Aldaran is much beset by strife with his kin; he bears neither loyalty nor grudge to either side. I am here to teach laran *to Lord Aldaran's foster-son while Renata cares for his daughter. . . .*

Is she very beautiful? In her thoughts, wordless yet unmistakable, he sensed rancor, jealousy. Was it for Renata or the unknown daughter? He heard her unspoken answer: *both. . . .*

Very beautiful, yes. . . . Allart kept his thoughts light, amused. *She is eleven years old . . . and no woman on the face of this world, not the Blessed Cassilda within her shrine, is half so beautiful as you, my beloved. . . .* Then another moment of the wholly blissful, ecstatic merging, joining, as if they were clasped together, with everything that they were, bodies, minds, souls. . . . He must break it. Cassandra could not long sustain this, not if she was working as a monitor. Slowly, reluctantly, he let the contact drop away, disappear, fade into nothingness, but his whole mind and body were still full of her as if he could feel the print of her kiss on his mouth.

Dazed, weary, Allart let himself come back to awareness of the matrix chamber, cold and blue, around him, of his own cramped and shivering body. Slowly, after a long time, he moved, rose, quietly tiptoed out of the matrix chamber, leaving the workers in the relay-nets undisturbed. As he made his way down the long twisting stairs, he did not know whether or not he was grateful for the chance to speak with her.

It has forged anew a bond which it would have been better to break. In that long joining he had picked up many things which he had not, with his conscious mind, really understood, but he sensed that Cassandra, too, had tried in her own way to break that bond. He was not resentful. They were still bound, more strongly than ever, with the bonds of desire and frustration.

And love? *And love?*

What is love, anyway? Allart was not sure whether the thought was his own, or one he had somehow picked up from the confused mind of his young wife.

Rosaura met him at the bottom of the stairs. If she noted his dazed face, the traces of tears around his eyes, she said nothing; there were certain courtesies among Tower telepaths, where no strong emotion could ever be concealed. She only said, quietly matter-of-fact, "After a contact across so much space, you will be drained and weary. Come, cousin, and refresh yourself."

Donal joined them at the meal, and half a dozen of the workers in the Tower who were not at their duties or resting. They were all a little manic with the relaxation of strain, the rare treat of company in their isolated place. Allart's sorrow and revived longing for Cassandra were swept away on a tide of jesting and laughter. The food was strange to Allart, though good; a sweet white mountain wine he had never tasted, mushrooms and fungus cooked in a dozen different ways, a soft white boiled tuber or root of some kind mashed into little cakes and fried in fragrant oil, but there was no meat. Rosaura told him that they had resolved to experiment here with a diet of no animal flesh and see if it sensitized their awarenesses. This seemed strange and a little silly to Allart, but he had lived for years with such a diet at Nevarsin.

"Before you go, we have a message for your foster-father,

Donal," Ian-Mikhail said. "Scathfell has sent embassies to Sain Scarp, to Storn, to Ardais and Scaravel, and to the Castamirs. I do not know what it is all about, but as overlord to Scathfell he should be told. Scathfell would not trust it to the relays, so I fear it is some secret conspiracy, and we had heard rumors of a breach between your father and Lord Scathfell. Lord Aldaran should be warned."

Donal looked troubled. "I thank you on my foster-father's behalf. Of course we knew some such things must be happening, but our household *leronis* is old, and has been much occupied with the care of my sister, so we had heard nothing by way of the overworld."

"Is your sister well?" Rosaura asked. "We should have liked to have her here with us at Tramontana for her testing."

"Renata Leynier has come from Hali to care for her during adolescence," Donal said, and Rosaura smiled.

"Renata from Hali; I know her well in the relays. Your sister will be well with her, Donal."

Then it was time to make ready and go. One of the monitors brought them neatly made-up packets of the chemicals which, mixed with water or other fluids, would expand enormously into a white foam that would cover an incredible expanse of fire. More would be sent as soon as land convoy could be arranged. Donal went up to the high walk behind the tower and stood there scanning the skies. When he descended, he looked grave.

"There may be storms before sunset," he said. "We should lose no time, cousin."

This time Allart felt no hesitation about stepping off, drifting on a rising current of air, using the power of his matrix to carry him up and up, soaring. Yet he could not wholly give himself to the enjoyment of the experience.

The contact with Cassandra, blissful as it had been, had left him drained and troubled. He tried to put aside all these thoughts, flying demanded concentration on his matrix; preoccupation with outside thoughts was a luxury he could not afford. Yet again and again he saw faces cast before him by his *laran*: a big hearty man who oddly resembled Dom Mikhail of Aldaran; Cassandra weeping alone in her room at Hali, then rising and composing herself to work in the relays; Renata facing Dorilys with angry challenge. . . . He brought himself back by force of will to the heights, the soaring rush of air past the glider, the air currents tingling painfully in his outstretched fingertips as if each finger were the pinion of a soaring hawk, himself neither man nor bird, swooping on the air. He knew that in this moment he shared Donal's inner fantasy.

"There are storms ahead," said Donal. "I am sorry to take you so far from our way when you are not used to flying, but we must go around them. It is not safe to fly so near a storm. Follow me, cousin." He caught a handy air current and let himself drift, matrix-aided, away from the straight line to Aldaran.

Allart could see the storm ahead of them, sensing rather than seeing the charges of electricity leaping from cloud to cloud. They circled in a long, slow spiral almost to the ground, and Allart sensed Donal's exasperation.

Are we going to have to land somewhere and wait out the storm? I would risk it, but Allart is unaccustomed to flying. . . .

I will risk what you risk, kinsman Donal.

Follow me, then. It is like dodging a rain of arrows, but I have done it more than once. . . . He dipped his wings, soared upward on a fast current, then darted swiftly between two clouds. *Quickly! A charge of lightning has just struck and there is a little time until another can build up!*

Allart felt the curious harsh tingle, and again they ran the gauntlet of darting lightning. He would have hung back, but he trusted Donal's *laran* to guide them through, Donal knowing where and precisely *when* the lightning would strike. Yet Allart felt cold chills strike him. They flew through a sudden small rain squall and he clung, drenched and icy, to the struts of the glider, his wet clothes freezing against his skin. He followed Donal on the long sickening swoop of downdraft, snatched up at the last minute to ride a current up and up till they hung circling above the heights of Castle Aldaran.

Donal instructed, a voice in his mind: *We cannot go down at once; there is too much charge on our gliders and clothing. When we put foot to ground it would knock us senseless. We must circle a while; soar, spread your hands to drain off the charge. . . .*

Allart, following instructions, drifting in lazy, dreamy circles, knew that Donal was in the hawk-persona again, projecting himself into the mind and thoughts of a great bird. Circling above the castle; Allart had leisure to look down at

Aldaran. In these months past it had become a second home to him, but now he beheld, with a sense of foreboding, a long caravan of riders winding up to the gates. Turning, Allart sent out a wordless cry of warning to Donal, as the caravan leader drew and brandished a sword, the sound of his yelling *almost* audible to Allart where he hung high above the battlements, above the steep tumbling waterfall.

"But there is no one there, kinsman," Donal said, troubled. "What ails you? What did you see? Truly, there is no one there."

Dazed, Allart blinked, a sudden giddiness making his wings flutter, and he tilted, automatically, to balance on the air. The road to Aldaran lay bare and deserted in the thickening twilight—neither riders, nor armed men, nor banners. His *laran* had shown him, only his *laran*, the foresight of what might, or might never, come to pass. It was gone.

Donal fluttered, swooped sidewise. His agitated alarm prompted Allart to follow him quickly. "We must get down, even if we are knocked senseless," he, shouted, then sent a swift, agitated thought to Allart: *There is another storm coming.*

But I see no clouds.

This storm needs no clouds, Donal thought in dismay. *This is the anger of my sister, generating lightning. The clouds will come. She would not strike us, knowing, but still we must get down as quickly as we can.*

He let himself drop on a swift current, shifting his weight on the glider so that he hung, vertically, using his weight and twisting his body like an acrobat to send the glider downward. Allart, more cautious and less experienced, followed a more conservative downward spiral, but he felt, still, the jolt of painful electricity as his feet touched the ground behind the castle. Donal, unbuckling his harness and shoving the glider in a jumble of ropes at the servant who came hurrying to take it, murmured, "What can it be? What has happened to upset or frighten Dorilys?" With a word of apology to Allart, he hurried away.

CHAPTER
EIGHTEEN

Renata, too, heard the muttering of the summer thunder, without thinking too much about it, as she moved through the castle halls on her way to Dorilys's apartments for their daily late-afternoon lesson.

Because Dorilys was younger than the novice workers in any Tower—and also because Dorilys had not, as they did, sought out this training of her own free will, pledging herself to endure uncomplaining all the discomforts and difficulties of the work—Renata had tried to make the teaching easy and pleasant, to devise games and amusements which would develop the girl's use of *laran* without tedious exercises to tire or bore her. Dorilys was still too young to be tested formally for telepathy which rarely developed much in advance of puberty, but other forms of *laran* were earlier to arise, and Renata judged that Dorilys had a considerable amount of clairvoyance and, probably, some telekinetic power in addition to her formidable gift of generating or controlling lightnings. So she had taught her with simple games: hiding sweets and toys and letting her find them with her *laran*, blindfolding her and having her find her way among intricate obstacle courses of furniture or unfamiliar parts of the castle; having her pick her own possessions, blindfolded, out of a jumble of similar ones, by the "feel" of her own magnetism attached to them. She was a quick pupil, and enjoyed the lessons so much that on two or three occasions Margali had actually controlled her rebellious young charge by threatening to deprive her of them, as she did with her music lessons, unless she satisfactorily finished the other tasks of which she was not so fond.

As far as Renata could tell, Dorilys was wholly without the two gifts which would have made her a trainable Tower worker: telepathy, defined as the ability to read or pick up deliberate thought; and empathy, or the ability to feel another's emotions or physical sensations in her own mind and body. But either might develop at adolescence—they often did—and if, at that time, she had some control of her own energy currents and flows, there would be less danger of the dreaded threshold sickness.

If it could only develop earlier—or later! It was the scourge of all the families with *laran* that these troubling facilities should develop at the same time the child was going through the physical and emotional upheavals of puberty. So many of those who bore these gifts found that the sudden onset of psi powers, developing sexuality, and the hormonal and temperamental liability of these times were an overload on body and brain. They developed enormous upheavals; sometimes crisis, convulsions, and even death followed. Renata herself had lost a brother to threshold sickness; no *laran* family survived unscathed.

Dorilys carried Aldaran blood on his father's side, not the relatively stable Delleray, which was akin to the Hastur. What Renata knew of the Aldaran and Rockraven lines did not make her entirely hopeful, but the more Dorilys knew of the energy currents in her body, the nerve flows and energon runs, the more likely she would be to survive these upheavals without undue difficulty.

Now, as she approached Dorilys's rooms, she sensed overtones of annoyance, weary patience (Renata herself considered the old *leronis* virtually a saint for putting up with this difficult and spoiled little girl), and the arrogance of Dorilys when she was crossed. Dorilys had seldom shown this pettish side to Renata, for she admired the young *leronis* and wanted her goodwill and liking. But she had never been disciplined firmly, and found it difficult to obey when her emotions went otherwise. It did not make it easier that, since Darren of Scathfell had been struck down, Margali was afraid of her charge, and could not conceal it.

I am afraid of her, too, Renata thought, *but she does not know it, and if I ever let her know, I will never again be able to teach her anything!*

Outside the door, she heard Dorilys's voice, just a petulant grumble. She heightened her sensitivity to hear Margali's firm answer.

"No, child. Your stitching is a disgrace. There will be no music lesson, nor any lesson with the lady Renata, until you have taken out all those clumsy stitches and done them properly." She added, in a coaxing tone, "You are not so clumsy as that; you are simply not trying. You can sew very neatly when you choose, but today you have decided you do not want to sew, and so you are deliberately making a mess of what you do. Now take out all of those stitches—no, use the proper ripping tool, child! Don't try to take them out with your fingers, or you will tear the cloth! Dorilys, what is the matter with you today?"

Dorilys said, "I don't like sewing. When I am Lady of Aldaran I will have a dozen sewing-women, and there is no reason I should learn. The lady Renata will not deprive me of my lesson because *you* say so!"

The rude and spiteful tone of her words decided Renata. The sewing was not important, but the self-discipline of working carefully and conscientiously at a task for which she had neither talent nor taste was a valuable teaching. Renata, a trained empath and monitor, felt as she opened the door the deep searing pain across Margali's forehead, the lines of weariness in the older woman's face. Dorilys was up to her old trick of giving Margali headaches when the older woman would not give her everything she wanted. Dorilys was sitting over the hated sewing, looking sweet and compliant, but Renata could see, as Margali could not, the triumphant smirk on her face as Renata came through the door. She flung the sewing to the floor, and rose, hurrying to Renata.

"Is it time for my lesson, cousin?"

Renata said coldly, "Pick up your sewing and put it away properly in its drawer—or better yet, sit down and finish it as you should."

"I don't have to learn to sew," Dorilys said, pouting. "My father wants me to learn those things which *you* can teach me!"

"What I can teach you best," Renata said firmly, "is to do what you have to do, when you have to do it, as well as you can do it, whether you want to do it or not. I do not care whether you can sew neatly or whether your stitches stagger like a *chervine* drunken on windfall apples"—Dorilys gave a small, triumphant giggle—"but you will not use your lessons with me to get the better of your foster-mother, or to evade what she wants you to do." She glanced at Margali, who was white with pain, and decided the time had come for a showdown.

"Is she giving you headaches again?"

Margali said faintly, "She knows no better."

"Then she shall learn better," Renata said, her voice icy. "Whatever it is that you are doing, Dorilys, you will release your foster-mother at once, and you will kneel and beg her pardon, and then *perhaps* I shall continue to teach you."

"Beg *her* pardon?" Dorilys said incredulously. "I won't!"

Something in the tilt of the small chin, though Dorilys was said to resemble her dead mother, suddenly made Renata think of Lord Aldaran himself. *She has her father's pride,* she thought, *but she has not yet learned to mask it in courtesy and expedient compromise and charm. She is still young and we can see this willfulness in all its naked ugliness. Already she does not care who she hurts, as long as she gets her own way. And to her, Margali is not much better than a servant. Nor am I; she obeys me because it pleases her.*

She said, "I am waiting, Dorilys. Beg Margali's pardon at once, and never do so again!"

"I will, if she will promise not to order me around anymore," Dorilys said sullenly.

Renata set her lips. So it was really a showdown, then. *If I back down, if I allow her to set her own terms, she will never obey me again. And this teaching may save her life. I do not want power over her, but if I am to teach her, she must learn obedience; to rely on my judgment until she can trust her own and control it.*

"I did not ask you on what terms you would beg her pardon," Renata said. "I simply told you to do it. I am waiting."

"Renata," Margali began.

But Renata said quietly, "No, Margali. Keep out of this. You know as well as I what the first thing is she must learn." To Dorilys she said, her voice a whiplash, using the trained command-voice, "Kneel down at once and beg pardon of your foster-mother!"

Dorilys dropped automatically to her knees; then, springing up, she cried out shrilly, "I have told you never to use command-voice on me! I will not allow it, and neither will my father! *He* would not see me humiliated by begging *her* pardon!"

Dorilys, Renata thought, *should have been thoroughly spanked before she was old enough, or strong enough, to get such exaggerated ideas of her own importance. But everyone has been afraid of her, and would not cross her. I do not blame them. I am afraid of her, too.*

She knew she faced an angry child whose anger had killed. *Yet I still have the upper hand. She is a child and she knows she is in the wrong, and I am a trained Tower technician and monitor. I must teach her, now, that I am stronger than she is. Because a day will come, when she is full-grown, when no one will be strong enough to control her; and before that time has come, she must be capable of controlling herself.*

Her voice was a whiplash. "Dorilys, your father gave me charge of you in all things. He told me that if you disobeyed, I had his leave to beat you. You are a big girl, and I would not like to humiliate you *that* way, but I tell you—unless you obey me at once, and beg pardon of your foster-mother, I shall do exactly that, as if you were a baby too small to listen to the voice of reason. Do as I tell you, and at once!"

"I will not," cried Dorilys, "and you cannot make me!" As if to echo her words, there was a harsh mutter of thunder outside the windows. Dorilys was too angry to hear it, but she sensed it, and flinched.

Renata thought, *Good. She is still a little afraid of her own power. She does not want to kill again. . . . .*

Then Renata felt across her own forehead the searing pain, like a tightening band . . . was she picking this up from Margali, with her own empath power? No; a quick look at the angry child showed her that Dorilys was taut, frowning, tense, concentrated with gritted anger. Dorilys was doing to her what she had done to Margali.

The little devil! Renata thought, torn between anger and unwilling admiration of the child's power and spirit. *If only all that strength and defiance can be turned to some useful purpose, what a woman she will make!* Focusing on her matrix—which she had never done before in Dorilys's presence, except to monitor her—Renata began to fight back, reflecting the energy at Dorilys. Slowly her own pain diminished and she saw the girl's face go white with strain. She kept her voice calm with an effort.

"See? You cannot serve me so, Dorilys. I am stronger than you. I do not want to hurt you, and you know it. Now obey me, and we will have our lesson."

She felt Dorilys strike out, angrily. Summoning all her own strength, she caught and held the child as if she had wrapped her physically in her arms, restraining body and mind, voice and *laran*. Dorilys tried to cry out, "Let me go," and discovered, in terror, that her voice would not obey, that she could not make a single move. . . . Renata, sensitive, empath, felt Dorilys's terror as if it were in her own body, and ached with pity for her.

But she must know that I am strong enough to protect her from her own impulses, that she cannot strike me down without thinking, as she did with Darren. She must know that she is safe with me, that I will not let her hurt herself, or anyone else.

Now Dorilys was really afraid. For a moment, watching her bulging eyes, the frantic small trapped movements of her muscles, Renata felt such pity that she could not endure it. *I do not want to hurt her, or to break her spirit, only to teach her . . . to protect her from her own terrible power! Someday she will know it, but now she is so frightened, poor little love. . . .*

She saw the small muscles in Dorilys's throat moving, struggling to speak, and released the hold on the child's voice; saw the tears starting from Dorilys's eyes.

"Let me go, let me go!"

Margali turned entreating eyes on her; she, too, was suffering, seeing her beloved nursling so helpless.

The old *leronis* whispered, "Release her, Lady Renata. She will be good; won't you, my baby?"

Renata said, very gently, "You see, Dorilys, I am still stronger than you. I will not allow you to hurt anyone, not even yourself. I know you do not really want to hurt or kill anyone for a moment's anger because you cannot have your own way in all things."

Dorilys began to sob, still held rigidly motionless in the grip of Renata's *laran*.

"Let me go, cousin, I beg you. I will be good. I will, I promise. I am sorry."

"It is not to me you must apologize, child, but to your foster-mother," Renata reminded her gently, releasing her hold on the little girl.

Dorilys dropped to her knees and managed to sob out, "I am sorry, Margali. I did not mean to hurt you; I was only angry," before she collapsed into incoherent crying.

Margali's thin fingers, gnarled now with age, gently stroked Dorilys's soft cheek. "I know that, dear heart. You would never hurt anyone; it is only that you do not think."

Dorilys turned to Renata and whispered, her eyes wide with horror, "I could have—could have done to you what I did to Darren—and I love you, cousin, I love you." She flung her arms around Renata, and Renata, still shaking, wrapped her arms around the thin, shaking child.

"Don't cry anymore, sweetheart. I won't let you hurt anyone. I promise," she said, holding her tight. "I won't ever let you hurt anyone." She took her kerchief, dried Dorilys's eyes. "Now put away your sewing properly, and we will have our lesson."

She knows, now, what she is capable of doing, and she is beginning to be wise enough to be afraid of it. If I can only manage to control her until she is wise enough to control herself!

Outside the window the storm had died to a distant rumble, and then to nothing, silence.

But, hours later, Renata faced Allart, shaking with long-suppressed tension and fear.

"I was stronger than she—but not enough," she whispered. "I was so frightened, kinsman!"

He said soberly, "Tell me about it. What are we to do with her?"

They were sitting in the drawing room of the small and luxurious suite of rooms which Lord Aldaran had ordered placed at Renata's disposal.

"Allart, I hated to frighten her that way! There should be a better way to teach her than fear!"

"I do not see what choice you had," Allart said soberly. "She must learn to fear her own impulses. There is more than one kind of fear." This discussion intensified many of his own old anxieties, roused by contact with Cassandra, by the long flight with Donal, the surroundings of the Tower at Tramontana. "My own battle was fought with fear, the kind of fear that paralyzed me and kept me from action. I find little that is good in that kind of fear. Until I mastered it, I could do nothing. But it seems to me that she knows too little of caution, and fear may have to serve her until she learns rational caution."

Renata repeated what she had thought during the battle of

wills. "If there were only some way to harness all that strength, what a woman she could be!"

"Well," said Allart, "that is, after all, why you are here. Don't be discouraged, Renata. She is very young and you have time."

"But not enough time," Renata said. "I fear puberty will come on her before the winter's end, and I do not know if that is enough time to teach her what she must learn, before that dreadful stress is placed on her."

"You can do no more than your best," Allart said, wondering if the images in his mind—a child's face circled by lightning, Renata's weeping in the vaulted room, her body swollen in pregnancy—were true images or fear alone. How could he distinguish between what would happen, what must happen, what might never happen?

Time is my enemy. . . . For everyone else it r͡ one way only, but for me it straggles and bends upon itself and wanders in a land where never is as real as now. . . .

But he banished self-pity and preoccupation again, looking into Renata's troubled eyes. She seemed so young to him, no more than a girl herself, and burdened with such dreadful responsibility! Searching for something to lighten her dread, he told her, "I spoke through the relays to Hali; I bear greetings and love for you from Arielle."

"Dear Arielle," Renata said. "I miss her, too. What news from Hali, cousin?"

"My brother has a son, born to his wife and therefore legitimate," Allart said. "And our king lies gravely ill and Prince Felix has summoned the Council. I know little more than that. Hali was attacked by incendiaries."

Renata shivered. "Was anyone hurt?"

"No, I think not. Cassandra would surely have told me if there had been any serious injuries. But they are all overwearied, working night and day," Allart said. Then he came out with what had been on his mind since he had spoken with his wife in the relays. "It weighs on me that I am here in safety when she must face such dangers! I should care for her and protect her, and I cannot."

"You face your own dangers," Renata said gravely. "Do not grudge her the strength to face her own. So she is full monitor now? I knew she had the talent, if she could endure the training."

"Still, she is a woman, and I am better fitted to endure danger and hardship."

"What troubles you, kinsman? Do you fear that if she is no longer dependent on you, she will not turn to you with love?"

Is it only that? Am I truly as selfish as that, that I want her weak and childlike, so that she will turn to me for strength and protection? He had picked up many things from Cassandra's mind in their long, intense rapport that she had not consciously told him, and which he was only now beginning to bring into awareness. The timid childlike girl, swayed by impulse, wholly dependent on his love and care, had become a strong Tower-trained monitor, a woman, a skilled *leronis*. She still loved him, deeply, passionately—their communion had left him no doubt of that—but he was no longer the only thing in her world. Love had taken its place among many forces now motivating her, and was not the only one she would act upon.

It was painful for him to realize this; more painful to realize how unhappy the thought made him.

Would I truly have wanted to keep her like that, timid, virginal, frightened, belonging to me alone, seeing the world only through my eyes, knowing only what I wanted her to know, being only what I desired in a wife? Custom, the traditions of his caste and his pride of family, cried out, *Yes, yes!* But the larger world he had begun to see prompted him to be ashamed of that.

Allart smiled ruefully, thinking this was not the first time Renata had interceded for his wife's own good. Now there were other roads for Cassandra besides the solitary one he had seen at the end of their love, that she must inevitably die in bearing his child. How could he resent anything which removed that continuing terror from his mind?

"I am sorry, Renata! You came to me for comfort, and as usual, you have ended by comforting and reassuring *me!* Indeed, I wish I knew more of Dorilys's *laran*, so I could advise you, but I agree with you that it will be a catastrophe if we cannot teach her in time. I saw Donal's in action today, and it is most impressive—more even than when he read which way the fire would move. Now that the fire season is starting," Allart suggested tentatively, "perhaps you could take her to the fire station, high on the peaks, and let Donal try to teach her a little of how to use this. He knows more of it than either you or I."

"I think perhaps I must do that," Renata agreed. "Donal, too, has survived the threshold, and it may give her confidence that she can do the same. I am glad that she does not read my thoughts; I do not want her to be terrified of what may come upon her with her womanhood, but she must be prepared to face that, too. . . . She wants more than anything else to learn to fly, as the boys in the castle do before they are anywhere near her age. Margali says it is unseemly for a girl, but since her *laran* has to do with the elements, she should learn to face them close at hand." Renata laughed and admitted, "I, too, would like to learn. Are you going to go all stiff and monkish on me and say it is unsuitable for a woman as for a young girl?"

Allart laughed, signaling with the gesture of a fencer who acknowledges a hit. "Are my years in Nevarsin still so plainly visible, cousin?"

"Dorilys will be so happy when I tell her," Renata said, laughing, and Allart realized again, suddenly, how very young she was. She had the self-imposed dignity and sober manners of the monitor, she had assumed formal manners and self-discipline to teach Dorilys, but she was really only a young girl herself who should be as lighthearted and carefree as Dorilys.

"Then, Donal shall teach you both to fly," he said. "I will speak with him, while you teach her to master a matrix and the art of levitating with it."

Renata said, "I think she is old enough to learn to use a matrix. Now she will learn quickly, and not waste her energies upon testing me."

"It will make it easier to go to the fire station," Allart told her, "since the ride is difficult, and many of the men who work there, watching for fires, find it simpler to fly to the peaks." He glanced self-consciously at the night beyond the windows. "Cousin, I must go; it is very late."

He rose, their hands touching with the fingertip-touch of telepaths, somehow more intimate than a handclasp. They were lightly in rapport, still, and as he looked down into her lifted face, he saw it aglow, warmed with passion. He was aware of her all over again as he had taught himself not to be; the close contact with Cassandra, barriers down, had broken the facade of monklike austerity, of indifference to women, which he kept so firmly in place. She blurred into a dozen women in that momentary touch, his *laran* showing him the possible and the likely, the known and the impossible; and almost without volition, before he was fully aware of what he was doing, he had drawn her into his arms, was crushing her to him, breathless.

"Renata, Renata—"

She met his eyes, with a troubled smile. They were in such close contact that it was impossible to conceal his sudden awareness and hunger for her, and her immediate and unashamed response to it.

"Cousin," she said gently. "What is it that you want? If I have roused you without meaning it, I am sorry. I would not knowingly have done so, simply to show my power over you. Or is it only that you are very much alone and longing for anyone who can give you comfort, and sympathy?"

He drew away from her, dazed, but struck by her calm, her complete lack of shame or confusion. He wished that he himself were as calm.

"I am sorry, Renata. Forgive me."

"For what?" she asked, her smile glinting deep in her eyes. "Is it an offense to find me desirable? If so, I hope I shall be offended that way many times." Her small hand closed on his. "It is not so serious a thing as that, cousin. I only wanted to know how seriously you intended it; that is all."

Allart muttered miserably, "I don't know." Confusion, loyalty to Cassandra, the memory of shame and disgust because he had been unable to resist the temptation of the *riyachiya* his father had pushed into his arms, overwhelmed him. Was it *this* which had led him to embrace Renata? The knowledge that she actually shared this upsurge of need and emotion confused him all over again.

A woman he could love without fear, one who was not wholly dependent on him. . . . Then came a shaming thought: *Or am I doing this because Cassandra is no longer wholly mine?*

She said, laughing up at him, "Why do you refuse for yourself a freedom you have given to her?"

He almost stammered, "I do not want to—to use you for my own need, as if you were no more than a *riyachiya*."

"Ah, no, Allart," she said in a small voice, clinging to him. "I, too, am alone and in need of comfort, kinsman. Only I have learned that it is nothing shameful to say so and acknowledge it, and you have not, that is all. . . ."

What Allart saw in her face shocked him with its openness.

He held her close to him, realizing suddenly that for all her strength, for all her invulnerable skill and wisdom, she was a girl, and frightened, and like himself facing troubles far beyond her ability to solve.

What have the men and women of the Domains done to one another, so that everything between us must be shrouded in fear or guilt for what has been or what may be. It is so rare that there can be simple kindliness or friendship between us, like this.

Holding Renata close in his arms, bending to kiss her very tenderly, he said almost in a whisper, "Let us comfort one another, then, cousin," and led her into the inner room.

CHAPTER
NINETEEN

Dorilys was wildly excited, chattering like a child half her age, but a little abashed when Margali dressed her in clothing borrowed from one of the young pages. Margali, too, was skeptical.

"Was this necessary, Lady Renata? She is hoyden enough already, without tearing about in boys' clothes!" She looked with frowning disapproval at Renata, who had borrowed a pair of breeches from the hall-steward's fifteen-year-old son.

Renata said, "She must learn to work with her *laran*, and to do that, she must confront the elements where they are, not where we might like them to be. She has worked very hard to master the matrix, so that I promised she might fly with Donal when she had done so."

"But is it really needful for her to wear those unseemly breeches? It seems not modest to me."

Renata laughed. "For flying? How modest would it be, do you think, if her gown should fill with the wind like a great sail and fly up about her ears? Those unseemly breeches seem to me the most modest garment she could possibly wear for flying!"

"I had not thought of that," the old *leronis* confessed, laughing. "I, too, longed to fly when I was a young girl. I wish I were coming with you!"

"Come along, then," Renata invited. "Surely you have skill enough to learn to control the levitators!"

Margali shook her head. "No, my bones are too old. There is a time to learn such things, and when that time is past, it is too late. It's too late for me. But go, Renata. Enjoy it—and you, too, darling," she added, kissing Dorilys's cheek. "Is your tunic fastened? Have you a warm scarf? It is sure to be cold on the heights."

Despite her brave words, Renata felt uneasy. Not since she was five years old had she showed the shape of her limbs in any public place. When they joined Allart and Donal in the courtyard, they, too, seemed abashed and did not look at her.

Renata thought, *I hoped Allart had more sense! I have shared his bed, and yet he looks everywhere but at me, as if it came as a great surprise to him that I had legs like everyone else! How ridiculous is custom!*

But Dorilys was quite without self-consciousness, strutting in her breeches, demanding to be noticed and admired.

"See, Donal! Now I will be able to fly as well as any boy!"

"And has Renata taught you to practice with the matrix, raising and lowering other objects before you tried it with yourself?"

"Yes, and I am good at it. Didn't you say I was good at it, Renata?"

Renata smiled. "Yes, I think she has a talent for it, which a little practice will sharpen into skill."

While Donal showed his sister the mechanism of the glider-toys, Allart came to help Renata with her straps. They stood side by side, watching Dorilys and her brother. The night they had spent together had cemented and strengthened their friendship; it had not really changed its nature. Renata smiled up at Allart, acknowledging his help, realizing with pleasure that she thought of him as she always did, as a friend, not a lover.

I do not know what love is. I do not think I really want to know. . . .

She was fond of Allart. She had liked giving him pleasure. But both had been content to leave it there, a single shared impulse of loneliness, and not to build it into anything it was not. Their needs were basically too different for that.

Donal was now showing Dorilys how to read the air currents carefully, how she could use the focus of her matrix to amplify them and make them more perceptible to her senses. Renata listened carefully; if lads in the Hellers mastered these tricks before they were ten years old, surely a trained matrix worker could do it, too!

Donal made them all practice a while on the flat windswept area behind the castle, running with the winds and letting themselves rise on the currents, soaring high and circling, swooping down. Finally he declared himself satisfied and pointed to the peak far above them, where the fire station commanded a view of the whole valley beyond Caer Donn.

"Do you think you can fly so far, little sister?"

"Oh, yes!" Dorilys was flushed and breathless, little tendrils of fine copper hair escaping from the long braid at her back, her cheeks whipped to crimson with the wind. "I love it. I would like to fly forever!"

"Come, then. But stay close to me. Don't be afraid; you can't fall, not as long as you keep your awareness of the air currents. Now, lift your wings, like this—"

He watched her step off and soar upward on a long rising current, rising and rising over a long gulf of sky. Renata followed, feeling the draft take her and toss her high, seeing Allart rising behind her. Dorilys caught a downdraft and was circling, hovering like a hawk, but Donal gestured her onward.

Higher and higher they flew, rising through a damp white cloud, emerging above it; now hovering and turning, soaring down until they came to rest on the peak. The fire watch station was an ancient structure of cobblestone and timbers; the ranger, a middle-aged man, long and lean, with pale gray eyes and the weathered look of one who spends much of his time peering into unfathomable distances, came to greet them, in surprise and pleasure.

"Master Donal! Has Dom Mikhail sent you with a message for me?"

"No, Kyril; it is only that we wished my sister to see how the fire station is managed. This is Lord Allart Hastur, and the lady Renata Leynier, *leronis* of Hali."

"You are welcome," the man said, courteously, but without undue servility; as a skilled professional, he owed deference to no one. "Have you ever been up to the peak before, little lady?"

"No. Father thought it too far for me to ride; also, he said you were too busy here during the fire season for guests."

"Well, he was right," Kyril said, "but I will be glad to show you what I can as I have leisure. Come inside, my dear."

Inside the station were relief maps of the entire valley, a replica in miniature of the tremendous full-circle panorama seen from the windows of the building on every side. He pointed out to her the cloud-cover over parts of the valley, the areas marked on his map which had been burned over in recent seasons, the sensitive areas of resin-trees which had to be watched closely for any stray spark.

"What is that light flashing, Master Kyril?"

"Ah, you have sharp eyes, little one. It is a signal to me, which I must answer." He took a mirrored-glass device with a small mechanical cover which could be opened and closed swiftly, and stepping to the opened window, began to flash a patterned signal into the valley. After a moment the flashing in the valley resumed. Dorilys started to ask a question, but he motioned her to be quiet, then bent over his map, marked it with chalk, and turned back to her.

"Now I can explain to you. That man signaled to me that he was building a cookfire there, while the herdmen take their count of his cattle. It is a precaution so that I will not think a forest fire has begun and call men together to fight it. Also, if the smoke remains more than a reasonable time for a herdman's cookfire, I will know it is out of control and can dispatch someone to help with it before it spreads too far. You see"—he gestured in a circle all around the fire-tower—"I must know at every moment where every wisp of smoke is, in all this country, and what causes it."

"You have the chemicals from Tramontana?" Donal asked.

"The first lot reached me just in time to stop a serious outbreak in the creek-bed there," he said, indicating it on the map. "Yesterday a consignment was brought here, and others stored at the foot of the peak. It is a dry year, and there is some danger, but we have had only one bad burn, over by Dead Man's Peak."

"Why is it called Deak Man's Peak?" Dorilys asked.

"Why, I do not know, little lady; it was so called in my father's time and my grandfather's. Perhaps at some time, someone found a dead man there."

"But why would anyone go there to die?" Dorilys asked, looking up at the far crags. "To me it looks more like a hawk's nest."

"There were hawks there once," Kyril said, "for I climbed to take some when I was a young man. But that was long, long ago." He looked at the distant sea of smoke and flame; to the others it was blurred by distance. "There have been no hawks there for years. . . ."

Renata interrupted the conversation, saying, "Dorilys, can you tell where the fire on that slope will move next?"

Dorilys blinked, her face going blank, staring into the distance. After a moment she gestured, and for a moment Allart, astonished, realized she was speaking so rapidly it was gibberish.

"What, child?" Renata asked, and Dorilys came back to herself.

She said, "It is so hard to say it in words, when I can *see* the fire where it was and where it is and where it is moving, from its start to its finish."

Merciful Avarra, Allart thought. *She sees it in three dimensions of time—past and present and future. Is it any wonder we find it hard to communicate with her!* The second thought that hit him, hard, was that this might somehow have some bearing on his own curious gift . . . or curse!

Dorilys was trying to focus down, to search, struggling, for words to communicate what she saw.

"I can see where it started, there, but the winds drove it down the watercourse, and it turned—look—into the. . . I can't say it! Into those net things at the edge of the windstream. Donal," she appealed, "*you* see it, don't you?"

He came and joined her at the window. "Not quite what you see, sister. I think perhaps no one sees it quite as you do; but can you see where it will move next?"

"It has moved—I mean, it will move *there*, where they will have the men all ganged together to fight it," she said. "But it will come there only because *they* come. It can feel—No, that isn't right! There aren't any words." Her face twisted and she looked as if she were almost crying. "My head hurts," she said plaintively. "Can I have a drink of water?"

"There is a pump behind the door," the man Kyril said. "The water is good; it comes from a spring behind the station. Be sure to hang up the cup when you have drunk, little lady." As she went in quest of her drink, Renata and Donal exchanged long looks of amazement.

Renata thought, *I have learned more about her* laran *now in a few minutes than I have learned in half a season. I should have thought to come here before.*

Kyril said in a low voice, "You know, of course, that there are not any men fighting the fire now; they controlled it and left it to burn out along the lower crags. Yet she saw them. I have seen nothing like this since the sorceress Alarie came here once with a fire-talisman to gain command of a great fire, when I was a young man. Is the child a sorceress, then?"

Renata, disliking the ancient word smacking so much of superstition, said, "No; but she has *laran*, which we are trying to train properly, to see these things. She took to the gliders like a young bird to the air."

"Yes," Donal said. "It took me far longer to master them. Perhaps she sees the currents more clearly than I can. For all we know, they are solid to her, something she can almost touch. I think Dorilys could learn to use a fire-talisman; the forge-folk have them, to bring metals from the ground to their forges."

Renata had heard of this. The forge-folk had certain especially adapted matrixes, which they used for mining and for that purpose only; a technique both more crude and more developed than the highly technical mining methods of the Towers. She had the Tower technician's distrust of matrix methods developed in this catch-as-catch-can, pragmatic way, without theory.

Kyril looked into the valley, saying, "The cookfire is out," and erased the chalk mark on his map. "One less trouble, then. That valley is all as dry as tinder. May I offer you some refreshment, sir? My lady?"

"We have brought food with us," Allart said. "Rather, we would be honored if you would share our meal." He began to unwrap the packages of dried fruit, hard-baked bread, and dried meat that they had brought.

"I thank you," Kyril said. "I have wine here, if I may offer you a cupful, and some fresh fruit for the little lady."

They sat near the window so that Kyril could continue his watch. Dorilys asked, "Are you alone here all the time?"

"Why, no, lady. I have an apprentice who helps me, but he has gone down the valley today to see his mother, so for the day I am alone. I had not thought I would be entertaining guests." He drew out his clasp-knife from his heavy boot and began to peel her an apple, spiraling the peel into delicately cut designs. She watched with fascination, while Renata and Allart watched the clouds moving slowly across the valley far below them, casting strange shadows. Donal came and stood behind them.

Renata asked him, in a low voice, "Can you, too, sense where the storms will move?"

"A little, now, when I can see them spread out this way before me. I think perhaps that when I am watching a storm I move a little outside of time, so that I see the *whole* storm, from start to finish, as Dorilys saw the whole fire a little while ago." He glanced back at Dorilys, who was eating her apple, chattering with the ranger. "But somehow at the same time I see the lightnings in sequence, one after another, so that I know where each one will strike and which first, because I can see the pattern of where they move *through* time. That is why, sometimes, I can control them—but only a little. I cannot *make* them strike anywhere, as my sister does," he added, lowering his voice so that it would not carry to the little girl. "I can only, now and again, divert them so that they will *not* strike where they have already begun to move."

Allart listened, frowning, thinking of the sensitive divisions of time which this gift took. Donal, picking up his thoughts, said, "I think this must be a little like your gift, Allart. You move outside time, too; do you not?"

Allart said, troubled, "Yes, but not always into *real* time. Sometimes, I think, a kind of probability time, which will never happen, depending on the decisions of many, many other people, all crisscrossing. So that I see only a little part of the pattern of what will be or what *may* be. I don't think a human mind could ever learn to sort it all out."

Donal wanted to ask some questions about whether Allart had ever tested his gift under *kirian,* one of the telepathic drugs in use in the Towers, for it was well known that *kirian* somehow blurred the borders between mind and mind so that telepathy was easier, time not quite so rigid. But Renata was following her own line of question, her mind again on her charge.

"You all saw how the fire troubled her," she said. "I wonder if that has something to do with the way she uses her gift—or strikes. Because in anger or confusion, she no longer sees a pattern of time clearly; for her there is nothing but that one moment, of rage, or anger, or fear. . . . She cannot see it as only one of a progression of moments. You spoke of a fever she had as a child, when storms raged around the castle for days, and you wondered what dreams or delirium prompted them. Possibly there was some damage to the brain. Fevers often impair *laran.*" She considered for a long moment, watching the slow inexorable drifting of the storm clouds below them, which now masked a sizable part of the valley floor.

Dorilys came up behind them, winding her arms around Renata like an affectionate kitten trying to climb into a lap.

"Is it me you are talking about? Look down there, Renata. See the lightning inside the cloud?"

Renata nodded, knowing the storm was just beginning to build up enough electrical potential to show lightnings; she herself had not seen lightning yet.

"But there are lightnings in the air even when there are no clouds and no rain," Dorilys said. "Can't you see them, Renata? When I use them, I don't really *bring* them, I just *use* them." She looked sheepish, guilty, as she added, "When I gave Margali a headache, and tried to do it with you, I was using those lightnings I couldn't *see*."

Merciful gods, Renata thought, *this child is trying to tell me, without knowing the words, that what she does is to tap the electrical potential field of the planet itself!* Donal and Allart, picking up the thought, turned startled eyes on her, but Renata did not see them, suddenly shuddering.

"Are you cold, cousin?" the child asked solicitously. "It is so warm. . . ."

All the gods at once be thanked that at least she cannot read minds as well. . . .

Kyril had come over to the window, looking with concentrated attention at the curdled mass of gray that was the storm center and the lightnings just beginning to be visible within it. "You asked about my work, little lady. This is a part of it, to watch where the storm center moves, and see if it strikes anywhere. Many fires are set by lightning, though sometimes no smoke can be seen for a long time after." He added, with an apologetic glance at the noblemen and Renata, "I think perhaps that some unknown forefather endowed me with a little foresight, because sometimes when I see a great strike I know that it will later blaze up. And so I watch it with a little more care, for some hours."

Renata said, "I would like to inquire into your ancestors, and find how even this diluted trace of *laran* came into your blood."

"Oh, I know *that*," Kyril said, again almost apologetic. "My mother was a *nedestro* of the old lord of Rockraven's brother—not he who rules there now, but the one before him."

So how can I say there is any laran *gift which is all evil, without potential use for good?* Renata thought. Kyril had turned his own small inherited gift to a useful, skilled, and harmless profession.

But Donal was following his own thoughts.

"Is it so, then, Kyril? Why, then, we are kinsmen."

"True, Master Donal, though I never sought to bring myself to their notice. Saving your presence, they are a proud people, and my mother was too humble for them. And I have no need of anything they could give."

Dorilys slid her hand confidingly through Kyril's. "Why, then, we are related, too, kinsman," she said, and he smiled and patted her cheek.

"You are like your mother, little one; she had your eyes. If the gods will, you will have inherited her sweet voice, as you have her pretty ways."

Renata thought, *How she charms everyone, when she is not being proud or sullen! Aliciane must have had that sweetness.*

"Come here, Dorilys," she said. "Look at the storm; can you see where it will move?"

"Yes, of course," Dorilys narrowed her eyes and squinted her face in a comical way, and Allart glanced at Renata for permission to question her pupil.

"Is its course fixed, then, not to be changed at all?"

Dorilys said, "It's *awfully* hard to explain, kinsman. It could go this way or that, if the wind changed, but I can only see one or two ways the wind could change. . . ."

"But the path is fixed?"

"Unless I tried to move it," she said.

"*Could* you move it?"

"It's not so much that *I* could move it," Dorilys frowned in fierce concentration as she fumbled for words she had never been taught and did not know existed. "But I can see all the ways it *could* move. Well, let me show you," she said.

Allart, sliding lightly into rapport with her mind, began to sense and see the thick gray high-piled storm clouds as she saw them, everywhere at once. Yet he could trace where the storm was now, where it had been, and at least four ways it *might* be.

"But what will be cannot be altered; can it, little cousin? It follows its own laws; does it not? You have nothing to do with it."

She said, "There are places I could move it and places I could *not*, because the conditions are not right for it to go there. It's like a stream of water," she said, fumbling. "If I put rocks in it, it would go around the rocks, but it could go either way. But I couldn't make it jump out of the stream-bed, or run back uphill; do you understand, cousin? I can't explain," she said plaintively. "It makes my head ache. Let me *show* you. See?" She pointed to the enormous anvil-shaped storm mass below. His sensitivity keyed into hers, he suddenly saw with his own gift, the probable track of the storm with others less probable *through* and *over* the most likely path; it faded into the nothingness of total unlikeliness and then impossibility at the far outer edges of his percep-tions. Then Dorilys's strange gift was *his own* gift, expanded, altered, strangely different, but basically the same: to see all the *possible* futures, the places where the storm *might* strike, the places where it might *not* because of its own nature. . . .

And she could choose between them like himself, to a very limited degree because of the forces outside herself which moved them. . . .

As I saw my brother on the throne, or dead, within seven years. There was no third choice, that he could choose to re-main content as Lord Elhalyn, because of what he is. . . .

He felt almost overwhelmed by this sudden insight into the nature of time, and probability, and of his own *laran*. But Renata was more practical.

"Can you actually control it, then, Dorilys? Or just tell where it will go?" Allart followed her thought. Was this sim-ply precognition, foreknowledge, or was it like the power of levitation, moving an inanimate object?

"I can move it anywhere it *could* go," she said. "It could go there or there"—she pointed—"but not *there* because the wind couldn't change that fast, or that hard. See?" Turning back to Kyril, she asked, "Is it likely to start a fire now?"

"I hope not," the man said soberly, "but if the storm should move down toward High Crags there, where the resin-trees grow so thickly, we could have a bad fire."

"Then we will not let it strike there," Dorilys said, laugh-ing. "It won't hurt anything if the lightning strikes down there, near Dead Man's Peak, where it is already all burned over; will it?" As she spoke a great blue-white bolt of lightning ripped from cloud to earth, striking Dead Man's Peak with a searing blaze, leaving a glare of sparks on all their eyes. After a second or two they heard the great crash of the thun-der rolling over them.

Dorilys laughed in delight. "It is better than the fire-toys the forge-folk set off for us at midwinter!" she cried, and

again the great flare of lightning arched across the sky, and
again, while she laughed excitely, pleased with the new ability to do what she would with the gift she had borne, not
knowing it, all her life. Again and again the great blue-white,
green-white bolts ripped and flamed down on Dead Man's
Peak, and Dorilys shrieked with hysterical laughter.

Kyril stared at her, his eyes wide with awe and dread.
"Sorceress," he whispered. "Storm queen. . . ."

Then the lightnings died, the thunders rumbled and rolled
into silence, and Dorilys swayed and leaned against Renata,
her eyes dark circled, smudged with fatigue. Again she was a
child exhausted, white and worn. Kyril lifted her tenderly
and carried her down a short flight of stairs. Renata followed
him. He laid her on his own bed.

"Let the little one sleep," he said.

As Renata bent over the child to pull off her shoes, Dorilys
smiled up at her wearily and was at once asleep.

Donal looked at her, questioning, as she came back to
them.

"She is already asleep," Renata said. "She could not fly
like this; she has exhausted herself."

"If you wish," Kyril said diffidently, "you and the little
lady can have my bed, *vai domna*, and tomorrow, when the
sun comes out, I can flash a signal for them to bring riding
animals for you to return home that way."

"Well, we shall see," Renata said. "Perhaps when she has
slept a while, she will have recovered enough to fly back to
Aldaran." She moved behind him to the window, watching as
his brow ridged in a worried frown.

"Look. The lightning has struck there, in that dry canyon,"
he pointed. Renata, with all her extended perception, could
not see the slightest wisp of smoke, but she did not doubt that
he saw it. "There is no sun for me to flash a signal. By the
time it comes out again the fire will have taken hold there,
but if I could reach anyone—"

Allart thought, *We should have telepaths stationed on these
watchtowers, so that they could reach others stationed below
at such times. If someone were standing by in the nearest village, armed with a matrix, Kyril or another could signal to
have the fire put out.*

But Donal was thinking of the requirements of the moment. He said, "You have the fire-fighting chemicals I
brought from Tramontana. I will fly there in my glider and

spread the chemicals where the lightning struck. That will damp the fire before it really starts."

The old ranger looked at him, troubled. "Lord Aldaran would be ill pleased if I let his foster-son run such a danger!"

"It is no longer a question of *letting* me, old friend. I am a grown man, and my foster-father's steward, and responsible for the well-being of all these people. They shall not be ravaged by fire if I can prevent it." Donal turned, breaking into a run, down the stairs and through the room where Dorilys still lay in her stunned sleep. Kyril and Renata hurried after him. He was already buckling himself into his flying-harness.

"Give me the chemicals, Kyril."

Reluctantly the ranger handed over the sealed water-cylinder, the packet of chemicals. When mixed together, they would expand into a foam that could cover and smother an extraordinary expanse of flames.

As he moved toward the open space, before he could break into the run of takeoff, she stopped him.

"Donal, let me go, too!" Would they really let him fly alone into such danger?

"No," he said gently. "You are too new to flying, Renata. And there is some danger."

She said aloud, and knew her voice was shaking, "I am not a court lady, to be sheltered against all dangers. I am a trained Tower worker, and I am used to sharing all the dangers I see!"

He reached out, took her shoulders gently between his hands. "I know," he said softly, "but you have not the experience of flying; I should be hindered by having to stop and make certain you knew precisely what to do, and there is need for haste. Let me go, cousin." His hands on her shoulders tightened and he pulled her into a quick, impulsive embrace.

"There is not as much danger as you think, not for me. Wait for me, *carya*." He kissed her, swiftly.

She stood, still feeling the touch of his lips, watching him run toward the edge of the cliff, wings tilted to catch the wind. Donal soared off, and she stood shading her eyes against the glare, watching the glider shrink to hawk-size, sparrow-size, a pinpoint dipping behind the clouds. When it was gone she blinked hard, turned, and made her way inside the fire station.

Allart was standing at the windows, watching intently. He

said as she joined him, "Since Dorilys showed me what she sees, I am somehow a little more able to control my foresight. It is a matter of shifting the perceptions for all times and seeing which is most real. . . ."

"I am so glad, cousin," she said, and meant it, knowing how painfully Allart had struggled with this curse of *laran*. But in spite of her very real concern for Allart, who was her kinsman, her lover, her friend, she discovered that she had no time to think of Allart now. All of her emotional tension was stretched outward, focused on that small distant fleck which was Donal's glider, hovering high above the valley, dipping slowly, slowly down, skirting the edge of the storm-pattern. And suddenly, all her emotion, all the empathic *laran* of a Tower-trained monitor, surged into awareness, identity, and she *was* Donal. She was . . .

. . . flying high above the valley, sensing the taut energy-net currents strung across the sky as if they were banners flying from the heights of the castle, snapped in the wind, trailing forces. He spread his fingertips to drain off the tingle of the electricity, hovering, soaring, all his attention focused on the spot on the forest floor that Kyril had pointed out to him.

A thin wisp of smoke, curling, half concealed by leaves and the long gray-green needles of evergreens, lying fallen and crisped by frost and sun on the ground. . . . It could smolder there unseen for days before blazing into a fire that could ravage all of the valley. . . . It had been well that he came. This was all too near the estate of High Crags which his foster-father had given him.

I am a poor man. I have nothing to offer Renata even if such a lady would be my wife . . . nothing but this poor estate, here in fire-country and ravaged again and again by fire. I had thought I could marry, establish a household. Yet now it seems to me all too little to offer my dear lady. Why do I think she would have me?

(Standing frozen, intent at the wide windows, Renata shivered, not really *there* at all. Allart, turning to speak, saw it and let her be.)

Again, Renata's awareness merged with his, Donal dropped down and down, hanging from the struts of the glider. He circled the small trailing wisp of smoke, studying it, unaware of how the storm above him moved and drifted and rumbled. The glider was dropping swiftly now, the wide wings slowing his fall just enough so that he could land on his feet, fall forward, braking his fall with his outstretched hands. He did not bother to unfasten the glider harness as he pulled the sealed water-cylinder from its place under the strut. After tearing it open with his teeth he tucked it under his arm while he ripped open the small packet of chemicals; then he dropped the chemicals into the water, held the pliable cylinder over the wisp of smoke, and watched as the green foam bubbled and surged out, foaming up and up endlessly, aiming and spilling around the forest floor, soaking quickly into the ground. The smoke was gone; only the last remnants of the oozing foam remained. Like all fire-fighters, Donal was astonished anew at how quickly a fire, once controlled at its source, could subside as if it had never been.

The most fickle of the elements, easiest to call, most difficult to control. . . . The words came from nowhere in his mind and were as swiftly gone again. He folded the limp bag which had once been the water-cylinder, its impermeable material still smelling faintly of chemical slime, and tucked it under one of the ropes of the glider harness.

This was so simple; why did Renata fear for me? Looking into the sky, he knew. The clouds had gathered again around him, and it was certainly no weather for flying. There was no rain here, the air still heavy and sullen, oppressive and thick; but above him on the slopes of Dead Man's Peak, the storm raged, heavy rain and black clouds laced intermittently by flares of lightning arching from cloud to the waiting ground. He was not really afraid, for he had been flying since he was a small boy. Frowning, he stood for a moment studying sky and air currents, the pattern of the storm, the winds, trying to calculate his best chances of return to the fire station with the least danger or difficulty.

At least the storm on Dead Man's Peak has drowned the last vestiges of the fire. . . . Scanning the sky, Donal whipped off the glider harness and tucked the contraption, wings folded, under his arm. Walking very far with the wings trailing offered too much drag, and there was also the danger of catching and snagging them on something. He climbed a small, steep hillside from where he knew he could catch a wind, strapped himself into the glider harness again, and tried to take off. But the winds were swirling, capricious. Twice he made a short run, tried to catch enough wind in his wings to take off, but each time the wind shifted around and spilled him, once with a painful tumble to the ground.

Picking himself up, bruised, Donal swore. Was Dorilys playing again with winds and air currents, shifting wind and magnetic fields without knowing he was down there? No, surely, Renata and Allart would keep her from trying any such tricks. But if she were still sleeping, still enormously nerved up from the excitement of the day, her first flight, the effort of controlling her gift? Did her dreaming mind shift winds and air at will, then?

Without enthusiasm he contemplated the distant peak where the fire station stood. Was he going to have to climb up there on foot? He could hardly do that before dark. The road was good enough, for supplies had to be brought up to the fire station every tenday; he had heard this road had been matrix-surfaced, in the time of Dom Mikhail's grandfather. But, still, he did not want to climb it. The best that could be said for it was that it was less trouble than scrambling up a rocky hillside. Yet if he could not catch a wind steady enough to lift him, with the aid of his matrix crystal, he must trudge up that road, carrying the glider under his arm!

He looked again at the sky, heightening his sensitivity to wind and air. The only wind steady enough to bear him up was blowing steadily toward the storm over Dead Man's Peak. Yet if he could ride up on this wind, catching a crosscurrent somewhere that would carry him back toward the fire station. . . there was some risk to it, yes. If the wind was too brisk, he would be carried along into the storm raging there.

Yet if he took the time to climb all that way, it would be dark and dangerous. He must risk the wind blowing toward the peak. He took a little extra time to make certain his straps were snug and secure, inspected the struts and their fastenings, and finally discarded the plastic fabric of the water-container. It could be reclaimed some other time, and even a little extra weight might make the difference in what was going to be a fairly tricky flying maneuver. Then he ran toward the edge of the hill, focusing on his matrix, letting the wind and the force of levitation bear him upward; felt, with relief, the wind catch in the broad edge-planes of his glider and carry him up and outward, along on the rising current of the solid draft.

He rose, soaring high, racing along on the wind with such

force that every strut and rope of the glider shuddered and he could hear a high singing note above the roar of wind past his ears. He felt a curious, cold, exhilarating fear, his senses strained to their limit, taken up with the delight of soaring on the wind. *If I fall I could be smashed—but I will not fall!* Like a hawk in its native element he circled, looking down at the valley below, the ragged rents in the clouds over the fire station, the thickly piled storm clouds, sullen with lightning, over Dead Man's Peak. Circling again, he caught a cross-draft which would take him in the general direction of the fire station; he tilted his wings into it, a bird in his element, every sense given into the ecstasy of the flight. He was not aware of Renata's mind linked with his, but he found himself thinking, *I wish Renata could see this as I see it.* Somehow in his mind he linked the ecstasy of that soaring long glide, the rush of wind past the struts, with the moment, all too brief, when he had held her and felt her mouth on his own. . . .

Lightning crackled ominously, the metal clips at the end of the struts gleamed, suddenly, with bluish light, and Donal, tingling with undischarged electricity, realized that the storm had begun to move, swiftly on the wind, down the valley toward the fire station. He could not even descend; carrying this much electrical charge, he could not touch ground or he would be killed. He must circle until the charge was drained away. Through the sudden thunder, he realized that he was very much afraid. The storm was moving the wrong way. It should have drifted out past Dead Man's Peak and now it was turning back. Suddenly he remembered the day of Dorilys's birth, the day of his mother's death. The storm had been wrong then, too! Dorilys, asleep, dreaming dreams of terror and power, reaching out to tap the forces of the storm. But why would she focus them on him, even in sleep?

Does she know that she is no longer the only female creature in my thoughts and in my heart? He fought to keep his place in the air, despite the stubborn downdraft that sought to carry him downward to the open space behind the fire station. He knew he must circle once more. Again the crackle of thunder in the air deafened him, and gusts and spurts of cold rain chilled him. Once again he felt the lightning moving around him, and with every last atom of his *laran* he reached out, *twisted* something, thrust it *elsewhere*. . . .

It was gone. Thunder crackled through his body and he fell like a stone, with his last strength catching a current which

could bring him in at the very edge of the open space behind
the fire station. Or would he miss it, go tumbling down the
side of the mountain to wind up, smashed, far below? Half-
unconscious, he saw someone running below him, running
toward where he would land. He fell heavily, staggering. His
feet touched ground, and Renata caught him in her arms and
held him, drenched and senseless against her for a moment
before his weight overwhelmed her and they fell, together.

Wrung, exhausted, Renata held the unconscious Donal
against her breast. His face was cold with rain and for a terrified moment she did not know if he were alive, then she felt
the warmth of his breath against her, and her own world
started to move again.

*Now do I know what it is to love. To see nothing ahead
except the one . . . to know, now, kneeling here as he lies
stricken in my arms, that if he had been killed, in a very real
sense I would have died here, too. . . .* Her fingers fumbled
on the straps, loosening the miraculously undamaged glider.
But his eyes opened; he pulled her down to him and their lips
met, in a sudden, profound quiet. They neither saw nor
heeded Allart and Kyril watching them. Once and for all,
now and forever, they knew they belonged to one another.
Whatever happened afterward would simply be confirmation
of what they already knew.

CHAPTER
TWENTY

As long as she lived, Renata knew, nothing in mind or memory would ever match the splendor of this season—high summer in the Hellers, and Donal at her side. Together they flew along the long valleys in their gliders, soaring from peak to peak, hiding beneath the crags from the summer storms, or lay side by side in the hidden canyons, hour after hour, watching clouds move across the sky, and turning from the sky to the green earth and to one another.

Day by day Dorilys came nearer to mastery of her strange gift, and Renata began to be more optimistic. Perhaps all would be well. Probably Dorilys should never risk bearing a child, certainly never a girl child, but she might survive puberty undamaged. In the flood of her own love, Renata felt she could not endure to rob Dorilys of that promise, that hope.

And I mocked Cassandra! Merciful Avarra, how young I was, how ignorant!

On one of the long, brilliant summer afternoons, they lay hidden in a green valley, looking up at the heights where Dorilys, with a few of the lads from the castle, was soaring like a bird, wheeling on the updrafts.

Donal said, "I am skilled enough with a glider, but I never could ride the winds as she does. I would not have dared. None of the boys is half so skilled or so fearless."

"None of them has her gift," Renata said, looking up into the dizzying violet depths of the sky, and blinking with sudden tears. Sometimes it seemed to her, in this first and last summer of their love, that Dorilys had become her own child, the girl child she knew she would never dare to bear to her lover;

225

but Dorilys was theirs, theirs to teach and train, theirs to love.

Donal leaned over suddenly and kissed her, and then touched her eyelashes with a light finger. "Tears, beloved?"

Renata shook her head. "I have been looking too long into the sky, watching her."

"How strange this is," Donal said, taking her hands in his and kissing the slender fingers. "I had never thought—" His voice trailed off, but they were so deeply in rapport that Renata could follow his unspoken thoughts.

I never thought love would come to me like this. I knew that someday, soon or late, my foster-father would find me a wife, but to love like this . . . it does not seem real. I must somehow find courage to tell him, sometime. . . . Donal tried hard to imagine himself going against custom and civilized behavior, walking into his foster-father's study and saying to him, "Sir, I have not waited for you to find me a bride. There is a woman I wish to marry. . . ." He wondered if Dom Mikhail would be very angry with him; or, worse, if he would blame Renata.

But if he knew that there would never again be any happiness in life for me, except with Renata. . . . He wondered if Dom Mikhail could possibly ever have known what it was to love. *His* marriages had been properly arranged by his family; what could he possibly know of the emotion that swept them both up this way? He felt the wind blow cold on him and shivered, feeling a distant premonitory breath of thunder.

"No," Renata said. "She knows the storm currents too well; she is not in any danger. Look! All the lads are following her now—" She pointed upward at the line of children, tipping and circling on the wings of the wind, arrowing back like a flight of wild birds toward the distant high crags of Aldaran. "Come, dear love. The sun will set soon, and the winds grow so strong at sunset; we must go back and join them."

His hands trembled as he helped her to fasten the straps of her glider.

She whispered, "Of all the things you have shared with me, Donal, perhaps this is the most wonderful. I do not know if any other woman in the Hellers has ever been able to fly like this." Donal saw, in the gathering sunset crimsons, the flicker of a tear on her lashes; but without a rebuff, she evaded his thoughts, tipping the wings of her glider and running away down the long valley, catching a swift draft and soaring up, up, and away from him, to hang on a long drift of air until he flew at her side.

That evening in the hall, when Dorilys had made her good nights and been sent away, Aldaran gestured to Allart and Renata to remain. The musicians were playing and some of the house-folk were dancing to the sound of the harps, but Dom Mikhail frowned as he spread out a letter.

"Look here. I sent an embassy to Storn to open negotiations for a marriage with Dorilys. Last year they were willing to speak of nothing else, but this year I receive only a reply that since Dorilys is so young, perhaps we should speak of it again when she is of an age to be married. I wonder—"

Donal said bluntly, "Dorilys has been handfasted twice, and both her affianced husbands met a violent death soon after. Dorilys is clever, and beautiful, and her dower is Castle Aldaran; but it would be surprising if it were not remarked that those who seek to wed her do not live long."

Allart said, "If I were you, Lord Aldaran, I would wait to think further of marriage until Dorilys has passed puberty and is free of the danger of threshold sickness."

Aldaran said, his breath catching in his throat, "Allart, have you foreseen . . . will she die of threshold sickness like the children of my first marriage?"

Allart said, "I have seen nothing of the kind." He had tried, very hard, not to look ahead. It seemed now that he saw nothing except disasters, many of which could not be tied down to time or place. Again and again he had seen Castle Aldaran under siege, arrows flying, armed men striking, lightnings aflare and striking down on the keep. Allart had tried to do as he did at Nevarsin—to barricade it all away from his mind, to see *nothing*; for most of what he saw were lies and meaningless fear.

"Foresight is useless here, my lord. If I should see a hundred different possibilities, still, only one of them can come to pass. So it is meaningless to see ahead and fear the other ninety-and-nine. But if it were inevitable that Dorilys should die in threshold sickness at puberty, I do not think I would be able to *avoid* seeing it; and I have not."

Dom Mikhail leaned his head in his hands, and said, "Would that I had some trace of your gift, Allart! For it seems to me that this is clear sign that the folk of Storn have

been in communication with my brother of Scathfell; and
they will not anger him because he still hopes to win Aldaran
somehow, if I die without son or son-in-law to hold it for me.
And *that*," he said, pausing and moving his head with that
quick hawklike movement, "will never be, while the four
moons ride in the heaven and snow falls in midwinter!"

His eyes fell on Donal, and softened, and all of them could
follow what he was thinking, that it was high time Donal, at
least, was wed. Donal tensed knowing this was not the time
to speak and cross him, but Dom Mikhail said only, "Go,
children, join the dancers in the hall, if you will. I must think
what to say to my kinsman of Storn," and Donal breathed
again.

But later that night, Donal said, "We must not delay much
longer, beloved. Or a day will come when he will summon
me and say, 'Donal, here is your bride,' and I will be put to
the trouble of explaining to him why I cannot marry whatever spiritless daughter of one of his vassals he has found for
me. Renata, shall I journey to the Kilghard Hills and make
suit, then, in my own name for your hand? Would Dom Erlend, do you think, give his daughter to a poor man, lord of
no more than the small holding at High Crags? You are
daughter to a powerful Domain; your kinsmen will say I was
quick to go wooing a rich dower."

Renata laughed. "I have but a small dower of my own; I
have three older sisters. And my father is so displeased that I
have come here without his consent that he may even refuse
me that! Such dower as I have is from Dom Mikhail, for my
care of Dorilys, and he will hardly be sorry to keep it in his
own family!"

"Still, he has been kinder to me than any father of my own
blood could have been, and he deserves better of me than this
double-dealing. Nor do I want your kinsmen to think I have
seduced you while you dwelt under my foster-father's roof,
perhaps for the sake of that very dower."

"Oh, that wretched dower! I know you do not care for
that, Donal."

"If it is necessary, my love, I will give up all claim on it
and take you in your bare shift," he said seriously.

Renata laughed and pulled his head down to her. "You
would take me better without it," she teased, loving the way
he still blushed like a boy half his age.

She had never believed she could be so wholly lost to everything except her love. She thought, *For all my years in the Tower, for all the lovers I have taken, I might as well have been a child Dorilys's age! Once I knew what love could be, all the rest meant nothing, nothing at all, less than nothing. . . .*

"Still, Renata," Donal said, resuming the conversation at last, "my foster-father should know."

"He is a telepath. I am sure he knows. But I think he has not yet decided what he means to do about it," Renata said, "and it would be quite unkind of us to force it upon his attention!"

Donal had to be content with that, but he wondered. How could Dom Mikhail ever have thought that Donal would go against custom this way, and turn his thoughts, unpermitted, upon a marriageable woman without the consent of her kin? He felt strange, alienated from the pattern he knew his life should have taken.

Looking at the troubled face of her lover, Renata sighed. In her solitary struggles with conscience in the Tower, she had realized that inevitably she must break away from the traditional patterns allotted to a woman of her clan. Donal had never, till now, faced the necessity for change.

"I shall send to my father, then, when it is too late for him to reply before midwinter, telling him that we are to be married at midwinter-night—if you still want me."

"If I still want you? Beloved, how can you ask?" Donal reproached, and the rest of their conversation was not held in words.

Summer drew on. The leaves began to turn, Dorilys celebrated her birthday, and the first of the harvest was gathered in. On a day when all of Aldaran's people had gone out to see the great wagons filled with sacks of nuts and jugs of the oil pressed from them borne into one of the outlying barns, Allart found himself standing next to Renata in an outlying part of the courtyard.

"Are you to remain for the winter, kinsman? I shall not leave Dorilys till she is safely past puberty; but you?"

"Donal has asked me to stay, and Dom Mikhail as well. I shall remain until I am summoned by my brother." Beyond the words Renata sensed weariness and resignation. Allart was painfully longing for Cassandra; in one of his secret dispatches he had asked leave to return, which Damon-Rafael had refused.

Renata smiled, an ironic smile. "Now that your brother has a legitimate son, he is in no hurry for you to rejoin your wife, and perhaps father sons who might contest that claim to the Domain."

Allart sighed, a sound too weary, Renata thought, for a man as young as Allart. "Cassandra will bear me no children," he said. "I will not bring that danger upon her. And I have sworn in the fires of Hali to support the claim of my brother's sons, legitimate or *nedestro*, to the Domain."

Renata felt the tears which had been so near the surface for days now welling up and brimming over in her eyes. To keep them back, she made her voice hard and ironic. "To the Domain—yes, you have sworn. But to the crown, Allart?"

"I want no crown," Allart said.

"Oh, I believe you," Renata's voice was waspish. "But will that brother of yours ever believe that?"

"I do not know." Allart sighed. Did Damon-Rafael truly believe that Allart could not resist the temptation to wrest the Domain—or the crown—from his hands? Or did he simply wish to place the powerful lord Aldaran under an obligation to Elhalyn? Damon-Rafael would need allies, if he chose to struggle with Prince Felix for the throne at Thendara.

That struggle would not come for a while. Old King Regis still clung to life, and the Council would not disturb his deathbed. But when the king lay in an unmarked grave at Hali beside his forefathers, as the custom was, then—*then* the Council would not be slow to demand that Prince Felix display his fitness to inherit his father's throne.

"An *emmasca* might make a good king," Renata said, following his thoughts effortlessly, "but he can found no dynasty. Felix will not inherit. And I read the last dispatch, too. Cassilde never recovered after the birth of her son, and died a few tendays after. So your brother has a legitimate son, but is seeking again for a wife. Now, no doubt, he repents he was so quick to marry you to Cassandra."

Allart's mouth curled in distaste, remembering what Damon-Rafael had said on that subject. "If Cassilde should die, as she has been likely to do any time these past few years, I would be free to take Cassandra myself." How could even his brother have spoken that way of the woman who had borne him a dozen children, only to see them die?

Allart said, "Perhaps it is better this way," but he sounded so dreary that Renata could not keep back the tears. He tipped her face gently up to his. "What is it, cousin? You are ever eager to comfort my troubles, yet you speak never of your own. What ails you, kinswoman?" His arms went out to encircle her, but it was the affectionate touch of a brother, a friend, not a lover, and Renata knew it. She sobbed, and Allart held her gently.

"Tell me, *chiya*," he said, as tenderly as if she were Dorilys's age, and Renata struggled to hold back her tears.

"I haven't told Donal. I wanted to have his child. If it were so with me, my father could not force me to come home to Edelweiss and marry whatever man he had chosen for me. . . . And so I conceived, but after a day or so, monitoring, I discovered that the child was female; and so I—" She swallowed, and Allart could feel her pain like a great agony within himself. "I could not let it live. I—I don't regret it; who could, with that curse on the line of Rockraven? And yet—I look at Dorilys and I cannot help but think, I have had to destroy what could have been like *that*, beautiful and—and—" Her voice broke and she sobbed helplessly for a moment against Allart.

And I thought I could force a choice like this upon Cassandra. . . . There was nothing Allart could say. He held Renata, letting her cry softly against him.

She quieted at last, murmuring, "I know I did right. It had to be. But I—I couldn't tell Donal, either."

What in the name of all the gods, are we doing to our women? What have we wrought in our blood and genes, to bring this on them? Holy Bearer of Burdens, it is your blessing, not your curse, that I am parted from Cassandra. . . .

Even as he spoke he seemed to see Cassandra's face, racked with fear, fear like Renata's. Trying to put it aside, he tightened his arms around Renata and said gently, "Still you know you have done right, and that knowledge will strengthen you, I hope." Then, slowly, searching for words, he told her of the moment of foresight, when he had seen her far advanced in pregnancy, terrified, despairing. "I have not seen that of late in my visions," he reassured her. "Probably that possibility existed only during the short time you were actually pregnant, and afterward—afterward, that future simply ceased to be; since you had taken the action which could prevent it. Don't be regretful."

Still, he was unsure: he had not seen *anything* of late. He had tried hard to blot out *any* use of his foresight and its dreadful thronging possible futures. Was it true that now, with the female child Renata had conceived already destroyed, there was no cause for fear? But he had reassured her. She looked calmer, and he would not disturb her again.

"I *know* I did right," Renata said. "Yet of late Dorilys has grown so sweet, so biddable and gentle. Now that she has some command of her *laran*, the storms seem to rage no longer."

Yes, thought Allart. *It has been long since my sleep or my waking was disturbed by those dreadful visions of a vaulted room, of a child's face framed in awful lightnings. . . .* Had all these tragedies, too, moved out of the realm of the possible, as Dorilys mastered her terrible gift?

"Yet, in a way, that makes it worse," Renata said, "to know there might have been another such child, and now she will never live . . . Well, I suppose I must simply think of Dorilys as the daughter I shall never dare to have. . . . Allart, she has invited her father and Donal to hear her play and sing this afternoon; will you come, too? She has begun to develop a truly fine singing voice; will you come and hear it?"

"With pleasure," Allart said sincerely.

Donal was there already, and Lord Aldaran, and several of the women of the household, including Dorilys's music-mistress, a young noblewoman of the house of Darriel. Darkly beautiful, with dark hair and dark-lashed eyes, she reminded Allart briefly of Cassandra, though they were not really much alike. Still, as Lady Elisa sat with her head bent over the *rryl*, tuning the strings, he noted that she, too, had six fingers on her hands. He remembered what he had said to Cassandra at their wedding, "May we live in a time when we can make songs, not war!" How brief that hope had been! They lived in a land torn with war among mountains and Domains alike, Cassandra in a Tower beset by air-cars and incendiaries, Allart in a land aflame with forest fire and raging lightnings, striking like arrows. Startled, he looked around the quiet room, out at the quiet skies and hills beyond. No sound of war, no breath. His damned foresight again, no more, in the calm room where Lady Elisa touched the side-bars of the harp, and said, "Sing, Dorilys."

The child's voice, sweet and mournful, began an old song of the far hills:

> "Where are you now?
> Where does my love wander?"

Allart thought such a song of hopeless love and longing ill placed on the lips of a young maiden, but he was entranced by the loveliness of the voice. Dorilys had grown considerably that autumn; she was taller, and her breasts, though small, were already well formed under her childish smock, the young body nicely rounded. She was still long-legged, awkward—she would be a tall woman. Already she was taller than Renata.

Dom Mikhail said as she finished her song, "Indeed, my darling, it seems you have inherited your mother's superb voice. Will you sing me something less mournful?"

"Gladly." Dorilys took the *rryl* from Lady Elisa. She adjusted the tuning slightly, then began to strum it casually and sing a comical ballad from the hills. Allart had heard it often at Nevarsin, though not in the monastery; a rowdy song about a monk who carried, in his pockets, as a good monk should, all the possessions he was allowed to own.

> "In the pockets, the pockets,
> Fro' Domenick's pockets.
> Those wonderful pockets he wore round his waist,
> The pockets he stuffed every morning in haste;
> Whatever he owned at the start of the day,
> He stuffed in his pockets and went on his way."

The audience was chuckling before long at the ever-increasing and ridiculous catalog of the possessions borne in the legendary monk's pockets.

> "Whatever he owned at the start of the day,
> He stuffed in his pockets and went on his way.
> A bowl and a spoon and a book for his prayers,
> A blanket to shield him against the cold airs,
> A pencase to write down his prayers and his letters,

A warm cozy kneepad to kneel to his betters,
A nutcracker handled in copper and gold . . ."

Dorilys herself was struggling to keep her face straight as
her audience began to chuckle, or giggle, or in the case of her
father, throw back his head and guffaw with laughter at the
absurdity of some of the contents of:

"The pockets, the pockets, Fro' Domenick's pockets . . ."

She had reached the verse which detailed:

"A saddle and bridle, some spurs and a rein
In case he was given a riding *chervine*,
A gold-handled basin, a razor of—"

Dorilys broke off, uncertainly, as the door opened, and
Lord Aldaran turned in anger on his paxman, who had entered with such lack of ceremony.

"Varlet, how dare you break into the room of your young
mistress this way!"

"I beg the young lady's pardon, but the matter is extremely
urgent. Lord Scathfell—"

"Come, come," Aldaran said irritably. "Even if he were at
our gates with a hundred armed warriors, my man, it would
not excuse such a lack of courtesy!"

"He has sent you a message. His messenger speaks of a demand, my lord."

After a moment Mikhail of Aldaran rose. He bowed to
Lady Elisa and to his daughter with as much courtesy as if
Dorilys's little schoolroom had been a presence-chamber.

"Ladies, forgive me. I would not willingly have interrupted
your music. But I fear I must ask permission to withdraw,
daughter."

For a moment Dorilys gaped; he asked *her* permission to
come and go? It was clearly the first time he had extended
this grown-up formal politeness; but then the beautiful manners in which Margali and Renata had schooled her came to
her aid. She dropped him so deep a curtsy that she nearly
sank to her knees.

"You are welcome to come and go at your own occasions,
sir, but I beg you to return when you are free."

He bent over her hand. "I shall indeed, my daughter.

Ladies, my apologies." he added, extending the bow to Margali and Renata, then he said curtly, "Donal, attend me," and Donal rose and hurried after him.

When they had gone, Dorilys tried to resume her song, but the heart had gone out of the occasion and after a little it broke up. Allart went down into the courtyard where the riding animals were stabled, and the escort of the diplomatic mission from Scathfell was tethered. Among them he could see other badges of different mountain clans, that armed men came and went in the courts, but they shifted like water and were not there when he looked again. He knew that his *laran* painted hallucinations for him of things that might never be. He tried to thread his way through them, to see into time, but he was not calm enough, and what he sensed—he was not consciously reading the minds of those who had brought Scathfell's demand, but they, too, were broadcasting their emotions all over the landscape—was not conducive to calm.

War? Here? He felt a pang of grief for the long beautiful summer, so irrevocably shattered. *How could I sit at peace when my people are at war and my brother prepares to strive for a crown? What have I done to deserve this peace, when even my beloved wife faces danger and terror?* He went to his room and tried to calm himself with the Nevarsin breathing disciplines, but he could not concentrate with the visions of war, storms, and riots crowding eyes and brain, and he was grateful when, after a considerable time, he was summoned to Aldaran's presence-chamber.

He had expected to confront the embassy from Scathfell, as he had seen them so often in his vision, but no one was there except Aldaran himself, staring gloomily at the floor in front of his high seat, and Donal, pacing nervously back and forth.

As Allart came in Donal gave him a quick look of gratitude and entreaty mingled.

"Come in, cousin," Dom Mikhail said. "Now indeed do we need the advice of kinsmen. Will you sit?"

Allart would have preferred to stand, or to pace like Donal, but he took the seat Dom Mikhail indicated. The old man sat with his chin in his hands, brooding. At last he said, "Do you sit, too, Donal! You drive me mad pacing there like a berserker possessed by a raging wolf," and waited for his foster-son to seat himself beside Allart. "Rakhal of Scathfell—for I will not yield him the name of brother—has sent me an envoy with demands so outrageous that I can no longer bear them in calm. He sees fit to demand that I shall choose without delay, preferably before midwinter, one of his younger sons—I suppose I should be honored that he leaves it up to me to choose which of his damned whelps I will have—to be formally adopted as my heir, since I have no legitimate son, nor, he says, am I likely to have one at my age." He picked up a piece of paper lying on the seat where he cast it, and crumpled it again in his fist. "He says I should invite all men to witness what I have done in declaring a son of Scathfell my heir, and then—will you listen to the insolence of the man!—he says, *then you may live out your few remaining years in such peace as your other deeds allow.*" He clenched the offending letter in his fist as if it were his brother's neck.

"Tell me, cousin. What am I to do with that man?"

Allart stared, appalled. *In the name of all the gods,* he thought, *what does he mean by asking me? Does he think seriously that I am capable of advising him on such a matter?*

Aldaran added, more gently, and also more urgently, "Allart, you were schooled at Nevarsin; you know all our history, and all the law. Tell me, cousin. Is there no way at all that I can keep my brother of Scathfell from grasping my estate even before my bones are cold in my grave?"

"My lord, I do not see how they can compel you to adopt your brother's son. But I do not know how you can keep Lord Scathfell's sons from inheriting after you; the law is not clear about female children." *And if it were,* he thought almost in despair, *is Dorilys truly fit to rule?* "When a female heir is given leave to inherit, it is usually because all concerned feel that her husband will make a suitable overlord. No one will deny you the right to leave Aldaran to Dorilys's husband."

"And yet," Aldaran said, with painstaking fingers smoothing out the crumpled letter, "look—the seals of Storn, and Sain Scarp, and even of Lord Darriel, hung about this letter, as if to lend their strength to this—this ultimatum he has sent. No wonder Lord Storn made me no reply when I sought his son for Dorilys. Each of them is afraid to ally himself with me lest he alienate all the others. Now, indeed, do I wish the Ridenow were not entangled in this war against your kin, or I should offer Dorilys *there.*" He was silent a moment, brooding. "I have sworn I will burn Aldaran over my own head ere it goes to my brother. Help me find a way, Allart."

The first thought that flashed into Allart's mind—and later, he was grateful that he had had sense enough to barricade it so that Aldaran could not read it—was this: *My brother Damon-Rafael has but lately lost his wife.* But the very thought filled his mind with erupting visions of dread and disaster. The effort to control them kept him silent in consternation, while he remembered Damon-Rafael's prediction that had sent him here: "I fear a day when all our world from Dalereuth to the Hellers will bow before the might of Aldaran."

Noting his silence, Dom Mikhail said, "It is a thousand pities *you* are wed, cousin. I would offer my daughter to *you.* . . . But you know my will. Tell me, Allart. Is there no way at all in which I can declare Donal my heir? It is he who has always been the true son of my heart."

"Father," Donal entreated, "don't quarrel with your kinsmen about me. Why set the land aflame in a useless war? When you have gone to join your forefathers—may that day be far from you, dear foster-father—what will it matter to you, then, who holds Aldaran?"

"It matters," said the old man, his face set like a mask in stone. "Allart, in all your knowledge of the law, is there no single loophole through which I might bring Donal into this inheritance?"

Allart set his mind to consider this. He said at last, "None, I think, that you could use, but these laws about blood inheritance are not yet so strong as all that. As recently as seven or eight generations ago, you and your brothers and all your wives would have dwelt together, and the eldest among you, or your chosen leader, would have chosen for heir the son who looked most likely and capable, not the eldest son of the eldest brother, but the *best.* It is custom, not law, that has foisted this rule of primogeniture and known fathering on the mountains. Yet if you simply proclaim that you have chosen Donal by the old law and not the new, then there will be war, my lord. Every eldest son in the mountains will know his position threatened, and his younger brother or his remote kinsmen more his enemy than now."

"It would be simpler," said Aldaran with great bitterness, "if Donal were a waif or an orphan, and not the son of my beloved Aliciane. Then could I wed him to Dorilys, and see my daughter protected and my estate in the hands of the one who knows it best and is best fitted to care for it."

Allart said, "That could still be done, my lord. It would be a legal fiction—as when the lady Bruna Leynier, sister of the heir who had been killed in battle, took her brother's widow and his unborn child under her protection in freemate marriage, so that no other marriage could be forced upon the widow and the child's rights set aside. They say that she commanded the guards, too, in her brother's place."

Aldaran laughed. "I thought that only a jesting tale."

"No," said Allart. "It happened, indeed. The women dwelt together for twenty years, until the unborn child was grown to manhood and could claim his rights. Folly, perhaps, but the laws could not forbid it. Such a marriage has a legal status at least—a half-brother and half-sister can marry if they will. Renata has told me it is best for Dorilys to bear no children, and Donal could father a *nedestro* heir to succeed him."

He was thinking of Renata, but Mikhail of Aldaran raised his head with a quick, decisive movement. "Legal fiction be damned," he said. "That is our answer, then, Donal. Allart is mistaken in what Renata said. I remember it well! She said Dorilys should not bear a *daughter*, but it would be safe for her to bear a son. And she has Aldaran blood, which would mean that Donal's son would be an Aldaran heir, and thus entitled to inherit after them. Every breeder of animals knows this is the best way to fix a desired trait in the line, to breed back with the same genetic materials. So that Dorilys will bear to her half-brother the son Aliciane should have given *me*—Renata will know how to make sure of that—and the fire-control and lightning-control talents redoubled. We must be careful for a few generations not to allow any daughters to be born, but so much the better, so that the line will flourish."

Donal stared at his foster-father, appalled. "You cannot possibly be serious, sir!"

"Why not?"

"But Dorilys is my sister—and only a little girl."

"Half-sister," Aldaran said, "and not such a little girl as all that. Margali tells me she will come to womanhood sometime this winter, so there is not even long to wait before we can tell them a true Aldaran heir is to inherit."

Donal stared at his father, stricken, and Allart could tell he

was thinking of Renata, but Mikhail of Aldaran was too intent on his own will to have the slightest scrap of *laran* left
over for reading his foster-son's thoughts. But as Donal
opened his mouth to speak, Allart saw, all too clearly, the old
man's face darkening and twisting, stricken, the roaring of
the brain. Allart clamped the boy's wrist in his hand, forcing
the picture of Aldaran's attack on Donal, hard, his thoughts
strong as the command-voice: *In the name of all the gods,
Donal, don't quarrel with him now! It would be the death of
him!* Donal fell back into his seat, the words unspoken. The
picture of Lord Aldaran stricken down at the words vanished
into the limbo of those things which now would not come to
pass, and Allart saw it thin out and vanish, relieved and yet
troubled.

*I am not a monitor, but if he stands so near to death, we
must tell Renata. He should be monitored. . . .*

"Come, come," Aldaran said gently. "Your scruples are
foolish, my son. You have known for many years that Dorilys
must marry as soon as she is grown, and if she must be wed
before she is full-grown, will it not be easier for her to marry
someone she knows and loves well? Would you not use her
more gently than some stranger? It is the only way I can
think of, that you should marry Dorilys and father a son
upon her—as things are now," he added, frowning a little.

Allart, startled and shocked, realized it was probably just
as well for Dorilys that Lord Aldaran was very old and considered himself past fathering an heir.

"As for this thing," Aldaran said, crushing Scathfell's letter
again and flinging it to the floor, "I think I shall use it to
wipe myself, and send it *so* to my brother, to show him what
I think of his ultimatum! At the same time I shall invite him
to witness your wedding."

"No," whispered Donal. "Father, I beg you—"

"Not a word, my son; my mind is made up." Aldaran rose
and embraced Donal. "Since first Aliciane brought you into
this house, you have been my beloved son; and this will make
it legitimate. Will you deny me that, dear lad?"

Donal stood helpless, unable to speak his protest. How
could he cast his foster-father's love and concern back at him
at that moment?

"Call my scribe," said Lord Aldaran. "I shall take pleasure
in dictating a letter to Lord Scathfell, inviting him to the
wedding of my daughter and heir with my chosen son."

Donal made a final plea. "You know, my father, that this is a declaration of war? They will come against us in force."

Aldaran gestured at the window. Outside the gray skies were blurring with the fall of daytime snow, the first of the year. "They will not come now," he said. "Winter is upon us. They will not come till spring thaw. And then—" He threw back his head and laughed, and Allart felt chills down his spine, thinking of the raucous scream of a bird of prey. "Let them come. Let them come when they will. We will be ready for them!"

CHAPTER
TWENTY-ONE

"But truly there is no woman in the world whom I wish to marry," Donal said, "except for you, my beloved." Until Renata had come into his life, he had never believed that he would have any choice in the matter—nor did he particularly want it, provided his bride-to-be was neither sickly nor a shrew, and he had trusted his foster-father to make sure of that. He had wasted very little thought on the matter.

Renata saw all these thoughts—and the almost unconscious resentment in Donal, that he had had to face this enormous change in his life pattern—and reached out to take his hand. "Indeed I am to blame, my love. I should have done as you wished, and married you at once."

"No one speaks of blame, *carya mea*, but what are we to do now? My foster-father is old, and today I truly feared he would be stricken down as I spoke, had not Allart prevented me. All the gods forgive me, Renata, I could not help thinking—if he should die, then would I be free of this thing he asks." Donal covered his face with his hands, and Renata, watching him, knew that his present upheaval was her doing. It was she who had inspired him to set himself against his foster-father's wishes.

At last she said, keeping her voice calm with considerable effort, "Donal, my beloved, you must do what you feel is right. The gods forbid I should try to persuade you against your conscience. If you think it wrong to go against your foster-father's will, then you must obey him."

He raised his face, struggling with the effort not to break down. "In the name of the merciful gods, Renata, how could I

241

possibly want to obey him? Do you think I *want* to marry my sister?"

"Not even with Aldaran as the dower?" she asked. "You cannot tell me that you have no desire to inherit the Domain."

"If I could do it justly! But not like this, Renata, not like this! I would defy him, but I cannot speak that word if it would strike him dead, as Allart fears! And the worst of it is—if you desert me now, if I should lose you—"

Quickly she reached out and took his hands in hers. "No, no, my love. I will not desert you, I promise it! That was not what I meant! I meant only that if you are forced into this marriage, it can be the legal fiction he wishes it to be, or wished it to be at first."

Donal swallowed hard. "How can I ask that? A noble-woman of your rank cannot become a *barragana*. This would mean I can never offer you what you should have in honor, the *catenas* and honorable recognition as my wife. My own mother was a *barragana*. I know what life would be for our children. Daily they taunted me, called me brat and bastard and things that made less pleasant hearing. How could I bring that upon any child of mine? Merciful Evanda, there were times I hated my own mother, that she had exposed me to such things!"

"I would rather be *barragana* to you than wear the *catenas* for another, Donal."

He knew she spoke truth, but confused resentment made him lash out, "Truly? What you mean, I suppose, is that you would rather be *barragana* to Aldaran than wife to the poor farmer of High Crags!"

She looked at him in dismay. *Already it has made us quarrel!*

"You do not understand me, Donal. I would rather be *yours*, as wife, freemate, or *barragana*, than marry some man my father chose for me without my knowledge or consent, were that man Prince Felix on his throne at Thendara. My father will be angry when he hears that I dwell openly in your house as *barragana*, but it will mean he cannot dispose of me to some other man, for there are those who would not have me upon such conditions, and I am beyond the reach of his anger—or his ambition!"

Donal felt guilty, knowing *he* could not so have defied his foster-father; and now, having defied *her* kin, Renata had nowhere else to go. He knew he should be equally brave, re-fuse Lord Aldaran's command, and insist upon marrying Renata at once, even if his foster-father were to disinherit him and drive him forth.

Yet, he thought, miserably, *I cannot quarrel with him. It is not only for my own sake, but I would not leave him at the mercy of the folk of Scathfell, and the other mountain lords who hover to pick his bones the moment they see him helpless!* His foster-father had no one else. How could he leave him alone? Yet it seemed that honor demanded he do just that.

He covered his face with his hands.

"I feel torn in pieces, Renata! Loyalty to you—and loyalty to my father. Is this, I wonder, why marriages are arranged by kinfolk, so that such terrible conflicts of loyalty cannot arise?"

As if Donal's tormented self-questioning could reverberate throughout Castle Aldaran, Allart, too, was troubled, rest-lessly pacing in his allotted chamber.

He thought, *I should have let Donal speak. If the shock of knowing he could not always have his own way should have killed Dom Mikhail, then we can well spare such tyrants, seeking always to impose their own will on others, despite their conscience. . . .* All the rage and resentment Allart had felt against his own father, he was ready to pour out on Lord Aldaran.

For this damned breeding program he will wreck Donal's life, and Dorilys's—before she is even out of childhood—and Renata's! Does he care about anything except a legitimate heir of Aldaran blood?

But then, belatedly, Allart began to be fair. He thought, *No, it is not all Dom Mikhail's fault. Donal is to blame, too, that he did not go at once to Dom Mikhail when first he fell in love with Renata, and ask for her in marriage. And I am to blame, that I listened to his request for some legal loophole. It was I who put it into his head that Donal and Dorilys could be married even as a legal fiction! And it was my damned foresight that made me prevent Donal from speaking out! Again I was swayed by a happening that might never have come to pass!*

My laran has brought this upon us all. Now somehow I must manage to master it, to thread my way and see through time, to discover what will happen among the many futures I see.

He had blocked it for so long. For many moons now, he had spent much of his emotional energy trying to see *nothing*, to live in the moment as others did, not letting himself be swayed by the shifting, seductive possibilities in the many futures. The thought of opening his mind to it all was terror, a fear that was almost physical. Yet that was what he must do.

Locking his door against intrusion, he went about his preparations with as much calm as he could summon. Finally he stretched out on the stone floor, closing his eyes and breathing quietly in the Nevarsin-trained manner, to calm himself. Then, struggling against panic—he *couldn't* do this, he had spent seven years in Nevarsin learning how *not* to do this—he lowered the self-imposed barriers and reached out with his *laran*. . . .

For an instant—timeless, eternal, probably not much more than half a second, but seeming like a million years inside his screaming senses—all of time rushed in on him, past and present, all of the deeds of his forefathers that had resulted in this moment. He saw a woman walking by the lake of Hali, a woman of surpassing beauty with the colorless gray eyes and moonlight hair of a *chieri*; he glimpsed memories of forests and peaks; he saw other stars and other suns, a world with a yellow sun with only a single pale moon in the sky; he looked out on a black night of space; he died in snow, in space, in fire, a thousand deaths crammed into a single moment; he fought and died screaming on a battlefield; he saw himself die curled into fetal position and withdrawing into himself beyond thought as he had almost done in his fourteenth year; he lived a hundred thousand lives in that one shrieking moment, and knew his body convulsing into spasms of terror, dying. . . . He heard himself cry out in agony and knew he was insane, that he would never come back. . . . He fought for a moment to slam the gates he had opened, knew it was too late. . . .

And then he was Allart again, and knew he had only this single life, *now*; the others were irrevocably past or had yet to be. But in this single life (and how narrow it looked, after those centuries upon centuries of split-second awareness that he *was*, he *had been*, he *would be*) still spread out before him, infinitely reduplicating itself, with every move he made hundreds of new possibilities were created and others were wiped out forever. He could see now how every move he had made since his childhood had either opened up opportunities or closed off other paths for all time. He could have taken the path of pride in strength and weaponry, set himself to best Damon-Rafael at swordplay and combat, become his father's most needed son. . . . He could have somehow arranged it so that Damon-Rafael died in childhood, become his father's heir. . . . He could have remained forever in the safe and sheltered walls of Nevarsin, disinherited. . . . He could have plunged into the world of the senses that he had discovered, an infinite temptation, in the arms of a *riyachiya*. . . . He could have choked out the life of his father, in his humiliated pride. . . . Slowly, through the crowding pasts, he could see the inevitability of the choices that had led him to this moment, to this crossroads. . . .

Now he was *here*, at this crucial moment in time, where his past choices, willing or unwilling, had led him. Now his future choices must be made in full knowledge of what they might bring. In that overloaded moment of total awareness, he accepted responsibility for what had been, and for what would be, and began to look carefully ahead.

Dorilys's words flashed through his mind: "It's like a stream of water. If I put rocks in it, it would go around the rocks, but it could go either way. But I couldn't make it jump out of the stream-bed, or run back uphill. . . ."

Slowly he began to see, with that curious extended perception, what lay ahead; the most likely thing straight before him, it seemed, fanning out to the wildest possibilities at the far edges of his awareness. He saw immediately before him the possibilities that Donal would accept; would defy; would take Renata and be gone from Aldaran; would take Dorilys and father *nedestro* children upon Renata. He saw that Dom Erlend Leynier might join forces with Scathfell against Aldaran in retaliation for the insult to his daughter. (He should warn Renata of that—but would she care?) Again and again, he saw the often repeated vision of Scathfell's armed men upon Aldaran in the spring, so that once again Aldaran must be kept by force of arms. . . . He saw remoter possibilities: that Lord Aldaran would indeed be struck down by a massive stroke, would die or lie helpless for months and years, while Donal struggled with his unwilling regency for his sister . . . that Lord Aldaran would recover and drive Scathfell away

with his superior armed might . . . that Lord Aldaran would
somehow be reconciled to his brother. . . . He saw Dorilys
dying in threshold sickness when womanhood came upon
her . . . dying while delivering the child Donal swore he
would never father upon her . . . surviving to give Donal a
son, who would inherit only the Aldaran *laran* and die of
threshold sickness in his teens. . . .

Painfully, painstakingly, Allart forced himself to thread his
way through all the possibilities. *I am not a god! How can I
tell which of these things would be best for all? I can only
say what would be least painful for Donal or for Renata,
whom I love. . . .*

Now, against his will, he began to see his own future. He
would return to Cassandra . . . he would not return but
would dwell forever in Nevarsin or, like Saint-Valentine-of-
the-Snows, alone in a solitary cave in the Hellers till death
. . . he would be reunited ecstatically with Cassandra . . . he
would die at the hands of Damon-Rafael, who feared treachery . . . Cassandra would dwell forever in the Tower . . .
she would die in bearing his child . . . she would fall into the
hands of Damon-Rafael, who had never ceased to regret that
he had given her to Allart instead of making her his own *barragana.* . . . This jolted Allart completely out of the reverie
of crowding futures and probabilities, to look more closely at
that one.

Damon-Rafael, his own wife dead, and his single legitimate
son dead before weaning. . . . Allart had not known that; it
was pure foresight, *laran.* But was it true or only a fear born
of his consciousness of Cassandra and of Damon-Rafael's un-
scrupulous ambition? Abruptly something his father had said
when speaking of his handfasting to Cassandra surged back
into his mind.

"You will be married to a woman of the Aillard clan, with
genes specially modified to control this *laran.* . . ." Allart
had heard his father, but he had not been listening. He had
heard only the voice of his own fear. But Damon-Rafael *had*
known. It would not be the first time that a Domain chief,
powerful and ambitious, had taken the wife of his younger
brother . . . *or his brother's widow. If I return to claim Cassandra for my wife, Damon-Rafael will kill me.* With a
craven pang, Allart wondered how he could avoid this fate,
the fate it now seemed he saw everywhere.

I shall return to the monastery, take vows there, never to return to Elhalyn. Then Damon-Rafael will take Cassandra for his wife, and seize the throne of Thendara from the faltering hands of the young emmasca who sits there now. Cassandra will mourn for me, but when she is queen at Thendara she will forget. . . .

And Damon-Rafael, his ambition satisfied, will be content.

Then horror flared upon Allart, seeing what kind of king his brother would be. Tyranny—the Ridenow would be wiped out wholly so that the women of Serrais could be bred into the line of Elhalyn, the Hasturs of Hali and Valeron would be assimilated into the single line of Elhalyn, so many alliances entered into that the Domains themselves would become only vassals to the Hastur of Elhalyn, reigning from Thendara. Damon-Rafael's greedy hands would reach out to bring all of the known world from Dalereuth to the Hellers under the domain of Elhalyn. All this would happen in the name of bringing peace . . . peace under the despotism of Damon-Rafael and the sons of Hastur!

Inbreeding, sterility, weakness, decadence, the inflow of barbarians from the Dry-towns and hill country . . . sack, looting, ravage, death. . . .

I do not want a crown. Yet no man living could rule this land worse than my brother. . . .

By main force Allart shut off the flow of images. Somehow, he must prevent this from occurring. Now for the first time he let himself think seriously of Cassandra. How casually he had almost stepped aside, leaving her to become Damon-Rafael's prey—for, queen or no, no woman would ever be more than this to his brother, a toy of lust and a pawn of ambition. Damon-Rafael had brought an almost certain death upon Cassilde, not caring as long as she bore him a legitimate son. He would not hesitate to use Cassandra the same way.

Then something in Allart that he had crushed and subdued and trampled suddenly reared up and said, *No! He shall not have her!*

If she had wanted Damon-Rafael, if she had even been ambitious for the crown, then, with agony never to be weighed or measured, Allart might have stepped aside. But he knew her too well for that. It was his responsibility—and his *right*, his unchallenged right—to protect and reclaim her for himself.

Even now, my brother might be reaching out his hand to take her. . . .

Allart could see ahead into all possible futures, but he could not see what was actually happening now at a distance—not without the aid of his matrix. Slowly, stretching cramped muscles, he stood up and looked around the chamber. The night had passed, and the snow; crimson dawn was breaking over the Hellers outside his window, showing snowclad peaks flashing red sunlight. With the weather-wisdom of the mountains, which he had learned at Nevarsin, he knew the storm was gone, for a time at least.

With the starstone in his hand, Allart resolutely focused on his thought, enormously amplified by the matrix, over the long spaces that lay between. *What befalls at Elhalyn? What is happening in Thendara?*

Slowly, pinpointed as if he were seeing it with his physical eyes through the small end of a lens, tiny and sharp-edged and brilliant, a picture formed before his eyes.

Along the shores of Hali, where the unending waves that were not water splashed and receded forever, a procession wound its way, with the banners and flags of mourning. Old King Regis was being carried to the burial ground at the shores of Hali, there to lie, as custom demanded, in an unmarked grave among the former kings and rulers of the Domains. In that procession, face after face flashed before Allart's eyes, but only two made any impression on him: One, the narrow, pale sexless face of Prince Felix, sad and fearful. It would not be long, Allart knew, looking at the rapacious faces of the nobles in his train, before Prince Felix was stripped naked and forced to yield his crown to one who could pass on blood and genes, the precious *laran*. The other was the face of Damon-Rafael of Elhalyn, next heir to the crown of Thendara. As if already tasting his victory, Damon-Rafael rode with a fierce smile on his face. Before Allart's eyes the picture blurred, not into what was now, but what would be, and he saw Damon-Rafael crowned in Thendara, Cassandra, robed and jeweled as a queen, at his side, and the powerful lords of Valeron, cemented in close alliance through kinfolk, standing behind the new king Damon-Rafael. . . .

War, decadence, ruin, chaos. . . . Allart suddenly knew he stood at the crux of a line of events which could alter forever the whole future of Darkover.

I wish my brother no harm. But I cannot let him plunge all of our world into ruin. There is no journey that does not begin with a single step. I cannot prevent Damon-Rafael from becoming king. But he will not cement the Aillard alliance by making my wife his queen.

Allart put the matrix aside, sent for his servants and had food brought, eating and drinking without tasting, to strengthen him against what he knew must come. That done, he went in search of Lord Aldaran. He found Dom Mikhail in high good humor.

"I have sent the message to my brother of Scathfell, inviting him to the wedding of my daughter and my beloved foster-son," he said. "It is a stroke of genius. There is no other man into whose hands I would so willingly give my little daughter for her safety and protection lifelong. I shall tell her today what we intend, and I think she, too, will be grateful, that she need not be given into a stranger's hands. . . . You are responsible for this splendid solution, my friend. I wish I could somehow repay you with some equal kindness! How I would like to be a fly upon the wall when my brother of Scathfell reads the letter I have sent him!"

Allart said, "As a matter of fact, Dom Mikhail, I have come to ask you a great favor."

"It would be a pleasure to grant you whatever you ask, cousin."

"I wish to send for my wife, who dwells in Hali Tower. Will you receive her as a guest?"

"Willingly," Dom Mikhail said. "I will send my own guard as escort, if you wish it, but the journey is precarious at this time of year; ten days' ride from the Lowlands with the winter storms coming on. Perhaps you could eliminate the time it would take my men to travel to the lake of Hali and fetch her, if you sent to Tramontana Tower with a message through the relays that she should set forth at once. I could send men to meet her on the way and escort her. I suppose she could find her own escort from Elhalyn."

Allart looked troubled. He said, "I do not want to trust her to my brother, and I am reluctant that her going should be known."

Dom Mikhail looked at him sharply. "Is it like that? I suggest, then, that you go at once with Donal to Tramontana, and try to persuade them to bring her here at once, through the Tower relays. It is not often done in these days—the expenditure of energy is out of all reason—unless the need is desperate. But if it is as important as that—"

Allart said, "I did not know that could still be done!"

"Oh, yes, the equipment is still there in the Tower, matrix-powered. Perhaps, with your help, they could be persuaded. I would suggest that you ride to Tramontana, however, rather than flying; the weather is not good enough at this season for that. . . . Still, speak with Donal. He knows all that there is to know about flying in the Hellers at any season." He rose, courteously dismissing the younger man.

"It will be a pleasure to welcome your wife as my guest, cousin. She will be an honored guest at my daughter's wedding."

"Yes, of course we can fly there," Donal said, glancing at the sky. "We will have at least a day free of snow, but of course we cannot return the same day. If there must be work done within the relays, you would be too exhausted, and so would your lady. I suggest that we leave for Tramontana as soon as we can, and that I give orders for mounts to be sent after us, including one for your wife, gentle and suited to a lady's riding."

They set forth later that morning. Allart did not speak of Donal's approaching marriage, fearing it might be a sore point with him, but Donal brought it up himself. "It cannot be before midwinter night," he said. "Renata has monitored Dorilys and she says she will not mature before that. And she has had such ill fortune with handfastings that even Father hesitates to subject her to another such ceremony."

"Has she been told?"

"Yes, Father told her," Donal said, hesitating, "and I spoke with her, a little, after. . . . She is only a child. She has only the haziest idea of what marriage means."

Allart was not so certain, but after all it was Donal's affair, and Renata's, not his. Donal turned to catch the wind, tilted his glider-wings with the control, and soared upward on a long drift of air.

Once airborne, as always, the troubles of the world slipped away from Allart's thoughts; he gave himself up to it without thought, riding the achingly cold air in a kind of ecstasy, matrix-borne, hawk-free. He was almost regretful when he came in sight of Tramontana Tower, but not quite. There lay his path to Cassandra.

As he turned the glider over to Arzi he pondered that. Perhaps, rather than bringing her here to a cowardly safety, he should return to Hali and face his brother. No, he knew with that cold new inner knowledge; if he should venture anywhere within Damon-Rafael's grasp his life would not be worth the smallest coin.

Inside himself he mourned. *How have we come to this, my brother and I?* Yet he put his grief aside, steadying himself to face the *tenerézu* of the Tower with his request.

Ian-Mikhail frowned, and Allart thought he would refuse out of hand. "The power is there," he said, "or can be summoned. Yet I am very reluctant to entangle Tramontana in the affairs of the Lowlands. Are you very sure there is danger to your wife, Allart?"

Allart found in his mind only the certain knowledge that Damon-Rafael would not hesitate to seize her, as he had seized Donal. Donal, close by, reading his thoughts, flushed with anger.

"*That* I had never known until this moment. It is well for Lord Elhalyn that my foster-father did not know!"

Ian-Mikhail sighed. "Here we are at peace; we make no weapons and take part in no wars. But you are one of us, Allart. We must safeguard your lady from harm. I cannot imagine it. I, too, was schooled at Nevarsin, and I would rather lie with a corpse or a *cralmac* than an unwilling woman. But I have heard that your brother is a ruthless man, and ambitious beyond measure. Go, Allart. Communicate with Cassandra through the relays. I will summon the circle for tonight."

Allart went to the matrix chamber, calming himself for the work, casting himself into the spinning darkness of the relays, riding the web of electrical energies as earlier that day he had ridden the air drafts of the winter sky. Then, without warning, he felt the intimate touch on his mind. He had not hoped for such luck; Cassandra herself was in the relays.

Allart? Is it you, love?

Surprise and wonder, an amazement that was near to tears. . . . *You are at Tramontana? You know we are all in mourning here for the old king?*

Allart had seen, though no one had thought to tell him formally here.

Allart, a moment before you begin whatever business brought you to Tramontana. I am—I do not want to trouble you, but I am afraid of your brother. He paid me a courtesy

*call, saying marriage-kin should know one another; and when
I spoke my sympathy at Cassilde's death and the death of his
young son, he spoke of a time gone by when brothers and sisters held all their wives in common, and he looked at me so
strangely. I asked what he meant and he said a time would
come when I would understand, but I could not read his
thoughts. . . .*

Until this moment Allart had hoped it was fantasy born of
his fear. Now he knew his foresight had been true.

*It was for this I came here, beloved. You must leave Hali
and come to me in the mountains.*

Ride there at this season? In the Hellers?

He could feel her fear. Nevarsin-trained, Allart had no
fear of the killing weather of the Hellers, but he knew her
fright was genuine. *No. Even now the circle is gathering, to
bring you here through the screens. You do not fear that, do
you, love?*

No. . . . But the faraway denial did not sound quite sure.

It will not be long. But go and ask the others to come.

Ian-Mikhail came into the matrix chamber, now wearing
the crimson robe of a Keeper. Behind him Allart could see
the girl Rosaura whom he had met here before, and half a
dozen of the others. The white-robed monitor was working
with the dampers, adjusting them to compensate for the
presence of an outsider, setting up the force-lock which made
it impossible for any outsider to intrude, body or mind, into
the space or time where they were working. Then Allart felt
the familiar body-mind touch and knew he was being monitored for his presence in the circle. He felt grateful to them,
not knowing how to express it, that they were willing to tolerate the presence of someone outside their closed and intimate
circle. Yet he was not wholly an outsider; he had touched
them more than once when he worked in the relay-nets. He
was *known* to them, and he felt obscurely comforted.

*I have lost my brother. Damon-Rafael is my enemy. Yet
will I nevermore be wholly brotherless, having worked in the
relays which touch mind to mind all over this world. I have
sisters and brothers in Hali and Tramontana, and at Arilinn
and Dalereuth and all of the Towers. . . .*

Damon-Rafael and I were never brothers in that sense.

Ian-Mikhail of Storn was gathering the circle now, motion-
ing each of them to his or her place. Allart counted nine in
the circle, and he came and sat in the ring of joined bodies,

not touching anywhere but close enough to feel one another as electrical fields. He saw the inner swirlings within force-fields that were the others in the circle; saw the field begin to build around Ian-Mikhail as the Keeper seized the tremendous energies of the linked matrices and began to twist and direct them into a cone of power on the screen before them. Having worked only with Coryn as Keeper, whose mental touch was light and almost imperceptible, by contrast Allart felt that Ian-Mikhail caught him, wrenched at him, almost brutally, placing him within the circle, but there was nothing of malice in the strength. It was simply the distinct way he worked; everyone used his or her psi powers in a particular way.

Once in the circle, locked into the ring of minds, individual thought faded, gave way to a humming awareness of joined, concentrated *purpose*. Allart could sense the force building inside the screen, a vast enormous singing silence. Dimly in the distance he touched other familiar minds: Coryn, like a brief handclasp; Arielle a riffle of air, wavering, perceptible; Cassandra. . . . They were *there*, they were *here*—then he went blind and deaf with the searing overload, the sting of ozone in his nostrils, the enormous flaring, searing energies like lightning crashing on the heights.

Abruptly the pattern broke, and they were separate individuals again, and Cassandra, dazed and white, was kneeling on the stones before the circle.

She reeled, about to fall, but Rosaura reached out and steadied her; then Allart was there, lifting her in his arms. She looked up at him in exhaustion and terror.

Ian-Mikhail said with a faint laugh, "You are as wearied as by the ten days' ride, kinswoman. There has been a certain amount of energy expended, however it was done. Come with us, then. We must eat and rebuild our forces. Tell us all the news from Hali, if you will."

Allart was faint with the terrible hunger of the energy-drain. For once, he found himself eating the heavily sweetened reserve foods in the matrix chamber without nausea or distaste. He was not enough of a technician to understand the process which had teleported Cassandra through space across the ten days' ride between the Towers, but she was here, her hand clasped tight in his, and that was enough for him.

The white-robed monitor came and insisted on monitoring them both. They didn't protest.

As they ate, Cassandra told the news from Hali. The death and burial of the old king; the Council summoned to test Prince Felix—not yet crowned, probably never to be crowned; the upheaval in Thendara among the people who supported the gentle young prince. There had been a renewed truce with the Ridenow which Hali Tower had been forced to use for the stockpiling of *clingfire*. Cassandra showed Allart one of the characteristic burns on her hand.

Allart listened with amazement and wonder. His wife. Yet he felt he had never seen this woman before. When last he had seen her she had been childlike, submissive, still sick with the recoil of her suicidal despair. Now, after a scant half year, she seemed years older; her very voice and gestures stronger, more definite. This was no timid girl but a woman, poised, confident, sure of herself, talking casually and competently with the other monitors about the professional requirements of their exacting work.

What have I to give to a woman like this? Allart wondered. *She clung to me, then, because I was stronger and she needed my strength. But now that she does not need me, will she love me?*

"Come, cousin," Rosaura said. "I must find you some clothes; you cannot travel in what you wear now."

Cassandra laughed, looking down at the loose, warm white monitor's robe which was her only garment.

"Thank you, kinswoman. I came away in haste without leisure to pack my belongings!"

"I will find you travel clothing, and a change or so of underlinen," Rosaura said. "We are much of a size. And when you reach Castle Aldaran, I am sure they can find you suitable garments."

"Am I going with you to Aldaran, Allart?"

Ian-Mikhail said, "Unless you would rather stay here with us . . . we are always in need of competent monitors and technicians."

There was something of the old childlike Cassandra in the way she clasped his hand.

"I thank you, kinsman. But I will go with my husband."

The night was far advanced, snow beating furiously around the heights of the Tower. Rosaura showed them to a room made ready on the lower floor.

Allart wondered again, when they were alone. *What have I to give a woman like this? A woman, and no longer in need of my strength!* But as he turned to her, he felt the barriers going down, one after another, so that their minds merged before he even touched her. He knew nothing was gone between them that could make a difference.

In gray dawnlight they were roused by a sudden knocking at the door. It was not really very loud, but somehow had a frantic sound, a commotion that made Allart sit up and stare wildly around him for some cause, some reason behind the violent disturbance. Cassandra sat up and looked at him in the dim light, frightened.

"What is it? Oh, what is it?"

"Damon-Rafael," Allart said, before realizing that this was madness. Damon-Rafael was ten days away in the Lowlands and there was no way he could intrude here. Yet, as he opened the door, the sight of Rosaura's pale, frightened face was a shock. Had he *really* expected to see his brother, armed for combat or kill, ready to break into the room where he slept, reunited with his wife?

"I am sorry to disturb you," Rosaura said, "but Coryn of Hali is in the relays and he says he must speak with you at once, Allart."

"At this hour?" Allart said, wondering who had suddenly gone mad, for the dawn was just beginning to merge into pink at the edge of the sky. Nevertheless he dressed in haste, and hurried up the long stairs to the matrix chamber because he felt too confused to trust himself to the rising-shaft.

A young technician Allart did not know was in the relays.

"You are Allart Hastur of Elhalyn? Coryn of Hali has insisted we waken you."

Allart took his place inside the relay circle, and reaching out, felt Coryn's light touch on his mind.

Kinsman? At such an hour? What can be happening at Hali?

I do not like it any better than you do. But a few hours past, Damon-Rafael, Lord Elhalyn, came raging to the doors of Hali, demanding that we turn your wife over to him, as hostage against your treachery. I knew not that there was madness in our kindred, Allart!

Not madness, but a touch of laran, *and a very little of my*

own foresight, Allart sent back in answer. *Did you tell him
you had sent her here?*

I had no choice, Coryn replied. *Now he has demanded that
we attack Tramontana Tower with our powers, unless they
agree quickly to send her back, and preferably you, too. . . .*

Allart whistled in dismay. Hali was bound, by law and custom, to use its powers for the Elhalyn overlord. They could
strafe Tramontana with psychic lightnings, till the workers in
the Tower were dead or mindless. Had he brought ruin on
the friends here who had brought Cassandra to him? How
could he have entangled them in his own family troubles?
Well, it was too late now to regret.

Coryn said, *We refused, of course, and he gave us a day
and a night to reconsider our answer. By the time he comes
again we must be able to tell him, in a way that will satisfy
his own* leronis *that neither of you is in Tramontana and that
such strafing would be useless.*

*Be very sure, we shall be gone from Tramontana before
daylight,* Allart assured him, and allowed the contact to
break.

CHAPTER
TWENTY-TWO

They set forth at the break of day, afoot, Tramontana kept no mounts and, in any case, their escort, with travel gear, had set forth yesterday at the same hour as Donal and Allart in their gliders. There was only one road, and sometime today they would meet the party from Aldaran on it.

The important thing was to be gone from Tramontana so that Hali could justly refuse to strafe the other Tower. *We cannot bring disaster upon our brothers and sisters of Tramontana, not when they have made themselves vulnerable for our sake.*

Cassandra looked up at him as they walked down the steep path side by side, and it seemed to Allart that the look she gave him was one of awful vulnerability. Once again, in life and death, he was responsible for this woman. He did not speak, but moved close to her.

"All the gods be thanked for the fine weather," Donal said. "We are but ill equipped to travel more than a day in these hills. But the party from Aldaran has tents and shelter, blankets and food; once we meet them, we could, if need struck us, camp for a few days should a storm come up." His trained eyes scanned the sky. "But it seems to me unlikely that there will be such a storm. If we meet with them on the road a little after midday, as we most probably will, we can reach Aldaran sometime tomorrow in the afternoon."

As he spoke a small thrill of dread struck inward at Allart. For a moment it seemed that he walked through whirling snow, a raging wind, and Cassandra was gone from his side... No! It was gone. No doubt Donal's words had roused fear of one of those remotely possible futures which

257

would probably never come to pass. As the sun rose above its mantle of crimson cloud on the distant peaks, he put back the cowl of his traveling-cloak—borrowed from Ian-Mikhail, for he had not been able to wear heavy garments in the glider, and all of his cold-weather gear was with the escort party from Aldaran; they had, of course, expected to wait in comfort at Tramontana until the escort came for them. Donal was similarly burdened with a borrowed cloak—for, although the weather seemed incredibly fine for the season, no one ventured forth in winter in the Hellers without clothing against a sudden storm, no matter how unlikely. Cassandra was dressed in clothing somewhat too short for her, borrowed from Rosaura. The colors, designed for the tawny-russet Rosaura, made her delicate dark beauty look quenched and colorless, and the short skirt displayed her ankles a little more than was strictly seemly, but she made a joke of it.

"All the better for walking on these steep paths!" She bundled up Rosaura's bright green travel-cloak and wadded it carelessly under her arm. "It is all too warm for this; I would as soon not be burdened with carrying it," she said, laughing.

"You do not know our mountains, Lady," Donal said soberly. "If even a little wind springs up, you will be glad of it."

But as the sun climbed the sky, Allart's confidence grew. After more than an hour of walking, Tramontana was lost to sight behind a shoulder of the mountain, and Allart felt relieved. Now indeed they were gone from Tramontana, and when Damon-Rafael came to Hali and demanded that they should be yielded up to him, Tramontana could honestly say they were out of reach.

Would he vent his wrath upon the Hali circle, anyway? Most probably he would not. He needed their goodwill for the war he was waging against the Ridenow, needed them to make the weapons which gave him tactical and military advantage—and Coryn was an inspired deviser of weapons. *All too inspired,* Allart thought. *If the Domain were in my hands I should make peace at once with the Ridenow, and truce lasting enough that we could settle our differences in a meaningful way. Aldaran is right; we have no cause to war with the Ridenow at Serrais. We should welcome them among us, and be grateful if the laran of Serrais is kept alive in the women they have wed.*

After several hours of walking, as the sun heightened to

noon, Donal and Allart, too, had taken off their heavy cloaks and even their outer tunics. The people at Tramontana had given them ample food for a meal or two by the way—"In case," they said, "your escort should be somewhat delayed by the road; riding-animals can go lame or rockfalls obstruct the roads for a little"—and they sat on rocks beside the road, eating hard flat cakes of journey-bread and dried fruit and cheese.

"Merciful Avarra," Cassandra said, gathering up the remnants, "it seems they have given us enough for a tenday! Surely there is no sense to carrying all this!"

Allart shrugged, stuffing the packets in one of the pockets of his outer tunic. Something in the gesture made him think of mornings at Nevarsin, stowing the few things he was allowed to possess in the pockets of his robe.

Donal, taking the remaining packages of food, seemed to share a part of the joke. "I feel like Fro' Domenick, with his pockets bulging," he said, and whistled a snatch of Dorilys's song.

Little more than a year ago, Allart thought, *I was resigned to living the rest of my life within the walls of a monastery.* He looked at Cassandra, who had tucked up her skirts almost to her knees and climbed a little stone wall to come at a stream that trickled down, clear and cool, from the heights. She bent to cup the water in her hands for a drink. *I thought I could spend all my life as a monk, that no woman could ever mean anything to me, yet it would rend me asunder now to be parted from her.* He climbed across the wall, and bent beside her to drink, and as their hands touched, he wished suddenly that Donal was not with them; then he almost laughed at himself. Surely there had been times in the summer past when Renata and Donal had suffered *his* presence as unwillingly as he now tolerated Donal's company.

They sat for a while beside the road, resting, feeling the warmth of the sun on their heads, and Cassandra told him about her training as a monitor, and of the work as a mechanic. He touched the bone-deep *clingfire* scar on her hand with a twinge of horror, glad suddenly that she was out of the reach of war. In return he told her a little of Dorilys's strange gift, touching lightly on the horror of the deaths following her handfastings, and talking of how they had flown among the storms.

"You shall try it, too, kinswoman," Donal said, "when the spring comes."

"I wish I might, but I do not know if I would care to wear breeches, even for that."

"Renata does," Donal said.

Cassandra laughed gaily. "She has always had more daring than I!"

Donal said, suddenly subdued, "Allart is my dear cousin and friend and I have no secrets from his wife. Renata and I were to be married at midwinter. But now my father has other wishes." Slowly, he told her of Aldaran's plan, that he and Dorilys should marry, so he might legally inherit Aldaran. She looked at him in kindly sympathy.

"I was fortunate. My kinfolk gave me to Allart when I had never seen him, but I found him such a one as I could love," she said. "Yet I know it is not always so, nor even very often, and I know what it is to be parted from a loved one."

"I will *not* be parted from Renata," Donal said, low and fierce. "This mockery of marriage with Dorilys will be no more than a fiction, to endure no longer than my father lives. Then, if Dorilys will have it so, we will find her a husband and go forth, Renata and I. Or if she has no will to marry, I will remain as warden in her time. If it is her wish to adopt one of my *nedestro* sons as her heir, well and good; and if not, well and good also. I will not defy my father, but I will not obey him, either. Not in this; not if he wishes me to take my half-sister to bed and father a son upon her!"

"I should think that should be as Dorilys wills it, kinsman. The lady of Aldaran, if she is lawfully wed to another, cannot create scandal by taking guardsmen or mercenaries to her bed . . . and she may not have any wish to live loveless and childless."

Donal looked away from her. "She may do as she wills, but if she has sons they will not be of my fathering. Allart has told me enough of what the breeding program and its inbreeding has already done among our people. My mother reaped that bitter fruit, and I will sow no more of it."

Before the fierceness of that, Cassandra recoiled. Allart, sensing her unease, picked up her cloak and said, "I suppose we should go on. The escort can travel faster than we can, but still, even an hour's walking to meet them will lessen the time we must spend on the road tomorrow."

The path was less steep now, but the sunshine was patched

with shadows as long feathery traces of gray cloud moved across the sky. Donal shivered and looked nervously toward the heights, darkening with thick gray masses, but he said nothing, only fastening the neck of his cloak.

Allart, picking up his apprehension, thought, *It would be well if we met with the escort as soon as might be.*

A little more walking, then, and the sky was hidden entirely with cloud, and Allart felt a snowflake strike his face. They were drifting slowly down, spiraling as they fell. Cassandra caught the snowflakes in her hand, marveling, childlike, at their size. But Allart had lived at Nevarsin and he knew something of the storms in the Hellers.

So Damon-Rafael may have had his way after all. By driving us forth in winter from the safety of Tramontana Tower, when storms are rather more likely than not, he may have rid himself without effort of a dangerous rival. . . . And if I die in this storm, then there is no one to stand against my brother's will to power. Allart's *laran* began to overpower him again, bringing him obsessive pictures of ruin and terror, wars raging, lands ravaged and burned, a true age of chaos all over Darkover from Dalereuth to the Hellers.

Scathfell, too, might fall upon Aldaran, and with Donal gone, there will be no one to stand against him. Between them, Scathfell and my brother will tear all this land asunder!

"Allart," Cassandra said, picking up from his mind some of the images of ruin and chaos, "what is wrong?"

And I have Cassandra to protect, not only against my brother, but against all the rage of the elements!

"Will it be a blizzard?" she asked, suddenly frightened, and he looked at the thickening snowfall.

"I am not sure," he said, watching Donal thrust up a wetted finger into the wind and turn it slowly around, trying to sense where the wind came from. "But there is some danger, though not immediate. We may meet the escort on the way before it gets any worse. They have food and clothing and gear for shelter, and then there will be nothing to fear."

But even as he spoke, he met Donal's eyes and knew that it was worse than he thought. The storm was coming *from* the direction of Aldaran; therefore it had probably already forced the escort to stop and make camp on the way. They would not be able to see the road ahead and the animals would not be able to find their footing in the heavy snow. There was no blame to the escort party; they would have be-

-lieved Allart and Donal and Allart's lady safe and among friends in Tramontana Tower.

How could they be expected to guess at Damon-Rafael's malice?

Cassandra looked terrified. *If she is reading my mind, no wonder,* Allart thought, and applied himself to the task of calming her fears. He had too much respect for her to offer her a pacifying lie, but things were not as bad as she feared, either.

"One of the first things I learned at Nevarsin, was the art of finding shelter in unlikely places, and how to come through these sudden storms without disaster. Donal," he said, "is there any man among the escort with a scrap of *laran*, so that you and I could reach him and tell the escort of our plight?"

Donal stopped to consider. At last he said regretfully, "I fear not, cousin. Although it would not hurt to try; some few men can receive thoughts, though they could not send them and do not think of it as *laran*."

"Try, then, to reach them," Allart instructed. "For they have every reason to believe us safe at Tramontana. They should know that this is not so. Meanwhile—" He cast his eyes around, searching for shelter, trying to think ahead along the road to see if there was an old building of any kind, a lean-to, a deserted barn, even some inhabited dwelling where they might be given shelter.

But as far as his clairvoyance could see, there was none. The country they traveled might have been virgin to all human feet for all time, for any traces of mankind's passing here. He had seen no print of habitation since the small stone wall near where they had eaten their midday meal.

It had been years since he had had to use his mountain-survival training; not since his third year at Nevarsin, when he had been sent forth barehanded in his monk's cowl into the teeth of the harshest season, to bring back proof of his fitness for the next level of training. The old brother who had taught him had said, "After some deserted human dwelling, next best is a thicket of trees close-set; after that, a rock-ledge facing away from the wind and with some vegetation." Allart wrinkled his forehead, trying to remember, searching out ahead of him, letting his *laran* have full play as he sought to spy ahead in time what lay along each of the directions they might take from here.

Is there time to return to Tramontana? Mentally retracing his steps, he saw along that line of probability only their three dead bodies, huddled and frozen at the side of the road.

For once in his life he was grateful for his *laran*, which allowed him to see clearly ahead on every choice they might make; because on the choices they made now, their very lives would certainly depend. He saw along the road directly ahead that the path narrowed; where blinded by the ever-thickening snow, they might miss their footing, go plunging into a chasm hundreds of feet deep, their bodies never found. They must go no farther along this road. Following his clear warning, Cassandra and Donal stopped and awaited his guidance. They were now only blurred cloaked shapes in the thickening snow, and a high wind had begun to scream down from the heights.

A little way ahead of them, a pathway led up to a clustered formation of rocks, close gathered to give almost as much shelter as a building. Allart started to direct them up to it, then hesitated, searching with his *laran* along that line of probability. He flinched, in panic; the cluster of rocks was the nest of banshee-birds, the evil flightless carnivores who lived above the timberline and were drawn by an unfailing tropism to anything with the body-heat of life. They must not go *that* way!

They could not remain here; the wind was strong enough to fling them off the ledge, and the snow thick around them. Already Cassandra was shivering, the borrowed travel-cloak never intended for a serious storm. Allart and Donal, more used to mountain weather, were not cold, but Allart was beginning to be frightened. They could not go back to Tramontana. They could not climb up where the banshees nested. They could not go ahead on the road to the narrowing path over the abyss. And they could not stay here. Was there no alternative to their death then? Was it ordained by fate that they should die in this blizzard?

Holy Bearer of Burdens, strengthen me. Help me to see a way, Allart prayed. He had almost forgotten how to pray since leaving the monastery, and fear for himself would not have done it, but Cassandra, shivering in his arms, spurred him to explore every avenue.

They could not return to Tramontana, but a little way back along the path was the stone wall. It was long abandoned and falling down, but it would provide better shelter than the open path; and behind it—he saw now with both memory and *laran*—a thick set clump of evergreens.

"We must go back to where we ate our midday meal," he said, pitching his voice carefully above the shriek of the wind.

Slowly, holding on to one another, for the snow was wet and slippery underfoot, they retraced their steps. It was slow, hard going. Donal, who had spent all his life in these mountains, was surefooted as a mountain cat, but Allart had been years away from the crags around Nevarsin, and Cassandra was wholly unaccustomed to these roads. Once she slipped and fell full length in the snow, her thin borrowed dress soaked to the knees, her hands torn on the rocks under their coat of snow, and she lay there chilled and sobbing with pain. Allart lifted her to her feet, his face set with determination. But she had twisted knee and ankle in the fall, and Donal and Allart had almost to carry her the last few hundred steps to the rock wall, to lift her over it and help her into the thick enclosure of the clumped trees. As they were down into it, Allart's *laran* screamed at him that this was the place of his death. He saw their three bodies, entangled, clutching one another for warmth, frozen and stark. He had to force himself down into the enclosure made by the trees.

Gnarled and old, twisted by the violence of mountain storms for half a century or more, the trees wove close, and inside their circle the wind was less, though they could hear it screaming outside, and there was a patch of ground unmarred by the heavy snow. Allart laid Cassandra down on the ground, folding her cloak so it kept the worst of the cold from her, and began to examine her injured leg.

"There is nothing broken," she said shakily, after a moment, and he remembered that she was a trained Tower monitor, skilled at penetrating the bodies of herself and others for whatever was wrong inside. "The ankle is painful but nothing is harmed; only a tendon pulled a little . . . but the kneecap has been twisted out of its place."

As Allart turned his attention to the knee he saw the kneecap wrenched to the side of the leg, the place rapidly swelling and darkening.

She said, drawing a terrified breath, "Donal, you must hold my shoulders, and you Allart, you must grasp my knee and ankle like this—" She gestured. "No! Lower down, with that hand—and pull hard. Don't worry about hurting me. If it is not returned to its place at once I could be lamed for life."

Allart steeled himself to follow her instructions. She was braced and tense, but despite her courage, a shriek was forced between her teeth as he gripped the dislocation and twisted it, hard, back into its place, feeling the grating as the kneecap slid back into its socket. She fell back in Donal's arms and for a moment it seemed she had fainted, but she had closed her eyes and was again monitoring to see what had happened.

"Not quite. You must turn my foot to one side—I cannot move it myself—so it will fall back into place. Yes," she said, between clenched teeth, as Allart obeyed her. "That will do. Now tear my under-petticoat and bandage it tightly," she said. Tears came to her eyes again, not only of pain, but of embarrassment as Allart lifted her to remove her under-garment, although Donal modestly turned away.

When the hurt knee had been tightly bandaged in strips of cloth, and Cassandra, white and shivering, had been wrapped in her cloak, and was resting on the ground, Allart soberly took stock of their chances here. Outside, the storm had not nearly reached its height, and night, as he imagined, was not far away, though already it was dark, a thick, heavy twilight that had nothing to do with the actual hour. They had with them only the remnants of their picnic lunch, enough for a couple of sparse meals. These storms sometimes lasted for two or three days, or more. Under ordinary conditions, any of them could have gone without a few meals, but not if the cold should become really severe.

They could probably manage for two or three days. But if the storm should last much longer than that, or if the roads should become impassable, their chances were not good. Alone, Allart would have wrapped himself tightly in his cloak, found the most sheltered spot possible, and let himself sink into the tranced sleep he had learned at Nevarsin, slowing his heartbeat, lowering his body temperature, all the requirements of his body—food, sleep, warmth—in abeyance. But he was responsible for his wife, and for young Donal, and they had not had his training. He was the oldest and the most skilled.

"Your cloak is the thinnest, Cassandra, and the least useful to us for warmth. Spread it on the ground like this, here, so it will keep the cold of the earth from rising," he directed. "Now, our two cloaks over the three of us. Cassandra is the least accustomed to the cold of the mountains, so we will put her between us." When they were all three huddled together, back to front, he could feel Cassandra's shivering subside somewhat.

"Now," he said gently, "the best thing to do is to sleep if we can; above all, not to waste energy in talking."

Outside the shelter where they lay, the wind howled, snow coming down endlessly in streaks white against the black night. Inside, only random flurries blew through the tightly laced branches. Allart let himself drift into a light trance, holding Cassandra close in his arms so that he would know if she stirred or had any need of him. At last he knew that Donal, at least, slept; but Cassandra, though she lay quiet in his arms, did not sleep. He was aware of the sharp pain in her injured leg, keeping her concentration at bay. At last she turned in his arms to face him, and he clasped her tight.

She whispered, "Allart, are we going to die here?"

Reassurance would have been easy—and false. No matter what, there must be truth between them, as there had been from the first moment they met. He fumbled in the dark for her slender fingers and said, "I don't know, *preciosa*. I hope not."

His *laran* showed him only darkness ahead. Through the touch of her hands he could feel the pain stabbing at her. She tried carefully to shift her weight without disturbing Donal, who was curled close against her body. Allart half rose, kneeling and lifted her, changing her position. "Is that easier?"

"A little." But there was not much he could do in their cramped shelter. This had been the worst of all mischances; even if there were a break in the weather, they could not now seek better shelter, for Cassandra would probably not be able to walk for several days. Tended, put at once into a hot bath, given massage and treatment by a matrix-trained *leronis* to halt the swelling and bleeding within the joint, it might not have been very serious; but long exposure to cold and immobilization did not promise well for swift healing. Even if conditions had been right, Allart had but small training in those skills. Rough and ready first aid he could give, indeed, but nothing more complicated.

"I should have left you safe at Hali," he groaned, and she touched his face in the darkness.

"There was no safety for me there, my husband. Not with your brother at my door."

"Still, if I have led you to your death—"

"It might equally have been my death to stay there," she said, and amazingly, even in this extremity, he caught a flicker of laughter in her voice. "Had Damon-Rafael sought to take me unwilling, he would have found no submissive woman in his bed. I have a knife and I know how—and where—to use it." He heard her voice tighten. "I doubt he would have let me live to spread the tale of that humiliation."

"I do not think he would have had to use force," Allart said bleakly. "More like, you would have been drugged into submission, without will to resist."

"Ah, no," she said, and her voice thrilled with an emotion he could not read. "In that case, my husband, I would have known where to turn the knife ere they brought me to *that*."

Allart felt such a thickening in his throat that he could not force an answer. What had he done to deserve this woman? Had he ever believed her timid, childlike, fearful? He caught her tightly against him, but aloud he only said, "Try to sleep, my love. Rest your weight against me, if it is easier. Are you too cold now?"

"No, not really, not close to you this way," she said, and was still, breathing long, calm breaths in and out.

But have I given her freedom or only a choice of deaths?

The night crawled by, an eternity. When day broke it was only a little lessening of the darkness, and for the three in the hollow, cramped and restless, it was torment. Allart cautioned Donal, crawling outside for a call of nature, not to go more than a step or two from the thicket, and when he staggered back inside, battered and already snow covered, he said that outside the wind was so heavy he could hardly stand. Allart had to carry Cassandra in his arms; she could not set her foot to the ground. Later he meted out most of the food from the day before. The snow showed no sign of abating; as far as Allart could tell, the world outside their tree-cluster ended an arm's length away in a white blur of snowy nothingness.

He let his *laran* range out cautiously ahead. Almost in every instance he saw their lives end *here*, yet there had to be other possibilities. If it were his ordained fate to die here, and if bringing Cassandra from Hali would lead inevitably to his death and hers in the snow, then why had his *laran* shown him no trace of it, ever, in any line of probability that he had foreseen to this time?

"Donal," he said, and the younger man stirred.

"Cousin . . ."

"You have more of the weather gift than I. Can you read this storm and discover how far it extends, and how long it will take to move past us?"

"I will try." Donal sank inward in consciousness, and Allart, lightly in rapport, saw again the curious extended sense of pressures and forces, like nets of energy upon the surface of the ground, and in the thin envelope of air above it. Finally, returning to surface consciousness, Donal said soberly, "Too far, I fear. And it is moving sluggishly. Would that I had my sister's gift, to control the storms and move them here and there at my will!"

Suddenly Allart knew that was the answer, as he began to see ahead again. His *laran* was real foresight, yes; he could dislocate time and stand outside it, but it was limited by his own interpretation of what he saw. For that reason it would always be unreliable as a sole guide to his actions. He must never be content with an obvious future; there was always the probability, however small, that interaction with someone whose actions he could not foresee would alter that future beyond recognition. He could rule his *laran*, but as with his matrix jewel, he must never let it rule him instead. Yesterday he had used it to find safety here and avoid the most obvious deaths lying in wait; it had worked to avert imminent death until he could explore some other probability.

"If we could somehow make contact with Dorilys—"

"She is not a telepath," Donal said, sounding doubtful. "Never have I been able to reach her with my thoughts." Then he lifted his eyes and said, "Renata . . . Renata is a telepath. If one of you two could manage to reach Renata—"

Yes, for Renata was the key to control of Dorilys's power.

Allart said, "*You* try to reach her, Donal."

"But—I am not so strong a telepath."

"Nevertheless. Those who have shared love, as you two, can often make such a link when no other can. Tell Renata of our plight, and perhaps Dorilys can read the storm, or help it to pass more quickly beyond us!"

"I will do what I can," Donal said. Drawing himself upright, the cloaks still hunched around him, he drew out his matrix and began to focus himself within it. Allart and Cassandra, clinging together beneath the remaining cloak, could almost see the luminous lines of force spreading out, so that

Donal seemed no more than a solid network of swirling energies, fields of force. . . . Then, abruptly, the contact flared and Allart and Cassandra, both telepaths, could not close away that amplified rapport.

Renata!

Donal! The joy and blaze of that contact spilled over to Cassandra and Allart, as if she touched them, too, embraced them.

I was fearful, with this storm! Are you safe? Have you remained at Tramontana, then? I feared when it broke that the escort would be forced to turn back; did they meet with you, then?

No, my beloved. Quickly, in rapid mental images, Donal sketched their plight. He interrupted Renata's horrified reaction. *No, love, don't waste time and strength that way. Here is what you must do.*

Of course, Dorilys can help us, and the swift touch, awareness. *I will find her at once, show her what to do.*

The contact was gone. The lines of force faded out and Donal shivered under the doubled cloaks.

Allart handed him the last of the food, and said, when he protested, "Your energy is drained with the matrix; you need the strength."

"Still, your lady—" Donal protested, but Cassandra shook her head. In the gray snowlight she looked pale, drawn, deathly.

"I am not hungry, Donal. You need it far more than I. I am cold, so cold. . . ."

Quickly Allart knew what she meant and what faced her now. He said, "What is it with the leg, then?"

"I will monitor and be sure," she said, a flicker of a smile touching her face, a wry smile indeed. "I have not wanted to know the worst, since there seems nothing I could do to mend it, however bad it may be." But he saw her look go abstracted, focused inward. Finally, reluctant, she said, "It is not good. The cold, the forced inactivity—and in the lower part of that leg the circulation is already impaired, so that it is more susceptible to chilling."

There was nothing Allart could say but, "Help may soon reach us, my love. Meanwhile—" He took off his outer tunic, began to wrap it around the injured knee to protect it, and wrapped her in his under-cloak, remaining in his undertunic and breeches. At their shocked protest, he said with a smile,

"Ah, you forget; I was a monk at Nevarsin for six years, and I slept naked in worse weather than this." Indeed, the old lessons took over; as the cold struck his now unprotected flesh, he began automatically the old breathing, flooding his body with inner warmth. He said, "Truly, I am not cold. Feel and see. . . ."

Cassandra reached out her hand, wondering. "It is true! You are warm as a furnace."

"Yes," he said, taking her chilly fingers in his and laying them under his arm. "Here, let me warm your hands."

Donal said, in astonishment, "I would that you could teach me that trick, cousin."

Feeling enormously genial with the sudden flooding warmth, Allart replied, "It needs little teaching. We teach it to the novices in their first season with us, so that before a few tendays have passed, they are romping half naked in the snow. Children who are crying with the cold in their first few days soon begin to run about in the courtyards without even remembering to put on their cowls."

"Is it a secret of your *cristoforo* religion?" Donal asked suspiciously.

Allart shook his head. "No, only a trick of the mind; it needs not even a matrix. The first thing we tell them is that cold is born of *fear*; that if they needed protection against cold, they would have been born with fur or feathers; that the forces of nature protect even the fruits with snow-pods if they need them; but man, being born naked, needs no protection against the weather. Once they come to believe that, that mankind wears clothes because he wishes to, for modesty or for decoration, but not to shelter against the weather, then the worst is over and soon they can adjust their bodies to cold or heat as they wish." He laughed, knowing the euphoria of the extra oxygen he was taking into his body was beginning to act upon him, to be converted into warmth. "I am less cold than I was last night under our shared cloaks and body warmth."

Cassandra tried to imitate his breathing, but she was in severe pain, and this inhibited her concentration, while Donal was wholly untrained.

Outside, the storm raged even more fiercely, and Allart lay down between the two, trying to share with them his warmth. He was desperately anxious about Cassandra; if she suffered much more pain and chilling, her knee might not heal for a long time, perhaps never wholly restore itself. He tried to conceal his anxiety from her, but the same closeness which had enabled Donal to reach Renata—without a Tower screen, through an open matrix-link alone—meant he and Cassandra were similarly linked and, especially at this close range, could not conceal a fear so strong from one another.

She reached for his hand and murmured, "Don't be frightened. The pain is not so bad now; truly it is not."

Well, when they reached Aldaran, Margali and Renata could tend her; for now there was nothing to be done. In the dimness he held the slight six-fingered hand in his, felt the knotted scar of the *clingfire* burn. She had endured war and fear and pain before this; he had not brought her out of peaceful life into danger. If he had simply substituted one danger for another, still, he knew, it was the danger which she had freely chosen for another less to her liking, and that was all any human being could ask in such days. Comforted a little, he dropped off, for a time, to sleep, held in her arms.

When he woke it was to hear a cry from Cassandra.

"Look! The storm has cleared!" He looked up, dazed, at the sky. It had stopped snowing entirely, and clouds were tearing across the sky at a wild pace.

"Dorilys," Donal said. "No storm ever moved across these hills at such a pace." He drew a long, shaking breath. "Her power—the power we have all feared so much—has saved all our lives."

Allart, sending his *laran* out across the country around, realized that the escort had been weathered in on the other side of the ledge he had hesitated to face in the storm. Now, as soon as they could bring their riding-animals across it—a matter of a few hours, certainly—help would be with them, food and shelter and care.

It had not been Dorilys's *laran* alone that had saved them, he thought soberly. The *laran* he had considered a curse had now proved its worth—and its limitations.

I cannot ignore it. But I must never wholly rely on it, either. I need not hide from it in terror, as I did all those years in Nevarsin. But I cannot let it wholly rule my actions.

Maybe I am beginning to know its limitations, Allart thought. It suddenly occurred to him that he had thought of Donal as very young, childishly young. Yet he himself, he realized, was no more than two years Donal's senior. With a completely new humility, free for once in his life of self-pity, he thought, *I am still very young myself. And I may not be given enough time to learn wisdom. But if I live, I may find that some of my problems were only because I was too young, and too foolish to know I was only too young.*

Cassandra was lying on his cloak, gray with pain and exhausted. He turned to her, and was touched that she tried to smile and appear brave. Now he could reassure her honestly, without hiding his own fear. Help was on the way and would reach them soon; there was only a little more time to wait.

CHAPTER
TWENTY-THREE

Donal Delleray, called Rockhaven, and Dorilys, heir to Aldaran, were formally married by the *catenas* on midwinter night.

It was not a festive occasion. The weather prevented, as often in the Hellers, inviting any but the nearest of Aldaran's neighbors; and of those invited, many chose not to come, in which Aldaran saw, rightly or not, a sign that they had chosen to align with his brother of Scathfell. So that the marriage was held in the presence of the immediate household alone, and even among these there was murmuring.

This kind of marriage, half-brother to half-sister, had once been commonplace in the early days of the breeding program, especially among the great nobles of the Domains— and imitated, like all such customs, by their inferiors. But it had fallen now into disuse and was regarded as mildly scandalous.

"They do not like it," said Allart to Cassandra as they went into the great hall where the festive supper, and the ceremony, and afterward the dance for the household, were all to be held. She was leaning heavily on his arm; she still walked with a dragging limp, memento of their ordeal in the snow, despite the best care Margali and Renata could give. It might heal with time, but it was still difficult for her to walk without help.

"They do not like it," he repeated. "Had anyone other than Dom Mikhail given orders for such a thing, they would have defied him, I think."

"What is it they do not like? That Donal shall inherit Aldaran when he is not of the blood of Hastur and Cassilda?"

273

"No," said Allart. "As far as I can tell from talking to Aldaran's vassals and household knights, that pleases them rather than otherwise; none of them has any love for Scathfell, nor any wish to see him rule here. If Dom Mikhail had given it out, true or not, that Donal was his *nedestro* son and would inherit, they would have stood by him to the death. Even if they knew it was false, they would have treated it as a legal fiction. What they do not like is this marriage of brother and sister."

"But this is a legal fiction, too," Cassandra protested.

Allart said, "I am not so sure of that. And neither are they. I still feel guilty that it was my own careless words which put this mad idea into Dom Mikhail's mind. And those who support Dom Mikhail in this—well, they do it as if they were humoring a madman. I am not so sure they are wrong," he added after a moment. "All madmen do not rave and froth at the mouth and chase butterflies in midwinter snow. Pride and obsession like Dom Mikhail's come near to madness, even if they are couched in reason and logic."

Since the bride was a little girl, the guests could not even hope to lighten the occasion with the jokes and rough horseplay which usually marked a wedding, culminating in the rowdy business of putting the bride and groom to bed together. Dorilys was not even full-grown, far less of legal age to be married. No one had wanted to rouse in Dorilys any bitter memories of her last handfasting, and so there had been no question of presenting her as a grown woman. In her childish dress, her copper hair hanging in long curls about her shoulders, she looked like a child of the household who had been allowed to stay up for the festivities, rather than like the appointed bride. As for the bridegroom, though he made an attempt to give decent lip service to the occasion, he looked grim and joyless, and before they went into the hall, the guests observed that he went toward a group of the bride's waiting-women and called Renata Leynier apart, talking with her vehemently for some minutes. A few of the house-folk, and most of the servants, knew the true state of affairs between Donal and Renata, and shook their heads at this indiscretion in a man about to be wed. Others, looking at the little bride, surrounded by her nurses and governesses, compared her mentally with Renata and did not censure him.

"Whatever he says, whatever mummery he may make with the *catenas*, this is no more than a handfasting, and not a legal wedding. In law, even a *catenas* marriage is not legal till it is consummated," Donal argued. Renata, about to tell him that this point was still being argued before the Council and the lawgivers of the land, knew that he needed reassurance, not reason.

"It will make no difference to me! Swear it will make no difference to you, Renata, or I will defy my foster-father here and now, before all his vassals!"

If you were going to defy him, Renata thought in despair, *you should have done so from the beginning, certainly before things went this far! It is too late for public defiance without destroying both of you!* Aloud she said only, "Nothing could make any difference to me, Donal; you know that too well to need any oaths, and this is neither the time nor the place. I must go back to the women, Donal." But she touched his hand lightly, with a smile that was almost pity.

We were so happy this summer! How could we come to this? I am not blameless; I should have married him at once. To do him justice, he wished for that. Renata's thoughts were in turmoil as she walked, with Dorilys's women, into the hall.

Dom Mikhail was standing by the fireplace, lighted with the midwinter-fires kindled that day with sunfire, token of the return of light from the darkest day, greeting each of his guests in turn. Dorilys made her father a formal curtsy, and he bowed to her, kissed her on either cheek, and set her at his right side, at the high table. Then, one by one, he greeted the women.

"Lady Elisa, I would like to express my gratitude for your work in cultivating the lovely voice my daughter has inherited from her mother," he said, bowing. "Kinswoman Margali, again at this season I am grateful to you that you have taken a mother's place with my orphaned child. *Damisela*"—he bowed over Renata's hand—"how can I express my pleasure in what you have done for Dorilys? It is the greatest pleasure to welcome you to my—to my festal board," he said, stumbling. Renata, a telepath and keyed to the highest level of sensitivity at this moment, knew with a moment of anguish that he had started to say, "to my family," and then had remembered the real state of affairs between herself and Donal, and forborne to speak those words.

I always thought he knew, Renata thought, blind with pain. *Yet it means more to him, to carry out this plan of his!* Now she even regretted the scruples that had prevented her from again becoming pregnant by Donal at once.

If I had come to midwinter night visibly pregnant with Donal's child, would he have had the insolence to give Donal in marriage to another before my very eyes? When he insists that I have been the salvation of Dorilys? Could I have forced his hand that way? She walked to her seat, blinded by tears, in a welter of regrets and anxieties.

Although Aldaran's cooks and stewards had done their best, and the feast spread before them was notable, it was a joyless occasion. Dorilys seemed nervous, twisting her long curls, at once restless and sleepy. At the close of the meal Dom Mikhail signaled for attention, and called Donal and Dorilys to him. Cassandra and Allart, seated side by side at the far end of the high table, watched in tension, Allart braced for some untoward explosion, either from Donal, guarded and miserable behind a taut facade of civility, or from one of the sullen stewards and household knights at high table or lower hall. But no one interrupted. Watching Dom Mikhail's face, Allart thought no one would have dared to cross him now.

"This is indeed a joyous occasion for Aldaran," said Dom Mikhail.

Allart, briefly meeting Donal's eyes, shared a thought with him, quickly barricaded again. *Like Zandru's hell it is!*

"On this day of revelry it is my pleasure to place the guardianship of my house and my only heir, still a minor, Dorilys of Aldaran, into the hands of my beloved foster-son Donal of Rockraven."

Donal flinched at the name which proclaimed him bastard, and his lips moved in inaudible protest.

"Donal Delleray," Dom Mikhail corrected himself, reluctantly.

Allart thought, *Even now he does not wish to face the fact that Donal is not his son.*

Aldaran placed the twin bracelets of finely chased copper—engraved and filigreed, and lined on the side nearest the skin with gold plating so that the precious metal would not irritate the skin—on Donal's right wrist and Dorilys's left. Allart, looking down at the bracelet on his own wrist, held out his hand to Cassandra. All around the hall married couples were doing the same, as Aldaran spoke the ritual words.

"As the left hand to the right, may you be forever at one;

in caste and clan, in home and heritage, at fireside and in council, sharing all things at home and abroad, in love and in loyalty, now and for all time to come," he said, locking the bracelets together. Smiling for a moment despite his disquiet, Allart fitted the link of his own bracelet into that of his wife and they clasped hands tightly. He picked up Cassandra's thought, *If only it were Donal and Renata . . .* and felt again a surge of anger at this travesty.

Aldaran unlocked the bracelets, separated them. "Separated in fact, may you be joined in heart as in law," he said. "In token I bid you exchange a kiss."

All through the hall, married couples leaned toward one another to proclaim again their bond, even those, Allart knew, who were not on good terms with one another at ordinary times. He kissed Cassandra tenderly, but he turned his eyes away as Donal bent forward, just touching Dorilys's lips with his own.

Aldaran said, "May you be forever one."

Allart caught Renata's eye, and thought, *Desolate. Donal should not have done this to her. . . .* He still felt a strong sense of closeness to her, of responsibility, and he wished he knew what he could do. *It is not even as if Donal himself were happy about this. They are both wretched.* He damned Dom Mikhail for his obsession, and guilt lay heavy on him. *This was my doing. I put it into his head.* He wished heartily that he had never come to Aldaran at all.

Later there was dancing in the hall, Dorilys leading the dance with a group of her women. Renata had helped her to devise this dance and danced with her in the first measures, hands interlaced with the child's as they went through the ornate measures.

Allart watched her and thought, *They are not rivals; they are both victims.* He saw Donal watching them both, and abruptly turned away, returning to the sidelines where Cassandra, still too lame for dancing, sat among a group of the old women.

The night wore on, Aldaran's vassals and guests dutifully trying to put some jollity into the occasion. A juggler performed magic tricks for the household, bringing coins and small animals from the unlikeliest places, scarves and rings out of nowhere; in the end he brought a live songbird from Dorilys's ear and presented it to her, then retired, bowing. There were minstrels to sing old ballads, and in the great hall, more dancing. But it was not like a wedding, nor like an ordinary midwinter feast. Every now and then someone would start to make the kind of rowdy joke suitable for a wedding, then remember the real state of affairs and nervously break off in mid-sentence. Dorilys sat beside her father in the high seat, Donal at her side for a long time. Someone had found a cage for her songbird and she was trying to coax it to sing, but the hour was late and the bird drooping on its perch. Dorilys seemed to droop, too. Finally Donal, desperate at the silent tension and the joyless gathering, said, "Will you dance with me, Dorilys?"

"No," said Aldaran. "It is not seemly that bride and groom dance together at a wedding."

Donal turned on his foster-father a look of fury and despair. "In the name of all the gods, this pretense—" he began, then sighed heavily and dropped it. Not at a feast, not before all their assembled house-folk and vassals. He said with heavy irony, "God forbid we should do anything out of custom, such as might cause scandal among our kin," and turned, beckoning Allart from his wife's side. "Cousin, take my sister out to dance, if you will."

As Allart led out Dorilys to the floor, Donal looked once at Renata, in despair, but before his father's eyes he bowed to Margali. "Foster-mother, will you honor me with a dance, I beg?" and moved away with the old lady on his arm.

Afterward he danced dutifully with other of Dorilys's women, Lady Elisa and even her aged, waddling nurse. Allart, watching, wondered if this was intended to lead up to a situation where it would seem obvious for Donal to dance with Renata; but as Donal returned old Kathya to the women, they came face to face with Dorilys, who had been dancing with the *coridom* of the estate.

Dorilys looked up at Donal sweetly, then beckoned to Renata and in a clear, audible voice, filled with a false and sugary sweetness, said loudly, "You must dance with Donal, Renata. If you dance with a bridegroom at midwinter, you, too, will be married within the year, they say. Shall I ask my father to find you a husband, cousin Renata?" Her smile was innocent and spiteful, and Donal clenched his teeth as he took Renata's hand and led her onto the dancing floor.

"She should be spanked!"

Renata was almost in tears. "I thought—I thought she understood. I had hoped she was fond of me, even that she had come to love me! How could she—"

Donal could only say, "She is overwrought. The hour is late for her, and this is a trying occasion. She cannot help but remember, I suppose, what happened at her handfasting to Darren of Scathfell. . . ." As if to underline his anger it seemed, though he could not be sure whether he really heard it or remembered it, that he heard a curious premonitory rumble of thunder.

Renata thought, *Dorilys has been on her good behavior of late. She cooperated with me on moving the storm which menaced Allart and Cassandra and Donal, and is now proud of her talent, proud that it saved lives. But she is only a child, spoiled and arrogant.*

Allart, across the room and seated at Cassandra's side, heard the thunder, too, and for a moment it seemed like the voice of his *laran*, warning him of storms to break over Aldaran. . . . For a moment it seemed that he stood in the courtyard of Aldaran keep, hearing thunders strike and break over the castle; he saw Renata's face pale and distraught with the lightnings . . . he heard the cries of armed men and actually started, wondering if the castle were truly under assault, until he recalled that it was midwinter night.

Cassandra clasped his hand. "What did you see?" she whispered.

"A storm," he said, "and shadows, shadows over Aldaran." His voice died to a whisper, as if he heard the thunders again, though this time it was only in his mind.

When Donal returned to the high seat of his foster-father he said firmly, "Sir, the hour is late. Since this will not end like a traditional wedding, with a bedding as well, I have given orders for the guesting-cup to be brought and the minstrels dismissed."

Aldaran's face turned dark with sudden flaring anger.

"You take all too much on yourself, Donal! I have given no orders to that effect!"

Donal was startled, mystified at the sudden rage. Dom Mikhail had left all such things in his hands for the last three midwinter feasts. He said reasonably, "I did as you have always bidden me to do, sir. I acted upon my own best judgment." He hoped that by quoting his foster-father's own words he could calm him.

Instead, Dom Mikhail leaned forward with clenched hands

and demanded, "Are you so eager to rule all in my place, then, Donal? That you cannot wait for my word—"

Donal thought, bewildered, *Is he mad? Is his mind going?*

Dom Mikhail opened his mouth to say more, but the servants had already entered bearing the jeweled cup containing a rich mixture of wine and spices, which would go around, shared from hand to hand. It was offered to Dom Mikhail, who held it motionless between his two hands for so long that Donal trembled. Courtesy finally conquered. Dom Mikhail set the cup to his lips, bowed to Donal, and handed him the cup. In his turn Donal barely tasted the mixture, but steadied it for Dorilys to taste, and passed it on to Allart and Cassandra.

The abortive scene had put a damper on what little remained of festivity. One by one, as they sipped from the cup, the guests bowed to Lord Aldaran and withdrew. Dorilys suddenly began to cry, noisy childish crying which suddenly escalated into screaming, bawling hysteria.

Dom Mikhail said helplessly, "Why, Dorilys, child," but she shrieked louder than ever when he touched her.

Margali came to enfold the child in her arms. "She is exhausted, and no wonder. Come, come, my little love, my baby. Let me take you away to your bed. Come, my darling, my bird, don't cry anymore," she crooned.

Dorilys, surrounded by Margali and Elisa and old Kathya, was half carried from the hall. The few remaining guests, embarrassed, slipped away to their beds.

Donal, crimson and raging, picked up a glass of wine and emptied it at a single swallow, then refilled it with angry determination. Allart went toward him to speak, then sighed and withdrew. There was nothing he could do for Donal now, and if Donal chose to get himself drunk, it was only a fitting end to this enormous fiasco of a festival. Allart joined Cassandra at the door, and went silently, at her side, down the hallway toward their own rooms.

"I do not blame the child," Cassandra said, painfully dragging herself upward on the stairs, holding to the railing. "It cannot be easy to be displayed as a bride before all these folk, and everyone staring and talking scandal about this wedding, and then to be put to bed in the nursery as if nothing had happened. Some wedding for the child! And some wedding night!"

Allart said gently, taking her by the elbow to steady her

lagging step, "As I remember, my beloved, you spent your wedding night alone."

"Yes," she said, turning her eyes on him and smiling, "but my bridegroom was not abed with someone he loved better, either. Do you think Dorilys does not know Donal shares Renata's bed? She is jealous."

Allart scoffed. "Even if she does know—at her age, would it mean anything to her? She may be jealous because Donal cares more for Renata than he does for her, but he is only her big brother; surely it does not mean to her what it would have meant to you!"

"I am not so sure," Cassandra said. "She is not so young as most people think. In years—yes, I grant you, she is a child. But no one with her gift, no one with two deaths behind her, no one with the training she has had from Renata, is really a child, whatever the years may indicate. Merciful gods," she whispered, "what a tangle this is! I cannot imagine what will come of it!"

Allart, who could, was wishing that he could not.

Very late that night, Renata, in her solitary room, was wakened by a sound at her door. Instantly knowing who was there, she opened it to see Donal, disheveled, swaying on his feet, very drunk.

"On this night—is it wise, Donal?" she asked, but she knew he was beyond caring for that. She could feel the despair like physical pain in him.

"If you turn me away now," he raged, "I shall throw myself from the heights of this castle before the dawn!"

Her arms went out to hold him against her, compassionately; to draw him inside, to shut the door after him.

"They may marry me to Dorilys," he said, with drunken earnestness, "but she will never be my wife. No woman living shall be my wife but you!"

Merciful Avarrà, what will become of us? she thought. Renata was a monitor; there could have been no worse time for him to come to her like this, and yet she knew, sharing with him all the rage and despair of the humiliating night past, that she could deny him nothing, nothing that could ease even a little the pain of what had happened. She knew, too, with a despairing foresight, that she would come from this night bearing his son.

CHAPTER
TWENTY-FOUR

Late in the winter, Allart met Cassandra on the stairway which led into the south wing of Castle Aldaran, where the women spent much of their time at this season in the conservatory rooms which caught the winter sun.

"It is a bright day," he said. "Why not come and walk with me in the courtyard? I see so little of you these days!" Then, laughing, he checked himself. "But no, you cannot—this afternoon is your festival in the women's quarters for Dorilys; is it not?"

Everyone at Castle Aldaran knew that in the last tenday Dorilys had first shown the signs of maturity—an official occasion for rejoicing. During the last three days she had been distributing her toys and playthings, her dolls and her favorite childish garments, among the children in the castle. The afternoon would be the private quasi-religious celebration among the women which marked leaving the company of the children and entering the society of the women.

"I know her father has sent her a special gift of some sort," Allart said.

Cassandra nodded. "And I am embroidering her some bands for a new shift," she said.

"What goes on at these women's affairs, anyhow?" Allart asked.

Cassandra laughed gaily. "Ah, you must not ask me that, my husband," she said, and then, with mock seriousness, "There are some things it is not good for men to know."

Allart chuckled. "Now there is a byword I have not heard since I left the company of the *cristoforos*. And I suppose we will not have your company at dinner either!"

"No. Tonight the women will dine together for her festival," Cassandra said.

He stooped to kiss her hand. "Well, then, bear Dorilys my congratulations," he said, and went out, while Cassandra, holding carefully to the railing—her lame knee had bettered somewhat, but was still troublesome on the stairs—went up toward the conservatory.

During the winter the women spent much of their time here, for these rooms alone caught the winter sun. They were bright with plants blooming in the light of the solar reflectors, and in the last tenday, in preparation for this celebration, branches of fruit-blossom had been brought inside and forced in the sunlight to adorn the gathering. Margali, as household *leronis* and also as Dorilys's foster-mother, was in charge of the ceremonies. Most of the women of the castle were present, the wives of the stewards and household knights and other functionaries, Dorilys's own waiting-women, a few of her favorites among the servant-women, and her own nurses, governesses, and teachers.

First she was taken to the chapel, and a lock of her hair was cut and laid upon the altar of Evanda, with fruit and flowers. After this Margali and Renata bathed her—Cassandra, as the highest in rank of the lady guests, had been invited to assist at this ritual—and dressed her from the skin out in new clothes, doing up her hair in a woman's coiffure. Margali, looking at her nursling, remembered how different she looked from when, less than a year ago, she had been masquerading in woman's garments at her handfasting.

Part of the purpose of this party, in earlier days, had been to make, for the new member of the woman's community, such things as she would need in her adult life; a remnant of a harsher time in the mountains. It was still, by tradition, a party at which all women brought their sewing, and everyone took at least a few stitches in items intended for the guest of honor. As they sewed, the harp went from hand to hand, each of the women being expected to sing a song, or tell a story, to amuse the others. Elisa had had the tall harp brought from the schoolroom and sang mountain ballads. A variety of dainties had been provided for refreshments, including some of Dorilys's favorite sweets, but Renata noticed that she only nibbled at them listlessly.

"What is the matter, *chiya?*"

Dorilys passed her hand over her eyes. "I am tired and my eyes hurt a little. I don't feel like eating."

"Come now, it is too late for that," one of them teased. "Two or three days ago was your time for headaches and vapors of that sort, if you must! You should be perfectly well again by now!" She examined the length of linen in Dorilys's lap.

"What are you making, Dori?"

Dorilys said with dignity, "I am embroidering a holiday shirt for my husband," and moved her wrist to display the *catena*s bracelet on it. Renata, watching her, suddenly did not know whether to laugh or cry. Such a traditional bridelike occupation, and the child had been given into a marriage which would never be more than a mockery! Well, she was still very young, and it would not hurt her to embroider a shirt for the big brother she loved and who was, in the eyes of the law, her husband.

Elisa finished her ballad, and turned to Cassandra.

"It is your turn. Will you favor us with a song, Lady Hastur?" she asked deferentially.

Cassandra hesitated, feeling shy, then realized that if she refused it might be taken as an indication that she considered herself above this gathering.

"With pleasure," she said, "but I cannot play on the tall harp, Elisa. If someone will lend me a *rryl*—"

When the smaller instrument was fetched and tuned, she sang for them, in a sweet husky voice, two or three of the songs of the Valeron plains, far away. These were new to the mountain women, and they asked for more, but Cassandra shook her head.

"Another time, perhaps. It is Dorilys's turn to sing for us, and I am sure she is eager to try out her new lute," she said. The lute, an elaborate gilded and painted one, adorned with ribbons, was Lord Aldaran's gift to his daughter on this occasion, replacing the old one of her mother's on which she had learned to play. "And I am sure she would welcome a rest from sewing!"

Dorilys looked up languidly from the mass of linen on her knees. "I don't feel like singing," she said. "Will you excuse me, kinswoman?" She drew her hand across her eyes, then began to rub them. "My head aches. Do I have to do any more sewing?"

"Not unless you wish, love, but we are all sewing here,"

Margali said. In her mind was a gently amused picture, which Cassandra and Renata could both read clearly, that Dorilys was all too ready to develop headaches when it came to doing the hated sewing.

"How dare you say that about me," Dorilys cried out, flinging the shirt in a wadded muddle to the floor. "I am really sick, I am not pretending! I don't even want to sing, and I *always* want to sing—" And suddenly she began to cry.

Margali looked at her in dismay and consternation. *But I didn't open my mouth! Gods above, is the child a telepath, too?*

Renata said gently, "Come here, Dorilys, and sit by me. Your foster-mother did not speak; you read her thoughts, that is all. There is no need to be troubled."

But Margali was not accustomed to barricading her thoughts from Dorilys. She had come to believe that her charge had no trace of telepathic power, and she could not prevent the swift thought that flashed through her mind.

Merciful Avarra! This, too? Lord Aldaran's older children so died when they were come to adolescence, and now it is beginning with her, too!

Dismayed, Renata reached out to try to barricade the thoughts, but it was too late; Dorilys had read them already. Her sobbing died and she stared at Renata in frozen terror.

Cousin! Am I going to die?

Renata said firmly, aloud, "No, of course not. Why do you think we have been training and teaching you, if not to strengthen you for this? I had not expected it quite so soon, that is all. Now don't try to read anymore; you haven't the strength. We will teach you to shut it out and control it."

But Dorilys was not hearing her. She was staring at them in a nightmare of panic and dread, their thoughts mirrored back at them in the first frightening moment of overload. She stared around her like some small trapped animal, her mouth open, her eyes so wide with terror that the whites showed all around the shrunken pupils.

Margali got up and went to her foster-child, trying to take her into a comforting embrace. Dorilys stood rigid, unmoving, unaware of the touch, unable to perceive anything but the massive onslaught of internal sensation. When Margali would have lifted her into her arms, she struck out unknowing, striking Margali with a painful shock that crumpled the old woman against the wall. Elisa hurried to her aid, lifting

Margali, and the woman sat there staring in shock and consternation.

To turn on me this way . . . on me?

Renata said, "She doesn't know what she is doing, Margali; she doesn't know anything. I can hold her," she added, reaching out to hold the girl motionless as she had done when Dorilys first defied her, "but this is serious; she must have some *kirian*."

Margali went for the drug, and Elisa, at a word from Renata, asked the guests to leave. Too many minds nearby would confuse Dorilys more frighteningly. She should be in the presence of only a few she trusted. When Margali returned with the *kirian*, only Renata, Cassandra, and Margali herself remained.

Renata went to Dorilys, trying to make contact with the terrified girl, isolated behind her panicked barricade of fear. After a time Dorilys began to breathe more easily, her eyes unlocked from their rigid, rolled-up unseeing position. When Margali held the vial of *kirian* to her lips she swallowed it without protest. They laid her on a couch and tucked a blanket around her, but when Renata knelt at her side to monitor her, she cried out again in panic and sudden terror.

"No, no, don't touch me, don't!" Thunder suddenly crashed around the heights of the castle, a rattling roar.

"*Chiya.* I won't hurt you, really. I only want to see—"

"Don't touch me, Renata!" Dorilys shrieked. "You want me to die, and then *you* can have Donal!"

Shocked, Renata recoiled. Such a thought had never crossed her mind, but had Dorilys probed to a level of which even Renata herself was unaware? Fiercely dismissing the guilt, she held out her arms to the girl.

"No, darling, no. Look—you can read my thoughts if you will and see what nonsense that is. I want nothing more than to have you well again."

But, Dorilys's teeth were chattering, and they knew she was in no state to listen to reason. Cassandra came and took her place; she could not kneel because of her lame knee, but she sat on the edge of the couch beside Dorilys.

"Renata would never hurt you, *chiya*, but we do not want you to upset yourself either. I am a monitor, too. I will monitor you. You are not afraid of me, are you?" She added to Renata, "When she is calmer, she will know the truth."

Renata moved away, still so horrified by Dorilys's sudden

attack that she was almost incapable of rational thought. *Has she lost her senses? Does threshold sickness presage madness also?* She had been prepared for Dorilys to show ordinary sisterly jealousy because Donal was no longer specially hers; she had not been prepared for the intense emotion of this.

Damn that mad old man, if he has encouraged her to believe this will be anything but a legal fiction! Although Renata had hoped very soon to reveal to Donal that she was bearing his son—for now she was certain, and she had monitored the unborn, germ-deep, to be certain it bore no lethals—she realized that it must be kept secret for a while longer. If Dorilys were sick and unstable, this would only hurt her more.

Cassandra went through the monitoring process; then, as the *kirian* began to take effect, lowering Dorilys's terrified defenses against the new sense which had frightened her so, Dorilys quieted, her breathing growing more steady.

"It's stopped," she said at last, and her face was calm, her heart no longer racing with panic. Only the memory of fear remained. "Will it—will it start again?"

"Probably," Cassandra said, but stilled Dorilys's look of swift panic with, "It will grow less troubling as you grow used to it. Each time it will be easier, and when you are fully mature, you will be able to use it as you do your sight, to look selectively as you wish, near and far, and to shut out everything you do not want."

"I'm afraid," Dorilys whispered. "Don't leave me alone."

"No, my lamb," Margali said. "I will sleep in your room as long as you need me."

Renata said, "I know Margali has been like a mother to you, and you want her near you, but truly, Dorilys, I am more skilled in this and I could help you more if you needed it for the next few nights."

Dorilys held out her arms, and Renata came into them. The girl hid her face against Renata's shoulder. "I'm sorry, Renata. I didn't mean it. Forgive me, cousin . . . you know I love you. Please, stay with me."

"Of course, darling," Renata said, holding her in a reassuring hug. "I know, I know. I have had threshold sickness, too. You were scared, and all kinds of wild ideas were flooding into your mind at once. It is hard to control when it comes on you so suddenly like that. From now on we must work a little every day with your matrix, to help you control it; because when it comes on you again you must be prepared."

I wish that we had her in a Tower. She would be safer there, and so would all of us, she thought. She felt Cassandra echo the wish as the thunder rolled again and crackled in the air outside the castle.

In the great hall Allart heard the thunder, and so did Donal. Donal never heard thunder, no matter how or where, without thinking of Dorilys; and Dom Mikhail evidently followed his thoughts.

"Now that your bride is become a woman, you can go about the business of fathering an heir. If we know there is to be a son with Aldaran blood, then we will indeed be ready to defy Scathfell when he comes on us—and spring is not far," Aldaran said with a fierce smile. But Donal's face was taut with rejection, and Dom Mikhail looked at him and scowled.

"Zandru's hells, lad! I do not expect that a child so young should attract you too much as a lover! But when you have done your duty to your clan, you can have as many other women as you will. No one will gainsay that! The important thing now is to give the Domain a legitimate, *catenas* heir, fathered in lawful marriage!"

Donal made a gesture of rejection. *Are all old people always so cynical?* At the same moment he felt his foster-father's thoughts crossing and reinforcing his, with a kind of rueful affection.

Are all young people always so foolishly idealistic? Mikhail of Aldaran reached out to clasp his foster-son's hand.

"My dear boy, think of it this way. This time next year there will be an heir to Aldaran, and you will be his regent lawfully," he said.

As he spoke Allart almost gasped aloud, for his *laran* clearly showed it. In this great hall where they now sat, he could see it as clearly as if it were at this moment present to his eyes: Dom Mikhail, looking older, stooped and aged, held up a blanketed child—newborn, only a small red oval of baby face between the folds of the fleecy shawl—proclaiming Aldaran's heir. The cries of acclamation were so loud that for a moment Allart could not believe the others could not hear them. . . . The images were gone, had yet to be. But he was deeply shaken.

Would Donal, then, actually father a child on his little sister? Would this be the heir to Aldaran? His foresight seemed so clear and unequivocal! Donal picked it up from his mind and sat staring at him, helplessly, but some hint of it spilled over to the old man and he grinned in fierce triumph, seeing in Allart's mind the heir with whom he was obsessed.

At that moment Margali and Cassandra entered the hall, and Aldaran looked at them with a benevolent smile.

"I had not thought your merrymaking would end so quickly, ladies. When the hall-steward's daughter came of age, there was dancing and singing in the women's rooms until midnight was past—" He broke off abruptly. "Margali, kinswoman, what is wrong?"

But he read the truth quickly in her face.

"Threshold sickness! Merciful Avarra!"

Suddenly, from ambition and paranoia, he was only a concerned father again. His voice shook when he said, "I had hoped she would be spared this. Aliciane's *laran* came on her early, and she had no crisis at puberty, but there is a curse on my seed . . . my older sons and daughter so died." He bowed his head. "I have not thought of them in years."

Allart saw them in his mind, reinforced by the memories of the old *leronis*: a dark, laughing boy; a smaller, more solid boy with a mop of riotous curls and a triangular scar on his chin; a delicate, dreamy dark girl who somehow, in the lift of her small head, had something of a look of Dorilys, too. . . . Allart felt in himself the anguish of the father who had seen them sicken and die, one after another, all their promise and beauty wiped out. He saw in the older man's mind a terrible picture, never to be effaced or forgotten: the girl lying arched, convulsed, her long hair matted, her lips bitten through so that her face was smeared with blood, the dreamy eyes those of an agonized maddened animal. . . .

"You must not despair, cousin," Margali said. "Renata has trained her well, to endure this. Often the first attack of threshold sickness is the most severe so that if she survives that, the worst is over."

"It is often so," Dom Mikhail said, his voice brooding inward on horror. "It was so with Rafaella, one day laughing and dancing and playing her harp; and the next day, the very next, a screaming, tormented thing going into convulsion after convulsion in my arms. She never opened her eyes again to know me. When at last she ceased to struggle, I did not know whether to be more grieved, or more glad that she had come to the end of her agony. . . . But Dorilys has sur- vived."

"Yes," Cassandra said compassionately, "and she did not even go into crisis, Dom Mikhail. There is no reason to think she will die."

Donal's voice was fierce, angry. "Now do you see, Father, what was on my mind? Before we speak of getting her with child, can we at least be sure she will live to womanhood?"

Aldaran flinched, as with a crushing blow. In the dying thunder past the windows, there was suddenly a crash and a rumble, and rain smote them, sluicing down and rattling, pounding, like the tramp of Scathfell's armies on the march toward them.

For now the spring thaw was upon the Hellers, and the war was upon them.

CHAPTER
TWENTY-FIVE

For the first moon of spring it rained incessantly, and Allart, welcoming the rain because he knew it would keep Scathfell's armies from the road, still fretted with indecision. Damon-Rafael had sent a message expressing kindly concern, which to Allart's perception read false in every line of it, and ended by ordering his brother home at the earliest moment when the roads were open and he was able to travel.

If I return home now, Damon-Rafael will kill me. It is as simple as that. . . . Treason. I am forsworn. I gave my oath that I would support his rule, and now I know I will not. My life is forfeit to him, for I have broken my oath, in thought if not in deed . . . yet. So indecision made him linger at Aldaran, glad of the spring rains which kept him there.

Damon-Rafael is not sure, not yet. But if the roads are open and still I do not come—then I am a traitor, my life forfeit. And he wondered what Damon-Rafael would do when there was no longer any room for doubt.

Meanwhile, Dorilys had had a few repeated attacks of threshold sickness, but they had not been very severe, and at no time had Renata considered her life to be in danger. Renata had stayed with her tirelessly—though on one occasion she said to Cassandra, with the wry lift of a smile, "I do not know if she truly wishes to keep me at her side—or whether she feels that when I am with her, at least I am not with Donal." Both women knew there was another thing, unspoken.

Soon or late, she must know that I am bearing Donal's child. I do not want to hurt her or cause her any more grief.

Donal, whenever he saw Dorilys—which was seldom, for

291

he was organizing the defenses of Aldaran against the attack which they knew would come with the spring—was kindly and attentive, the loving elder brother he had always been. But whenever Dorilys spoke the words "my husband," he never answered with anything except an indulgent laugh, as if this were indeed a childish game they were playing, and he humoring her in it.

During these days when Dorilys was subject to recurring attacks of disorientation and upheaval—her telepathic sense, not yet under control, plunging her into a nightmare of terror and overload—she and Cassandra had become very close. Their shared love of music cemented this bond. Dorilys was already a talented player on the lute; Cassandra taught her to play a *rryl* as well, and she learned from the older woman some of the songs of Cassandra's faraway homeland at Valeron.

"I cannot see how you can endure to live in the Lowlands," Dorilys said. "I could not live without the mountain peaks surrounding me. It must be so dismal there, and so dull."

Cassandra smiled. "No, sweetheart, it is very beautiful. Sometimes here I feel the mountains are closing around me so that I can hardly breathe, as if the peaks were the bars of a cage."

"Really? How strange! Cassandra, I cannot play that chord as you do at the end of the ballad."

Cassandra took the *rryl* from her hand and demonstrated. "But you cannot finger it as I do. You will have to ask Elisa to show you the fingering," Cassandra said, and spread out her hand before Dorilys. The girl stared, wide-eyed.

"Oh, you have six fingers on your hand! No wonder I cannot play it as you do! I have heard that is a sign of *chieri* blood, but you are not *emmasca* as the *chieri* are; are you, cousin?"

"No," Cassandra said, smiling.

"I have heard—Father told me that the king in the Lowlands is *emmasca*, so they will take the throne from him this summer. How terrible for him, poor king. Have you ever seen him? What is he like?"

"He was only the young prince when I saw him last," said Cassandra. "He is quiet, and sad faced, and I think he would have made a good king, if they had been willing to let him reign."

Dorilys bent over the instrument, experimentally fingering the chord she could not play again and again. Finally she gave up the attempt. "I wish I had six fingers," she said. "There is no way I can play it properly! I wonder if my children will inherit my musical talents, or only my *laran*."

"Surely you are too young to be thinking yet about children," Cassandra said, smiling.

"In a few more moons, I will be capable of bearing. You know there is a great need for a son of Aldaran blood." She spoke so seriously that Cassandra felt a great wrench of pity.

This they do to all the women of our caste! Dorilys has hardly put away her dolls, and already she can think of nothing but her duty to her clan! After a long silence, hesitating, she said, "Perhaps—Dorilys, perhaps you should not have children, with this curse of *laran* you bear."

"As a son of our house must risk death in war, so a daughter of a great house must risk everything to give children to her caste." She repeated it simply and positively, and Cassandra sighed.

"I know, *chiya*. Since I was a child younger than you, I, too, heard that day in and day out, as a religion it was impious to doubt, and I believed it as you do now. But I feel you should be old enough to decide."

"I *am* old enough to decide," said Dorilys. "You do not have that kind of problem, cousin. *Your* husband is not heir to a Domain."

"You did not know?" Cassandra said. "Allart's elder brother will be king, if the *emmasca* of Hali is dethroned. This brother has no legitimate sons."

Dorilys stared at her. She said, "You could be queen," and her face held awe. Evidently she had had no idea of Allart's caste; he was only her brother's friend. "Then Dom Allart, too, stands desperately in need of an heir, and you are not yet bearing him one." Her eyes held a hint of reproach.

Hesitant, Cassandra explained the choice they had made. "Now, perhaps, with what I know, it might be safe, but we will wait till we are sure. Till we are very sure. . . ."

"Renata said I should bear no daughters," Dorilys said, "or I might die as my mother died in giving me birth. But I am not sure I trust Renata anymore. *She* loves Donal, and she does not want me bearing his children."

"If that is true," Cassandra said very gently, "then it is only that she fears for you, *chiya*."

"Well, in any case, I should have a son first," Dorilys said, "and then I will decide. Perhaps, when I give him a son, Donal will forget Renata, because I will be the mother of his heir." Her young arrogance was so great that Cassandra felt troubled, and again assailed by doubts.

Could she cement her bond with Allart best by giving him the son he must have, if they were not to deny him the throne like Prince Felix? They had not spoken of this seriously for some time.

I would give anything, to be so sure of myself as Dorilys! But she changed the subject firmly, taking the *rryl* on her lap again, and placing Dorilys's fingers on the strings.

"Look. I think perhaps if you hold it this way, you can play that chord, even with only five fingers," she said.

Again and again, as the days passed, Allart wakened to the awareness of Aldaran under siege, then knew that the reality was not yet with them, that it was only his foresight which spread the inevitable visibly before him. That it was inevitable he knew perfectly well.

"At this season," Donal said one morning, "the spring storms would have subsided in the Lowlands, but I do not know how the weather goes at Scathfell or Sain Scarp, or whether their armies can move. I shall go up to the watchtower, which commands all the country around, and see if there is any suspicious movement on the roads."

"Take Dorilys with you to the watchtower," Allart advised. "She can read the weather even better than you."

Donal hesitated and said, "I am reluctant, always, to meet with Dorilys now. Especially now that she can read my thoughts a little, as well. I am not happy that she has become a telepath."

"Still, if Dorilys feels she can be of use to you somehow, that you are not altogether avoiding her . . ." Allart suggested.

Donal sighed. "You are right, cousin. Besides, I cannot avoid her entirely." He dispatched a servant to his sister's rooms, thinking, *Would it be altogether bad, then, to give Dorilys what my father wishes of me? Perhaps, if she has what she wants of me, she will not grudge me Renata, and we need not struggle so hard to keep it from her. . . .*

Dorilys looked like the springtime itself, in a tunic embroidered with spring leaves, her shining hair braided low on her neck and caught with a woman's butterfly-clasp. Allart could see the dissonance in Donal's mind between his memories of the child, and the tall, graceful young woman she had become. He bowed over her hand, courteously.

"Now I see that I must call you *my lady*, Dorilys," he said lightly, trying to make it a joke. "It seems that my little girl is gone forever. I have need of your talents, *carya*," he added, and explained what he wanted of her.

At the very topmost spire of Castle Aldaran, the watchtower shot up for the height of another floor or two, an astonishing feat of engineering, and one which Allart could not figure out. It would have had to be done by matrix, working with a large circle. This great height commanded all of the country around to a great distance. While they climbed to the Tower, the window-slits showed them it was wrapped in fog, and cloud, but by the time they emerged into the high chamber, the clouds were already thinning and moving away. Donal looked at Dorilys in delighted surprise, and she smiled, almost a smug smile.

"To dispel fogs of that sort—even as a baby I think I could do *that*," she said. "And now it is nothing. It takes only the lightest thought, without effort, and if you wish to see clearly—I remember when I was little you brought me up here, Donal, and let me look through Father's collection of big spyglasses."

Allart could see the roads below them aswarm with movement. He blinked, knowing they were not there, not yet; then shook his head, trying to clarify present from future. It was true! Armies moved on the road, though not yet at the gates of Aldaran.

"We need not fear," Donal said, trying to reassure Dorilys. "Aldaran has never been captured by force of arms. We could hold this citadel forever, had we food enough; but they will be at our gates within a tenday. I will put on a gliderharness and go out to spy where they go, and bring back news of how many men move against us."

"No," Allart said. "If you will let me presume to advise you, cousin, you will not go yourself. Now that you are to command, your place is here where any one of your vassals who needs to consult with you can find you at once. You must not risk yourself on a task which any one of your lads could do for you."

Donal made a gesture of repugnance. "It goes against

me—to order any man into a danger I will not face myself,"
he said, but Allart shook his head.

"You will face your own dangers," he said, "but there are
dangers for the leaders and dangers for the followers, and
they are not interchangeable. From now on, cousin, your flying must be a recreation for times of peace."

Dorilys touched Donal's arm very lightly. She said, "Now
that I am a woman—can I still fly, Donal?"

Donal said, "I do not see why you should not, when there
is peace again, but you must ask our father about that, *chiya*,
and Margali."

"But I am your wife," she said, "and it is for *you* to give
me commands."

Caught between exasperation and tenderness, Donal sighed.
He said, "Then, *chiya*, I command you to seek Margali's advice in this, and Renata's. I cannot advise you." Her face had
clouded ominously at the mention of Renata, and Donal
thought, *Someday I must tell her, very clearly, how it stands
with me and Renata.* He said aloud, an arm gently about her
shoulders, "*Chiya*, when I was fourteen and my *laran* was
coming on me, as it is upon you now, I was forbidden to fly
for more than half a year, since I was never sure when an attack of disorientation and giddiness would come upon me.
For that reason, it would please me better if you did not seek
to fly until you are sure you can master it."

"I will do exactly as you say, my husband," she said, looking up at him with a look of such adoration that he quailed.

When she had gone away, Donal looked at Allart in
despair. "She seems not like a child! I cannot think of her as
a child," he said, "and that is my only defense now, to say
she is a child and too young."

Allart was painfully reminded of his own emotional con-
flict over the *riyachiyas*, with this difference—that they were
sterile and not altogether human and whatever he did with
them could affect only his own self-esteem and not the
riyachiyas themselves. But Donal had been placed in the position of playing a god with the life of a real woman. How
could he advise Donal? He had consummated his own marriage, against his own better judgment, and for much the
same reasons—because the girl wished for it.

He said soberly, "Perhaps it would be better not to think
of Dorilys as a child, cousin. No girl given the training she
has had can be altogether a child. Perhaps you must begin to

think of her as a woman. Try to come to agreement with her in that way, as a woman old enough to make her own decisions; at least when the threshold sickness has left her free of impulse and sudden brainstorms."

"I am sure you are right." Almost gratefully, Donal recalled himself to duty. "But come—my father must be told that there is movement on the roads, and someone must be sent to spy out where they are!"

Aldaran greeted the news with a fierce smile.

"So it has come!" he said, and Allart thought again of the old hawk, mantling, spreading his wings, eager for a last flight.

As armed men crossed the Kadarin and moved northward into the Hellers, Allart, seeing them with his *laran*, knew with a sinking heart that some of these men moved northward against *him*; for among the armed men there were some with the fir-tree badge of the Hasturs of Elhalyn, with the crown that distinguished it from the Hasturs of Carcosa and Castle Hastur.

Day after day, he and Donal returned to the watchtower, awaiting the first sign of the armies' imminent approach at the castle.

But is this real, or does my laran *show me what might never come to pass?*

"It is real, for I see it, too,'" Donal said, reading his thoughts. "My father must be told of this."

"He wished to keep from entanglement in Lowland wars," Allart said. "Now, by sheltering me and my wife, he has made an enemy, and Damon-Rafael has made common cause with Scathfell against him." As they turned to go down into the castle, he thought, *Now, truly, I am brotherless. . . .*

Donal laid a hand on his arm. "I, too, cousin," he said.

On an impulse, neither moving first, but simultaneously, they drew their daggers. Allart smiled, laid the hilt of his to the blade of Donal's; then slid Donal's into his own sheath. It was a very old pledge; it meant that neither would ever draw steel against the other in any cause whatever. Donal sheathed Allart's dagger. They embraced briefly, then, arms linked, went down to Dom Mikhail.

Allart, comforted by the gesture, felt a moment's hesitation.

Perhaps I was wrong. I must be careful what alliances I

*make, do nothing it would embarrass me to retract should I
one day sit on the throne.* . . . He broke off the thought impatiently.

Already, he thought with a flare of self-hatred, *I am thinking in terms of what is expedient, like a politician—like my brother!*

As they came into the courtyard and began to cross it, one of the servants suddenly pointed upward.

"There—there! What is that?"

"It is only a bird," someone said, but the man cried out, "No, that is no bird!"

Shading his eyes, Allart looking up into the sun, seeing *something* there, wheeling, slowly spiraling down, a slow and ominous descent. Fear and agony clutched at him. *This is some work of Damon-Rafael's, an arrow launched by Damon-Rafael at my heart,* he thought, almost paralyzed. In a spasm of dread he realized, *Damon-Rafael has the pattern of my matrix, of my soul. He could aim one of Coryn's fearful weapons at me, without fear it will kill any other.*

In that moment he felt Cassandra's thoughts entangled in his own; then there was a blaze of lightning in the clear sky, a cry of pain and triumph, and the broken thing that was *not* a bird fell, like a stone, arrested in midair, splattering fire from which the servants edged back in terror. A woman's dress had been caught in the terrible stuff. One of the stablemen grabbed her and shoved her bodily into one of the washing-tubs that stood at the end of the court. She screamed with pain and outrage, but the fire sizzled and went out. Allart looked at the fire and the broken bird still squirming with dreadful pseudo-life as he came near.

"Bring water, and douse it wholly," he ordered.

When the contents of two or three laundry-tubs had been flung on it and the fire was wholly out, he looked at the faintly squirming thing with terrible repugnance. The woman who had been pushed into the first laundry-tub had hauled herself out, dripping.

"You were fortunate," Donal said before she could protest. "A drop of *clingfire* splattered on you, my good woman. It would have burned up your dress and burned through your flesh to your bones and gone on burning until the burned flesh was cut away."

Allart stamped on the broken thing of metal coils and wheels and pseudo-flesh, again and again, until it lay in shattered fragments which were still, faintly, moving. "Take this," he directed one of the stablemen. "Pick it up on your shovels. Do not touch it with your bare hands, and bury it deep in the earth."

One of the guardsmen came and looked, shaking his head.

"Gods above! Is *that* what we must face in this war? What devilry sent *that* against us?"

"The lord Elhalyn, who would be king over this land," said Donal, his face like stone. "If it were not for my sister's command of the lightning, my friend and my brother would now lie here burning!" He turned, sensing Dorilys running down the inner stairs, Cassandra following more slowly, with all the haste her lamed leg would allow. Dorilys ran to Donal and caught him close in her arms.

"I felt it! I felt it hovering over us. I have struck it down," she cried. "It did not strike at you or Allart! I saved you, I saved you both!"

"Indeed you did," Donal said, holding the girl in his arms. "We are grateful to you, my child, we are grateful! Truly you are what Kyril called you that day at the fire station—queen of storms!"

The girl clung to him, her face lighted with such joy that Allart felt sudden fear. It seemed to him that lightnings played all over Castle Aldaran, though the sky was wholly clear again, and that the air was heavy with fire.

Was *this* what lay ahead in this war? Cassandra came to him, holding him, and he felt her fear like his own, and remembered that she had known the pain of a *clingfire* burn.

"Don't cry, my love. Dorilys saved me," he said. "She struck down Damon-Rafael's evil contrivance before it reached me. I suppose he would not believe I could escape this one, so it is not likely he will send another such thing against me."

But even as he comforted her, he was still afraid. This war would not be ordinary mountain warfare, but something quite new and terrible.

CHAPTER
TWENTY-SIX

If there had ever been room for doubt in Allart's mind about the coming war, there was none now. On every road leading to the peak of Aldaran, armies were gathering. Donal, massing the defenses, had stationed armed men ringing the lower slopes, so that for the first time in Donal's memory Castle Aldaran was actually the armed fortress it had been built to be.

A messenger had come into the castle under truce-flag. Allart stood in Aldaran's presence-chamber, looking at Mikhail of Aldaran on his high seat, calm, impassive, menacing. Dorilys sat beside him, with Donal standing at her side. Even Allart knew that Dorilys's presence was no more than the excuse for Donal's.

"My lord," the messenger said, and bowed, "hear the words of Rakhal of Scathfell, demanding certain observances and concessions from Mikhail of Aldaran."

Aldaran's voice was surprisingly mild. "I am not accustomed to receive demands. My brother of Scathfell may legitimately require of me whatever is customary from overlord to vassal. Say therefore to Lord Scathfell that I am dismayed that he should demand of me anything which he has only to request on the proper terms."

"It shall be so spoken," said the messenger. Allart, knowing that the messenger was a Voice, or trained speaker who would be able to relay up to two or three hours of such speech and counter-speech without the slightest variation in phrasing or emphasis, was certain the message wold be relayed to Scathfell in Aldaran's very intonation.

"With that reservation, my lord Aldaran; hear the words of

Rakhal of Scathfell to his brother of Aldaran." The stance and the very vocal timbre of the messenger altered slightly, and although he was a small man, and his voice light in texture, the illusion was eerie; it was as if Scathfell himself stood in the hall. Donal could almost hear the good-humored bullying voice of Lord Rakhal of Scathfell as the messenger spoke.

"Since you, brother, have made of late certain unlawful and scandalous dispositions regarding the heritage of Aldaran, therefore I, Rakhal of Scathfell, warden and lawful heir to the Domain of Aldaran, and pledged to support and uphold the Domain should your illness, infirmity, or old age make you unfit to do so, declare you senile, infirm, and unfit to make any further decisions regarding the Domain. Therefore I, Rakhal of Scathfell, am prepared to assume wardenship of the Domain in your name. Therefore I demand"— Lord Aldaran's fists clenched at his side at that repeated word, *demand*—"that you deliver up to me at once possession of Castle Aldaran, and the person of your *nedestro* daughter Dorilys of Rockraven, in order that I may suitably bestow her in marriage for the ultimate good of the realm. As for the traitor Donal of Rockraven, called Delleray, who has unlawfully influenced your sick mind to do malice and scandal to this realm, I, warden of Aldaran, am disposed to offer amnesty, provided that he leaves Castle Aldaran before sunrise and goes where he will, never to return or to step within the borders of the realm of Aldaran, or his life shall be forfeit and he shall be slain like an animal by any man's hand."

Donal stiffened, but his mouth took on a hard, determined line.

He wants Aldaran, Allart thought. Perhaps at first he was willing to step aside for Aldaran's kinsmen. But now it was obvious that Donal had become accustomed to thinking of himself as his foster-father's lawful successor and heir.

The Voice went on, and his voice altered faintly, his very posture changing somewhat. Although Allart had seen the technique before, it was now as if a quite different man stood before him, even the lines of his face changing. But what they had in common was arrogance.

"Furthermore, I, Damon-Rafael of Elhalyn, rightful king of the Domains, demand of Mikhail of Aldaran that he shall at once deliver to me the person of the traitor Allart Hastur of Elhalyn and his wife Cassandra Aillard, that they may be duly charged with plotting against the crown; and that you,

Mikhail of Aldaran, present yourself before me to discuss
what tribute shall be paid from Aldaran to Thendara that
you may continue during my realm to enjoy your Domain in
peace."

Still again the messenger's voice and bearing altered, and
again it was as if Rakhal of Scathfell stood before them.

"And should you, my brother of Aldaran, refuse any of
these demands, I shall feel empowered to enforce them upon
your stronghold and yourself by force of arms if I must."

The messenger bowed a fourth time and remained silent.

"An insolent message," Aldaran said at last, "and if justice
were done, he who spoke it should be hanged from the
highest battlement of this castle, since in serving my brother
you are also pledged to serve his overlord, and I am he. Why,
then should I not treat you as a traitor, fellow?"

The messenger paled, but his face betrayed no twitch of
personal reaction, as he said, "The words are not mine, Lord,
but those of your brother of Scathfell and His Highness Elhalyn. If the words offend you, sir, I beg of you to punish
their originators, not the messenger who repeats them upon
command."

"Why, you are right," Aldaran said mildly. "Why beat the
puppy when the old dog annoys me with barking? Bear *this*
message, then, to my brother of Scathfell. Say to him that I,
Mikhail of Aldaran, am in full enjoyment of my wits, and
that I am his overlord by oath and custom. Say to him that if
justice were done, I should dispossess him of Scathfell, which
he holds by my favor, and proclaim him outlaw in this realm
as he has presumed to do with the chosen husband of my
daughter. Say further to my brother that as for my daughter
Dorilys, she is already wedded by the *catenas*, and he need
not trouble himself to find a husband for her elsewhere. As
for the lord Damon-Rafael of Elhalyn, say to him that I neither know nor care who reigns within the Lowlands across
the Kadarin, since within this realm I acknowledge no reign
save my own, but that if he who would be king in Thendara
should invite me as his equal to witness his crowning, we will
then discuss the exchange of diplomatic courtesies. As for my
kinsman and guest Allart Hastur, he is welcome at my household and he may make to Lord Elhalyn such answer as he
chooses, or none at all."

Allart wet his lips, too late realizing that even this gesture
would be faithfully reproduced by the messenger standing be-

fore him, and wished he had not betrayed that small weakness. At last he said, "Say to my brother Damon-Rafael that I came here to Aldaran as his obedient subject and that I have faithfully performed all that he asked of me. My mission completed, I claim the right to domicile myself where I choose without consulting him." *A poor answer*, he thought, and cast about for the best way to continue. "Say further that the climate of Hali did not agree with my wife's health and that I removed her from Hali Tower for her health and safety." *Let Damon-Rafael chew on that!*

"Say at last," he added, "that, far from plotting against the crown, I am a faithful subject of Felix, son of the late king, Regis. If Felix, lawful king of Thendara, bids me at any time to come and defend his crown against any who would conspire to seize it, I am at his command. Meanwhile I remain here at Aldaran lest the lawful king Felix accuse me of conspiring to seize his rightful throne."

Now, he thought, *it is done and irrevocable. I could have sent a message of submission to my brother, and pleaded that as Aldaran's guest I could raise no hand against him. Instead, I have declared myself his foe.*

Allart resisted the temptation to look ahead and see, with his *laran*, what might befall when Damon-Rafael and Lord Scathfell received that message. He might foresee a hundred things, but only one could come to pass, and there was no sense in troubling his mind with the other ninety and nine.

There was silence in the presence-chamber while the trained Voice digested the message. Then he said, "My lords, those who dispatched me foresaw some answer such as this and bade me say thus:

"To Donal of Rockraven, called Delleray, that he is declared outlaw in this realm and that any man who slays him shall do so from this day forth without penalty. To Allart Hastur, traitor, we offer nothing save the mercy of his brother should he come and make submission to him before sundown of this day. And to Mikhail of Aldaran, that he shall surrender Castle Aldaran, and all those within it, to the last woman and child, forthwith, or we shall come and take it."

There was another of those long silences. At last Aldaran said, "I do not plan to visit my Domain in the near future. If my brother of Scathfell has nothing better to do with his seed-time and harvest than sit like a dog outside my gates, he may stay there as long as it pleases him. However, should he injure man or woman, child or animal lawfully under my protection, or should he step beyond the line of my armed men so much as the width of my smallest finger, then I shall hold that as reason to annihilate him and his armies, and declare his holding of Scathfell forfeit. As for him, if I take him here I shall certainly hang him."

Silence. When it was obvious that he had no more to say, the messenger bowed.

"My lord, the message shall be delivered faithfully as spoken," he said. Then, the truce-flag before him, he withdrew from the room. Even before he had reached the door, Allart knew that there was no mistaking what the future would be.

It was war.

But then, he had never been in any doubt of that.

It was not long in coming. Within an hour of the departure of the Voice, a flight of fire-arrows winged up from below. Most of them fell harmlessly on stone, but a few landed on wooden roofs or on bales of fodder stacked within the courtyard for the animals, and the laundry-tubs of water were again put into play for extinguishing them before the fire could spread.

After the fires had been put out, silence again. This time it was an ominous silence, the difference, Donal thought, between warfare impending and warfare begun. Donal ordered all the remaining fodder doused down heavily with water from the inside wells. But the fire-arrows had only been the formal answer to the challenge, ". . . should he step beyond the line of my armed men so much as the width of my smallest finger. . . ."

Inside the courtyard, all were ready to repel a siege. Armed men were stationed at the head of every small path leading upward, in case anyone should break through the outer ring of men around the entire mountain. Food and fodder had been stockpiled long since, and there were several wells within the enclosure of the castle, living springs in the rock of the mountain. There was nothing to do but wait. . . .

The waiting continued for three days. Guards stationed in the watchtower, and those in the line around the lower peaks, reported no activity in the camp below. Then, one morning,

Donal heard cries of consternation in the courtyard and hurried out to see what had happened.

The guardsmen were cooking their breakfast around fires kindled within hearthstones laid at the far end, but the cooks, and those who were carrying water to the animals, stared in fear at the water flowing from the pipes: thick, red, and sluggish, with the color, the consistency, and even the smell of freshly spilled blood. Allart, coming to see, looked at the frightened faces of the guardsmen and soldiers, and knew that this was serious. The success in outlasting a siege depended almost entirely on the water supply. If Scathfell had somehow managed to contaminate the springs which watered the castle, they could not hold out more than a day or two. Before sunset some of the animals would begin to die; then the children. There was nothing but surrender before them.

He looked at the stuff flowing from the pipes. "Is it only this spring? Or is the other one, which runs into the castle, contaminated also?" he asked.

One of the men spoke up. "I went into the kitchens, Dom Allart, and it's just like this."

Dom Mikhail, hastily summoned, bent over the stuff, let it run into his hand, grimacing at the thick texture and the smell; then experimentally lifted his hand to his mouth to taste. After a moment he shrugged, spit it out.

"How did they get at the wells, I wonder? The answer to that is that they *could* not; and therefore they *did* not." He touched the matrix about his neck. He took another mouthful and when he spit it out the water ran clear from his lips.

"Illusion," he said. "A remarkably realistic and disgusting illusion, but illusion nevertheless. The water is clean and wholesome; they have only set a spell on it so that it looks, and tastes, and worst of all smells like blood."

Allart bent to sip the stuff, feeling the surge of nausea because to all appearances he was drinking a stream of fresh blood . . . but it was water to the texture and feel, despite the sickening smell and taste.

"Is this to be witch-war, then?" the guard demanded, shaking his head in consternation. "Nobody can drink *that* stuff."

"I tell you, it's water, and perfectly good water," Aldaran said impatiently. "They've just made it *look* like blood."

"Aye, Lord, and smell and taste," said the cook. "I tell *you*—none will drink of it."

"You'll drink of it or go dry," Donal said impatiently. "It's all in your mind, man; your throat will feel it as water, whatever the look of it."

"But the beasts will not drink of it, either," said one of the men, and indeed they could hear the noises of restless animals from inside the barns and stables, some of them kicking and rearing.

Allart thought, *Yes, this is serious. All beasts fear the blood-smell. Furthermore, the men here are afraid, so we must show them quickly that they need not fear such things.*

Aldaran said, sighing, "Well, well, I had hoped we could simply ignore it, let them think their spell had no effect." But while they might at last coax or persuade the men to ignore the look and taste of the water, the effort of this would sap their morale. And the animals could not be persuaded by reason to ignore it. To them, smell and taste *were* the reality of the water, and they might easily die of thirst within reach of all the water they could drink, rather than violate their instincts by drinking what their senses told them was freshly spilled blood.

"Allart, I have no right to ask you to aid in the defense of my stronghold."

"My brother has seized the crown and makes common cause with *yours*, kinsman. My life is forfeit if I am taken here."

"Then see if we can find what in Zandru's seven hells they are doing down there!"

"There is at least one *laranzu* bearing a matrix," Allart said, "and perhaps more. But this is a simple spell. I will see what I can do."

"I need Donal here for the defense of the outwalls," Aldaran said.

Allart nodded. "So be it." He turned to one of the servants, who stood staring at the water that still flowed, like fresh blood, in a crimson stream from the pipe, and said, "Go to my lady, the lady Renata, and Margali, and ask that they join me in the watchtower as soon as they may."

He added, turning to Dom Mikhail, "By your leave, kinsman, it is isolated enough that we can work in peace."

"Give what orders you will, kinsman," Aldaran said.

Within the watchtower, when the women joined him, he said, "You know?"

Renata made a wry face, saying, "I know. My maid came shrieking in when she went to draw my bath, screaming that blood flowed from the taps. I suspected even then that it was illusion, but I could not convince my servingwomen of that!"

"I, too," Margali said. "Though I knew it illusion, I felt I would rather go dirty than bathe in the stuff, or thirsty than drink of it. Dorilys was terrified. Poor child, she has had another attack of threshold sickness. I had hoped she was past it, but with all this emotional upheaval—"

"Well, first we must see how it is done," Allart said. "Cassandra, you are a monitor, but you, Renata, have had the most training. Do you wish to work central to what we are doing?"

"No, Allart. I—I dare not," she said reluctantly.

Immediately Cassandra picked up her meaning. She put her arm around her kinswoman. "I had not known . . . you are pregnant, Renata!" Cassandra said, in astonishment and dismay. After all Renata had said to them . . . but it was done, and nothing to argue now. "Very well. You can monitor outside the circle, if you wish, though I do not think it is needed for this. . . . Margali?"

A blue light began to glimmer from the three matrixes as they focused upon them; after a moment Cassandra nodded. It had been, indeed, the simplest of spells.

"There is no need for anything," she said, "except to reinforce nature. That water shall be what it is, and nothing more."

Joined, they sank into the surrounding energy patterns, repeating the simplest of the awarenesses, the old elemental pattern: *Earth and air and water and fire, soil and rock and wind and sky and rain and snow and lightning.* . . . As the rhythm of nature moved within them and over them, Allart felt even Renata drop into the simple spell . . . for this, in tune with nature instead of wrenching it to their patterns, could do nothing but good even to her unborn child. It repeated simply that he must be what nature had made him. As they searched out the fabric of the vibration that had set the illusion on the springs below the castle, they knew that every spring and every tap and pipe now flowed clear spring water from the rock. Remaining for a moment in the smooth resting rhythm of nature, they felt Dorilys, too, and Donal and Lord Aldaran—everyone within the castle who bore a matrix and could use *laran*—reinforced and strengthened by it. Even those who had not this awareness sensed the smooth rhythm, to the lowliest beasts in the courtyards and stables.

The sun, too, seemed for a moment to shine with a more brilliant crimson light.

All of nature is one, and all that one is harmony. . . . To Cassandra, the musician, it was like a great chord, massive and peaceful, lingering and dying away into silence, but still heard, somewhere. . . .

Dorilys came softly into the watchtower room. After a moment the rapport fell quietly apart, without any tactile break, and Margali smiled and stretched her hand to her foster-daughter.

"You look well again, sweetheart."

"Yes," Dorilys said, smiling. "I was lying on my bed, and suddenly I felt—oh, I don't know how to tell you—*good*, and I knew you were working here, and I wanted to come and be with you all." She leaned against her foster-mother, with a sweet and confiding smile. "Oh, Kathya said I must tell you that the water flows clean again in bath and pipes, and you can break fast when you will."

The healing-spell was made, Allart knew. It would be that much harder for Scathfell's hordes to use the powers of sorcery or matrix science against them, when these did any violence to nature. The best thing was that they had done this without even harming the *laranzu* who had set the spell; for his attempted evil he had been returned good.

Holy Bearer of Burdens, grant it stops at this, Allart thought. But despite the flow of happiness and well-being in every nerve, he knew it could not stop here. Having barred their attack by illusion, the forces commanded by Scathfell and Damon-Rafael must turn, at least for now, to more conventional warfare.

He said as much to Dom Mikhail, later that day, but Lord Aldaran looked pessimistic.

"Castle Aldaran can stand through any ordinary siege, and my brother of Scathfell knows it. He will not be content with that."

"Yet I foresee," Allart said, hesitating, "that if we use ordinary warfare only, it will go hard with both sides. It is not even sure that we shall win. But if they manage to lure us into a battle by matrix technology, then nothing can come but catastrophe. Lord Aldaran, I have pledged that I will do what I can to aid you. Yet I beg you, Dom Mikhail. Try to keep this warfare to ordinary methods, even if the victory comes harder in this way. You have said yourself that this castle can withstand any ordinary siege. I beg you not to let them force us into doing their kind of battle."

Lord Aldaran noted that Allart's face was pale, and that he was trembling. Part of him understood and took in fully all that Allart was saying; the part of him that had been repelled when Allart spoke of *clingfire* used in the Lowlands. Yet a part of him, the skilled old soldier, veteran of many forays and campaigns in the mountains, looked at Allart and saw only the man of peace, afraid of the desolation of war. His sympathy was not unmixed with contempt, the contempt of the natural warrior for the man of peace, the soldier for the monk. He said, "I wish it might be kept, indeed, to lawful weapons of war. Yet already your brother has sent evil birds and *clingfire* against us. I fear he will not be content to throw catapults against us and storm our walls with scaling ladders and armed men. I will pledge you this; that if he does not use his dreadful weapons against us, I will not be the first to use *laran* against him. But I have no Tower circle at my command to stockpile ever more frightful weapons against my enemies. If Damon-Rafael has brought Tower-created weapons to place at the command of my brother of Scathfell, I cannot hold him off forever with men armed only with arrows and dart-guns and swords."

That was only reasonable, Allart thought in despair. Would he allow Cassandra to fall into the hands of Damon-Rafael, simply because he was reluctant to use *clingfire*? Would he see Donal hanged from the castle wall, Dorilys carried off to a stranger's bed? Yet he *knew*, beyond all shadow of a doubt, that if *laran* were used, beyond this simple spell which reaffirmed that nature was one and nothing out of harmony with it could long exist, then . . .

Allart's ears were full of cries of future lamentation . . . Dom Mikhail stood before him bowed with weeping, aged beyond recognition in a single night, crying out, "I am accursed! Would that I had died with neither daughter nor son." Renata's face swam before him, convulsed, anguished, dying. The terrible flare of lightning stunned his senses, and Dorilys's face showed livid in the storm's glare. . . . He could not endure the possible futures; neither could he shut them out. The weight of them cut off speech, cut off everything but dread. . . .

Shaking his head despairingly at Lord Aldaran, he went away.

But for a time indeed, it seemed that the attackers had been frustrated and must fall back on ordinary weapons. All that day, and all through the night, catapults thudded against the castle walls, some varied with flights of fire-arrows. Donal kept men with tubs of water continually on the alert, and even some of the women were pressed into service watching for fires and hauling tubs of water where they could be used at once to extinguish fires in the wooden outbuildings. Just before dawn, while most of the castle's guard were busy scurrying here and there putting out a dozen small fires, an alarm was suddenly sounded calling every able-bodied man to the walls to repel a party on scaling ladders. Most of them were cut down and thrown from the heights, but a few managed to break inside, and Donal, with half a dozen picked men, had to face them in the first hand-to-hand battle of the inner courtyard. Allart, fighting at Donal's side, took a slight slash in one arm, and Donal sent him to have it tended.

Allart found Cassandra and Renata working alongside the healer-women.

"All the gods be thanked it is no worse," said Cassandra, very pale.

"Is Donal hurt?" Renata demanded.

"Nothing to worry about," Allart said, grimacing as the healer-woman began to stitch his arm. "He cut down the man who gave me *this*. Dom Mikhail did never better for himself or Aldaran than when he had Donal trained in warfare. Young as he is, he has everything under complete control."

"It is quiet," Cassandra said, with a sudden deep shudder. "What devilry are those folk down there contemplating now?"

"Quiet, you say?" Allart looked at her in astonishment; then realized that it was indeed quiet, a deep ominous quiet both inside and out. The screaming sound of the shells and missiles breaking against the castle wall had ended. The sounds he heard so clearly were all inside his own head, were the possibles and might-never-be's of his *laran*. For the moment it was quiet indeed, but the sounds he could *almost* hear told him this was only a lull.

"My beloved, I wish that you were safe at Hali, or in Tramontana."

She said, "I would rather be with you."

The healer-woman finished bandaging his arm and

strapped it in a sling. She handed him some reddish sticky fluid in a small cup. "Drink this; it will keep your wound from fevering," she said. "Rest your arm if you can; there are others who can bear a sword into the fight." She drew back in dismay as the cup fell from Allart's suddenly lax hand, the red fluid running like blood on the stone floor.

"In Avarra's name, my lord!"

But even as she stooped to mop up the mess the outcry Allart had already heard through his *laran* broke out in the courtyard; unceremoniously Allart rose and ran down the inner stairs, hearing the commotion. There was a crowd in the inner court, edging back from a burst container which lay on the stone, oozing a strange-looking yellow slime. As the slime spread, the very stone of the courtyard smoked and burned and fell away into great gaping holes, eaten away like cold butter.

"Zandru's hells!" burst out one of the guardsmen. "What is *that*? More wizard hellcraft?"

"I know not," Dom Mikhail said, sobered. "I have never seen anything like it before."

One of the courageous soldiers came forward, to try to heave some fragments of the container aside. He fell back, howling in agony, his hand seared and blackened with the stuff.

"Do *you* know what this is, Allart?" Donal asked.

Allart pressed his lips tight. "No sorcery, but a weapon devised by the Towers—an acid that will melt stone."

"Is there nothing we can do about it?" Lord Aldaran asked. "If they throw many of those against our outwalls, they will melt the very castle about our ears! Donal, send men to check the boundaries."

Donal pointed to a guardsman. "You, and you, and you, take your paxmen and go. Take straw shields; it will not harm the straw—See where it has splashed on the fodder—but if it touches metal you will be stifled by the acid fumes."

Allart said, "If it is acid, take the ash-water you use for mopping in the dairy and stables, and perhaps it will stop the acid from eating through the stone." Although the strong alkali did indeed neutralize the acid and keep it from spreading, several of the men were splashed by the strong lye. Where the courtyard had been eaten by the acid, even where treated afterward with the lye-water, holes were eaten in boots and whole areas had to be fenced off so that the men would not be injured by trespassing on them. There had been a few direct hits on the stone of the outwalls, and the stone was eaten away and crumbling; worse, the supply of lye-water was soon exhausted. They tried to use substitutes, such as soap and animal urine, but they were not strong enough.

"This is dreadful," Dom Mikhail said. "They will have our walls down at this rate. Surely this is Lord Elhalyn's doing, kinsman. My brother of Scathfell has no such weapons at his command! What can we do, kinsman? Have you any suggestions?"

"Two," Allart said, hesitating. "We can put a binding-spell on the stone, so that it cannot be eaten away by any unnatural substance, but only by those things intended to destroy stone. It would not stand against earthquake or time or flood, but I think it may stand against these unnatural weapons."

So once again the Tower-trained personnel took their place in the matrix chamber. Dorilys joined them, pleading to take a hand.

"I can monitor," she begged, "and Renata would be free to join you in the circle."

"No," Renata said quickly, thanking all the gods that Dorilys's telepathy was still untrained and erratic. "I think, if you will, you can take a place in the circle, and I will monitor from outside."

As monitor for the circle Dorilys would know at once why Renata could not join it now.

It goes against me to deceive her this way. But a time will soon come when she is strong and well, and then Donal and I will tell her, Renata thought.

Fortunately, Dorilys was sufficiently excited at being allowed to take a place inside the circle, her first formal use of a matrix except to levitate her own glider, that she did not question Renata. Cassandra held out her hand and the girl took her place beside Cassandra. Again, the circle formed, and once again they sent out the spell that was only a strengthening of nature's own forces.

The rock is one with the planet on which it is formed, and man has so shaped it as it was determined. Nothing shall change it or alter. The rock is one . . . one . . . one. . . .

The binding-spell was set. Allart, individual consciousness lost behind the joined consciousness of his circle, was aware of the shaped rocks of the castle, of their hard integrity; of the fact that the impact of explosive shells and the chemical slime was harmlessly bouncing away, repelled, the yellow slime rolling down the outside, leaving long, evil-looking streaks, but not crumbling stone or melting it.

The rock is one . . . one . . . one. . . .

From outside the circle, a careful thought reached them.

Allart?

Is it you, brédu?

It is Donal. I have stationed men on the outwalls to pick off their cannoneers with arrows, but they are out of range. Can you make a darkness about them so that they cannot see where to shoot?

Allart hesitated. It was one thing to affirm the integrity of nature's creation by forcing water to remain, untampered, as water, and stone to remain impervious to things nature had never intended to destroy stone. But to tamper with nature by creating darkness during the hours of light . . .

Dorilys's thoughts wove into the circle. *It would be in tune with the forces of nature if a thick fog should come up. It often happens at this season, so that no man on the hillside can see beyond the reach of his own arms!*

Allart, searching a little way ahead with his *laran*, saw indeed that there was a strong probability of thick fog arising. Focusing on the joined matrixes again, the workers concentrated upon the moisture in the air, the nearing clouds, to wrap the whole of the mountainside in a thick curtain, rising from the river below, until all of Castle Aldaran and the nearby peaks lay shrouded in darkening fog.

"They will not lift this night," said Dorilys with satisfaction.

Allart dissolved the circle, admonishing his group to go and rest. They might be needed again soon. The sound of shelling had stopped, and Donal's men below had a chance to clean up the residue of acids and lye. Renata, running the body-mind monitor's touch over Dorilys, was struck with something new in her.

Was it only the healing-spell earlier? She seemed calmer, more womanly; no longer even a little like a child. Renata, recalling how she herself had grown swiftly into adulthood in her first season in the Tower, knew that Dorilys had made some such enormous leap into womanhood, and inwardly gave thanks to all her gods.

If she has stabilized, if we need no longer fear her childish explosions, if she is beginning to have judgment and skill to match her power—perhaps then, soon, soon, it will be over and Donal and I will be free. . . .

With a surge of the old love for Dorilys, she drew the girl close and kissed her. "I am proud of you, *carya mea*," she said. "You have acquitted yourself as would a woman in the circle. Now go and rest, and eat well, so that you will not lose your strength when we need you again."

Dorilys was glowing.

"So I am doing my part, like Donal, in the defense of my home," she exclaimed, and Renata shared her innocent pride.

So much strength, she thought, *and so much potential. Will she win through after all?*

The thick fog continued to shroud the castle hour upon hour, enclosing in mystery what the attacking armies were doing down below. Perhaps, Allart thought, they were simply waiting—waiting, as were those in the besieged castle, for the fog to lift so that they could resume the attack. For Allart's part, he was wholly content to wait.

This breathing spell, after the hectic opening days of the siege, was appreciated by them all. At nightfall, since even the watch on the castle walls could do little, Allart went to dine alone with Cassandra in their rooms. By common consent they avoided speaking of the war; there was nothing they could do about it. Cassandra called for her *rryl*, and sang to him.

"I said upon the day of our wedding," she said, looking up from the instrument, "that I hoped we might live in peace and make songs, not war. Alas for that hope! But even in the shadow of war, my dearest, there can still be songs for us."

He took the thin fingers in his hands and kissed them.

"So far, at least, the gods have been good to us," he said.

"It is so still, Allart! They might have all gone away in the night, it is so quiet below!"

"I would that I knew what Damon-Rafael was doing," Allart said, roused to new unquiet. "I do not think he will be content to sit there at the bottom of the hill, without throwing some new weapon into the gap."

"It would be easy for you to find out," she hazarded, but Allart shook his head.

"I will not use *laran* in this war unless I am forced to do so. Only to defend us from certain catastrophe. Damon-

Rafael shall not make of me the excuse to bring his frightful kind of war to this country."

About midnight the sky suddenly began to clear, the fog first thinning, then blowing away in little wisps and ragged shreds. Overhead three of the four moons floated, brilliant and serene. Violet Liriel was near the zenith, full and brilliant. Blue Kyrrdis and green Idriel hung near the western edge of the mountains. Cassandra was sleeping, had been sleeping for hours, but Allart, seized by strange unease, slid quietly from bed and into his clothes. Hurrying down the hallway, he saw Dorilys in her long white chamber-robe, her hair hanging loose down her back. She was barefoot, her snub-nosed face a pale oval in the dimness.

"Dorilys? What is Margali thinking of to let you wander like this in your night-garb at this hour?"

"I could not sleep, Dom Allart, and I was uneasy," the girl said. "I am going down to join Donal near the outwall. I suddenly woke and felt that he was in danger."

"If he is truly in danger, *chiya*, the last place he would want you is beside him."

"He is my husband," the child said adamantly, raising her face to Allart. "My place is at his side, sir."

Paralyzed by the strength of her obsession, Allart could do nothing. After all, this was the only thing she could share with Donal. Since Allart himself had been reunited with Cassandra, he had been highly sensitized to loneliness. It struck him at that moment that Dorilys was almost wholly alone. She had left the society of children irrevocably. Yet among the adults she was still treated as a child. He did not protest, but began to move toward the outer stairs, hearing her behind him. After a moment he felt her small dry hand, a child's hand and warm like a little animal's paw, slide into his. He clasped it, and they hurried together across the courtyard to Donal's post at the outwalls.

Outside, the night had grown bright and cloudless, with only a single low bank of cloud hanging at the horizon. The moons floated high and clear, in a sky so brilliantly lighted that no single star was visible anywhere in the sky. Donal was standing, arms folded, atop the outwall, but as Allart hurried toward him, someone spoke in a low, reproachful voice.

"Master Donal, I beg you to come off the wall. You are all

too good a target standing there," and Donal slid down off the wall.

Not too soon; an arrow came whistling out of the darkness, harmlessly flying past where Donal had just been standing. Dorilys ran and caught him around the waist.

"You must not stand there like that, Donal. Promise me you will never do so again!"

He laughed noiselessly, bending to kiss her, a light brotherly peck, on the forehead. "Oh, I am in no danger. I wanted to see if anyone was still down there and awake, after all, or if they had all gone away; as in that quiet and fog it seemed they might well have done."

It had been Allart's own thought—that they were too quiet, that some devilry was afoot. He asked Donal, "Did the fog lift of itself?"

"I am not sure. They have more than one *laranzu* down there, and it lifted, indeed, all too quickly," Donal said, wrinkling up his forehead. "But at this season the fog does blow away sometimes, exactly like that. I cannot tell."

Suddenly, to Allart, the air was filled with cries and exploding fire. "Donal! Call the watch!" he cried. Almost before the words escaped his lips, an air-car flashed by overhead, and several small shapes fell slowly toward the ground, almost lazily, like snowflakes, falling open as they moved and pouring liquid streaks of fire toward the castle roofs and the court.

"*Clingfire!*" Donal leaped for an alarm bell, but already several of the wooden roofs were blazing up and fire was lighting the whole courtyard. Men poured into the court, only to be stopped, screaming, by the streams of unquenchable fire. One or two went up like human torches, shrieking all the time, until the howls died away and they lay, their corpses still smoking and flaming, lifeless on the stone. Donal leaped to push Dorilys under an overhanging stone cave, but drops of the liquid fire rolled off and caught her chamber-robe, which blazed up wildly. She screamed in terror and pain, as Donal dragged her toward a tub of water and literally flung her into it. Her dress sizzled and went out, but a drop of the stuff had fallen on her skin and was burning, burning inward. She kept shrieking, a wild, almost inhuman sound, maddened with the pain.

"Keep back! Keep in the lee of the building," Donal yelled. "There are more of them overhead!"

Dorilys was screaming and struggling between his hands, maddened with agony. Overhead, thunder suddenly crackled and flared, lightnings seared and struck here, there. . . . Abruptly one of the air-cars overhead went up in a great burst of fire and fell, a flaming ruin, into the valley. Another great bolt struck a second air-car in midair, exploding it into showers of fire. Rain sliced down hard, drenching Allart to the skin. Donal had fallen back from Dorilys in terror. Screaming, maddened, the child was shaking her fist at the sky, striking with great sizzling bolts here, there, everywhere. A final air-car split with a huge explosion and fell apart over the attacking camp below, sending forth shrieks and howls of pain as the *clingfire* fell back on its launchers. Then silence, except for the heavy, continuing rumble of the rain, and Dorilys's stabbing screams of pain as the *clingfire* continued to eat inward on her wrist, penetrating to the bone.

"Let me take her," Renata said, running up barefoot in her nightgown. The girl sobbed and cried out and tried vainly to push her away. "No, darling, no. Don't struggle! This must be done or it will burn your arm away. Hold her, Donal."

Dorilys screamed again with pain as Renata scraped away the last remnants of the *clingfire* from the burned flesh, then collapsed against Donal. All around the courtyard men were gathering, silent, awed. Renata tore Dorilys's charred chamber-robe to bandage her arm. Donal held her against him, soothingly, rocking her.

"You saved us all," he whispered. "Had you not struck at them, so much *clingfire* could have burned Aldaran over all our heads!"

Indeed, Allart thought. Damon-Rafael and Scathfell had thought to take Aldaran unawares, unprepared for this kind of attack. Had the contents of three air-cars all carrying *clingfire* struck them, all of Castle Aldaran would have been burned to the ground. Had they exhausted their arsenal, then, hoping to win at one stroke? Had Dorilys decisively defeated them, then, in this one stroke? He looked at the child, weeping now in Renata's arms with the pain of her burns.

She had saved them all, as she had saved him, before, from Damon-Rafael's evil bird-weapon.

But he did not think this would be the end.

CHAPTER
TWENTY-SEVEN

There were still fires to be put out, where the *clingfire* had set buildings alight. Five men were dead, and a sixth died as Renata knelt to look at him. Four more had *clingfire* burns deep enough that even Allart knew they would not live out the day, and a dozen more had minor burns which must be treated and every scrap of the terrible stuff scraped away, disregarding screams and pleas for mercy. Cassandra came and took Dorilys away to be put to bed, her bandages soaked in oil. But when all had been done, Donal and Allart stood on the outwall, looking down at the camp of the besiegers where fires still raged and flared.

The rain had subsided as soon as Dorilys was calm, and in any case it would take long, heavy soaking rain to put out *clingfire* blazes. Now Donal had no fear of arrows out of darkness. He said, stepping down from the wall, "Scathfell and his folks will have more than enough to do this night in their own camp. I will leave a small watch, but no more. Unless I am gravely mistaken, they will have no leisure to mount another attack for a day or so!"

He set a few picked men as guards, and went to see how Dorilys fared. He found her abed, restless, her eyes bright and feverish, her arm freshly bandaged. She reached with her free arm for his hand and pulled him down at her side.

"So, you have come to see me. Renata was not being cruel to me, Donal. I know it now; she was scraping away the fire so that it would not burn my arm to the bone. It nearly did, you know," she said. "Cassandra showed me. She has a scar almost exactly like mine will be, and from *clingfire*, too."

318

"So you, too, will bear an honorable scar of warfare from the defense of our home," Donal said. "You saved us all."

"I know." Her eyes flickered, and he could see the pain in them. Far away he could hear a distant rumble of thunder. He sat beside her, holding the small hand that stuck out below the heavy bandage.

"Donal," she said, "now that I am a woman, when shall I be really your wife?"

Donal turned his eyes away, grateful that Dorilys was still a very erratic telepath. "This is no time to speak of that, *chiya*, when we are all fighting for survival. And you are still very young."

"I am not so young as all that," she insisted. "I am old enough to work in a matrix circle as I did with Allart and the others, and old enough to fight against those who are attacking us."

"But, my child—"

"Don't call me that! I am not a child!" she said with a small, imperious flare of anger; then laid her head against his arm, with a sigh that was not, indeed, childlike. "Now that we are entangled in this war, Donal, there should be an heir to Aldaran. My father is old, old, and this war ages him day by day. And today—" Suddenly her voice began to shake uncontrollably. "I don't think I had ever thought of this before, but suddenly I knew you could die—or I could die, Donal, young as I am. If I should die before you, never having borne you a child, you could be driven forth from Aldaran, since you are not blood-kin. Or if—if you should die, and I had never had your child, I could be flung into some stranger's bed for the dower of Aldaran. Donal, I am afraid of *that*."

Donal held her small hand in his. All this was true, he thought. Dorilys might be the only way he could hold this castle which had been his only home from childhood. It was not even as if she were unwilling. He, too, after the long days of battle and siege, was all too aware of the vulnerability of his own body. He had seen men blaze up like living flames, seen them die fast and slow, but die nonetheless. And Dorilys was his, legally given in marriage with the consent of her father. She was young, but she was moving quickly, quickly, into womanhood. . . . His hand tightened on hers.

"We shall see, Dorilys," he said, drawing her close for a minute. "When Cassandra tells me that you are old enough to bear a child without danger, then, if you still wish for it, Dorilys, it shall be as you desire."

He bent down and would have kissed her on the forehead, but she clung to him with surprising strength, pulling him down so that their lips met, with passion that was not at all childlike. When at last she released him Donal was dizzy. He straightened up and left the room quickly, but not before Dorilys, with her erratic telepathic sense, still unreliable, had picked up his thought, *No, Dorilys is a child no more.*

Quiet. Quiet. All was silent in Castle Aldaran . . . all was silent in the camp of the besiegers below. All day the dreadful silence hung over the land. Allart, high in the watchtower, setting again a binding-spell on the castle walls, wondered what new devilry this quiet presaged. So sensitized had he become by this prolonged warfare by matrix that he could almost *feel* them plotting—or was it an illusion?—and his *laran* continued to present pictures of the castle falling in ruins, the very world trembling. Toward midday, all over the castle, all at once, men began shrieking and crying out, with nothing visible the matter with them. Allart, in the tower room with Renata, Cassandra, and the old sorceress Margali—Dorilys had kept her bed, for her arm still throbbed with pain, and Margali had given her a strong sleeping draft—had his first warning when Margali raised her hands to her head and began to weep aloud.

"Oh, my baby, my little one, my poor lamb," she cried. "I must go to her!" She ran out of the room, and almost at the same moment Renata caught her hands against her breast, as if struck by an arrow there, and cried out, "Ah! He is dead!" While Allart stared at her in amazement, at the slammed door still quivering behind Margali, he heard Cassandra screaming. All at once it seemed to him that she was gone, that the world grew dark, that somewhere behind a locked door she fought a deathly battle with his brother, that he must go to her and protect her. He had actually risen and taken a step to the door on a mad dash to rescue Cassandra from the ravisher, when he saw her across the room, kneeling, swaying in anguish and tearing at herself, keening as if she knelt above a corpse.

A tiny shred of rationality struggled for what felt like hours inside Allart. *Cassandra is in no need of rescue, if yonder she sits wailing as if the one she loved best lay dead be-*

fore her. . . . Yet within his mind it still seemed that he heard screams of terror and anguish, that she was calling to him, crying out.

Allart! Allart! Why do you not come to me? Allart, come come quickly . . . and a long, terrified shriek of desperate anguish.

Renata had risen, and was making her way on faltering feet to the door. Allart caught her around the waist.

"No," he said. "No, kinswoman, you must not go. This is bewitchment. We must fight it; we must set the binding-spell."

She fought and struggled in his arms like a mad thing, kicking, scratching at his face with her nails as if he were not Allart at all but some enemy bent on murder or rape, her eyes rolled inward in some wholly interior terror, and Allart knew she neither saw nor heard him.

"No, no, let me go! It's the baby! They're murdering our baby! Can't you see where they have him there, ready to fling him from the wall? Ah, merciful Avarra . . . let me go, you murdering devils! Take me first!"

Icy chills chased themselves up and down Allart's spine as he realized that Renata, too, fought against some wholly internal fear, that she saw Donal, or the child who was not yet even born, in deadly danger. . . .

Even while he held her he struggled against the conviction that, somewhere, Cassandra was screaming his name, weeping, pleading, begging him to come to her. . . . Allart knew that if he did not quickly still this he would succumb also and run wildly down the stairs seeking her in every room of the castle, even though his mind told him she knelt there across the room, wholly caught up into some such internal ritual of terror as held Renata.

He snatched out his matrix, focused into it.

Truth, truth, let me see truth . . . earth and air and water and fire . . . let Nature prevail free of illusion . . . earth and air and water and fire. . . . He had no strength for anything but this, the most basic of spells, the first of prayers. He strove to drive out the nonexistent, dying sound of Cassandra's screams for mercy in his ears, the terrible guilt that he lingered here while she struggled somewhere with a ravisher. . . .

Quiet spread through his mind, the silence of the healing-spell, the silence of the chapel at Nevarsin. He entered into the silence and, for a timeless moment, was healed. Now he saw only what was there in the room, the two women in the grip of terrifying illusion. He focused first on Renata, willing her to quiet with the pulse of the healing-spell. Slowly, slowly, he felt it enter her mind, calm her, so that she stopped struggling, stared around her with a great amazement.

"But none of it was true," she said in a whisper. "Donal—Donal is not dead. Our child—our child is not even born. Yet I *saw* Allart, I saw where they held them and I could not reach them."

"A spell of terror," Allart said. "I think everyone saw what he or she most feared. Come quickly—help me to break it!"

Shaken, but strong again, Renata took her matrix, and at once they focused on Cassandra. After a moment her smothered cries of terror stopped, and she looked at them, dazed with dread, then blinked, realizing what had happened. Now with three minds and three matrixes focused, they sent the healing-spell beating out through all the castle, and from cellar to attic and everywhere in the crowded courtyard, servants and soldiers and guardsmen and stableboys came out of the dazed trance wherein each had heard the cries of whoever he loved best and fought blindly to rescue that one from the hands of a nameless enemy.

At last all the castle lay under the rhythm of the healing-spell, but now Allart was shaking in dread. Not, this time, the dread of nameless persecution, but something all too real and frightful.

If they have begun to fight us this way, how can we hold them at bay? Here within the castle Allart had only the two women, old Margali, the still older Dom Mikhail, and Donal, if he could dare to take him from the defense of the castle against attackers who were all too tangible. In fact, Allart feared that this was just the tactic they would use—to distract the fighting men while they attacked, under cover of the great fear they could project. He hurried in search of Dom Mikhail, for a council of war.

"You know what we have had to fight," he said. The old lord nodded, his face grim, his eyes hawk-bright, menacing.

"I thought I stood and watched my best-loved die again," he said. "In my ears was the curse of a sorceress I hanged from these walls thirteen years gone by, jeering at me that a day would come when I would cry out to the gods in grief that I had not died childless. Then he seemed to start awake and shake himself like a mantling hawk on the block. "Well, she is dead and her malice with her."

He pondered for a time.

"We must attack," he said. "They can wear us down quickly, if we must be alert night and day for that kind of attack, and we cannot be ever on the defense. Somehow we must send them howling. We have only one weapon strong enough to rout them."

"I did not know that we had any such weapon," Allart said. "Of what do you speak, my lord?"

Dom Mikhail said, "I speak of Dorilys. She commands the lightning. She must strike them with storm, and utterly destroy their camp."

Allart looked at him in consternation.

"My lord Aldaran, you must be mad!"

"Kinsman," Aldaran said, his eyes flaring displeasure, "I think you forget yourself!"

"If I have angered you, sir, I beg your pardon. Let my love for your foster-son—yes, and for your daughter, too—be my excuse. Dorilys is only a child, and the lady Renata—yes—and my wife also have done their utmost to teach her to master and control her gift, never to use it unworthily. If you ask her now to direct it in rage and destruction on the armies below us, can you not see, my lord, you wipe out all we have done? As a young child, twice, she killed, striking with a child's uncontrolled anger. Can you not see, if you use her this way—" Allart stopped, trembling with apprehension.

Dom Mikhail said, "We must use such weapons as we have to hand, Allart." He raised his head and said, "You did not complain when she struck down the evil bird your brother sent against you! Nor did you hesitate to ask her to use her gift to move the storm which had you trapped in the snow! And she struck down the air-cars which would have spread enough *clingfire* here to burn Castle Aldaran into a smoking ruin!"

"All this is true," Allart said, shaking with earnestness, "but in all this she was defending herself or others against the violence of another. Can you not see the difference between defense and attack, sir?"

"No," Aldaran said, "for it seems to me that in this case attack is the only defense, or we may be struck down at any moment by some weapon even more frightful than those they have loosed on us already."

Sighing, Allart made his last plea.

"Lord Aldaran, she has not yet even recovered from her threshold sickness. I saw, when we were at the fire station, how over use of her *laran* left her sick and weak, and then she was not yet come to the threshold of maturity this way. I am really afraid of what may happen if you put further strain on her powers just now. Will you wait, at least, until we truly have no other choice? A few days, even a few hours—"

The father's face contracted with fear, and Allart knew that for the moment, at least, he had won his victory.

"Cassandra and I will go again to the watchtower and keep vigil so they will not take us unaware again. No matter how many *leroni* they have down there, they must have exhausted themselves with that spell of terror. I think they must rest before they try anything more like *that*, or worse."

Allart's prediction proved true, for all during that day and night, only a few flights of arrows flew against the walls of the castle. But at dawn the next morning, Allart, who had snatched a few hours of sleep, leaving Cassandra on watch in the tower room, was wakened by ominous rumbling far away. Confused, trying to flood away sleep by splashing cold water on his face, he tried to identify the sound. Cannon? Thunder? Was Dorilys angered or frightened again? Had Aldaran broken his pledge not to use her except in extremity? Or was it something else?

He hurried up the stairs to the watchtower, but as he went, the stairs seemed to sway under his feet and he had to clutch at the handrail, his *laran* suddenly envisioning the cracks spreading in the tower walls, the tower splitting and crumbling, falling.

He burst into the tower room, his face white, and Cassandra, seated before the matrix, looked up at him in sudden terror, picking up his dread.

"Come down," he said quickly. "Come out of here, at once, my wife." As she hurried down the stairs he saw again the great cracks widening in the staircase, the rumbling. . . . They fled down the stairs, hand in hand, Cassandra stumbling on her lame knee, and at last Allart turned back, caught her up in his arms and carried her down the last few steps, not stopping even to breathe, hurrying along the hall. Out of breath, he set her on her feet and stood clinging to a door-frame in the corridor, her arms around him. Then the floor beneath their feet swayed and rumbled, there was a great sound like the splitting asunder of the world, and the floor of the tower they had just left heaved and buckled upward. The stairs broke away from the wall, stones fell outward, crumbling, and then the whole tower split and fell, crashing in heavy thunder down upon the roofs of the keep, stones cascading into the courtyards, falling into the valley below, touching off rockfalls and landslides. . . . Cassandra buried her face in Allart's chest and clung to him, shaking with dread. Allart felt his knees buckling and they slid together to the floor, as it swayed and shook under them. Finally the noise died away, leaving only silence and strange, ominous grumbles and crunching sounds from the ground under them.

Slowly they clambered to their feet. Cassandra had injured her lame knee freshly in their fall; she had to cling to Allart to stand. They stared up at the great gap and thick foggy dawn where once a tall tower had risen, by a near-miracle of matrix engineering, three flights of stairs toward the sun. Now there was nothing but a great pile of stone and rubble and plaster fallen inward, and a huge gap through which the morning rain was drizzling in.

"What, in the name of all the gods was *that?*" Cassandra finally inquired, stunned. "An earthquake?"

"Worse, I fear," Allart said. "I do not know what kind of *leroni* they have down there, or what they are using against us, but I am afraid it is something worse than even Coryn would invent."

Cassandra scoffed, "No matrix known could do *that!*"

"No single matrix, no," Allart said, "and no technician. But if they have one of the great matrix screens, they could explode this planet to its core, if they dared." His mind clamored, *Would even Damon-Rafael risk laying waste this land he seeks to rule?* But his mind provided him with a grim answer.

Damon-Rafael would not be at all averse to showing his power over a part of the world for which he had no immediate need and which he considered expendable. And after this, no one would dare to challenge him.

Scathfell might be malicious and eager to rule in his brother's shoes, but Damon-Rafael was the culprit this time. Scathfell wished to rule in Castle Aldaran, not to destroy it.

Now they became aware, through the gap in the castle walls, of cries and commotion below, and Allart recalled himself to duty.

"I must go and see if anyone has been hurt by falling stones, and how it fares with Donal, my sworn brother," he said, and hurried away. But even as he went he felt the castle trembling again beneath him, and wondered what new devilry was afoot. Well, Cassandra could warn the women without his help. He hurried down into the courtyard, where he found chaos unbelievable. One of the outbuildings had been buried entirely beneath the falling stones of the tower, and a dozen men and four times as many animals were dead in the ruins; others had been crushed by falling debris.

Dom Mikhail was there, leaning heavily on Donal's arm. He was still in his furred bed-gown, his face gray and fallen in; Allart thought he looked twenty years older in a single night. He clung to his foster-son as he moved carefully among the ruin in his courtyard. As he saw Allart his thin mouth stretched in a travesty of a smile.

"Cousin, the gods be thanked, I feared that you and your lady had fallen with the tower and been killed. Is the lady Cassandra safe? What, in the name of all Zandru's demons, have they done to us now? It will take us half a year to clear away this chaos! Half the dairy animals have been killed; the children will go wanting milk this winter. . . ."

"I am not certain," Allart said soberly, "but I must have every man or woman in this stronghold who is able to use a matrix, and organize our defenses against it. We are but ill prepared, I fear, for this kind of warfare."

"Are you sure of that, my brother?" Donal asked. "Surely earthquakes have been known in the mountains before this!"

"It was no earthquake! I am as sure of that as if Damon-Rafael stood before me laughing at what he had done!"

Dom Mikhail knelt beside the body of a fallen man, only crushed legs protruding from a block of fallen stone larger than a man. "Poor fellow," he said. "At least his death must have been swift. I fear that those buried in the stables had a death more fearful. Donal, leave the guardsmen to bury the dead; Allart has more need of you now. I will send everyone with *laran* to you, so that you can see what has been sent us."

"We cannot meet in the tower now," Allart said grimly. "We must have a room somewhat isolated from the grief and fright of those who are clearing away the ruin, Lord Aldaran."

"Take the women's conservatory; perhaps the peace of the flowering plants there will create an atmosphere you can use."

As Donal and Allart entered the castle once again, Allart could feel, through the soles of his feet, a renewed faint tremor. Again he wondered what happened. He felt a spasm of dread, remembering how near Cassandra had come to being trapped in the falling tower.

Donal said, "I wish that our friends in Tramontana were here. They would know how to deal with this!"

"I am glad that they are not," Allart replied. "I would not have the Towers drawn into the wars in this land!"

The sun was just coming through the clouds as they entered the conservatory, and the calm brilliance of the sun light, the solar collectors spreading light, the faint, pleasant damp smell of herbs and flowering leaves, felt strangely at odds with the dread and fear Allart could feel from the men and women who were joining him there. Not only Cassandra, Renata, Margali, and Dorilys, but two or three of the women he had not seen before, and half a dozen of the men. Each one bore a matrix, though Allart sensed that more than half of these had only minimal talent and could do little more than open a matrix-lock or operate some such toy as the gliders. After a time Dom Mikhail, too, came in.

Allart glanced at Cassandra. She had been in a Tower longer than he, she was, perhaps, better trained, and he was willing to allow her to conduct this search, but she shook her head.

"You are Nevarsin-taught; you are less subject to fear and confusion than I."

Allart was not so sure, but he accepted her decision and looked around the circle of men and women.

"I have no time to test you one by one and assess the level of your training; I must trust you," he said. "Renata, you were four years a monitor. You must set a guard around us, for we expose ourselves to those who are trying to destroy this castle and all those in it, and we are vulnerable. I must find what they are using against us, and if there is any defense against it. You must lend us your strength, and our lives are in all of your hands."

He looked around the room, at the men and women who

shared with him a spark of this gift of the great families. Did they all have some trace of the far-off kin to the gods; were they all somehow descended via the breeding program from the blood of Hastur and Cassilda? Or did all men, in truth, have some trace, more or less, of these powers? Always before he had depended on his equals, his kinsmen; now he was in the hands of commoners, and it sobered him, and humbled him, too. He was afraid to trust them, but he had no choice.

He linked his mind first with Cassandra, then with Donal; then, one by one, with the others in the circle, picking up traces of their emotion as he did so . . . fear, anger at what was being sent against them, disquiet at this unusual operation, strangeness. . . . He felt Dorilys drop into the linkage, sensing her fury at the attackers who had dared to do this to her home. . . . One by one, he picked up every man and woman in the circle, and sank into the joined consciousness, moved outward and outward, searching sifting. . . .

It seemed a very long time before he felt the link fall apart and Allart raised his head, looking sobered.

"It is no natural matrix they are using against us," he said, "but one constructed artificially within the Towers by a technician. With it, they are seeking to alter the natural vibration of the very rock of the mountain beneath us." As he spoke, he put out a hand and he could feel through the walls the very faint trembling of the walls which reflected the deeper trembling within the foundations and the veined metal and layers of old rock beneath.

Dom Mikhail had not shaved; beneath the untidy stubble of grayish beard his face was deathly pale. "They will bring down the castle about our heads! Is there no defense, Allart?"

"I do not know," Allart said. "All of us together could hardly stand against a matrix that size." Was there indeed any hope, or should Aldaran capitulate and surrender before his entire castle collapsed in ruin around him? "We could try to put a binding-spell upon the rock of the mountain," he said, hesitating. "I do not know if it would hold. Even with all of us, I am not sure it would hold. But it seems our only hope."

Dorilys sprang to her feet. She had come to the conservatory, with her matrix, not bothering to dress; she sat in her long-sleeved childish nightgown, her hair unbraided and falling about her shoulders like a cascade of new copper.

"But I have a better idea," she cried. "*I* can break their concentration; can I not, Father? Donal, come with me."

Allart watched, in consternation, as she hurried from the room. In a whisper, from the men and women, commoners, around the room, he heard again the name they had given her.

"Stormqueen. Our little lady, our little sorceress, she can raise a storm and give those folk down there something else to think about, indeed!"

Allart appealed to Dom Mikhail.

"My lord—"

Slowly, the old lord of Aldaran shook his head. "I see no other choice, cousin. It is that, or surrender at once."

Allart lowered his eyes, knowing that Dom Mikhail spoke no more than truth.

Already, as he followed toward the high battlement where Dorilys stood with Donal, he could see the clouds thickening and gathering. Then he shrank from the open window as Dorilys raised her arms, crying out wordlessly. Power seemed to burst from her, so that she was no longer only a young woman in a nightgown, her hair falling about her shoulders; above their heads the storm burst like one of the explosive shells, with a great thunderbolt and a flare of lightning that seemed to split the sky asunder. Torrential rains poured down, wiping out eyesight below, but through the welter of noise, the crash upon crash of thunder and the glare that hurt his eyes and split the heavens apart, Allart sensed what was happening below.

Floodwaters washing down on the camp at the foot of the mountain. Thunder, deafening and stampeding their riding-animals, spreading panic in human and nonhuman alike. Lightning ripping through the tent where the matrix workers sat over their great unnatural stone, searing them blind and deafened, some of them burned out or dead. Rain, pouring soaking rain, pounding and drumming, beating their camp into the ground, driving around every rock or tree where they might take shelter, reducing everything that had life in that camp to naked, soaked animal humiliation. Lightning again kindling fires to roar through their tents, searing, raging, beating everything to the ground.

Never had Allart known such a storm. Cassandra clung to him, as it raged on and on over their heads, burying her head and sobbing in fear. Allart held himself tensed against the noise and devastation, as if it raged through his whole body. But Dom Mikhail's face held a fierce exultation as he stood there, hour after hour, watching the storm wreak desolation and ruin in the camp of Scathfell and Damon-Rafael below them.

At last, at long last, it began to subside. Small rollings and rumblings of thunder remained, dying away in shudders of sound on the distant hills, and the rain began to grow weaker. As the sky cleared to whitish shreds of cloud, Allart looked down into the valley. The valley lay stunned, quiet, a few fires still roaring out of control in the camp, side by side with flooding streams which had left their beds and raged over the countryside. There seemed no sign of life below.

Dorilys swayed, her face very white, and fell against Donal in a faint. He picked her up tenderly and carried her inside.

She has saved us, Allart thought, *at least for now. But at what cost?*

CHAPTER
TWENTY-EIGHT

It was high noon before there was any sign of life from the camp of Lord Scathfell below. There were still more rumbles and noise of ominous thunder high above them, crashing around the peaks, and Allart wondered if Dorilys, in her exhausted sleep, still dreamed of the dreadful battle, if these thunders reflected her nightmares.

Renata said that Dorilys taps the magnetic potential of the planet, he reflected. *I can well believe it! But with all that power flowing through her poor little body and brain, can she survive it undamaged?*

He wondered if Aldaran, in the long run, would not have done better to surrender. What kind of father love would expose a beloved child to that?

But near midday the thunders died away, and Cassandra, who had been summoned to monitor Dorilys and care for her, reported that she had wakened and eaten and fallen into normal sleep. Still, Allart felt a dreadful unease, and it seemed to him that unending lightnings still played around the castle. Donal, too, looked deeply troubled, and although he had gone to supervise the men who were burying the dead and clearing rubble from the fallen tower, he kept returning, stealing up to the door of her room and standing there to listen to her breathing. Renata came to look at him, in dread and pleading, but he avoided her eyes.

The woman wondered, in dread, *Has he been seduced at the thought of all this power? What has happened to Donal?* And she, too, was afraid for Dorilys, wondering what the use of that blasting force had done to the girl she loved.

An hour or two past noon, a messenger appeared on the

road leading up to the castle, still washed-out and runneled with water flooding from the heights, partially blocked with stones that had fallen when the tower collapsed. The message was relayed to Donal, who took it to Dom Mikhail at once.

"Father, your brother of Scathfell has sent a messenger asking if he may come to negotiate terms with you."

Aldaran's eyes glinted, fierce and bright, but he said calmly, "Tell my brother of Scathfell I will hear what he has to say."

After a time, the leader of the opposing army came up the path, afoot, followed by his paxman and two guards. As he crossed the line of siege he said to the single man stationed there, "Wait till I return." Donal, who had come to escort him into Aldaran's presence, received the most contemptuous glare, but Scathfell looked beaten nevertheless, and they all knew he had come to surrender. There was too little left of his army, and nothing of Damon-Rafael's weaponry. He had come, Donal knew, to try to save what little he could out of defeat.

Lord Aldaran had made ready to receive his brother in his presence-chamber, and he entered the room with Dorilys on his arm. Donal thought of the last time they had all been together in this room. Scathfell looked older, grimmer, aged by the crushing weight of defeat. He glared at Donal, and at Dorilys in her blue gown, and looked with grim appraisal at Allart when he was named. Even though Allart had been styled traitor and rebel, Scathfell still looked on him with the habitual respect, amounting to awe, of a younger son and minor noble before a Hastur lord.

"Well, my brother," Aldaran said at last. "Much has passed between us since last you came into this hall. I had never thought to see you here again. Tell me—why have you asked for my presence? Have you come to surrender yourself and beg my pardon for your rebellion against my lawful demands?"

Scathfell swallowed heavily before he could speak. At last he said with great bitterness, "What other choice have I now? Your witch-daughter there has routed my armies and killed my men as she struck down my son and heir. No man living can stand against such sorcery. I have come to ask for compromise."

"Why should I compromise with you, Rakhal? Why should I not strip you of your lands and honors, which you hold at my pleasure, and send you forth naked and yelping like a beaten hound, or hang you from my battlements to show all men how I shall deal henceforth with all rebels and traitors?"

"I do not stand alone," Rakhal of Scathfell said. "I have an ally who is, perhaps, even more powerful than you and your witch-brat together. I am bidden to say that if I do not return before sunset, Damon-Rafael will gather his forces and shake apart this mountain beneath you, and Aldaran will fall over your head. You had a taste of that power this morning at sunrise, I think. Men and armies can be scattered and beaten, but if you wish this land to be rent in a dozen parts by sorcery, it will be your doing and not mine. However, he has no desire to destroy you now that you know his power. He asks only that he shall be allowed to speak with his brother, both unarmed, in the space between our armies, before sunset."

"Allart Hastur is my guest," Aldaran said. "Should I deliver him over to his brother's sure treachery?"

"Treachery? Between brethren and Hasturs both?" asked Scathfell, and his face showed honest outrage. "He would make peace with his brother as I, Mikhail, would make peace with mine." Clumsily, unaccustomed, he bowed to one knee.

"You have beaten me, Mikhail," he said. "I will withdraw my armies. And, believe me, it was none of my doing that broke your tower. Truly, I spoke against it, but the lord Damon-Rafael wished to display his power before the northlands."

"I believe you." Aldaran looked at his brother with a great sadness. "Go home, Rakhal," he said. "Go in peace. I ask only that you take oath to honor the husband of my daughter as next heir after me, and never to raise hand or sword against him, openly or by stealth. If you will take this oath in the light of truthspell, you may enjoy Scathfell forevermore, without harassment from me or mine."

Scathfell raised his head, rage and contempt vying on his face.

Donal, watching him, thought, *My father should not have pressed this now! Did he think I could not hold Aldaran after him?* Yet it seemed that Scathfell would capitulate.

"Call your *leronis* and set the truthspell," he said, his face set and unsmiling. "Never did I think I would come to this at your hands, my brother, or that you would exact such humiliation from me." He stood restless, as Margali was summoned, shifting from foot to foot. As the *leronis* came, he made as if to go to his knees before Donal and Dorilys. Then suddenly he cried, "No!" and bounded to his feet.

"Take oath never to contest the bastard of Rockraven, and that hell-brat of yours? Zandru take me first! Rather will I strike and rid the earth of their sorcery," he cried, and suddenly there was a dagger in his hand. Donal cried out and flung himself in front of his sister, but there was a shrill shriek from Dorilys, an exploding blue flare of lightning in the room, searing the air white, and Scathfell fell, convulsing briefly into an agonized arch, then lay still, half his face blackened and burned away.

There was silence in the room, the silence of shock and sheer horror. Dorilys cried out, "He would have killed Donal! He would have killed us both! You saw the dagger," and she covered her face with her hands. Donal, struggling to control his nausea, unfastened the cloak around his throat and cast it mercifully over the blackened body of Scathfell.

Mikhail of Aldaran said hoarsely, "It is no dishonor to kill a man forsworn, who seeks to do murder on the very ground of surrender. There is no shame to you, daughter." But he left his high seat and came down into the room, kneeling by his brother's body, pulling back the cloak from his face.

"Oh, my brother, my brother," he mourned, and his eyes were blazing and tearless. "How did we come to this?" He bent, kissing the blackened brow; then gently drew the cloak over Scathfell's face again.

"Bear him down to his men," he said to Scathfell's paxman. "You are witness that there was no treachery save his own. I will take no revenge; his son may hold Scathfell after him. Though it would be only fair if I gifted Donal with Scathfell for amends, and gave them only the farm at High Crags in its stead."

The paxman, knowing that what Aldaran said was true, bowed silently.

"It shall be as you say, Lord. His eldest son Loran is turned seventeen and shall assume rule over Scathfell. But what am I to say to the lord Hastur?" He amended quickly, "To His Highness, Damon-Rafael, king over this land?"

Allart suddenly left his place. He said, "My brother's quarrel is with me, Lord Aldaran. I will go down and meet him, unarmed, as he has asked."

Cassandra cried out, "Allart, no! He means treachery!"

"Still, I must face him," Allart said. It was his doing which had entangled the house of Aldaran in this Lowland war, when they had enough trouble of their own. Now, unless Allart went to him, Damon-Rafael would destroy Aldaran around their heads. "He said that he wished to compromise with his brother as Lord Scathfell wished to come to terms with *you*; and I think, at that moment, Scathfell spoke only truth. I do not think he moved against Donal by foresight but upon impulse, and he has paid for it. It may be that my brother wishes only to persuade me that he is indeed rightfully king over this land, and ask my support. It is true that before I knew what I did, I pledged to support him in this. He is right to call me traitor, perhaps. I must go down and speak with him."

Cassandra came and clutched at him, holding him motionless.

"I will not let you go! I will not! He will kill you, and you know it!"

"He will not kill me, my wife," said Allart, putting her away with more force than he had ever before used against her. "But I know what I must do, and I forbid you to hinder me."

"You forbid me?" She stood away from him, angry now. "Do what you feel you must, my husband," she said, her teeth set, "but say to Damon-Rafael that if he harms you, I shall raise every man, every woman, and every matrix in the Hellers against him!"

Yet as he went slowly down the mountainside, Cassandra's face seemed to go with him, and his *laran* spread pictures of disaster before him.

Damon-Rafael will almost certainly try to kill me. Yet I must kill him first, as I would kill a maddened beast, raging and ready to bite. If he becomes king over this land, then there will be ruin and disaster such as the Domains have never known.

I never wanted to rule. I never wanted power; I have no ambitions of that kind. I would have been content to dwell within the walls of Nevarsin, or within the Tower at Hali or Tramontana. Yet now that my laran *has shown me what must come to pass if Damon-Rafael comes to the throne, I must somehow stop that from happening. Even if I must kill him!*

The hand he had thrust into the fires of Hali throbbed, as

if reminding him of the oath he had sworn and was now breaking.

I am forsworn. But I am a Hastur, descendant of the Hastur who was said to be son to a god; and I am responsible for the well-being of this land and its people. I will not loose Damon-Rafael upon them!

It was not long to the camp, but it seemed the distance to the world's end, and his *laran* spread dissolving pictures before him, of things which might be, which would be, which could be if he did not take care, which would never be. In all too many of these futures he lay lifeless among the stones fallen from the tower, with Damon-Rafael's knife in his throat, and Damon-Rafael went on to level the walls of Aldaran, to possess northlands and Domains, to reign in tyranny and power for many years, riding roughshod over all the remaining freedoms of men, razing their defenses with weapons ever more powerful, and at last invading even their very minds with his *leroni*, making them all obedient slaves to his will, their own wishes and enterprises burned away.

His heart cried out, as Mikhail of Aldaran had cried out a little while ago, *Ah, my brother, my brother, how did we come to this?*

Damon-Rafael was not an evil man. But he had pride, and a will to power, and he felt honestly that he knew what was best for all men.

He is not unlike Dom Mikhail. . . . But Allart shuddered away from that thought. He was lost again in terrifying vision, blotting out the present, of this land under the rule of the tyrant Damon-Rafael.

Yet my brother is not evil. Does he even know this?

At last he came to a stop, and he saw that he stood on a leveled place in the road, with fallen debris of the tower all around him. At the far end of the leveled space, his brother Damon-Rafael was standing and watching him.

Allart bowed, without speaking.

His *laran* was screaming, *This is the place, then, of my death.* But Damon-Rafael was alone, and seemed unarmed. Allart spread his hands to display that he was unweaponed, too, and the brothers advanced, step by step, toward one another.

Damon-Rafael said, "You have a loyal and a loving wife, Allart. It will grieve me to take her from you. Yet you were reluctant to wed her, and even more reluctant to bed her, so I suppose it will not trouble you much to give her up to me. The world and the kingdom are full of women, and I shall make sure you are wed to one you will like just as well. But Cassandra I must have; I need the support of the Aillards. And I have discovered that her genes were modified before puberty, so that she can bear me a son with the Hastur gift controlled by the Aillard."

Allart cleared his throat and said, "Cassandra is my wife, Damon-Rafael. If you loved her, or if she were ambitious to be queen, I would step aside for you both. But I love her, and she loves me, and you care nothing for her, save as a pawn of political power. Therefore I will not yield her up to you. I will die first."

Damon-Rafael shook his head. "I cannot afford to take her over your dead body. I would greatly prefer not to come to the throne over a brother's death."

Allart smiled fiercely. He said, "Then I can inconvenience you somewhat in coming to the throne, if only by my death!"

"I do not understand this," Damon-Rafael said. "You asked me to spare you this marriage to the Aillard woman, and now you speak romantically of love. You swore to support me for the throne, and now you refuse your support and strive to hinder me! What has happened, Allart? Is that what love for a woman can do to a man? If so, I am glad I have never known such love!"

"When I pledged my support to you," Allart said, "I did not know what would befall if you were to be king. Now I have pledged myself to support Prince Felix."

"An *emmasca* cannot be king," Damon-Rafael said. "That is one of our oldest laws."

"If you were fit to be king," Allart retorted, "you would not be on the road with an army, trying to extend your reign to the northlands! You would wait until the Council offered you the throne, and seek their advice."

"How could I better serve my kingdom, than by extending its might and power across the Hellers as well?" Damon-Rafael said. "Come, Allart, there is no reason we should quarrel. . . . Cassandra has a *nedestro* sister, as like to Cassandra as twin to twin. You shall have her for your wife, and be my chief councillor. I shall need someone with your foresight and strength. *Bare is back without brother* . . . that is what they say, and believe me, it is true. Let us amend our differences, embrace and be friends."

Then it is hopeless, Allart thought. Even as Damon-Rafael held out his arms for the offered embrace, Allart was aware of the dagger concealed by stealth in his brother's hand.

So he would not even face me openly, but would embrace me and stab me to the heart even while I went to his arms, he mourned. *Oh, my brother.* . . . As he moved into Damon-Rafael's embrace, he reached out with his *laran,* trained and honed to skill in the Tower and at Nevarsin, and held Damon-Rafael motionless, the dagger revealed now in his hand.

Damon-Rafael struggled, held motionless, but Allart shook his head sadly.

"So you seek to embrace and stab at once, brother? Is this the kind of statecraft you think will make you king? No, Damon-Rafael," he said sorrowfully, and reaching out into Damon-Rafael's mind, made contact. "See what kind of king you would make, my brother who has renounced the tie of brotherhood."

He felt his *laran* flooding the future through Damon-Rafael's mind; conquest, blood and rapine, the relentless rise to power, laying waste the Domains to wilderness and a stunned conquest they called peace by default . . . men's minds burned into blind obedience, the land shattered and torn with war waged with greater and greater weapons, all men bowing down before a king who had become not the just ruler and protector of his people, but their tyrant, despot, hated as no man had ever been hated within the realm. . . .

"No, no," Damon-Rafael whispered, struggling with the dagger in his hand. "Show me no more. I would not be like that."

"No, my brother? You have the Hastur *laran* which sees all choices; see for yourself what manner of king you would be," Allart said, releasing his hold on his brother's mind but holding him motionless. "Face no man's judgment but your own. Look within."

He watched Damon-Rafael, saw the look of dread and horror spreading over his face, slow dawning of awareness, conviction. Then, with a maddened effort, Damon-Rafael freed himself from Allart's hold and raised the dagger. Allart stood his ground, knowing that within a moment he might lie at his brother's feet—or had Damon-Rafael seen himself clearly enough to take warning?

"I will not be such a king," Damon-Rafael whispered, just

loud enough for Allart to hear. "I tell you I will *not*," and with one swift movement he raised the dagger and plunged it deep into his own breast.

He crumpled to the ground, whispered, "Even your foresight cannot see all ends, little brother," and coughed out a stream of bright red blood. Allart felt his brother's dying mind fade into silence.

CHAPTER
TWENTY-NINE

The armies in the valley below had departed, but thunder
still rolled and crunched around the heights, and stray bolts
of lightning ripped across the mountains. As she went into
the lower hall of Castle Aldaran, Cassandra gave Allart a
quick, frightened look.

"It has not stopped thundering—not once, not for a moment—since she struck Scathfell down. And you know she
will not let Renata near her."

Donal sat with Dorilys's head in his lap; the girl looked ill
and feverish. She held Donal's hand tightly clasped in hers
and would not release it. The blue eyes were closed, but she
opened them, painfully, as Cassandra came to her side.

"The thunder hurts my head so," she whispered. "I can't
make it stop. Can't you help me turn off the lightning, Cassandra?"

Cassandra bent over her. "I will try. But I think it is only
that you are overwearied, *chiya*." She took the lax fingers in
hers, fell back with a cry of pain, and Dorilys burst into violent crying.

"I didn't mean to do that, I didn't! It keeps happening and
I cannot stop it! I hurt Margali; I did it to Kathya while she
was dressing me. Oh, Cassandra, make it stop, make it stop!
Can't anybody make the thundering go away?"

Dom Mikhail came and bent over her. His face was drawn
and troubled. "Hush, hush, my precious, no one is blaming
you!" He turned a look of agony on Cassandra. "Can you
help her? Donal, you have that kind of *laran*, too; can you do
nothing for her?"

"I wish indeed that there was something I could do," Donal said, cradling the girl in his arms. She relaxed against him, and Cassandra, steadying herself, braced and took the girl's hand in her own again. This time nothing happened, but she felt frightened, even while she tried to relax herself into the calm detachment of a monitor. She looked once at Renata, over Dorilys's head, and Renata picked up her thought: *I wish she would let you do this; you have so much more experience than I.*

"I will give you something to make you sleep," she said at last. "Perhaps all you need is rest, *chiya*."

When Renata brought the sleeping draft, Donal held the vial to her lips. Dorilys swallowed it obediently, but her voice was plaintive when she said, "I am so afraid to sleep now. My dreams are so dreadful, and I hear the tower falling, and the thunder is inside me. The storms are all inside my head now. . . ."

Donal stood up, Dorilys in his arms. "Let me carry you to your bed, sister," he said, but she clung to him.

"No, no! Oh, please, please, I'm afraid to be alone. I'm so afraid. Please stay with me, Donal! Don't leave me!"

"I will stay with you until you are asleep," Donal promised, sighing, and signaled to Cassandra to come with them.

She followed as he carried Dorilys along the hall and up the long staircase. At the end of the hallway the roofing had been roughly repaired. but a great pile of stone and fallen plaster and debris still blocked the hall. Cassandra thought, *It is no great wonder she hears it in her nightmares!*

Donal carried Dorilys into her room, laying her on the bed and summoning her women to loosen her clothing, remove her shoes. But even when she was tucked under her quilts she would not release his hand. She murmured something Cassandra did not hear. Donal stroked her forehead gently, with his free hand.

"This is no time to speak of that, *chiya*. You are ill. When you are well and strong again, and wholly free of threshold sickness—then, yes, if you wish it. I have promised you." He bent to kiss her lightly on the forehead, but she pulled at his head with both hands so that their lips met, and the kiss she gave him was not a child's kiss or a sister's. Donal drew away, looking troubled and embarrassed.

"Sleep, child. sleep. You are wearied; you must be strong and well tonight for the victory feast in the Great Hall."

She lay back on her pillow, smiling.

"Yes," she said drowsily. "For the first time I shall sit in the high seat as Lady of Aldaran . . . and you beside me . . . my husband. . . ."

The drowsiness of the strong sleeping medicine was already taking her. She let her eyes fall shut, but she did not loosen her grip on Donal's hand, and even when she slept it was some time before her fingers relaxed enough so that he could draw his hand free. Cassandra, watching, was embarrassed at having witnessed this, even though she knew perfectly well that this was one reason Donal had wanted her there.

She is not herself. We should not blame her for what happens when she is under such stress, poor child. But inside herself Cassandra knew that Dorilys was perfectly well aware what she was doing, and why.

She is too old for her years. . . .

When they returned to the hall, Renata raised questioning eyes to them, and Donal said, "Yes, she sleeps. But in the name of all the gods, cousin, what did you give her to work so quickly?"

Renata told him, and he stared at her in consternation.

"*That*? To a child?"

Dom Mikhail said, "That would be a dose overlarge for a grown man dying of the black rot! Was that not dangerous?"

"I dared give her nothing less," Renata said. "Listen." She held up a hand for silence and overhead they could hear the crackle and crumble of thunder in the cloudless sky. "Even now she dreams."

"Blessed Cassilda, have mercy!" Dom Mikhail said. "What ails her?"

Renata said soberly, "Her *laran* is out of control. You should never have allowed her to use it in the war, my lord. Her control was broken down when she loosed it against the armies. I first saw it in the fire station, when she played with the storms, and became overexcited and dizzy. You remember, Donal! But she had not then come to her full strength or womanhood. Now—all the control I taught her has faded from her mind. I do not know what we can do for her." She turned, made a deep reverence to Aldaran.

"My lord, I asked you this once before, and you refused. Now, I think, there is no choice. I implore you. Let me burn out her psi centers. Perhaps now, while she sleeps, it could still be done."

Aldaran looked at Renata in horror.

"When her *laran* has saved us all? What would that do to her?"

"I think—I *hope*," Renata said, "that it would do no more than take away the lightnings that torment her so. She would be without *laran*, but she wishes for that now. You heard her beg Cassandra to take away the thundering. She would perhaps be no more, and no less, than an ordinary woman of her caste, ungifted with *laran*, yes, but having her beauty, still, and her talents, and her superb voice. She could still—" She hesitated, choked over the words, and went on, looking straight at Donal, "She could still give an heir of Aldaran blood to your clan, gifted with the *laran* in her genes. She should never bear a daughter, but she could give Aldaran a son, if need be."

Donal had told her of the promise he had made to Dorilys, during the siege of Castle Aldaran.

"It is no more than fair," Renata had said then. *If Dorilys must be bound all her life by the catenas in a marriage forced on her before she is old enough to know anything of marriage or of love, where she will have the name and dignity of a wife but never a husband's love, it is only fair that she should have something of her very own, something to love and cherish. I do not grudge her a child for Aldaran. It would be better if she would choose some other than Donal for the fathering, but as her life must be ordered, it is not likely she will come to know any man well enough for such a purpose. And it is Lord Aldaran's will that Donal's son should reign here when he is gone. I do not begrudge Dorilys a child of Donal's. It is I who am his wife, and we all know it, or will know it, in time to come.*

Now Renata looked at Lord Aldaran, pleading, and Allart remembered the moment when he had seen with his *laran*, in this very hall, the vassals of Aldaran acclaiming a child whom he held up before them, proclaiming the new heir of Aldaran blood. Why, Allart wondered, should his foresight show him only this one moment? It seemed that all else was blurred into nightmare and thundercloud. But they saw it in Allart's mind, all the telepaths there assembled, and Aldaran said "I told you so!" with that fierce, hawklike glance.

Donal lowered his head and would not meet Renata's eyes.

"It seems terrible to do that to her, when she has saved us

all. Are you sure it would do no worse to her than this—to
destroy the psi centers and leave the rest undamaged?" Lord
Aldaran said.

Renata said reluctantly, "My lord, no *leronis* living could
make such a pledge. I love Dorilys as if she were my own,
and I would give her the uttermost of my skill and strength.
But I do not know how much of her brain has been invaded
by the *laran*, or damaged by these storms. You know that
electrical discharges *within* the brain reflect themselves as
convulsive seizures in the body. Dorilys's *laran* somehow
translates the electrical discharges *in* the brain to thunder and
lightnings in the electrical field of the planet. Now that is out
of control. She said the thunders were *inside* her now. I do
not know how much damage has been done. It might be that
I would have to destroy some part of her memory, or of her
intelligence."

Donal was white with dread. "No!" he said, and it was a
prayer. "Would she be an idiot, then?"

Renata would not look at him. She said, very low, "I cannot swear that the possibility is beyond belief. I would do my
best for her. But it could indeed be so."

"No! All gods help us—no, kinswoman!" Aldaran said, the
old hawk roused. "If there is the slightest chance—no, I cannot risk it. Even if all should go for the best, cousin, a
woman who is heir to Aldaran cannot live as a commoner,
without *laran*. She would be better dead!"

Renata bowed, a submissive gesture. "Let us hope it does
not come to that, my lord."

Lord Aldaran looked around at them all. "I shall see you
tonight at the victory feast within this hall," he said. "I must
go and give orders that all is done as I command." He went
from the hall, his head erect and arrogant.

Renata, watching him go, thought, *It is his moment of triumph. He has Aldaran now, unchallenged, despite the ruin of
the war. Dorilys is a part of that triumph. He wants her at
his side, a threat, a weapon for the future.* Suddenly she
shuddered, hearing the thunders, soft and dying overhead.

Dorilys slept, her terror and rage diminished by the drug.

But she would wake. And what then?

The thunders were still silent late that evening, as the sun
set. Allart and Cassandra stood on the balcony above their
suite, looking down into the valley.

"I can hardly believe the war is over," Cassandra said.

Allart nodded. "And most likely the war with the Ridenow as well; it was my father and Damon-Rafael who wished to conquer them and drive them back to the Dry-towns. I do not think anyone else cares if they remain at Serrais; certainly the women of Serrais, who wedded them and welcomed them there, do not."

"What is going to happen in Thendara now, Allart?"

"How should I know?" Her husband's smile was bleak. "We have had proofs enough of the inadequacy of my foresight. Most likely Prince Felix will reign until the Council declares his heir. And you know, and I know, whom they are likely to choose."

She said, with a little shiver, "I do not want to be queen."

"Nor I to be king, beloved. But we both knew, when we became entangled in the great events of our time, that there would be no help for it." He sighed. "My first act, if it is so, will be to choose Felix Hastur as my principal Councillor. He was born to the throne, and reared to the knowledge of ruling; also, he is *emmasca* and long-lived, as with those of *chieri* blood, and he may live through two or three reigns. Since he can raise up no son to supplant me, he will be the most useful and disinterested of advisers. Between the two of us, he and I may together make something like a king."

He put his arm around Cassandra, drew her close. Damon-Rafael had reminded him; with Cassandra's modified genes, the blend of Hastur and Aillard might, after all, be viable in a child of theirs. Cassandra, following his thoughts, said aloud, "With what I have learned in the Tower I can make certain I will conceive no child who will kill me in the bearing, or carry lethal genes which will destroy him at puberty. There will be some risk, always. . . ." She raised her eyes to his and smiled. "But after what we have survived together, I think we can risk that much."

"There will be time for that," he said, "but if there should be no such good fortune, Damon-Rafael has half a dozen *nedestro* sons. One of them, at least, should have the stuff to make a king. I think I have had lesson enough in the pride that drives a man to seek a crown for his own sons." He could see, shadowy and blurred in the future, the face of a lad who would follow him to the throne, and that it was a child of Hastur blood. But whether it was a son of his own, or the son of his brother, he did not know, or care.

He was weary, and more grieved than he wanted to let himself know, at his brother's death. He thought, *Even though I had resolved to kill him if I must, even though it was I who held up the mirror of his own heart and thus forced him to turn the knife on himself, I am grieved.* He knew he would never be wholly free of grief and guilt for the decision which had been, whether anyone else ever knew it or not, the first conscious act of his reign. And he knew he would never cease to mourn—not for the power-hungry potential tyrant he had driven to suicide, but for the big brother he loved, who had wept with him at their father's grave.

But *that* Damon-Rafael had died long ago, long ago—if he had ever lived outside Allart's own imagination!

Faint thunder rumbled in the sky, and Cassandra started, then, looking at the rain falling, a dark streak, across the valley on the peaks, she said, "I think it is only a summer storm. Yet I can never hear lightning now—" She broke off. "Allart! Do you think Renata was right? Should you have persuaded Dom Mikhail to let Renata destroy her *laran* as she slept?"

"I do not know," Allart said, troubled. "After what has befallen, I am not eager to trust my own foresight now. But I, too, found my *laran* a curse, when I was a boy on the threshold of manhood. Had any offered me such a release then, I think I would have taken it with gladness. And yet—and yet—" He reached out for her, drew her to him, remembering those agonized days when he had cowered, paralyzed, under the *laran* which had become such a dreadful curse. It had stabilized when he came to manhood; he knew now that he would never have been more than half alive without it. "When she comes to maturity, Dorilys, too, may find stability and strength, and be the stronger for these trials."

As I have been. And you, my beloved.

"I should go to her," Cassandra said uneasily, and Allart laughed.

"Ah, that is like you, love—you who are to be queen, to rush off to the bedside of a sick maiden, and one who is not even to be one of your subjects!"

Cassandra raised her small head proudly.

"I was monitor, and healer, before ever I thought of being a queen. And I hope I shall never refuse my skill to anyone who stands in need of it!"

Allart raised her fingertips to his lips and kissed them.

"The gods grant, beloved, that I shall be as good a king as that!"

Within the castle, Renata heard the thunder, and thought of Dorilys as she readied herself for the victory feast.

"If you have any influence with her at all, Donal," she said, "you will try to persuade her that I mean her well. Then, perhaps, I can work with her, to rebuild the control I had begun to teach her. It would be easier to retrace what she and I had done than to begin again with a stranger."

"I will do that," Donal said. "I do not fear for her; never once has she turned on me, nor on her father, and if she has control enough for that, I have no doubt she can learn control in other things. She is weary now, and frightened, and in the grip of threshold sickness. But when she is well again, she will recapture her control. I am sure of it."

"God grant you are right," she said, smiling, trying to hide her fears.

Abruptly, he said, "At the victory feast, beloved—I want to tell my father, and Dorilys, how it stands with us."

Renata shook her head vehemently. "I do not think it is the right time, Donal. I do not think she can bear it yet."

"Yet," Donal said, frowning, "I am reluctant to lie to her. I wish it had been you, rather than Cassandra, who saw how she clung to me, when I carried her to her bed. I want her to know that I will always cherish her and protect her, but I do not want her to misunderstand, either, or to have a false impression of how things are to be between us. At this feast—when she sits at my side as my wife—" He stopped, troubled, thinking of the kiss Dorilys had given him, which was not a sister's kiss at all.

Renata sighed. At least a part of Dorilys's trouble was threshold sickness, the emotional and physical upheaval which often disturbed a developing telepath in adolescence. Aldaran had lost three nearly grown children that way. Renata, a monitor, and Tower-trained, knew that part of the danger in threshold sickness was the enormous upsurge, at the same time, of telepathic forces, mingled with the stresses of developing, not yet controlled, sexuality. Dorilys had come young to that, too. Like a plant in a forcing-house, the use of her *laran* powers had created all the other upheavals and up-surges, too. Was it any wonder, filled with all this new power and awareness, that she turned to the older boy who had been her special champion, her idol since she was a baby, her protector—and now, by this cruel farce she was too young to understand, her husband as well?

"It is true that she survived her first attack of threshold sickness, and the first attack is often the worst. Perhaps, if she wakes well and coherent—but at this victory feast, Donal? When first she sits at your side, acknowledged your wife? Would you spoil her pleasure in *that*, then?"

"What better time?" Donal asked, smiling. "But even before Dorilys, I want you to tell my father how it is to be with us. He should know that you bear my *nedestro* child. It is not the heir he wants for Aldaran. But he should know that this child will be shield-arm and paxman to Aldaran house as I have been since my mother brought me here as a child. Truly, my dear love, we cannot keep it secret much longer. Pregnancy, like blood-feud, grows never less with secrecy. I would not have it thought that I am cowardly, or ashamed of what I have done. Once known and acknowledged, beloved, your status is protected. Even Dorilys, by civilized custom, knows it is a wife's duty to see to the well-being of any child her husband may father. At this point in her life, I think, any duty properly belonging to a wife will please Dorilys. She was so pleased when Father said she should sit as heir at the victory feast, beside her consort."

"Perhaps you are right," Renata said, remembering Dorilys, who hated sewing, proudly embroidering a holiday shirt for Donal—a traditional bride's task. Donal was right; his marriage to Dorilys was a legal fiction, but custom should be observed, and it was his duty to tell Dorilys that another woman bore his child.

Donal remembered that he had been present—a boy just turned ten years old—when Dom Mikhail had informed Lady Deonara that Aliciane of Rockraven was pregnant with his child. Deonara had risen, embraced Aliciane before all the house-folk, and led her from the women's table to the high seat, formally sharing a drink of wine from the same cup, in token that she would accept the coming child. Renata laughed uneasily at the thought of this ritual with Dorilys.

"Yet you have loved her tenderly," Donal urged, "and I think she will remember that. Also there is this to consider. Dorilys is impulsive and given to fierce tempers, but she is also very conscious of her dignity before the house-folk, as Lady of Aldaran. Once she has been forced to be polite to you at a formal occasion, like this, she will remember how kind you have been to her. Nothing would please me more than to see you reconciled. She will know that I love her, I honor her, I will always care for her. I will even, if it is really her will, give her a child. But she will know what she can expect from me, and what she cannot."

Renata sighed and took his hands.

"As you will, then, beloved," she said. "I can refuse you nothing."

There was a time, not a year past, when I was proud to say to Cassandra Aillard that I did not know what it was to love a man, to suspend my own better judgment to do his will. Do all women come to this, soon or late? And I dared to judge her for that!

Later that evening, when Donal met her at the door of the feasting hall, and himself conducted her to her seat at the women's table, Renata thought that she might as well have shouted it aloud before all the assembled house-folk of Castle Aldaran. She did not care. If all had gone rightly, she and Donal would have been married at midwinter night, and worn the *catenas*. Aldaran had forced another marriage on Donal, but she was neither the first woman nor the last to cling to a lover forced into an expedient marriage with someone else.

She watched Donal as he took his seat at the high table. He had looked handsome to her even in the old rubbed-leather riding-breeches and faded jerkin he had worn during the siege, but now he had put on his finest garments. Firestones hung gleaming at his throat and a jeweled sword at his side. His hair was curled and there were rings on his fingers; he looked handsome and princely. Old Dom Mikhail, in his long furred robe of dark green, with wide sleeves and a jeweled belt, looked proud, but benevolent, too. Dorilys's chair was empty, and Renata wondered if she were still in her drugged sleep. No doubt sleep would do her more good than feasting. Beside Donal and Lord Aldaran at the high table were only Allart and Cassandra, as honored guests of highest rank, and the *leronis* Margali, who was a noblewoman and Dorilys's foster-mother. Under ordinary conditions, Renata sat there herself, as Dorilys's companion and teacher, and so did the *coridom* or estate steward, the chief of the hall-stewards, the castellan, and three or four other functionaries of Castle Aldaran. But at such a solemn feast, only the immediate family and any guests of rank equal to Aldaran's own, or higher, were seated beside the lord Aldaran. The nobles and functionaries were seated either at the women's table where Renata sat, with Lady Elisa and the other women of the estate, or at the men's table with the household knights and important men of the castle.

The lower hall was crowded with those of lower rank, soldiers, guardsmen, servants, everyone down to the stablemen and dairy-women.

"Why are you looking like that at Dorilys's empty chair?" Cassandra asked.

"I thought for a moment that she was there," Allart murmured, disquieted. He had seen for a moment a strange flare of lightning, and thought, *I am weary. I still start at shadows. Perhaps it is only the aftermath of the siege!*

Dom Mikhail leaned toward Margali, asking what had delayed Dorilys. After a moment he nodded, rose from his chair, and addressed the folk assembled in the Great Hall.

"Let us give thanks to the gods that the armies which surrounded us are vanquished and gone to their own place. What they have destroyed will be rebuilded; what they have broken shall be mended." He raised his cup. "First let us drink to honor those who have given their lives in this warfare."

Allart rose with the others, drinking silently from his cup in honor to the dead.

"Now I shall speak of the living," Lord Aldaran said. "I hereby state that any child of any man who died in the siege of this castle shall be fostered in my house, or the household of one of my vassals, according to his father's rightful station, commoner or noble."

There was an outcry of thanks for the lord Aldaran's generosity; then he spoke again.

"Furthermore, if their widows wish to marry again, my stewards shall see to finding them suitable husbands, and if not, they shall be helped to respectable livelihoods."

When the outcry had died down this time, he said, "Now let us eat and drink, but drink first in honor of him who best defended the castle—my foster-son Donal of Rockraven and husband of my daughter, Dorilys, Lady of Aldaran."

Under the cover of the cries of acclamation, Cassandra

said, "Would that Dorilys were here, to know herself so honored."

"I do not know," Allart said slowly. "I think perhaps she has already too much pride in her own power and station."

Dom Mikhail glanced to where Allart sat with Cassandra. "I would that you might remain to help me set my Domain in order, cousin. Yet I have no doubt that before very long they will summon you to Thendara. With your brother dead, you are heir to the Domain of Elhalyn." He looked at Allart, suddenly cautious. Dom Mikhail had become aware that he was no longer dealing with a kinsman, a friend, a fellow noble, but with a future ruler with whom he must one day soon have careful, tactical diplomatic dealings. A Hastur lord, one who might before midsummer day sit on the throne of Thendara.

It seemed to Allart that every word Dom Mikhail spoke was fenced about with sudden caution.

"I hope we will always be friends, cousin."

Allart said, heartfelt, "I hope, indeed, that there will always be friendship between Thendara and Elhalyn." But he wondered, *Can I never again know any real friendships, any simple personal relationships?* The thought depressed him.

Dom Mikhail said, "It will take us half a year to clear away the rubble of the fallen tower; perhaps twice that to rebuild, if we do it by ordinary means. What do you think, Donal—shall we send for a matrix crew, perhaps from Tramontana, perhaps from the Lowlands, to come and clear away this rubble?"

Donal nodded. "We must think of the folk who have had to be away from their homes because of the armies; already the spring planting is delayed, and if it must wait much longer, we will have hunger in these hills at harvest."

Dom Mikhail said, "Yes, and they can design the tower anew, and raise it again by matrix. It would be costly and long, but it would give pride to Castle Aldaran, and when your children and Dorilys's rule here someday, you will wish for a point of vantage to command the country around. Though, indeed, I think it will be long, very long, before anyone sends armed might against the stronghold of Aldaran!"

"May that day be far," Donal said. "I hope you will sit in this high seat for many years to come, my father." He rose and bowed. "By your leave, sir," he said, and left his seat, going to the women's table where Renata sat.

"Come with me, love, and speak with my father. Then, when Dorilys comes later to join us, he will know the truth, and there will be honesty among us all."

Renata smiled and took his offered hand. Part of her felt naked and exposed by the way in which he had sought her out, but she realized that this was a part of the price she paid for her love. She could have chosen to go away, to return to her family, when Donal was married to another. A conventional woman would have done so. She had chosen to remain here as Donal's *barragana*, and she was not ashamed of it. Why should she hesitate to cross the little space between the women's table and the high seat, to sit at Donal's side?

Allart watched with apprehension, wondering what would happen when Renata and Dorilys came face to face. No . . . Dorilys was not here; she had not come into the hall. Yet his *laran* showed him weird out-of-focus pictures of Dorilys's face, of Renata, distraught. He started to rise from his seat, then realized in despair that there was nothing he could do, nothing to focus on, nothing had happened *yet*; but the noise and confusion in the hall, pictured by his *laran*, paralyzed him. He stared around, bewildered by the pandemonium of his *laran*, and the actual present Great Hall, with only the cheerful noises of many people loudly eating and drinking at a holiday feast.

Renata said, "I love Dorilys well. I would not for worlds step on the hem of her garment. I still feel we should not tell her this until we are sure that she is free of threshold sickness."

"But if she finds it out of herself, she will be very angry, and rightly so," Donal argued, leading Renata toward the high seat. "We should tell my father, even if there is no need to tell Dorilys at once."

"What is it that you will say to my father and not to me, my husband?"

The light, childish voice dropped into the silence, shattering it like breaking glass. Dorilys, in her holiday gown of blue, her hair coiled low on her neck, and somehow looking more childish than ever in her woman's garments, came walking across the floor, dazed, almost as if she were sleepwalking. Allart and Margali rose, and Dom Mikhail held out his hand to Dorilys, saying, "My dear child, I am glad you are well enough to join us," but she paid no attention, her eyes fixed on Donal and Renata, hand in hand before her.

She cried out suddenly, "How dare you speak like that about me, Renata!"

Renata could not conceal a start of surprise and guilt. But she looked at Dorilys and smiled.

"Dear child," she said, "I have said nothing about you except what shows my love and concern, as always. If there is anything we have not told you, it has been only to save you distress while you were overwearied and ill with threshold sickness." But her heart sank as she saw the look in Dorilys's eyes, dark, strained, clutching sanity about her with painful concentration, and she realized that Dorilys, as she had done on the day of her festival, was reading thoughts again; not clearly like a skilled telepath, but erratically, with crazy, patchy imcompleteness. Then Dorilys cried out in rage and sudden comprehension, turning on Donal.

"*You!*" she cried, in a frenzy. "You have given to *her* what you denied to *me!* Now you think—you scheme that *she* will bear the new heir to Aldaran!"

"Dorilys, no," Renata protested, but Dorilys, beside herself, would not hear.

"Do you think I cannot see it? Do you think I do not know that my father has always schemed that *your* child should be heir? He would let you father a child on some outsider to supersede *mine.*"

Donal reached for her hands, but she wrenched them away.

"You promised, Donal," she cried shrilly. "You promised, and tried to soothe me with lies, as if I were a child to be petted and told fairy tales, and while you lied to me, all that time you planned that *she* should bear your first son. But she shall not, I swear it! I will strike her first!"

Lightning flared in the hall, a crash of thunder, loud and almost deafening. In the shocked silence as it died away, Cassandra rose, taking a frantic step toward Dorilys.

"Dorilys, dear child, come to me."

"Don't touch me, Cassandra!" Dorilys shrieked. "You have lied to me, too. You are *her* friend, not mine! You schemed with her, knowing what she planned behind my back. I am alone here; there is none to love me."

"Dorilys, there is none here does *not* love you," Donal said.

But Dom Mikhail had risen, somber and angry. He raised a hand and said, using command-voice, "*Dorilys!* I say, *be still!*"

The girl stood motionless, shocked into silence.

"This is an outrage!" Lord Aldaran said, towering over the child. "How dare you create such an unseemly uproar at a festival? How dare you speak so to our kinswoman? Come and sit here in your proper place by me, and be silent!"

Dorilys took a step toward the high table, and Renata thought, her heart churning with relief, *After all, even with her power, she is a child; she is accustomed to obey her elders. She is still young enough to obey her father without question.*

Dorilys took another step under the command-voice; then she broke free.

"No!" she cried out, whirling, stamping her foot in the willful fury Renata had seen so often in her first days at the castle. "I will not! I will not be humiliated this way! And you, Renata, you who have dared to step on my garment this way, in pride of what you have had from my husband when I have had only empty words and promises and a child's kiss on the forehead, you shall not flaunt your belly at me. You shall not!" She whirled, her face ablaze with the lightning flare.

And Allart saw what once he had foreseen in this hall, a child's face all ablaze with lightning. . . .

Renata took a panicked step backward, tripping over a piece of furniture. Donal cried out, "Dorilys, no! No! Not at her!" and flung himself between Renata and Dorilys, shielding Renata with his body. "If you are angry, speak your anger to me alone—" Then he broke off, with an inarticulate sound, and staggered and his body twitched, caught in the lightning flare. He jerked violently, convulsed, fell, his body crisped and blackened like a blasted tree, twitched again, already lifeless, and lay without moving on the stone pavement.

It had all happened so swiftly that there were many in the lower hall who had heard nothing except cries and accusations. Margali still sat with her mouth open, staring stupidly at her charge, not believing what she saw. Cassandra still stood with her arms extended toward Dorilys, but Allart caught her and held her motionless.

Dom Mikhail took one step toward Dorilys, and staggered. He stopped, swaying, holding himself upright with both hands on the edge of the table. His face was congested and dark with blood, and he could hardly speak. His voice held a terrible bitterness.

"It is the curse," he said. "A sorceress foretold this day, that I should cry out to the gods above and below, would to all of the gods that I had died childless." Moving slowly, an old, broken-winged hawk, he came slowly to where Donal lay, fell to his knees beside him.

"Oh, my son," he whispered. "My son, my son . . ." and raised his face, set and rigid as if carved in stone, to Dorilys.

"Strike me down, too, girl. Why do you wait?"

Dorilys had not moved; she stood as if turned to stone, as if the lightning which had struck Donal down had struck her, too, turning her motionless. Her face was a terrible, tragic mask, her eyes blank and unmoving. Her mouth was open, as if in a soundless scream, but she did not move.

Allart breaking the frozen stasis, began to move to Dom Mikhail's side, but a wild flare of lightning suddenly blazed in the hall, and Dorilys disappeared in its flare. Allart fell back dazed by the shock. Another and another lightning bolt crackled in the room, and they could see Dorilys now, her eyes mad and blazing. Another lightning bolt and another seared at random around the room, and in the lower hall a man leaped up, twitched, and fell dead. One by one, everyone edged back, step by step, from where Dorilys stood, surrounded by the crazed flare of lightning, deafened by thunder; back, and back from where she stood like a statue of some terrible goddess etched in lightning. Her face was not a child's face. It was not even human anymore.

Only Renata dared the lightning. Perhaps, Allart thought in some horrified corner of his mind where he could still think, perhaps Renata simply had no more to lose. She took a step toward Dorilys; another. Another. Dorilys moved for the first time since she had struck Donal down, a menacing gesture, but Renata did not pause or flinch, advancing step by step toward the core of those terrible lightnings where Dorilys blazed like some figure of legendary hells.

Dom Mikhail said brokenly, "No, Lady Renata. No, no—stand back from her. Not you, too, Renata—not you, too."

Allart heard in his mind a clamor, a confusing babble, a wild interplay of confused possibilities there—gone, retreating, surging up again—as Renata moved, slowly and steadily, toward Dorilys, where she stood over Donal's dead body. He saw Renata fall blasted, saw her strike Dorilys with her own *laran* and hold her motionless, as she had done when Dorilys was a willful child; he heard her cursing Dorilys, pleading with her, defying her, all at once in the wild surge of futures from this moment that would be, might be, would never be. . . .

Renata spread her arms wide. Her voice was anguished but steady, clearly audible.

"Dorilys," she said in a whisper. "Dorilys, my little girl, my darling—"

She rose from where she had fallen and took a step and another, and Dorilys came into her arms, was folded close to her breast. The lightnings died. Suddenly Dorilys was only a little girl again, clasped in Renata's arms, sobbing tempestuously.

Renata held her, soothing her, stroking her, murmuring soft love words, tears raining down her own face. Dorilys looked around her, dazed.

"I feel so sick, Renata," she whispered. "What has happened? I thought this was a festival. Is Donal very angry with me?" Then she shrieked, a long, terrible cry of horror and realization, and crumpled, a limp, lifeless-looking unconscious heap in Renata's arms.

Overhead the thunder muttered and died and was still.

CHAPTER
THIRTY

"It is too late," Renata repeated. "I do not know if it will ever be safe to let her wake again."

Overhead the thunder rattled at random, striking sudden searing bolts around the towers of Aldaran, and Allart wondered, with a shudder, what dreams disturbed Dorilys's sleep. Dreadful ones, no doubt.

In the stunned moment following Dorilys's realization of what she had done, Renata had managed to get her to swallow a dose of the same strong drug she had given her before. Almost as soon as she had swallowed it, the moment of sanity had faded from her eyes and the terrible core of lightning had begun to build up around her again. But the drug had taken over with merciful quickness before more than a few random bolts had struck, and she had sunk into her present unquiet stupor, the storms raging overhead but not striking near.

"We cannot give her that drug again," Renata repeated. "Even if I could get her to take it again—and I am not sure of that—it would almost certainly kill her."

Aldaran said, with terrible bitterness, "Better that, than that she should destroy us all as she destroyed my boy." His voice broke and the terrible glazed brightness of his eyes was worse than weeping. "Is there no hope, Renata? None?"

"I am afraid that even when I asked you, before," Renata said, "it was too late. Too much of her mind, too much of the brain itself has been destroyed and invaded by the lightnings. It is too late for Dorilys, my lord. I fear you must accept that; our only concern now is to make sure she does not destroy too much outside herself, in her own death."

The father shuddered. Finally he said, "How can we make sure of that?"

"I do not know, my lord. Probably no one with this lethal gift has ever survived so near maturity, and so we have only the faintest notion of its potential. I must consult with those in Tramontana Tower, or perhaps at Hali, to be certain what we can do, and how we can best make her harmless during"— Renata swallowed, struggling to control herself—"during what little time remains to her. She can tap the whole electrical potential of the planet, my lord. I beg you not to underestimate the damage she can still do, if we frighten her."

"I am cursed," said Aldaran, softly and bitterly. "I was cursed the day she was born, and I did not know it. You tried to warn me, and I did not hear. It is I who deserve death, and it took only my children, my innocent children."

"Let me go and consult my colleagues in the Towers, Lord Aldaran."

"And spread far and wide the news of the shame of Aldaran? No, Lady Renata. It was I who brought this awful curse to our world; without malice, and in love, but still it was I. Now I shall destroy it."

He drew his dagger, raised it above Dorilys, and brought it suddenly striking down. But from the prostrate form there came a blue flash and Aldaran fell back, knocked half across the room, the breath gone from his body. When Allart picked him up he struggled for breath and for a moment Allart feared he was dying.

Renata shook her head sadly.

"Had you forgotten, my lord? She is a telepath, too. Even in her sleep, she can sense your intent. Although I do not think she would want to live if she knew, there is something in that brain that will protect itself. I do not think we can kill her. I must go to Hali or to Tramontana, my lord."

Lord Aldaran bowed his head.

"As you will, kinswoman. Will you make ready to ride?"

"There is no time for that—and no need. I will go through the overworld."

Drawing out her matrix, Renata composed herself for the journey. With one part of herself she was grateful for this disturbance, this desperate need; it deferred the moment when she must face the unendurable fact of Donal's death. Unasked, Cassandra came to keep watch beside Renata's body while she made the journey through the intangible realms of the mind.

It was like stepping out of a garment suddenly grown unimaginably too large. For an instant, in the grayness of the shadow-world overlaying the solid and tangible world, Renata could see her body, looking as lifeless as Dorilys's, wearing the elaborate gown she had put on for the victory feast which had turned to defeat, and Cassandra motionless beside her. Then, moving with the swiftness of thought, she stood on the high peak of Tramontana Tower, wondering why she had been drawn here . . . then, in the crimson garment of a Keeper, she saw Ian-Mikhail of Tramontana.

He said gently, "So Donal is dead, suddenly and by violence? I was his friend, and his teacher. I must seek him out in the Realms Beyond, Renata. If he died suddenly, and by violence, he may not know he is dead; his mind may be trapped near to his body and he may be helplessly trying to reenter it again. I was uneasy about him; yet I did not know what had befallen him until I saw you, cousin."

In the intangible spaces of the overworld, where a physical touch could register only as an idea, he gently touched her hand.

"We share your grief, Renata. We all loved him; he should have been one of us in Tramontana. I must go to him." She saw the small premonitory stirring of the gray spaces which presaged Ian-Mikhail's withdrawing of his thoughts and presence from her, and caught at his presence with a despairing thought that disturbed the overworld like a cry.

"What of Dorilys, kinsman? What shall we do for her?"

"Alas, I do not know, Renata. Her father would not entrust her to us, and we do not know her. It is a pity; we might have found a way to help her control her *laran.* But the records of the breeding programs are at Hali and Arilinn. Perhaps they have had some experience, or some advice. Delay me no more, sister; I must go to Donal."

Renata watched his image in the overworld recede, grow distant. He was going to seek out Donal, dead so suddenly by violence, make certain he did not linger, trapped, near his useless body. Dully Renata envied him. She knew that contact between the dead and the living was perilous for both, and thus forbidden. The dead must not be encouraged to remain too near the grief of the bereaved: the living must not be drawn into realms where, as yet, they had no business. Ian-

Mikhail, trained from adolescence to the detachment of a Keeper's vows, could safely perform this office for his friend without being drawn into overmuch concern. Even so, Renata knew, had Donal been a member of his immediate family, Ian-Mikhail would have ceded this task to another, less personally concerned.

Weary, uncertain, remembering only Donal and her loss, Renata turned her thoughts toward Hali. She struggled for calm, knowing that too much emotion would force her off this plane altogether, but it threatened to overcome her. She knew that if she did not banish the tormenting memories she would break altogether, retreat in to the dream-stuff of the overworld, and never return.

But the grayness of the overworld seemed unending, and while she could see the dimness of the Tower of Hali in the distance, it seemed that although she tried to move toward the Tower, her limbs would not obey her, nor her unruly thoughts. She moved forever in gray uninhabited mental wastelands. . . .

Then, very far away, in the distance, it seemed that she saw a familiar figure, young, laughing, very far away, too far to reach. . . . Donal! Donal, so very far from her! In this realm where thoughts were pliable, something survived. . . . She began to hurry after the retreating figure, sending out a cry of joy.

Donal! Donal, I am here! Wait for me, beloved. . . .

But he was very far away. He did not turn or look at her. She thought, with a last moment of rationality, *No; it is forbidden. He has gone into a realm still denied, still inaccessible. This could draw me after him . . . too far. . . .*

I will not go too far. But I must see him again. I must see him only this once, say the good-byes of which we were so cruelly cheated . . . only this once, and then nevermore. . . .

She hurried after the retreating figure, her thoughts seeming to bear her along swiftly through the grayness of the overworld. When she looked around all the familiar landmarks, the last sight of Hali Tower, had vanished, and she was wholly alone in grayness, with nothing but the small, retreating figure of Donal just at the horizon, drawing her on. . . .

No. This is madness! It is forbidden. I must return before it is too late. She had known this from her first years in the

Tower, that there could not be, *must* not be, any intrusion by the living into whatever realms belonged to the dead, and she knew why. But caution was almost gone in her now. In the despair of grief, she thought, *I must see him once more, only once, must kiss him, must say good-bye. . . . I must or I cannot live! Surely it cannot be forbidden, only to say good-bye. I am a trained matrix worker. I know what I am doing, and it will give me the strength to go on living without him. . . .*

A final touch of intruding sanity made her wonder if it were truly Donal there on the horizon, leading her away. Or was it an illusion, born of grief and longing, unwillingness to accept the irrevocability of death? Here in the realms of thought, her mind could build an illusion of Donal and follow it till she joined him in those realms.

I do not care! I do not care! It seemed that she was running, running after the retreating form, then more slowly, more despairing, her pace slackening. Unable to move, she sent out a final despairing cry:

Donal! Wait—

Suddenly the grayness lightened, thinned, a shadowy form barred her way, and a voice spoke her name; a familiar, gentle voice.

"Renata. Kinswoman, cousin—Renata, no."

She saw Dorilys standing before her, not the terrifying inhuman lightning flare, not the queen of storms, but the old Dorilys, the little Dorilys of that summer of her love. In this fluid world where all things were as the mind pictured them, Dorilys was the little girl she had been, her hair in a long plait, one of her old childish dresses barely reaching her ankles.

"No, Renata, love, it is not Donal. It is an illusion born of your longing, an illusion you would follow forever. Go back, dear. They need you, *there*—"

Suddenly Renata saw the hall in Castle Aldaran, where her lifeless body lay, watched by Cassandra.

Renata stopped, looking at Dorilys before her.

She had killed. Killed Donal. . . .

"Not I, but my gift," Dorilys said, and the childish face was tragic. "I will kill no more, Renata. In my pride and willfulness I would not listen, and now it is too late. You must go back and tell them; I must never wake again."

Renata bowed her head, knowing the child spoke truth.

"They need you, Renata. Go back. Donal is not here," Dorilys said. "I, too, could have followed him forever over that horizon. Only, perhaps, now, when there is no pride or desire to blind me, I can see clearly. All my life, I never saw more of Donal than *that*, an illusion, my own willful belief that he would be what I wanted him to be. I—" Renata saw her face flicker and move and she saw the child Dorilys might have been, the woman she was becoming, would now never be. "I knew he was given to you; I was too selfish to accept it. Now I have not even what he would have given me, willingly. I wanted what he could give only to you."

She gestured. "Go back, Renata. It is too late for me."

"But what will become of you, child?"

"You must use your matrix," Dorilys said, "to isolate me behind a force-field like the ones at Hali . . . you told me of them, shielding things too dangerous to use. You cannot even kill me, Renata. The gift in my brain works independent now of the real *me*—I do not understand it, either—but *it* will strike to protect my body if I am attacked. Even though I no longer desire to live. Renata, cousin, promise me you will not let me destroy any more of those I love!"

It could be done, Renata thought. *Dorilys could not be killed. But she could be isolated, her life-forces suspended, behind a force-field.*

"Let me sleep so, safe, until it is safe for me to wake," Dorilys said, and Renata trembled. This would isolate Dorilys in the overworld, alone, behind the force-field which would barricade èven her mind.

"Darling, what of you, then?"

Her smile was childish and wise.

"Why, with such a long time—although time, I know, does not exist *out here*—I shall perhaps learn wisdom, at last, if I continue to live. And if I do not"—a curious, distant smile—"there are others who have gone before me. I do not believe wisdom is ever wasted. Go back, Renata. Do not let me destroy anyone else. Donal is gone beyond my reach, or yours. But you must go back, and you must live, because of his child. He deserves some chance at life."

With those words Renata found herself lying in the chair in the Great Hall at Castle Aldaran, with the storms breaking above the castle heights. . . .

"It can be done," Allart said at last quietly. "Among the three of us, it can be done. Her life-forces can be lowered to where she is no danger. Perhaps she will die; perhaps, only, they will be in abeyance and someday she may wake in safety, in control. But more likely she will sink and sink, and finally, perhaps many years or centuries from now, she will die. In either case she is free, and we are safe. . . ."

So it was done, and she lay as Allart had foreseen with his *laran*, motionless on the bier in the great vaulted room which was the chapel of Castle Aldaran.

"We shall bear her to Hali," Allart said, "and there lay her within the chapel, forever."

Lord Aldaran took Renata's hand. "I have no heir; I am alone and old. It is my will that Donal's son shall reign here when I am gone. It will not be long. Kinswoman," he added, looking into her eyes, "will you wed me by the *catenas*? I have nothing to offer you save this: that if I acknowledge your child my son and heir, there is none alive who can gainsay me."

Renata bowed her head. "For the sake of Donal's son. Let it be as you will, kinsman," and Aldaran held out his arms and folded her in them. He kissed her, tenderly and without passion, on the forehead; and with that the floodgates broke, and for the first time since Donal had been stricken down before her, Renata began to weep, crying and crying as if she would never cease.

Allart knew at last that this death would not strike down Renata also. She would live, and someday she would even recover. A day would come when Aldaran would proclaim Donal's son heir to Aldaran in this very room, as Allart's *laran* had foreseen. . . .

They rode forth the next morning at daybreak, Dorilys's body sealed in her force-field within its casket, to bear her to Hali, there to lie forever. Allart and Cassandra rode beside her. Above them, on the highest balcony of Aldaran, Renata and old Dom Mikhail watched them go, silent, motionless, bowed with mourning.

Allart thought, as they rode down the pathway, that he could never cease to mourn—for Donal, struck low in the midst of victory; for Dorilys, in her beauty and willfulness and pride; for the proud old man who stood above them, broken; and for Renata at his side, broken by grief.

I, too, am broken. I will be a king, and I do not want to

reign. Yet I alone can save this realm from disaster, and I have no choice. He rode, head bowed, hardly seeing Cassandra at his side, until at last she reached to him and closed her slender six-fingered hand over his as they rode.

"A time will come, my dear love," she said, "when at last we may make songs, not war. My *laran* is not as yours. But I foresee it."

Allart thought, *I am not alone . . . and for her sake I must not grieve.* He raised his head, setting his face firmly against the future, and threw up a hand in final farewell to Castle Aldaran, which he would never see again, and in parting from Renata, from whom, he knew, he parted only for a little while.

As he rode down the path from Aldaran, following the cortege that bore the stormqueen to her last resting place, he prepared himself to meet on the road the men who were, even now, riding toward him to offer him the unwanted crown. Overhead the sky was gray and still, and it seemed that no thunder had ever troubled those quiet spaces.

DAW PRESENTS MARION ZIMMER BRADLEY

Darkover Novels

DARKOVER LANDFALL	#UE1806—$2.25
THE SPELL SWORD	#UE1675—$1.95
THE HERITAGE OF HASTUR	#UE1744—$2.95
THE SHATTERED CHAIN	#UE1840—$2.95
THE FORBIDDEN TOWER	#UE1752—$2.95
STORMQUEEN!	#UE1951—$3.50
TWO TO CONQUER	#UE1876—$2.95
SHARRA'S EXILE	#UE1836—$3.50
HAWKMISTRESS!	#UE1958—$3.50
THENDARA HOUSE	#UE1857—$3.50

Friends of Darkover Anthologies

THE KEEPER'S PRICE	#UE1931—$2.50
SWORD OF CHAOS	#UE1722—$2.95

Others

HUNTERS OF THE RED MOON	#UE1713—$1.95
THE SURVIVORS	#UE1861—$2.95
GREYHAVEN	#UE1815—$2.50

PHILIP K. DICK

"The greatest American novelist of the second half of the 20th Century."

—*Norman Spinrad*

"A genius . . . He writes it the way he sees it and it is the quality, the clarity of his Vision that makes him great."

—*Thomas M. Disch*

"The most consistently brilliant science fiction writer in the world."

—*John Brunner*

PHILIP K. DICK

In print again, in DAW Books' special memorial editions:

- ☐ **WE CAN BUILD YOU** (#UE1793—$2.50)
- ☐ **THE THREE STIGMATA OF PALMER ELDRITCH**
  (#UE1810—$2.50)
- ☐ **A MAZE OF DEATH** (#UE1830—$2.50)
- ☐ **UBIK** (#UE1859—$2.50)
- ☐ **DEUS IRAE** (#UE1887—$2.95)
- ☐ **NOW WAIT FOR LAST YEAR** (#UE1654—$2.50)
- ☐ **FLOW MY TEARS, THE POLICEMAN SAID** (#UE1624—$2.25)

Attention:

DAW COLLECTORS

Many readers of DAW Books have written requesting information on early titles and book numbers to assist in the collection of DAW editions since the first of our titles appeared in April 1972.

We have prepared a several-pages-long list of all DAW titles, giving their sequence numbers, original and current order numbers, and ISBN numbers. And of course the authors and book titles, as well as reissues.

If you think that this list will be of help, you may have a copy by writing to the address below and enclosing one dollar in stamps or coins to cover the handling and postage costs.

DAW BOOKS, INC. Dept. C
1633 Broadway
New York, N.Y. 10019

A GALAXY OF SCIENCE FICTION STARS!

LEE CORREY Manna	UE1896—$2.95
TIMOTHY ZAHN The Blackcollar	UE1959—$3.50
A. E. VAN VOGT Computerworld	UE1879—$2.50
COLIN KAPP Search for the Sun	UE1858—$2.25
ROBERT TREBOR An XT Called Stanley	UE1865—$2.50
ANDRE NORTON Horn Crown	UE1635—$2.95
JACK VANCE The Face	UE1921—$2.50
E. C. TUBB Angado	UE1908—$2.50
KENNETH BULMER The Diamond Contessa	UE1853—$2.50
ROGER ZELAZNY Deus Irae	UE1887—$2.50
PHILIP K. DICK Ubik	UE1859—$2.50
DAVID J. LAKE Warlords of Xuma	UE1832—$2.50
CLIFFORD D. SIMAK Our Children's Children	UE1880—$2.50
M. A. FOSTER Transformer	UE1814—$2.50
GORDON R. DICKSON Mutants	UE1809—$2.95
BRIAN STABLEFORD The Gates of Eden	UE1801—$2.50
JOHN BRUNNER The Jagged Orbit	UE1917—$2.95
EDWARD LLEWELLYN Salvage and Destroy	UE1898—$2.95
PHILIP WYLIE The End of the Dream	UE1900—$2.25